"I BELIEVE in the large simplicities, in the human urges at the back of all of us. I believe in love, courage and compassion. I suppose that is why the people who are out first after cleverness fail to see that life is a complex of the great simplicities. We are apt to look at little bits of the pattern, and not at the whole garment."

This credo explains the enormous success of
Warwick Deeping's novels:

SORRELL AND SON

DOOMSDAY   KITTY

UTHER AND IGRAINE

OLD PYBUS   ROPER'S ROW

THE TEN COMMANDMENTS

EXILE   SMITH

OLD WINE AND NEW

TWO BLACK SHEEP

SEVEN MEN CAME BACK

THE MAN ON THE WHITE HORSE

THE GOLDEN CORD   NO HERO—THIS

BLIND MAN'S YEAR

THE WOMAN AT THE DOOR

MALICE OF MEN

BLUEWATER

FOLLY ISLAND

Also by Mr. Deeping, an omnibus volume:

STORIES OF LOVE, COURAGE AND
COMPASSION

These are Borzoi Books, published by
ALFRED · A · KNOPF

THE MAN
WHO WENT BACK

WARWICK DEEPING

THE MAN
WHO
WENT BACK

NEW YORK
ALFRED·A·KNOPF
1940

THE MAN
WHO WENT BACK

CHAPTER ONE

I WILL not attempt to explain anything. Such an experience cannot be explained, save by the mystics, or by some of our mathematical dreamers whose feet are washed by the waters of other dimensions.

It will not appear even credible to my generation, though, a thousand years hence, our thinkers may have knowledge and understanding of these matters.

Psychologists would say that I had dreamed a very elaborate and lengthy dream.

What happens in sleep, or in dreams? Does anyone know? What happens when a man lies unconscious for days or weeks? Does anything happen? Or is he no more than a chrysalis wrapped up in bed?

Is man a spirit?

I shall always believe so after the things I have suffered.

Always, I have been a great dreamer and my dreams have been vivid and spacious, and for a young man sometimes peculiarly logical. I have had what I can describe as fourth dimensional dreams, but what to call this other piece of existence I do not know. I can remember being immensely piqued and challenged by that most exquisite play, *Berkeley Square,* but my jump into the past was not willed and planned, and it exceeded that hero's experience by many hundreds of years. I had read Mr. Dunne's suggestive and fascinating works upon dreams and Time. I had seen one of Mr. Priestley's plays. I had read Ouspensky and dabbled in psychical research, but my job in life was completely utilitarian. I was a young consulting engineer, aged thirty-one. I had been married for five years.

At a time when the Dictators were presenting us with a series of crises, and those murderous little brutes, the Japs, were creating a new sort of Mongoloid terror, I, like most young married men, lived in a state of worry and suspense. The future seemed so black and problematical. Business was bad, and the weather as bad as business. Moreover, one's soul could never possess itself in peace, even in one's garden, or in one's favourite chair. Aeroplanes reminded one perpetually that it was a waspish world, and one turned on the wireless, wondering whether another crisis was flaring up. The Germans had put both hoofs in Prague. The tragedy of the *Thetis* had shocked me. I had joined up as a Territorial, and, in five months, my wife was expecting her first baby.

She was away, staying for a week with her people. We lived at Weybridge in a little white house near the Heath. That particular Sunday happened to be fine, and feeling that I wanted to lose myself in the country, I took the car out, meaning to leave it in the Newland's Corner car-park, and walk. One of my hobbies was exploring old trackways and earth-works. I had an ordnance map with me, and some sandwiches and a thermos in my haversack, and my plan was to follow the sunken lane down to Albury, and strike an old pack-horse trail that led up to Farley Heath. It was a warm Spring day, and the thorns must have been in blossom on the Downs and the bluebells out in the woods by Newland's Corner. Actually, I must have changed my mind, and driven down past the Silent Pool and the gates of Albury Park, and up the steep hill to Black Heath. It was here, where the road to Ewhurst joins the Shamley Green Farley road that the crash occurred. I have no recollection of it. The last thing I can remember was getting the car out of the garage of White Lodge at Weybridge.

I had been asleep.

I woke, staring at the sheeted blue of the sky. I was lying on my back on a little mat of rabbit-nibbled grass in a sea of heather. It was old heather, high and clotted, shutting me in like a low hedge, but above it, towards the east I could see a clump of Scotch firs with the sun shining upon their red throats and rich green polls. My head ached slightly. Beyond that I was not conscious of any strangeness. I supposed that I had just fallen asleep, though I could not remember having spread myself here. I sat up. I could see nothing but heather and the Scotch firs. I felt thirsty. I looked round for my haversack, and then it was that something very odd struck me. My haversack was not there. It was not its absence that was strange. I could have explained that to myself. I had left it in the car, or some tramp might have pinched it. The surprising fact was that something else was lying there in its place, a kind of leather wallet with a rawhide strap or thong.

I was conscious of surprise, curiosity. Fear had not yet gripped me. Had someone been playing a trick? I reached for the thing, opened it and saw a curious-looking knife, a piece of brownish bread, and one or two little metal things.

Coins, money! I picked up one of them. It was of silver, and though only very slightly tarnished, it had for me the appearance of an antique. The coins in the wallet were Roman coins.

I believe I said: "Well, I'm damned!"

But what was the meaning of this? In a dream one may accept the most fantastic details without questioning them, but I was asking questions. How had this wallet with the Roman coins managed to substitute itself for my haversack? Had some errant archæologist played a trick on me? Were Cinema people "shooting" on these Surrey hills, and had they left me a piece of property-stuff, and borrowed my haversack? Both suggestions seemed absurd. And then I became aware of something else that shocked me into a staring, gaping stillness.

The last thing a man may notice may be his clothes. They may be so much part of himself on a ramble that he is unconscious of them, provided they are comfortable. I sat staring at my own feet. They were shod in queer, leather shoes that suggested sandals. My legs were bare, and covered with bruises and scratches as though I had been blundering through brambles and undergrowth. I had set out from Weybridge wearing old plus-fours, rough stockings, and a pair of brown, crêpe-soled shoes. I sat and stared. What the devil? My glance travelled higher. I was wearing a pair of white linen drawers, and a greenish tunic. I fingered the things. Yes, they were real enough. And then I began to be frightened.

I stood up and looked about me. Apparently I was in a little hollow, and the ground, rising round me, showed me nothing but heather and sky. A winding path led through the heather. I followed it, and it brought me to a dip in the ground where water oozed into a little black brown pool surrounded by rushes, and shaded by alders. I felt very thirsty, and I suppose my feeling frightened made my mouth more dry. I put the wallet down and knelt, and in that very still water I saw my own reflection. It startled and scared me. My hair was a black mop, and looked as though it had not been cut for months. I had black stubble all over my chin and my upper lip. My face looked strangely haggard and starved. There was a dark mark on my forehead, and when I put my hand to my head I felt that something had clotted itself into my hair.

And suddenly, I was afraid, acutely afraid. I wanted to see things, things that were familiar and reassuring. I drank from my palm, dashed water in my face, picked up the wallet and ran. I ran up the long, low hill that seemed to end in a dark ridge, and as I topped the rise I saw the great swell of the North Downs spreading across the valley. Yes, there they were, familiar and friendly and serene. I stood still, realizing that I was panting. I saw the grey-green slopes, and the yews and thorns. Yes, Newland's Corner was just over there. Thank God! Then, a certain strangeness about that landscape surprised me. Many people must know those two chalk mounds with their clumps of beech trees. The trees were not there, but the two mounds stood out white and clear like markers. Moreover, I saw on the hill-side below a kind of white gash running straight up the hill-side like an arrow pointing to the gap between the two white mounds.

What the devil?

I gave a shake of the head, closed my eyes for a moment, and then looked again.

No, there was no doubt about it. I saw those two great tumuli and the white pointer like a finger on the hill-side.

But the Ridgeway was there. I could pick out in places its broad green track.

And St. Martha's? Yes, of course I should see St. Martha's on its hill in the valley. I waded on through the heather and paused, with my heart beating hard.

Yes, there was the hill, a green pyramid with sandy scars in it.

St. Martha's chapel was not there!

I think I have never known such fear as the panic that seized me as I stood there in the heather. The feeling was penetrated by a kind of terrible premonition, and a sense of desolation. I think I cried out: "Lucy, Lucy, wake me up." Lucy was my wife. I felt like a terrified child in the anguish of some nightmare.

I began to run. I came to a road, a narrow road of gravel. Thank God, for a road! I wanted to see a car. I followed the road, and suddenly I knew where I was, on Farley Heath. Over there should be the mass of bracken, and the solitary thorn bush which marked the site of the Roman temple.

The thorn tree was not there.

A little, white-pillared building with a red-tiled roof stood in the tree's place. The Roman temple!

Again I shook my head, closed my eyes, waited and looked a second time. The temple was there with the sunlight shining upon it. The road ran up and past it, cutting through the grass banks which marked out the enclosure.

I was more and more afraid. I shivered. I think I shook at the knees, and though I had just drunk at the pool my mouth felt dry. I was conscious of desolation, of being alone in a strange world, a dream-world that was, somehow, terrifyingly real. I kept saying to myself: "Wake up, wake up. O

God, let me wake up!" I wanted that building to disappear, the thorn-bush to take its place, and St. Martha's to pop up again on its hill-top.

The temple did not disappear.

I felt drawn to it, pulled by a bitter curiosity. I must go and look and touch. Perhaps when I touched the thing the little building would vanish, and my own world would come back. But I was afraid of that building. It seemed to challenge me. I could see no human figure anywhere in this strange yet familiar scene. I left the road, and wading through the heather, got my back to the sun and approached the building from the west. It had a little portico at each end, and suddenly I stood still. I saw a figure in the northern portico, leaning against one of the pillars. It had an arm round the pillar. I could see the line of a purple dress, and the back of a dark head. It seemed to be a woman's figure.

Here was something alive in this strange, dead world, something that could speak to me. I think I was yearning to hear the sound of a human voice. I moved forward and to the left so that I could see more of the figure. I was within twenty yards of the temple. I could see the girl now. She was leaning against the pillar, her right arm round it, and she was looking northwards towards the Downs and those two white tumuli. She was utterly still, and yet her very stillness suggested suspense, a watchfulness that was so concentrated upon something that might happen over yonder, that she was quite unaware of my presence. She was a very dark girl, tall and slim, with one of those creamy skins faintly tinted with an olive brownness. Her mouth was a red thread. Her eyes stared away into the distance with a kind of black fierceness. It was not a gentle face, though very lovely. There was pride in the nostrils of her little beak of a nose. I saw that she was wearing red leather shoes strapped across the instep, a purple-coloured robe-like garment fastened on the left shoulder by a brooch. She wore her very black hair in coils upon her head. A green girdle encircled her loins, and from it hung a pouch, and a little dagger in a gilded sheath. I stood and stared and stared at her, finding in her strangeness something poignantly familiar. It was as though she and I had met before.

She must have become conscious of being watched, for, suddenly she turned her head and saw me. Her arm slipped from the pillar. Her face became alive; her very dark eyes seemed to flash.

"Pellias!"

She was down off the podium and coming towards me.

She gave me the name with the I in it lengthened to an E. Pell-e-as. Pellias! Was I Pellias? My bewilderment was absolute. I must have stood and gaped at her.

"Why do you not speak?"

She was giving me Latin, and though my Latin was as dusty as death, I understood her, which was strange.

"Why don't you speak? Where are the others?"

I heard myself say: "I do not remember," and I realized that I was answering her in Latin.

She had paused about two yards from me, and so vivid was she to me that my bewilderment increased. She was staring at my face with those fierce dark eyes of hers, and I seemed to divine in her a quality that was different from the rather tepid and dreary casualness of twentieth-century England. She seemed more vivid, more poignantly alive, more capable of being played upon by the passionate things of life, its loves and its angers, its loyalties and its hates. She was looking me in the face with a frank, challenging intentness as though my face could reveal something to her, even though I stood mute. And then those disturbing eyes of hers looked me over from my unshaven jowl to my bruised, scratched legs.

"Where is your armour? Where is your sword?"

Good God, what did she mean? I was feeling so utterly lost and bewildered that I blurted those words at her again.

"I do not remember."

Which was true, but the mordant truth of it was beyond her comprehension and beyond mine! She stared me straight in the eyes. Then her glance lifted to my forehead and remained there for a moment. She seemed to see something that made her face grow more gentle, something that explained to her my dazed, loutish helplessness.

"You have been wounded. There is dry blood in your hair."

"I do not remember."

She spoke to me as she might have spoken to a child, and with the air of one accustomed to being obeyed.

"Kneel down! Let me look!"

I went down on my knees, feeling that I was being carried along by happenings which had the inevitableness of things that had happened, and over which I had no control. I seemed to be part of a pattern, a figure in a picture that had been painted long ago, and yet it was a moving-picture. Surrender seemed to be my only resource, to let myself drift, to repeat those words: "I do not remember." She bent over me, and I felt her fingers touch my hair and I could smell some perfume that she used. But her touch both thrilled and frightened me. I became conscious of a strange, exquisite anguish. I trembled. Even the soft sward seemed to quiver under my knees.

"A sword cut. Poor Pellias. So, the battle was lost. Those accursed savages!"

I raised my face to hers. So helpless did I feel that I realized that my only hope lay in accepting helplessness. Let her take the tragedy or whatever it was, as it had happened, and assume that I was a poor devil who had been broken by it, and who had forgotten. So, I had had a blow on the head! I had been fighting savages. What savages? And where and why?

I said: "I have forgotten everything."

She drew back and looked at me consideringly, and again her face grew fierce. She turned again to the hills across the valley. I saw her hand go to her bosom. The fingers seemed clenched over her heart. She was hating something, defying something. Her head went back; her nostrils seemed to dilate and quiver.

"Those German swine!"

A shock went through me. Those words might have been uttered by some of the moderns. Good God, was I dreaming? I seemed to remember something. It was like a beam of light passing, pausing and disappearing. She was looking at me again with a kind of passionate impatience.

"So, you remember nothing? Were many slain?"

"I remember nothing."

She gave a shrug of the shoulders and seemed to despair of me. I was a poor thing to be pitied, a fugitive, a fellow who had thrown away his arms. I had a sudden feeling that I did not want to be pitied by her, or be treated with tolerant and tragic scorn. She was so vital and vibrant that her eyes and her lips and her proud black head could set the man in me alight.

"Wait. They are waiting for news down yonder. I came up here to watch."

She turned away and mounting the steps of the podium passed along the little portico and disappeared into the temple. I knelt there watching, wondering whether this dream, or whatever it was, would end. Would the temple vanish, and she with it? I was conscious of a fierce desire to see her again. I knelt and wondered whether the little, pillared building would vanish like a picture from a screen, and the thorn tree take its place, but the white pillars and the red roof remained solid and real against the green of the woods and the hills. I heard a voice, her voice. She seemed to be praying aloud.

To whom did she pray? Christ? But this was no temple sacred to the Man of Galilee. Her gods were Roman gods, or British gods, or perhaps the Unknown God. I heard her voice utter the words, "Dea Mater."

I wanted to see her again, and when I saw her again she looked different. She stood on the edge of the platform, and spoke to me.

"Pellias, come here."

I rose and went to her, and looking up into her eyes, saw pity in them.

"Pellias, I have prayed that you may remember. I will you to remember."

She reached out and touched my forehead with her finger.

"Close your eyes. Remember."

I closed my eyes. How hopeless was all her praying! Were we two ghosts who had met in some strange, twilight world? I shook my head.

"I cannot remember."

CHAPTER TWO

❧

$\mathcal{S}$HE gathered up the folds of her robe, came down from the podium, and took to the road. It ran diagonally across the temple enclosure, and seemed to head in the direction of Guildford and the crossing of the Wey. I followed her, limping a little, for now that the first excitement had passed, I realized that I was very footsore. She had taken the lead, as though born to it, and I followed her half a pace behind, feeling, I know not how or why, that I was neither quite her equal nor her servant. Dear God, who and what was Pellias, this other I? What manner of man was I supposed to be? My gaze and my thought went to the place I knew as Guildford, that steep street with the confusion of its cars, its shops and shoppers. Was it over there as I knew it?

She was walking fast yet with an easy glide, a young stateliness that seemed part of her young splendour. How she might despise a man who was weak, a man who had thrown away his harness! And I, the child of democracy, deeming myself an intellectual, a Leftish person, dared to draw level

14

with her and to walk at her side. I was aware of the quick turn of her head, and the look she gave me. It put me in my place, and yet there was a kind of compassionate comprehension in it. Almost it said: "You have forgotten other things, what you are and what I am; but, poor creature, that sword-blow must be remembered." The sense of humiliation was quick and hot in me, but I fell back and followed on her left, half a pace behind.

Then a gradual and new curiosity stirred in me. Whither were we going? What was I to see down yonder in the valley that held what were for me Shere, Albury and Chilworth? I remembered that Martin Tupper lay buried in the new Albury churchyard, the Martin Tupper of flowery poetical platitudes who had dug trenches through and round that very temple, and had caused later explorers to curse him as an interfering busybody. If I had been shot by some trick of time back into Romano-British England, where was the soul of Martin Tupper? Where were the things he had found on the site of that Roman temple? In museums? But had a bronze urn or an unguent bottle souls that could manifest both here and there, then and now? This fantastic drama left me dizzy.

We were going down hill now, and we left the road for a path or pack-trail that plunged down into the woods. Here were birches, firs, an occasional oak, and this sandy track seemed to me very familiar. I was sure that I had passed along it before. It was one of those timeless tracks whose only evidence of age may lie in the hollow ways they trench where the ground slopes up and down from a valley. I saw a great ants-nest at the foot of a Scotch fir, just such a nest as I once had stirred up with my stick. There were stretches of heather, pools where the crooked bracken was showing

through the blackish peaty crust. A couple of jays scolded
at us, and in one green glade a yaffle flew away, uttering its
laughing, mocking cry. The girl had not spoken to me since
we had left the road, but when the woodpecker laughed at
us, she turned and looked into my face.

"Has the bird no voice for you?"

I think I smiled at her.

"What name would you give it?"

She frowned.

"Do you not remember even that?"

There was a flick of scorn in her voice. What a poor, limping sloven was this Pellias! I flashed back at her.

"No more than I remember your name."

That seemed to startle her. She paused, looked at me
steadily as though to challenge some lie.

"What is my name?"

"I have forgotten."

"You might be a fool or a newly-born babe."

"I am that."

"I wonder! It may be wise to forget some things."

Irony! What was she suggesting? That I was playing a
part, which God knows I was. She moved on again and I
followed her along the track that swung up and down
through the woods and heather. I felt that we must be nearing the great valley, the valley which has seemed to me the
most beautiful in England, and suddenly the trees thinned
and we came out on to the shoulder of a hill, and I saw ewes
grazing, their lambs with them. But even they were not like
the sheep I knew, though I cannot claim much knowledge
of sheep. These animals looked smaller, rougher, longer in
the leg. The ewes nearest to us set up a maternal bleating,
and their lambs ran to their mothers.

I felt that I wanted to break the silence that this haughty young woman had imposed upon me.

"A good season for lambs, I gather?"

She answered me curtly over her shoulder.

"You should remember that. You and your father numbered them."

Good God, had I a father in this world, another ghost to be confronted!

"My father! I have forgotten his name."

She answered me again over her shoulder.

"Almost, it seems to me, that you have forgotten to be man."

That was a devastating snub, and it galled me more than my tired feet. I heard a sudden piping, and saw the shepherd, a mere lad, sitting under a thorn tree and playing upon his pipe. He was looking towards the Downs, and he had neither seen nor heard us, nor had he been disturbed by the bleating of the ewes. The girl called to him, and her voice was the voice of young authority.

"Alban."

The lad took the pipe from his lips, turned, stared and started to his feet. He had fair hair and very blue eyes, and was dressed in a woollen smock that reached below his knees. His feet were bare.

"Is that how you guard your sheep?"

He flushed up, gave her a kind of bob or curtsey, and then he stared at me. His eyes grew rounder and rounder, and seemed to bulge like blue pebbles. Obviously my sudden manifestation in his world was as startling and as tragic to him as it had been to the girl. His mouth hung open. I might have been a figure of fate, terrifying and ominous. I did not know then that his father and my father had marched to fight those invading Saxons, and that both his father and my father were dead.

But my lady was not for lingering or for explaining my presence and my wild look to this shepherd lad. She swept on, and I followed behind her, only to find the shepherd lad at my elbow.

"Master, speak to me. What of my father?"

His beardless, boyish face, with its frightened eyes, bothered me. How was I to tell him anything? And he had called me "master," which made me assume that my unknown father and I were men of some weight in the valley.

I pointed to my head.

"Alban, forgive me; I do not remember."

I can recall being surprised by this peasant lad speaking to me in the Latin tongue, for I, like most people, had given little thought to the realities of the Roman life in Britain. And here was I speaking Latin like a native! I left the poor shepherd wringing his hands, and hurried on after my Mistress, for that was how I had begun to visualize her. Also, I was pricked by curiosity; I wanted to look down into that valley, and compare it with the valley that I knew.

We had come to the shoulder of the hill where the ground began to fall steeply, and now I could see into the valley. I judged that we were just above the village I knew as Albury, and at the first glance the valley did not appear to be very different from the valley that I knew. I saw woods of beech and of oak on the upper hill-sides, groves of thorn and of yew, poplars rising in the bottom. There were little meadows, very green in the spring of the year, and yellowing up with buttercups. I could see the glitter of water, the Tillingbourne flashing here and there, and a great mere with water-flags abloom about it. This was no wild valley, but rich, and ordered, and cared-for. Then I saw the buildings, a great, long, low, white house roofed with pantiles, a courtyard before it, and its pebble-glass lattices catching the light. It seemed to be surrounded by gardens and orchards. I saw a great yew hedge, clipped like an English hedge, a flint wall, a gatehouse. There were other buildings scattered along the valley, barns, granaries, stables, the cottages of the peasant folk, and a smaller white house that also had its garden. A Roman manor! It was all very beautiful, and rich and serene, lying peacefully there in the May sunshine, yet somehow filling me with a kind of anguish.

Nothing that I knew or yearned to see was there!

So, I followed her down the steep green slope into the valley, feeling that Time had played a fantastic and paralysing trick upon me, and bundled me into this dream-box without a key or a password. How would the people down yonder receive me? What was I to do and say? Still cling to the pretence that my wits had been scattered by a blow on the head? And which self was I to parade before this other world, John Hallard the engineer, or Pellias the—I knew not what? What a hell of a problem! Were I to try and talk to these people like twentieth-century man they would think me madder than I seemed. No, a nice cunning was the thing; silence, mere blank stupidity. I had to get my bearings, play for time, keep my wits about me, yet at the back of my bewilderment was the thought that all this would pass. I had to play up to this dream world, walk delicately, conceal that other secret self. Somehow, I would escape from it back into my own world. This fantastic dream-state could not last. The thing was ridiculous, ridiculous yet enthralling.

A grass path between hedges and orchards brought us

down to the manor road which followed the stream much
as the Albury-Chilworth road followed it. I saw some children playing in the road. They stood, stared, ran, screaming
as English children might have screamed. The news was
out, news of the ominous thing that must have been hanging
over the village. I could feel fear in this valley. This little
world had been waiting upon rumour, listening, watching,
and here was I a beaten man and a fugitive, with death and
disaster in my wounded silence.

The thatched, white-walled cottages were strung along the
lane much as in an English village. They had their hedges
and their gardens, and were part of the peaceful scene in a
land that had grown up under the shield of the Pax Romana.
These tragic days were like strange, raw wounds in the green
silence. People came running, women and old men; they
seemed to appear from nowhere. I saw a man in a leather
apron come out of the village smithy, a gnarled, swarthy,
fierce old man, hairy as to chest and arms. The little crowd
waited for us by the mill where a water-wheel was going
round and round and making a moist rumble. All those
faces seemed to wait for us, beholding me as a messenger of
woe and of disaster.

I saw a woman rush forward.

"Mistress, what news?"

The girl stood still, head up, looking steadily into the
woman's face.

"What you see, you see, Fanta."

She turned and pointed a finger at me, and the gesture
said: "Behold the man, the man without sword or harness,
the poor, hunted sloven. Look at him and understand."

There was a murmur from the crowd. I felt all those eyes
fixed on me, a kind of breathlessness, fear. They were wait-

ing for me to speak, and I was mute. I understood that old phrase, one's tongue clinging to the roof of one's mouth. The mill-wheel rumbled round and round; the water splashed. I was aware of that grim old smith glaring at me like a red-eyed dog.

"Has he lost his tongue?"

"Yes, like his sword!" screeched a woman.

The girl raised her arm in a gesture that made me think of the Fascist salute.

"Listen, my children. Pellias has been wounded. He has lost his memory. He says that he cannot remember."

I could see no pity on those faces. The suspense had been too sharp for them. They had been waiting, waiting, and here was I, the symbol of disaster, a poor dumb idiot, soiled, unshaven and bruised. These people were provoked by a passionate impatience. They wanted news, and I had nothing to give them but a silly, oafish silence.

It was the smith who came up and clutched me by the arm.

"Speak, man, speak."

I just stared at him and mumbled. His impatience seemed to become a fury.

"Where is Mabon my son?"

I shook my head, and he let out a savage snarl, and struck me with his open hand. He struck me twice in the face.

"Will that make you remember? Speak, you fool."

Those smacks hurt and angered me, but he was an old man, and beside himself, and then I heard the girl's voice fly at him like some fierce bird. "Niger!" I saw the rage go out of his eyes, and suddenly he became a whimpering old man.

"Pardon, Lady Meona. It was love that got the better of me."

That was the first time I heard her name. Meona! Moreover, Niger the Smith's words might have been prophetic. Love and Time may get the better of us all.

The crowd followed us up the village to the manor house, as though hoping that my memory might recover itself, or because these women, children and old men looked to the great house for succour and guidance. The courtyard gates were open, and in the porter's lodge sat a very old man with a head that shook like a pea on a wire thread. A big brown hound lay at his feet. The dog was up and nosing against Meona's knees, and licking her hands; she spoke to him more gently than I had heard her speak to any living thing. The porter stood up and bobbed his bald head to her, and squinted at me as though I were some horrid apparition.

"Hail, Master Pellias."

The dog looked up at me with great, solemn eyes, sniffed at my tunic, and seemed suspicious. Had he alone divined the fact that the man whom he knew and the man wearing the body of that Pellias who had been dead in Time for fifteen hundred years or more, were not the same creatures?

We crossed the courtyard to the house. The courtyard was paved with local stone, much like the crazy-paving in my garden, and between the stones dwarf herbs had been planted, so that when a foot crushed them a sweet scent rose up. There were clipped yews and box-trees, and great earthen vases in which green things were growing, a water-cistern in the centre stocked with fish. The great house, built in two storeys, had a loggia between its two outjutting wings, and up the pillars climbed vines and roses. It was a rich and lovely house, stately and serene, its windows looking south across the valley at the uplands and the woods.

Three steps led to the loggia, and I saw two women in

white smocks standing in the doorway. Meona paused on the second step, and turned to speak to me.

"You will stay here."

It was an order and I bent my head to her, but my spirit was beginning to resent her serene young arrogance. Forlorn and desolate I might be, but I was man and young, and in my own world thinking no small beer of myself. She waved to the women, and they disappeared like mutes. I sat down on the steps, and saw the crowd grouped outside the gate, watching me with a kind of ominous, silent curiosity. The old porter had joined them, and was bobbing his head and shuffling about among them as though trying to pick up crumbs of comfort. The dog came and sat at my feet, and stared at me with huge brown eyes. A disconcerting beast! I spoke to him, but he showed no sign of friendliness.

What a situation! I felt both angry and bewildered. My courage was down in my boots, or rather, in those damned sandal-like shoes. I was a ghost in a live body, a spirit embalmed in the carcase of another man long since dead. Good God, when should I wake up, escape from this dream that was so horribly actual and vivid? Should I wake up? Had I been pitched back to the lower curve of some Time Spiral? Was I dead? Had I to climb that spiral all over again, find myself forking muck on some medieval farm, or washing dishes in an Elizabethan kitchen? I felt like cutting my throat.

I had heard voices in the house, and a woman came out to me. She was a youngish wench, like a dark pansy, and she looked at me as though I had the evil eye.

"You are to come before my lord."

I rose and followed her into the house, and I noticed that she kept glancing back at me, and that every time she looked

she made some sort of gesture that might be meant to repel
an evil spirit. The vestibule had a mosaic floor in blue and
white and red, and from the floor a huge Bacchic face leered
at me. The vestibule opened into a corridor that ran the
whole length of the house on its northern side, and it was lit
by narrow windows high up in the wall. Its floor was of plain
red tesseræ. I had no doubt but that I was walking in a
Roman villa, a museum piece that had become alive to harass
the soul of a poor mortal who was dead or dreaming. I stared
at the nape of the girl's neck. It was real enough, with her
dark hair hanging down in two plaits, and a comb tucked
into the crown of it. She shuffled along in slippers, waggling
broad hips.

I saw a gold-coloured curtain closing the end of the corridor.
The girl drew it aside, and shrinking against the wall, spread
her first and little finger at me. Yes, I was evil, something
sinister and under a curse, a bearer of bad news, a ghost
wrapped in blood and horror.

I found myself in what was the summer-room, a stately
chamber that occupied the whole west wing. It had windows
looking both north and south, and a little apsidal cell recessed
in its west wall, and in this recess a lamp was burning. The
walls were frescoed, the floor a fine mosaic, depicting the four
seasons of the year, but all this was vague background to me
for the moment. The human figures alone mattered. I saw
a very old man seated in a curule chair, his hands resting
upon a white stick set like a sword between his knees. Meona
stood behind him, leaning upon the back of the chair. Here
was my Roman master, and never in my life had I looked
upon any creature so fine and masterful as this old man. He
had a great head, and a mane like a snow-white lion, a clear,
fine, sanguine skin, black eyes of peculiar brightness. They

were eyes that held you and fascinated you, jocund, wise, and somehow all-seeing. I got the feeling that this old autocrat was what we should have called a super-man, and that he was more than a mere tyrant. There was humour, a touch of mischief in that long-lipped, mobile mouth. He sat and looked at me, and through me, and over me, until I felt like a boy in the presence of some Olympian and spell-binding "Head."

"Well, my lad, you have been in the wars, I see."

Magnificent he might be, but there was something about him that succoured my soul. This old gentleman was human, infinitely so. Almost, I felt that I could blurt things out to him, and that even if he thought me mad, he would tolerate and comprehend such madness.

"Yes, sir."

He looked at me steadily as a physician might look at a case, sitting very still, with the light playing upon his fine white mane. Then he raised one of his hands, and spoke to his daughter.

"Leave us. Pellias and I have matters to talk of."

She passed round his chair, and I, daring to look at her, saw her somehow differently. She seemed to have become more gentle, more compassionate, more like her name, which had a dark loveliness. She smiled at me, and something happened to me when she smiled in that way. Her dark, swift loveliness became a spell.

The old man sat and looked at me, almost as though he understood my secret, though the thing he suspected was not the thing I was concealing.

"Sometimes, my son, it is wise to forget."

I echoed that one word.

"Sometimes."

"When fools and babes are filled with fear. Tell me, Pellias, how much do you remember?"

This was not a man to whom you could lie, and I found myself calling him lord.

"I can remember nothing, lord."

"What do you remember?"

"Waking up in the heather on Farley Heath."

The words slipped out before I could smother them, an English tail to the dog-Latin I was talking. I saw him frown. Farley Heath must have sounded gibberish to him.

"No more?"

"I felt dazed, lord, and my head ached."

His eyes were keen but kind.

"Come hither, my son. Kneel down."

I knelt at his feet, close to his knees, and putting his stick aside he examined my head, passing his hands over it. His hands were cool and soft, and not like an old man's hands. Then, he took me by the chin, raised my face, and looked into my eyes, as though examining their pupils. He felt my forehead, and my pulse. I might have been in Harley Street.

"A scalp wound. You bled. That cut must have sliced through your helmet. And your father, Gerontius, my steward?"

He may have intended to surprise me, but I looked him straight in the face.

"What of my father, lord?"

"Do you not remember?"

I shook my head. He was very patient with me.

"My son, when the savage terror flamed, the levies of these many manors marched into Kent. Twenty men went from this valley, and your father led them. There were men from the White Ford, men even from Venta. There should have been men from Londinium also, though they are a cowardly, self-seeking people. You remember nothing of all this?"

"Nothing."

He gazed at me intently, and then, putting his hands on the arms of his chair, rose to his feet.

"Stand up, my son."

I rose and standing, found him, old though he was, taller than I was, though I am six feet.

"Come."

He walked to the recess or alcove, and then, I realized its nature. It was the house's lararium, and in its niches were the busts of three gods. The lamp burned steadily on a shelf above the little altar. I remember feeling astonished, for I had believed that Britain in those days had become Christian, and here were the old gods of Rome, not the rustic British deities, but Jupiter, the Sacred Mother, the Genius of Imperial Augustus. Or, so, I took them to be.

The old man placed himself in front of the altar, and facing his gods, raised his right arm.

"O Mysterious Ones, be merciful and strong for our sakes. Let that which has been be."

He turned to me, and moving to one side, bade me kneel in front of the gods.

"Behold, my son, the faces of the Great Ones. Before the gods one does not lie. One may remember."

I knelt down as he bade me, feeling a desperate fool. I shut my eyes, and remembering that favourite play of mine, *Berkeley Square,* I realized that were I to confess to this old man the knowledge that was in me, I might appear as some disturbing spirit of evil, a creature of fantastic and ominous malice. New wine was not for old bottles. I must dream my dream to the end.

"My lord, I cannot remember."

I opened my eyes again and looked at the lamp, and not at those serene, stone faces. How was I to convince him that I could not remember the things that Pellias the son of Gerontius should know?

"My lord, believe me, even your name has gone from me."

He was silent, so silent, that I turned my head and looked at him. He smiled at me as he might have smiled at a sick child.

"That, indeed, is forgetting. You will have to go to school again, my son."

CHAPTER THREE

✤

$\mathscr{I}$ WAS indeed, what we moderns describe as "A Case." My white-headed master might call upon his gods, but I was to discover in him that universality which is the prerogative of all fine and intuitive intelligences in all ages. Somehow, great minds do not date, and I suspect that Plato and Einstein could have strolled together up and down some portico and discussed the eternal mysteries and the manifestations of that otherness that we call God. Stone images are for the crowd and the conventions. My Romano-British philosopher and autocrat understood the uses and the significance of such conventions, but his spirit both accepted and transcended them. He would have said that man must have his Book of the Law, and a conviction that the simple verities matter. Let there be fruitful earth under man's feet, not a cloud of sophistry. Faith must leap over the eternal cliff, while the sophists pelt it with words like peas thrown at a wall. He would have said—and did say—that a people began to slip back into the morass of decadence and pessimism when the clever little apes began to chatter too cleverly. He was to

29

say to me: "Words, my son, may be man's undoing, little bright pebbles with which we play. Look at the sun and the moon and the stars, and marvel."

I often wonder what was at the back of those bright and infinitely sage old eyes. He treated me with great gentleness and understanding. I had lost my memory. Such an erasing of the pattern on the tablets of the mind must have been known to him. I was a case, not a mental one, but a clean slate that had been sponged. I must have interested him, and profoundly so. He treated me rather like a lost child. I was to remain in the great house for that night, and not return to the empty house of my father, that other house further up the valley. I was to eat, sleep, and be rested. He himself saw me settled in a dim little room like a cell where a narrow window showed me the green of the valley. I was given bread and meat, a cup and a jug of water. There was a bed in the room, and a basin and a ewer on a kind of tripod stand.

"Eat and sleep, my son," and he closed the door, and left me.

It grew dark, and very silent, and with the darkness despair came to lie with me in that narrow room. Never have I known such misery. It was more than mere desolation. I felt like a man buried alive in the body of some stranger. I could not sleep. I tried to lie still and face this horror, and to reason it out, and to assure myself that I was dreaming. I kept on saying to myself: "You will wake up, you will wake up." But so acute did this anguish of loneliness become that I left the bed and walked up and down my cell. If I tired myself out, if I slept, I might wake up and find myself back in my old familiar world, that mechanical, noisy, confused and half crazy world to which I had been born. I was frightened, most terribly frightened. So desperate and terrified did I become, that I remember cracking my head against the wall in the hope that the jolt might jar me back into sanity. It did nothing of the kind. The crack left me sick and dizzy, and I had to lie down on the bed.

I lay and listened. The house and the valley had become immensely still. They and I might have been fathoms deep in dark water. There was no moon. Was I dead, and the whole world with me? Had my dream ended in nothingness? I felt my heart beating. And then I thought I heard footsteps in the corridor. They seemed to come to my door and pause there. Someone was listening. I sat up and swung my legs over the edge of the bed, for my impulse was to rush out and seize that listener, and cry out fiercely: "Am I alive? Am I dreaming? Who am I? Who are you?" I sat and shook like a poor, palsied, panic-stricken thing. I heard the footsteps fade away. I lay down again, prone, and drove my face into the pillow. It was soft and warm, and must have been stuffed with down. I wanted either to die or to wake up.

When I opened my eyes again, I was in that half-way-house state between sleeping and waking. It was my twentieth-century self that lay and sleeked itself in that feeling of lazy relaxation. What was the day? Oh, Monday, and no black Monday for me, for I was interested in my job, especially so in the job that was mine at the moment. Moreover, Lucy was coming back to-morrow. What time was it? Time for early morning tea? The room seemed darker than usual, and I turned on my side and reached for my watch which spent the night on the table beside my bed. There was no table, no watch. And then, the horror rushed back on me. I sat up, stark yet shivering. I saw the narrow window, and the green woods streaked with early sunlight, and the red tesserae of the floor, and the pale ochre-coloured walls, and that strange tripod stand with its basin and ewer. My God, I was still in this other world, imprisoned in the body of another man!

I went flat, closed my eyes, and tried to reason the thing out. I wasn't awake; I was still dreaming. Lucy was coming home to-morrow. In five minutes I should hear Mary's knock, and her correct voice saying: "Your early tea, sir." I lay and listened, with my eyes closed. I swore to myself that I could not be in this Roman house; it was a nightmare, a preposterous illusion. When I opened my eyes again I should see all the familiar things about me, Lucy's dressing-table, her wardrobe, her bed with the rose-coloured quilt. I lay in the darkness, and willed myself back into sanity. I had to will myself into opening my eyes. I was cold with fear. I opened my eyes, and saw that damned window, and the green hill-side, and the strange furniture.

I turned over and wept.

How long that frightened-child phase lasted I do not know. Daylight came about four, and it must have been about six o'clock when I pulled myself out of that pit of despair. I felt that I must do something, escape from this place, thrash my way back to that grassy space in the heather where I had been born into this other world. I was obsessed by the childish hope that if I went to sleep on that hill-side I might sleep myself back into my own world. Moreover, this dream-valley was coming to life. I could remember hearing the birds singing up the sun. A bell began to clang as though calling the valley to its labour. I heard stirrings in the house, a woman's voice, the shuffle of feet.

I rose, and pouring water into the basin, sluiced my hands and face. There was no mirror in the room, but my fingers told me of all that stubble on my chin. I was touched by a twinge of vanity. Was it possible to get a shave in this damned place? I did not want to meet Meona, looking like a tramp. But, good God, did it matter? I was going to shake the dust off my shoes.

I plastered my hair down with water, opened the door—it had a queer wooden latch—and looked out into the corridor. I saw a woman on her hands and knees swabbing down the tessellated floor. She raised her head and looked at me, and her eyes were round and unfriendly. Confound the jade! I was moved by a sudden passionate petulance. Was I such a scarecrow? I would try English on her, and see how she reacted. My other self asked that question: "What time is breakfast?" I remembered feeling astonished when I heard my voice asking her in the Latin tongue at what hour we broke our fast.

She stared at me, muttered something, and went on with her work. I think I laughed, as much at myself as at anything, and it was not pleasant laughter. The woman kept her head down as though she had no desire to meet my eyes. I walked past her and found myself in the vestibule with its mocking, Bacchic face. The doors were open, and I saw two pillars of the loggia, and the courtyard, the cistern and clipped trees. The courtyard seemed empty, and the gates were open. My mood was to make a dash for it.

I had reached the loggia when I heard those voices, a sudden ominous clamour. There were the deep voices of men, angry, sullen men. A woman's shrill cry rose in a kind of siren note. Another voice, a woman's, set up a wild wailing. I felt scared, penetrated by a premonition of evil. Good God, what now?

They marched into the courtyard, those returning warriors, surrounded, so it seemed to me, by all the women and old men and children in the village. Four of them carried a litter upon which lay a man who was wounded. They looked a dirty and unshaven and desperate lot of blackguards, a veritable Treasure Island crowd, and yet there was a fierce, wild-eyed impressiveness about them that was to make the approaching scene all the more bitter for me. Their weapons were broken, their harness dusty, scarred, and splashed with blood. One fellow's face was all red bandage; another had his arm lashed to his body. These men had fought and been beaten, but they were not mere cowed fugitives.

I saw a woman in the crowd pointing at me, but there was no need for her to point me out. These fierce, weary and bloody men saw me, and their eyes flashed and their mouths spewed scorn. They shouted at me.

"Hail, coward."

"Hail, the cur who turned his tail."

A horror of this new horror seemed to paralyse me. Had I inherited, not only the body of another man, but his frailties, his poltroonery, his panic in the face of the enemy? I stood leaning against a pillar, and looking into these fierce faces of these survivors. I made myself confront them. Whatever my fate might be, I felt I had to grasp it.

The four men set the litter down near the cistern. There was one old fellow who appeared to be the leader, a grim, thick-set boar of a man. His name was Constantine, and I was to learn that he was an old soldier, a legionary, a veteran who had remained behind upon his farm when Rome had abandoned the island. He had teeth like tusks, and a bristling black beard. He marched up to the loggia steps, stared me in the face and spat.

"Hail, coward! There was valour in your legs!"

The crowd howled.

"Yah, coward."

"He left his father to die."

"The good Gerontius."

"Yes, neighbours, one clip on the head, and he ran. I saw it. He had a face like a frightened girl."

How ironic was all this! I suppose I should have been stricken with shame, but the mockery of the thing began to fill me with fury. I wanted to fly in the face of my own fate as it was expressed by the faces of these other men. I believe I folded my arms, and stood up straight, and tried to look haughty.

"You lie."

That enraged them. They shouted at me. I was bold enough among the women and children, was I? They came crowding to the steps as though they would pull me down and savage me. I suppose no man can say how stout he is or what stuff he has in him until he finds himself in a tight corner, but I had boxed for my school, and until my marriage I had played pretty rough rugby football. I put up my fists and dared them to touch me, but I was to be rescued in a way that was not pleasing to my pride.

There was sudden silence. I saw all those faces lose much of their anger. Their eyes were looking at something behind me. And then I heard her voice, and turned and saw her. She had come to the top of the steps, and stood there confronting these angry men. She looked very pale, and to me very lovely, though there was a fierceness about her beauty, a tinge of scorn that was not comforting to my soul. I should have said that her sign was fire, a pale and stinging flame that made one's pride wince, and one's heart beat hard and harshly.

"Constantine, you shall speak."

She looked them over, forlorn and fierce as they were. She

seemed to be counting them. Her eyes rested for a moment on the stretcher and its burden. I saw her lips move.

"Who lies there?"

"The smith's son, lady."

"So, Gerontius fell."

"Yes, lady, and seven others. We were too few. It was a battle with wild beasts."

She turned and looked at me, and my humiliation was complete. I, the son of Gerontius, had fled the fight. I had left my father to die, and deserted these other men. Ye Gods, how was one to confront such shame, especially when one was innocent? I felt like going berserk and fighting the crowd to show her I was no coward.

"What has Pellias to say?"

What could I say? Every eye was watching me. I was a thing to be scorned and mocked at.

"Have you forgotten?"

Her irony scourged me, and I was mute, but the crowd was not mute, and the women were more bitter than the men. She held up a hand for silence, but I was to be given nothing but sarcasm.

"It seems that Pellias has forgotten. It is sometimes easy to forget. You, Constantine, will tell us what happened to this young man."

The old soldier glared at me.

"Lady, he ran away."

"Without a blow at those wild beasts?"

"Lady, those sea-rovers have fierce faces. They fight like the mad. It takes a brave man to look them in the eyes without flinching."

"And Pellias flinched."

"He had one blow on the head, lady. He fought next me.

I stabbed the man who slashed him. But when I looked to my right, Pellias had gone. We fought in two ranks, lady, the spears behind and thrusting through to break the rush for us swordsmen."

Another man broke in, the one with the bandaged arm.

"I was behind Pellias, lady. He pushed me aside and ran. I saw his white face, and blood."

"Yes," said another, "he ran."

There was silence, and she turned again and looked at me, and my face must have been as stark and as white as the face of the man who had fled in panic.

"Have you forgotten that, also?"

I felt sullen. The injustice of the thing was too damnable.

"Yes, I have forgotten."

The crowd laughed, and its laughter was not pleasant to my pride.

"Let him be put into women's clothes and wash floors."

But a woman in the crowd protested.

"No, no, we women are not like that. Let him go naked and feed the swine."

Meona raised her hand again.

"People, go about your labours. Constantine, and you, Felix, you will stand before my father. And you—"

I drew myself up to meet that blow.

"And you, Pellias, will go to your room and stay there until Aurelius Superbus, my father, chooses to speak with you. Go."

Her voice was a whip, and for a moment I was moved to flout her, to leap down and charge through the crowd, and run for the woods, but I smothered that impulse. Those fierce men would stop me. I could see that they were lusting to lay hands upon the coward. I should be ducked, beaten, pelted, thrown upon a dungheap, and I had had as much shame as

I could stomach. I turned and walked into the house. No one spoke or jeered, and the silence was more bitter than any mocking or cursing. I passed up the corridor, and into my cell, and closed the door, and sat down on the bed.

What a bloody riddle had I to solve!

Was this dream to persist, and was I to be a shameful ghost in the centre of the picture?

And what would Aurelius make of it?

Aurelius? Aurelius Ambrosius was a great name shining strangely out of those dim, old, tragic days. Was my white-maned philosopher a member of that notable Romano-British clan? I felt myself enveloped in those twilight idylls, and sharing in the sunset cries of conquered Kings. Aurelius Ambrosius, Uther Pendragon, Arthur, Guinevere! I sat on my bed with my head in my hands, and my blood felt like water in me.

CHAPTER FOUR

❧

An hour or more must have passed while I sat on that bed, trying to remember the little I knew of the history of Roman Britain, to make some sort of pattern of the world in which I found myself. I had read Haverfield and other experts on the subject, and I did know that the period intervening between the passing of Rome and the dominance of the Saxons was obscure, a wilderness of legend and conjecture. Still, the Roman cult had flowered in the island for nearly four hundred years, and that is a long time. I had read that the level of civilization was higher then until, perhaps, the period of the Jacobeans. Nor had the Romano-British culture tumbled after the passing of the legions. It had fought, and often successfully so, for two hundred years, only gradually to be dispossessed of the fertile, civilized south, and driven into Cornwall, Wales, and Strathclyde.

But where was I in this ancient pattern? In the house of a Romano-British notable, one Aurelius Superbus, who might be an uncle, a brother or a cousin of that other Aurelius who had rallied Britain and driven back the sea-rovers, and the

39

Scotch and Irish? The barbarians had invaded Kent. I remembered the stories of Vortigern and Hengist and Horsa. Had I, as Pellias, marched to repulse one of these many raids? Who had led us? Had the disaster been utter? Would those blond savages come ravaging along the Downs and the Valley of the Thames, and pour with fire and sword into this Surrey valley? The Weald, I supposed, was a wilderness. Londinium might be too tough a nut for them. Silchester or Calleva, that rich little town amid the woods, might prove a lure. There were villas and manors to be plundered in West Sussex and on the Hampshire borders. And this valley? Had the Jutes occupied Kent? Was this a mere raid, or a deliberate advance, a conquering and settling of new lands?

Good God, but what a strange way of learning history, to be tumbled back into it, to live it with every sort of emotion tearing out one's vitals! I was history in the making. I was a blood-stained and desperate participator in one of those dim tragedies of which the learned write with tepid and dispassionate detachment. Maybe I was to listen to the wailing of women, and see houses and cities go up in flames, know fear in the dark woods. Maybe I was to go down to my death in shame and anguish. Maybe, I was to look into the scornful eyes of a girl. Damnation, if I was to share, even dreamfully, in these confused and poignant happenings, was I to play the part of coward? Was this the Roman *fatum*? Was I a ghost following a pre-ordained path, walking some prescribed gallery, or was the part mine, to play it as I pleased, even in a dream?

Free Will and Destiny, one can argue those problems interminably, but my furious groping into the past and into the future was broken by a sound. I heard footsteps in the corridor. Someone was coming to my door.

There was a click of the wooden latch, and a face looked in, a face I had not seen before, a moon face fringed with pale hair. It lisped at me. This was a mannerish person, affected, precise, inadequately supercilious, and I seemed to divine the scribe.

"My lord awaits you."

I followed this gentleman's gentleman along the corridor to the summer-room, noting the baldish head and the finicky movements of the creature. He walked like a woman. There was no stride about him. This was Gildas, my lord's secretary. He drew the curtain aside, and I saw that he wore a signet ring, a most Byzantine-looking ring. He announced me.

"The man Pellias, my lord."

The man, indeed! Damn him! I felt more than man to this blowfly.

Aurelius was sitting in his chair. His eyes seemed to remain fixed upon me from the moment that I entered, but, somehow, the depth and steadfastness of that gaze did not vex me. I bent my head and shoulders to him, and there was a naturalness in the homage that I gave him. This old man was a serene and princely person. Master Gildas placed himself beside his lord's chair, and produced his tablets and a style. The occasion was to be official so far as this scribbling functionary was concerned.

The old man raised a hand, but without taking his eyes off me.

"You can leave us, Gildas."

The secretary bowed, and looking primly peeved, shuffled out of the room. The door closed, and there was silence. I waited, only to hear Aurelius say a most unexpected thing to me, and to say it with a smile that was like the touch of a friend's hand.

"Go to the door and look. Go softly."

I went and opening it, found our friend, half smothered up in the curtain, waiting to play the interested listener. I smiled at him, and he snapped a vicious look at me, and assuming the attitude of a man who was about to draw the curtain across the door, did so, and minced off.

My lord's eyes were jocund.

"A man's affairs, my son, may become the property of his servant. Gildas was there?"

"He was, sir."

My lord did not laugh, but his eyes enjoyed the joke. Thank the lord, my Roman master had a sense of humour and a taste in wit. I was conscious of a strange sense of relief, in that I was in touch with a personality, and a mind that had a modern flavour, which, God forgive me, sounds like priggery. I had a feeling that there was greatness and wisdom and a calm courage in this magnificent old man. He was both timeless and dateless. He was Jove and Jehovah, and Aristotle and Galileo, Walt Whitman and Lloyd George. Something seemed to laugh in me as those names poured out, and God knows, I needed laughter.

He bent his brows on me.

"There is something strange in you to me, my son."

My heart gave a leap. Should I tell him? Could I tell him? I was wild to unburden myself to some human soul, and after all, he could only think me mad.

"You have great wisdom, sir."

He smiled at me almost roguishly. I was not to flatter.

"I know what I do not know. The gods are figures on a curtain and beyond that lies mystery. But let us remember that the mystery must have meaning. No Euclidian figure that, my son, but divination."

I looked him straight in the face.

"My lord divines something."

He was silent, surveying me.

"My son, you have not the eyes of a coward."

I moistened my lips. The confession was on my tongue.

"My lord, I am no coward."

"You do not remember?"

"I am not that Pellias who fled."

He leaned forward, and his face was like white light.

"Who are you?"

I wanted to blink under his gaze.

"You would not believe, lord. It is not credible."

He answered me sharply.

"Granted that there is mystery, everything is credible. Who are you?"

I felt my legs trembling under me. Should I tell him? And if I did confess, would he think me some evil spirit, a thing to be cast out? Would he have my body crucified, torn asunder, burnt and thrown to the winds? I felt I had to dare it.

"Lord, I will tell you. I am a man yet to be born. I am a man who lived hundreds of years hence. I am a ghost out of the future, somehow thrown back into the body of your steward's son."

His hands gripped the chair arms. I could hear his breathing in that supernatural silence. His eyes seemed to look right through me.

"A ghost out of the future! Poor ghost."

There was such gentleness, such understanding in those two words that suddenly I fell on my knees before him. I stretched out my hands.

"Master, I am lost, bear with me. I dream, and yet my

dream is real. I am alone, ye Gods, how alone. And yet, to you, this must seem madness."

He put out his hands and drew me to him.

"My son, I too have dreamed dreams. There is more in this strange world than one wots of. I believe souls pass. But in dreaming one thinks of souls as passing on, not back. How did it begin with you?"

I raised my face to his.

"Is it possible that you believe me?"

"My son, I listen. One can do no more than listen, and marvel, and ask of The Mystery questions it will not answer. How did it begin with you?"

I told him.

"In the year nineteen hundred and thirty-nine I drove out in the horseless chariot we used in those days. I remember no more. I woke up in the heather, wearing strange clothes. I was afraid. I looked for the things I know, and they were not there. I saw things that were strange to me, a temple, your daughter, a landscape that was the same and yet different."

He continued to look steadily into my eyes like some diviner gazing into a crystal.

"Are such things possible, or is the man moon-struck? And where, my son, is the spirit of that other Pellias, my Pellias?"

That was a problem that had puzzled me. If I had stolen the body of that other man, where was his spirit?

"Who knows? If I am a ghost—"

He laid his hands on my shoulders, and bore heavily on them.

"It is a very solid ghost. But this is beyond human understanding. Do you remember the life in the world from which you came?"

"Everything. That is the strangest part of it. I am a new man in the body of one—" And then I paused, remembering *Berkeley Square,* and the way the long-since dead had flinched from the ghost unborn.

His face seemed to grow very old. I think he had caught my meaning.

"So, to you, my son, I have been dead a thousand and a half years. And to you, our little tragedies and wars and terrors must be the dust of history. You know what we fear, the to-morrow."

He gripped my shoulders and stared me in the face.

"Does Rome still stand?"

I nodded.

"And Byzantium?"

"Yes, master. But—"

I felt his fingers pressing into my flesh. If he was afraid of me, as well he might be, he feared other things, the horror of knowing that which might be to him disaster, and to me, mere history. He rose, and going to the window looked right and left, and then he closed the lattice. He passed to the door, opened it, pulled the curtain aside, and stood listening. Then he closed the door, and began to walk up and down. I felt his eyes upon me as upon some fatal thing. I might be a lantern in a dark house, or a cup of poison. I felt accursed.

Presently, he came and stood over me.

"In your days do you speak the Latin tongue, my son?"

"No. We learn it in our schools, as a—"

I caught myself up. Nearly had I said: "A dead language."

"And yet you speak it."

"That is part of the strangeness."

He looked hard at me, walked to the alcove, and stood before his gods. Mystery! Those little stone busts were impotent, mute, helpless. He came back and stood over me again, as though reflecting fiercely upon this problem.

"Is the lad possessed? Is it a dream? Ye Gods, but there is peril in such dreaming."

I understood him.

"You would have me dead and silent, master."

"Not dead, my son, but silent. My soul is torn by a dreadful curiosity, but even I do not dare—"

I looked up at him as a gentle ghost might look at a mortal and apologize for haunting him.

"I will be silent."

"Is there that strength in you?"

"I will attempt it."

"That is well, my son. Otherwise, even we might will you to be dead. Words can slay; words can make men mad. We have other things to fear."

I nodded at him, for I understood. Violence might be very near to this valley and its ordered life, and my lord was no man to quail or to surrender to a crowd of savages. But how ironical it all was, for I was a descendant of the savages! None the less, his need was courage, courage for his people if they were to defend what was theirs and make head against invasion.

He was still standing over me.

"By the Gods, my son, it puzzles me what to do with you. Are you a meteor, heralding disaster? Or have you been sent to succour us? I must think, I must think."

He tossed his great white mane, and I, still kneeling there, was moved by his emotion.

"Master, some strange turn of time's wheel has brought you and me together. What is there to do but accept the mystery. I will swear silence. I will answer no questions save the questions that you ask me."

He looked hard at me again.

"My son, I will trust you. Stand up, and come with me before my gods, and swear by the God behind the gods that you will be silent."

I stood with him in the little sanctuary, raised my arms, and swore, and then, holding me by the shoulders, he kissed me upon the forehead.

"There is my seal, Pellias. You and I must keep faith with each other."

Having put me upon my honour he straightway treated me as a man of honour. He told me that I should remain in his house for the next few days, and eat at his table. His kindness both comforted and disarmed me, though I did suspect that were I to break faith with him he could be ruthless. He asked me whether I wished to be alone and to shape myself in solitude for the strange part I had to play, and I, remembering my foul face, asked if I could be barbered. He was amused, and he was Roman in his cleanliness. A barber should be sent to me; I should be shown the bath.

In fact he treated me like a privileged guest. I was shaved by a fat little man who served me with circumspection; and who seemed to fear that I might try and snatch the razor from him and cut my throat or his. The fine temper of the razor surprised me. I was given a robe and taken to the bath, a fair chamber off the east wing. It had a hot bath and a cold plunge, and the water had been heated for me. The floor and the lining of the baths were of mosaic, white and slate-blue tesseræ, the walls distempered yellow. I bathed, and my barber friend dealt with me, planking me on a marble slab, and massaging me and rubbing in perfumed oil. He examined my cracked head, washed away the clotted blood, and applied some ointment to the wound which had sealed itself up cleanly. When I went back to my sleeping cell I found clean clothes laid out on the bed, a white tunic, a kind of purple cloak, new shoes, and a green girdle. I put them on and rather wished I had a mirror to see how I shaped as a Roman Briton.

I heard a knock at my door.

"My lord awaits you in the garden."

I followed the barber. He led me to a little door at the end of the corridor, and passing through it, I found myself in the garden. And what a garden! It astonished me. It seemed so English. It had a high flint wall, and gravel paths, and box edging, and a pergola covered with vines and roses and wild clematis. Fruit trees were trained against the high grey walls. There were few flowers in it as yet, for the year was young, but some of the fruit trees were still in blossom. At the end of the pergola I saw a great stone seat set in an arbour made of clipped yews. Aurelius was sitting there, leaning upon his stick, his white head looking as though it carried a garland.

I could see his eyes studying me as I walked up under the vines. The garden backed upon a steep meadow and the high woods, and I was to learn that the high wall was to keep out the deer. There were wild boars and wolves in the Weald, but the wolves were not many, and were dangerous only in winter. I am something of a gardener, and a garden is always associated in my mind with a pipe, but my hand did not go into a non-existent pocket for the ghost of a pipe and pouch. I had not smoked, for how long was it? God knows! But in this other man's body the craving was unborn in me. I think I smiled. No nicotine, no tea, no coffee! In heaven, it is suggested, one gets one's whisky and one's cigar, if one needs them, but in this dream-world my drink was to be wine and water, and a home-made brew like beer.

We men are vain creatures, and I was no weed. I had fancied myself in football togs, and the body of Pellias was that of a tough fellow. My lord was eyeing me with approval. I was shaved and washed and dressed, and my new girdle was tight round tough loins. Was my spirit tougher than my double's, and capable of making more use of a comely body? I must have smiled at my master, and perhaps swaggered just a little. He bade me stand before him, and I did.

"You have not the eyes of a coward, my son."

"That is to be proved."

"Tell me, do you new men carry swords?"

"No, sir. We go unarmed, save for the professional soldiers."

"Your legions. So it was in this island until recently. No man was allowed to bear arms unless he was a soldier. That has been one of our misfortunes. We had the Roman peace, but when the legions left us we were tame, untrained men. Our young men had not been hardened to war."

How strange was this! It put me back into my other life and our reaction to the German menace and the sudden awakening to it of an unarmed England. Here was yet another German menace, for the Saxons were of the same stock. I could have pushed a platitude at him, and observed that history repeated itself, but with bombs and poison-gas and propaganda, instead of with swords and spears.

He bade me sit down beside him.

"How like you this garden, Pellias?"

I did not say that its beauty and order surprised me, but he must have divined my thought, for he spread a hand as though blessing the sacred and secret place.

"We of the Roman spirit love beauty and order, or the beauty of order. We ask to control what is round us, either as peasant or as prince. An old man must cultivate his garden. So, have we cultivated this valley. And now we have these half-naked savages let loose on us. Attila scourges the world, and these sea-wolves, escaping from the greater beast, fall upon us."

Had we in my England not confronted the same spectre of ruin, cities blown to pieces, houses wrecked, women and children lying dead in the streets? The order and the liberty and the happy, playful fancy of a free man's life sacrificed to a booted fanaticism!

I said: "Such good things should not pass."

I felt him watching me.

"And what would you do, my son?"

"Fight."

He laid a hand upon my shoulder.

"You are not that other Pellias, it seems. And yet his fate is upon you. Consider what was, what is, and what might be. Can a ghost out of the future strive to serve the past?"

His words moved me very strangely.

"My fate, perhaps, is now and here."

"Consider it, my son. I make you free of my garden, and my trust."

He rose, and I stood beside him.

"Master, that which was—is, and yet perhaps differently so."

He left me to walk in his garden and to meditate upon these things.

CHAPTER FIVE

〄

*H*AD all this happened before?

How had my poor ghost-brother Pellias responded to the challenge of his fate? Had he continued in cowardice, or had he discovered in that cowardice the spur of courage? A man is not always brave, or always a coward. Circumstance casts its spell, the web of happenings in which he may find himself.

But what of myself? If I was imprisoned in the body of another man in a dead-live dream world, was I to play the man or the coward? Did I wish these dream-people to think well of me? Did I desire to shine, or be howled at and treated with savage scorn?

I walked round that walled garden, and looked at the sky and the woods, and those blue distances, and felt the thing we call romance stirring in my blood. What an adventure was this, no tame world, no catching of the inevitable train, no daily paper, no office-chair. What had one's adventure been? Some car-scuffle with a week-end cad on the Portsmouth Road, and since I possessed some sense and decency the cad usually had had the best of it. He could do things which the sportsman in me could not do. Also, if one crashed because of a cad, one's wife might suffer.

Yes, Lucy!

Had she suddenly grown dim to me? Was I forgetting? Would this Roman world prove to be reality, and my other life a dream? The old anguish stabbed me. My bowels yearned suddenly for all those other human contacts, people to whom I could talk, not ghosts who would not understand. This silence seemed too dreadful, too crushing. It was like being buried alive.

I went and sat on the seat under the arched yews, with my head in my hands.

How had that other Pellias answered the challenge?

Cut his throat, fallen upon a sword, hanged himself?

Was that my choice, silence in death, or silence in daring to live?

For the moment I could find no answer.

The answer was to be discovered for me, or thrust upon me as an emotional spasm. I was staring across the garden, when I saw that door open, and a figure appear. Meona! She was dressed in some saffron-coloured stuff, and her black and brilliant hair was loose upon her shoulders. It was plain to me that she thought herself alone in this walled place, though an old, round-backed man had come in by another door and was busy with a long-handled spade in a distant corner. It was like a modern French spade, a tool with a long handle. But my eyes were on Meona. She came up the broad path under the climbing vines, sometimes in the sunlight, sometimes in the shadow. Her face had a gentleness that I had not seen before, a beautiful, douce pallor. Her eyes looked larger, darker in the broad soft oval of her face, her mouth

less of a hard red streak. She was looking up at the sky and
the pattern of the vine leaves, and her young beauty wounded
me. That haughty little nose of hers looked less cruel about
the nostrils. But how impossible it is to describe a face, especially a face that is sensitive and swift, and so strangely significant as hers was. All I can say is that the exquisite outlines
of her, her symmetry, her poise, the sharp sweet flavour of
her colouring, the very way she moved, filled me with a kind
of wounded sadness.

I stood up, and then she saw me. Never have I seen a face
change its mood more swiftly. Her head went up, her eyes
flashed, her nostrils seemed to swell. She looked at me as
at something that was less than man, less than that lumpy
old fellow digging over yonder. Her scorn stabbed me. I
understood that in a wild world such as hers might be, a
woman had no use for cowards.

"Who gave you leave to be here?"

I must have reddened up like a boy.

"My lord, your father."

That might be news to her, but she stood as though waiting
for some mean thing to remove itself. I was less than a flea-
ridden cur. And I was angry, angry with the deep and
urgent anger of primitive, male pride.

"You do me no justice, Meona."

When I spoke her name she gave me such a lift of·the head,
and a look of such devastating scorn that I knew my place.
That vulgar phrase "Hoity-toity" flashed into my consciousness. One might have said to a modern wench: "Cut it out,
old thing, cut out the pose and the Dietrich business." But
my lady was not a modern wench, nor was I a lad in sloppy
grey bags and a coloured pullover. Her prides and her scorns
were actual and vivid, and so would her passion be, like light-

ning or the rush of rain, or the wind sweeping the tree-tops. I was her father's servant, and a sorry and a futile one at that. I had no honour in her eyes, not even the honour of crude courage.

I stood aside, and she swept into the arbour and sat down, and since I did not immediately remove myself, she looked at me steadfastly and with a sharp serenity that left me in no doubt as to my duty. This garden was no place for me while she chose to walk or sit in it. Had I been toiling with a spade, like the old gardener over yonder, she might have tolerated me, but as it was I was a poor, spunkless lout who did not know his place. And I had rather fancied myself in my new tunic and cloak and girdle.

She said: "It would seem, fellow, that you have forgotten many things."

Fellow! I felt furiously hot about the ears, but her natural scorn was too much for me. Her eyes said: "Remember to go," and I went, and tried to do it with dignity, though I imagine that my reactions were of no more interest to her than the flutterings of a sparrow.

I got back into my cell, and shut myself in, and wondered what her response would have been had I broken my promise to her father, and told her the incredible truth.

Damn it, I was moved to go back and tell her the truth. And what would she have thought? That I was completely and insolently out of my senses?

I am ashamed to say that her stabbing scorn pushed me into a mood of agonized self-pity. I did not see red for long, but pale primrose. That a creature so indubitably lovely and untouchable as she was should regard me as less than man, and not even as a valued lackey, threw me into such desperate petulance that I did not ask myself how else she could regard me. What had that damned fellow Pellias done to deserve even her tolerance? I sat on my bed and hated my Roman self and her, this black-eyed young tigress to whom I was less than a sheep. I wanted to be back in my own world, oh, terribly so. If I could only turn that mysterious corner and find myself in the 5.37 from Waterloo, reading the *Evening Standard,* and the last example of egregious Fascist insolence. No, not even that. The Wimbledon results would be more familiar and soothing. I simply was not up to the standard of this haughty and wounded young woman, the daughter of a Romano-British petty noble, and for the moment I was as bitter an example of the inferiority complex as any little raging Red.

How long I sat there I do not know, but someone, a servant, came to my door and told me that dinner was served. Good God, was I expected to sit at her father's table with her, and bear her silent surprise and her scorn? She would not understand that her father and I shared a secret. No doubt she might think that the old gentleman had gone potty. But the servant was waiting, a little contemptuously so. If my lord chose to be foolishly magnanimous to his dead steward's son, well, that might be the strange privilege of the gentry! I got off my bed, and followed the fellow along the corridor to the summer-room. An oak table stood by the south window, an oblong table. My lord's chair was placed at the head of it, and he was sitting in it. Meona was standing by a chair on the right. I saw a vacant stool on the opposite side. That was to be my pillory.

There was a feeling of unrest in the room, and I imagine that there had been some high argument between Aurelius and his daughter. Probably she had scorned the idea of sit-

ting down with the agent's son when that person was so poor
a specimen of the fighting man, and after she had shown him
the height of her pride. Possibly, my lord had been reasoning
with her, describing me as a man sick of soul who was deserv-
ing of compassion. My lord smiled at me and waved me to
my stool. Meona took her chair, and did not so much as look
at me. In truth, through all that dreadful meal she looked
past me and over me with a calmness and a contempt that
were complete.

I felt like a lout, and I blurted like one.

"I see, sir, you use Castor ware."

Castor ware it was, and I had recognized it, and the pattern of animals with big eyes, and slim flowing bodies. My
lord lifted me out of that indiscreet venture, while I was
bothered about my table manners. We were provided with
little silver-handled knives and tiny two-pronged forks. So,
one did not use one's fingers!

"I see that you are beginning to remember, my son."

I glanced at Meona's face, and its utter aloofness challenged
me. Could I not show myself as a somewhat responsible
person, a grown man capable of confronting the very terrible
threat that hung over their world? The manservant who had
brought me from my room, served us from a little side-table,
which, I gather, was carried in from the kitchen.

"Wine or beer, sir?"

I chose wine, and red wine was poured into a glass beaker.
My lord was watching me, and I was watching how he dealt
with his food, cooked meat and a green vegetable like spin-
ach, and a brownish bread. I reminded myself that potatoes
were confined to that as yet undiscovered New World. I
felt that I ought to make conversation, for the silence was
smothering.

"Is there any news, sir?"

My lord gave me a sharp look. There was a warning in it, and to cover the lapse, I raised my beaker and drank. The wine was good, though a little sweet as though it had been treated with honey. The silence continued. And then I heard a horn blown, and the clatter of a horse's hoofs on the stones of the courtyard. With one swift movement, Meona rose from her chair and crossed to the window.

"Festus is back from Pons Albus."

Aurelius looked at me steadily behind his daughter's back, and shook his great white head at me, but if this was a reprimand, it was a kind one. His very wise eyes seemed to say to me: "There is more virtue in silence than in speech. Silence can answer every question. Silence can be both armour and a cloak." I felt very small and futile, like a junior clerk sitting at a managing director's table, who, in trying to show that he was not self-conscious, had blurted himself into profound foolishness. Yes, silence was the thing. Meanwhile, Meona, without waiting for her father's word, had given her orders to those in the courtyard. "Send Festus in." This young woman carried life swiftly on her imperious, confident shoulders.

She returned to her chair, and for the first time she glanced at me directly. It was the look one gave to a person who was superfluous, and who might be crassly insensitive as to that superfluity. I pushed back my stool, as though to rise and leave them, but my lord said quietly and with authority: "Stay where you are."

The man Festus came into the room. He was a very dark man, about my own age, with an alert, lean face, and humorous eyes. He was dusty and hot, and wearing harness, and breast-plate and greaves and a kind of leather tunic. A sword

was belted to him. I liked the look of Festus. I thought him
a fine, well-tempered figure of a man, taut and tall and lean
and mordant, such a man as I might wish to be, and carrying
arms and carrying them as though he could use them. He
was wearing a peaked leather cap, rather like a jockey's. He
saluted Aurelius.

"Well, what news, Festus?"

"Pons Albus lost seven men, lord. I had a talk with their
dux. He said that the men of Londinium left them in the
lurch."

"Paltry fellows. Any news of the savages?"

"No, lord. Pons Albus sent two horsemen along the Ridgeway this morning. They rode as far as Cæsar's Head. No
smoke, no sign of the barbarians."

Aurelius nodded his white head.

"In what strength were they? My fellows talk of thousands."

"Hundreds, lord, but very fierce and strong. One of our
scouts rode round their host. He said that there were women
and wagons in the rear."

That, I gathered, was grave news. This was no mere raid,
but an advance in force to take land and hold it.

"Which way will they march, Festus?"

"Maybe along the Ridgeway, lord. Or they may come
along the river, or if they strike the great road, turn away
towards Regnum. Londinium is too strong for them."

"We must watch, Festus, keep scouts on the hills. If our
neighbours will gather we may hold them off."

I noticed that Festus kept looking at me with curiosity. I
suppose that he had heard my story, and yet his glances were
not unfriendly. I had behaved like a coward, and maybe to

him I looked stouter than my reputation.

It was Meona who spoke next.

"Let someone ride to Londinium and see what their spirit is. I will go, if Festus will ride with me."

Her father shook his head.

"No. I will have out my chariot and drive to speak with the Aquilas and Pontius of Pontes. We must act together if our country-side is to be saved."

Much of this was mere gibberish to me, though it might be grim gibberish, and devastatingly significant to these dwellers in Surrey. I could suppose that the Saxons had conquered Kent, and had established themselves there, and were now pushing forward into Surrey, Middlesex and Sussex. I had read of the storming of Anderida and the slaughter of the Britons therein, but my dates were as confused as my emotions. Someone had written of London as a city holding out like a citadel, while the barbarians pushed past it into Surrey and Berkshire, and that London in its death-rattle was a deserted place. And what of Christianity? I had supposed that Britain was Christian, but as yet I had seen no sign of the Cross. What of Pelagius, that gentle heretic?

Festus went out to order my lord's chariot. I was to learn that Festus was a farmer and a breeder of horses on the Downs above what was to be Guildford. I was feeling dreadfully out of things, but I sat glued to my stool. I could suppose that good manners would not permit me to rise before my lord.

Meona was standing by the window, perhaps wishing that she was a man and suffered to ride out armed against these invaders. She looked fierce, frustrated, petulant.

"I go with you in the chariot. I can handle the horses."

I had no doubt that she could, and her father did not gainsay her.

"Festus will ride with us."

"Ah, he is a man."

Did she turn her head and look at me? I sat there, not knowing what to do with my face or my hands. My lord rose from his chair, and took pity on me.

"Rest that head of yours, Pellias."

I rose and walked to the door. I wanted to be alone, even with my loneliness, and yet I wanted to see that chariot, with Meona handling the reins.

I went out into the corridor, and the old man followed me.

"Patience, my son."

There was a stone bench in the corridor, and I flopped down on it and put my head in my hands. I wanted to escape. I wanted to follow a last desperate impulse that took control and swept me along. If I could see my own country might not this dream-horror pass? If I found myself in that little familiar corner, might not everything come back to me?

Aurelius laid his hand on my head.

"Is your soul lost, my son?"

I shivered. I raised my face.

"Lord, let me go for a few hours. In my world I lived over beyond those hills. I would go and look and search."

He eyed me steadfastly, compassionately.

"Go, my son, if your spirit is in darkness. But, if—"

I pulled myself together.

"If it has all gone, I will come back."

I made him that promise, praying that I should not have to keep it. Anything and everything might happen if I could see the old Wey and those familiar fields and scraps of heath.

Yes, the Brooklands woods, and Vickers, and the grey spire of Weybridge church, and my own little white house, and aeroplanes flying overhead.

He patted me on the shoulder.

"Well, go, my son. But, remember, danger is abroad."

Danger! What did I care? I was mad to go, and try to stagger back into the future.

But I wanted to see them sally. I sneaked back into the summer-room and stood at the window. The chariot was waiting in the courtyard with a couple of white horses harnessed to the pole. It made me think of an old-fashioned dog-cart set low between the wheels, which had carved spokes painted white and blue. The hubs were gilded. It was certainly a luxury machine, its dash-board painted yellow, and its broad seat padded with leather. Reins and harness were of red leather, and fitted to the dash-board was a long, trumpet-shaped basket in which were a bow, arrows, and a hunting spear. The chariot had neither springs nor mud-guards, and you entered it by a little side door fitted into the body.

Festus and two other fellows were mounted and ready. They carried spears and wore swords. I'll confess there was a part of me that envied Festus on his great black horse. Festus was a fighting-man, and I less than a camp-follower. I saw Meona come down the steps. She was wearing a Phrygian cap and a soft, green leather jerkin buttoned tight to her throat. She carried a whip. My God, she could handle other kinds of whips! My lord followed her, helping himself with his stick. Meona took charge of the chariot. She did not sit, but stood to her work like a charioteer, and she made me think of a figure of Winged Victory. Aurelius took his seat. The white horses needed no urge from the crack of the short-handled whip, for they felt the spirit of the girl whose hands held the reins. Festus and his men turned their horses and rode out through the gateway. The blue and white wheels revolved, and Meona, leaning back with her weight on the reins, checked the impatience of those two beasts as the chariot made for the gate. Then, the wall hid them from my eyes, but they came into view again a little way down the valley, where the mill stood among willows and poplars. Festus and his men were cantering, and Meona had given the white horses their heads. I saw dust flying, and the chariot bumping and rolling, its yellow hubs flashing. That fierce young woman was a speed-merchant, and I wondered how her father felt about her chariot-charge. Was he holding to the seat, and pressing his feet against the floor-boards? But I was to learn that my lord could be as impetuous and fear-free as his daughter, with a white head that was, perhaps, a little cooler than her black one.

CHAPTER SIX

✂✂

No ONE hindered my going, or flattered me by attempting to interfere with my freedom. I walked across the courtyard and out of the great gate into the village street, if one can call it a street. I suppose that to the people I was Pellias the coward, or Pellias the nit-wit, and that in such times as these tame lunatics are not given garlands.

I heard Niger the Smith hammering away in his smithy, and I imagined that he was beating out sword blades or spearheads. Children were looking in at the door at the spark-spurting, roaring forge, and watching Niger hammering white-hot metal. One of the children, a boy, turned and saw me pass, and all he did was to put out his tongue at me. So that was that!

I had in mind the sunken lane that cut its way up out of the valley to the North Downs and Newland's Corner. Was it there still? It was, though a much more shallow trackway, and its persistence cheered me. I felt that I was in a valley of dreams—Honey Village was its name in those days—and that if I escaped from it I might shed my ghost-self. I wanted to run, but there was a cunning in me that remembered that I

63

had a dozen or so miles to go across wild country and that I had better take the climb steadily. I passed a farm, and a large yellow dog came and barked at me. I was polite to him, for I had not so much as a stick in my hand.

"Hallo, old fellow."

He was an unfriendly dog, and he barked the harder, adding growls to his get-off-my-earth warning.

It seemed dark and gloomy in this hollow way with its smother of bushes and trees, but when I came out on to the uplands I found that the sky had changed with that stealthy suddenness that is England. A wind had sprung up, and a greyness had spread over the landscape, though the distant hills retained a tinge of blue. How familiar was this clearness before rain, this grey and gusty sadness! I stood on the hill-side and looked at the familiar scene, Hascombe, Hazlemere, the three blobs that mark Hindhead. I could see Farley Heath, and the little temple very white against the gloom of heather and firs. No, there was no doubt about that temple, and the absence of Albury's bald new church, and the uncrowned head of St. Martha's. No silver smoke over Guildford, no trains running in the valley, the Weald a wilderness. I turned north, and saw the yews and thorns and scattered beeches, gorse, and the broad green ribbon of the Ridgeway. And there were those two white chalk knolls with a grass trackway running between them. I understood their significance now. They were great guide-posts that could be seen through the gap in the green-sand ridge and right across the Weald to the South Downs. They must mark the way over the chalk hills down into the Thames Valley, and the bridge at Staines, or the fords at Weybridge or Kingston. It was so. When I stood between the two tumuli I saw a trackway heading north, and following it found it becoming a gravelly lane that went down into the valley. I saw the low ground spread before me, not as I knew it, but wilder, more wooded, with no familiar blobs of tile and brick stippling it. No tall Woking chimney, no St. George's Hill, no distant gasometers, no Newland's Corner Hotel. The absence of that bizarre white building hurt me rather absurdly, for I was rather fond of the place. Lucy and I had dined and danced there.

I took a long look at the landscape, trying to find some marker for my route, and I saw one whitish building in the middle distance that seemed to lie in the way I should take. The rough road travelled in that direction, and it occurred to me that this track might head for the junction of the Wey and the Thames and a passable ford there. I did know that one main Roman road to the west had run from London to Staines, and so on to Silchester, and this track might cross the river and join it. I was going down hill now, and I started to trot. I was still buoyed up by the hope that now that I had escaped from that enchanted valley the landscape would suddenly revert to the landscape that I knew.

The trackway took me across the lower ground somewhere between the two Clandons, but most of it was wild country, all woods and heather. The only human being I met was a peasant boy leading a donkey with panniers full of charcoal. He smiled at me as though he knew me, but I, not knowing him at all, smiled back and trotted on. I passed two or three small farms, little secret places hidden in what were glades, but though I saw cattle grazing, no one came out to speak with me. My one duty lay in following this track, for had I tried to cut across country I should have lost myself. Whether it was my own feeling of suspense, or the sudden greyness of the day, but I got the impression that fear was abroad, and that the very clouds were heavy with menace.

The track dived into a deep wood, climbed out of it, and arrived at the edge of a low, flat hill. There were open fields here, and orchards, and I saw ahead of me the white house that I had spotted from the Downs. My mood was to avoid it, but the track ran directly past it, and the fields were hedged and ditched like English fields. Well, what had I to fear? Yet, as I neared the place I became aware of human activities, of clumsy wains and carts parked on a grassy space near the wall of this Surrey villa. Men were loading furniture and gear into these wagons with a furious haste that was significant. I saw a herd of cattle pour out of a big, walled yard, with drovers and dogs behind them. A man on a horse was riding hither and thither as though directing the men and urging them on. Women fluttered in and about, carrying things and passing them to the men who were loading. I stood under a tree and watched what was, obviously, a panic flight, a country exodus. These people were stricken with fear, fear of the Saxons.

Well, I did not want to be involved in their flurry, to be stopped and questioned. It was more than possible that Pellias of the Honey Valley was known to these people. There was some open woodland west of the estate, and cutting along a hedge I gained the wood and keeping just within the trees, cast a half circle round the place, and striking the track well beyond it, I ran. Some of those wagons might soon be on the road, and I did not want to be caught up by the fugitives. But their fierce, busy panic had infected me. God, into what a land of strange tragedy and terror my dream-state had landed me! I ran, as though those savage men from beyond the sea were close upon my heels.

There was more heathland interspersed with woods of birch and of Scotch fir. It was all so familiar in its colouring and its contours that I might have been on Ockham Common, or the heathland by Wisley, with the black band of the Portsmouth Road vibrant with traffic. What would I have given to have seen that stretch of tarmac, or heard the rumble of a lorry, but this country was silent, so silent that it made me more afraid. The track took me past a sheet of water that was very like the big pool by the Hut Hotel, and a little further on I sighted one or two familiar knolls capped with fir trees, knolls that are familiar to all those Londoners who picnic or pause and leave litter among the Ockham heather. Had I stumbled upon a Wall's ice cream carton I think I should have gone down on my knees, picked the thing up and kissed it.

The track turned past one of these knolls, and taking me through a birch wood and across some rough grassland gave me a sudden glimpse of a river. My God, the Wey! But not the Wey as I knew it, a decorous little stream, but a more turgid affair swelling its way through boggy ground set with alders and willows, reeds and water-plants. The track kept away from it, turning right and edging along the shoulder of a low hill, with marshland and rough meadows on its left.

Where was I now? This might be St. George's Hill on the right, and down there in the flats should be Brookland's Track. I was beginning to feel horribly depressed. There was nothing here to shock me back into my own century. Trees, gorse, heather, soggy meadows, a grey and dolorous sky. I could not follow the river, for the land looked too marshy down there. It began to drizzle. The track brought me to a great heathy space that dipped to the north and the river, and the lie of the land here was so familiar that I stood under a thorn tree and looked and looked. Not a house was to be seen, and yet this heathy slope with its birches and thorns and patches of gorse was terribly mine. I was standing just below Weybridge Station, and gazing down towards what should be Weybridge, with that distant landscape much as I remembered it, and hanging like a backcloth across the horizon.

An anguish of suspense gripped me. I left the track which appeared to be making for the junction of the Wey and the Thames, and went charging through the gorse and heather. I was a little mad, and I ran downhill, seeing nothing but heather and gorse and birch trees, yet the sandy soil had a wounding intimacy. How many times had I walked from the Southern station down this heath to my home. I think that to the very last I hoped that my dream would suddenly dissolve, and that I should see the place as I knew it, the row of cottages, the red villas, the particularly hideous police station, Weybridge spire, the old group of cottages with their gardens on the edge of the Brooklands woods. There was nothing, nothing but trees and heather, gorse, rough grass and sand. I could see the Wey just across the flats, shaggy with alders, sallow and willows.

Sweating, and breathing hard, with my heart knocking against my ribs, I came to a gentle slope where the heath tailed out and became marsh grass. I was—here. I was sure of the place. This was where the white house was to stand fifteen hundred years hence. And there was nothing here, nothing, nothing, nothing. I flopped down on some rough grass under a young birch tree, and lay prone, and hid my face. I dug my nails into my throat. I was in such mental anguish that I wanted to hurt myself, to struggle like a man in deep water, to fight my way back to light, air, and reality.

Presently, I sat up and made myself look again at the scene, like a man preparing to be judged and condemned. There was no escape from this other reality, and yet the lie of the land was so terribly familiar that almost I could recreate the scene as I knew it. Yes, I must be sitting on the slope of turf between the loggia and Lucy's particular parterre, that oblong bed which she had loved to crowd with colour. The house would be behind me. The big herbaceous border and the lawn would lie in front, shut in by the high holly hedge, with the flowering trees we had planted closing the vista. Yes, and the garage, and its screen of treillage covered with honeysuckle and ramblers. One ought to be able to see the big cedar in the cemetery.

I got up and wandered over the ground, like some mad archæologist searching for fragments of the future instead of the past. I walked a little way up the heath, and down again. The drizzly rain grew heavier, and was wetting my hair and face, and suddenly an insufferable anguish smote me. I wanted to escape from this desolation, this inhuman wilderness that mocked me. I was a ghost, a frightened ghost, hunting for a home that was not there. I wanted to end this horror. I would go down to the river and drown myself.

Even that wishful exit from this dead world was denied me. I went plunging down over the rough grassland towards the Wey, only to find myself in a morass that sucked at my feet and legs, but was not sympathetic towards my thirst for deep water. There were shallow, stagnant pools, sinister oozy patches. I found myself up to my knees in slime, with the river eluding me. And if that desolate heath had scared me, this sour, bubbling morass scared me still more completely. I squelched and blundered out of it back to the solid earth, shaken and overwrought. I realized that I did not want to die in that way, even as Pellias the Romano-Briton. It was both better to feel the wind and the rain in one's face, and to struggle back—whither? Yes, where was I, a poor ghost, to go? Back to this other world into which the summersault of time had thrown me?

My legs were all black slime, and I pulled some grass and wiped myself down. I was like a sponge sodden with self pity. I realized that I should have to go back to the one place where I was known, nor was that knowledge very consoling. I started to climb the heath, thinking of the boys who played football there, and of the various ladies with their various dogs. What if I met old Soper with his bowler hat and Pickwick face toddling down the sandy path and carrying the inevitable umbrella? A prim, dry, bumptious old bore was Soper, but had he appeared to me I should have kissed him. No umbrellas, no Chamberlain, no A.R.P. And then I caught my leg in the loop of a stout bramble, and the thing scratched and hurt me. I swore. I clutched at the bramble cane and gave it a savage tug, and the thorns dug into my hand. I was like an angry child, but anger was good for me. I was sodden with desolation and despair, and I needed pricking or scourging.

Something in me seemed to say: "Damn it, be a man." I had a sudden vision of Meona in the chariot, leaning on the reins, and driving those white horses like a figure of Winged Victory. A strange, primitive thrill went through me. Was I man, or a poor sap of a creature who could neither love nor hate, dare nor forget? I became conscious of a sudden surge of emotion in me, a desire to swagger. I was thinking with my blood, as the Germans put it. In this other world, this world of old, dim, tragic things the vapourings of a cultured "Dreary" were of no account. Arms and the man! Had I no guts for this monstrous adventure? Could I not be man instead of ghost? If some fantastic, topsy-turvy trick of Time had tumbled me into this tragedy, could I not find the stuff in me to tackle it?

I began to draw deep breaths, put my head back, square my shoulders. I had gained the top of the heath and the trackway, and I turned to look back. I began to feel—Roman. I raised my arm and shouted.

"Vale."

My shout sounded good. It was like a trumpet-cry to self. It tingled and gave out defiance. Damn it, why should I not be such a man as Festus, tough and lean, a dangerous fellow, a cool swordsman who could smile and kill? I had never killed anything but a marauding cat, and mosquitoes and greenfly. And suddenly, I wanted to kill. It was as though the primitive in me had pushed up through the thin, tame crust of custom. I was man.

I must be describing all this very crudely, but the fact remains that when I turned my face away from that which was in the future, I seemed to become more acclimatized to the past. As I followed the sandy track back towards the white house I remembered the exodus I had watched, those frightened folk loading their wagons and herding their cattle. If they were making for the ford across the Thames I might meet them, unless, of course, they had turned south to strike the North Downs and the Ridgeway. I did not meet them. I saw no live things but a yaffle, and a weasel that bolted across the track, and an occasional rabbit. The wind soughed in the trees. I was no more than a wild man in wild country, and my senses seemed to sharpen, for this was no country ramble, with one's only possible peril that of being accused of trespassing. I began to wish that I had some sort of weapon. I found myself listening, and watching the ground ahead of me, and sometimes fancying that a figure flitted behind a tree. There were glooms in these woods where mystery was like the black mouth of a cave. When a jay scolded at me sharply and suddenly, my head went up with a jerk and my heart leaped in me.

Yes, wild country, with wild men not so far away. What did these Saxons or Jutes look like? Blond, big, hairy men with fierce, bulging blue eyes? More and more did I wish that I had some sort of weapon, even a stout stick. I tried to break off an oak sapling, but it was too tough for me. Even a solid stone would be something to fling or to strike with, but I could not find such a stone. Also, I was feeling tired and hungry. The drizzle had ceased, and there was a break in the sky above the tree tops. Sunlight splashed here and there upon the young green of the birches and the oaks. I passed a big thorn that was in blossom, and the smell of it was sweet.

I came at last to the more open and gentle country where the white house stood. There were no fresh wheel-tracks in the sand, and no hoof slots, so I could suppose that the fugitives had trekked south or west. I worked my way into the open wood, and slipped from tree to tree, until I had a good view of the place. I leaned against the trunk of a beech.

Nothing can look more desolate than a deserted house, and this homestead had been stripped of men and beasts. It was a long, one-storied building with a high, thatched roof like the roof of a Devonshire cottage. The windows had shutters and the shutters were closed. No smoke rose from it, or any sound. The out-buildings and yard were as deserted as the house, and a patch of sunlight falling upon the place made its desolation seem more complete. I think the blind eyes and muteness of this homestead made me realize the nature of the tragedy that was menacing this island world. I felt drawn towards that abandoned house. I wanted to explore it, though the shuttered windows promised to keep me out. Moreover, I was hungry and thirsty, and in need of some sort of weapon. I walked out of the wood and across the meadowland to this Romano-British farmstead.

The one live thing I saw about the place was a brown hen scratching in the yard. She paid no attention to me, nor did she appear worried by the late exodus and her abandonment. A fence of wattles surrounded the white house and its garden, separating it from the farmyard and outbuildings, and I passed through the open gate of this fence, and found myself in the middle of a grass-plot that was edged with herb-beds and roses that were not yet in flower. I saw lavender, sage, mint, tansy and southernwood in this deserted garden. The rose bushes looked like the old-fashioned cabbage rose, rather pale of leaf, with a few fat flower-buds showing.

The house had a thatched portico sheltering the door, which was of oak, and studded with nails like an old church door. I walked up and gave the door a push, not for a moment expecting it to open, but open it did, with a melancholy creaking. I was so surprised that I just stood and stared into the vestibule with its floor of worn red tessaræ. The walls were plastered and coloured an ochrish yellow, and hanging on the left hand wall I saw a hunting-spear. Strange that they should have forgotten that spear, but here was a weapon with which I could arm myself. I took the spear and wandered down a darkish corridor with rooms opening from it. The doors were open, and I could see that the rooms had been stripped of most of their furniture, but in one dim room I saw a table standing, with the remains of a meal on it, bread, a meat bone with some meat left on it, a large brown pitcher.

Plates, dishes, cups, knives had disappeared.

Well, here was food of a sort. I was about to walk into that silent and almost sinister room when something rubbed against my leg. I let out a hiss like a snake, and jumped to one side, which only goes to show how overwrought I was and not yet hardened to strange places and strange perils. I looked down and saw a cat, a very ordinary tabby cat. It mewed up at me, and went on rubbing round my legs. Obviously, it was more dependent upon human associations than was that hen!

I laughed at myself, and then bent down to stroke the cat, and the beast purred round me with tail erect. Then, I went into the room. The shutters were pierced with round holes which let in pencils of light, but I asked for more light, and I turned the shutter-bar back and opened the two leaves. I remembered that I had not shut the oak doors, and since I was both trespasser and thief, and did not wish to be surprised in this deserted house, I walked down the corridor and shut and barred the door. The cat followed me, still rubbing against my legs. Now, for an uninterrupted meal. Since there was no stool or bench to sit on, I sat side-saddle on the table, and inspected the remains of the meal. The bread was brown and fresh, but the meat did not look appetising; it suggested the scrag-end of a leg of mutton, but I was hungry, much more hungry than I had ever known myself to be as modern man. I tore off a piece of bread, and placed it on my knee, and picking up the meat-bone, gnawed at the meat. I had no knife, and nature's knives had to serve. I found that the jug was a quarter full of some sort of beer. I drank from the jug, and found the stuff warming and pleasant, if a little sweet. The cat rubbed against my left leg and set up a meowling that reminded me that she, too, was hungry, though why the beast had not jumped on the table and welshed that meat I cannot say. I tore off a strip near the bone end and threw it on the floor, and the cat, head down and paws tucked in, fell to chewing it.

My back was to the window, with the sunlight shining in and through into the corridor and painting an oblong patch on the yellow wall and red floor. I had left the hunting-spear leaning against the end of the table, and I remember noticing a little patch of rust on its blade that might have been dried blood. I was feeling much less jumpy, and rather pleased with myself and my wild-man meal, and the cat was as busy as I was, when I heard that sound which brought me up taut on the table. Voices, but not very near, voices that seemed to drift from the distance and into the open window.

Were those fugitives coming back? Had they repented of their panic or gathered reassuring news upon the road? I got off that table with a chunk of bread in my hand, and keeping close to the wall, slipped along it to the window. I wanted to see without being seen, and it was fortunate for me that I showed such caution.

I saw three men standing on the edge of the open wood under the young green selvage of the beeches. They were tall men, bare legged, with long fair hair and portentous moustachios. In fact, they were so hairy that they made me think of sheep-dogs. They wore conical steel caps on their heads, and they carried shields and spears. The shields were round, painted in bright colours, blue and white and red, with metal bosses. I stared at these men, flattening myself against the wall, and not showing more than the edge of a face. Who the devil were these fellows? And then it dawned on me with shattering suddenness. These men were sea-pirates, savages, Saxons.

I saw one of the three, a huge fellow with legs like bolsters, raise his spear and point. Had he seen my face at the window? The three of them set up a fierce shouting which sounded to me like the sharp baying of dogs. The sound was savage enough to scare me, more especially so as their howling seemed to echo in the wood and to produce an answering uproar. I thought of a pack of wolves suddenly giving tongue. The dark wood became alive; I saw figures moving among the trees, with bits of sunlight splintering upon their metal head-pieces and their spear-points. Their coloured shields were like great round flowers. But I did not wait for more. I swung round, picked up the spear, and dived for the door, feeling myself trapped in the house. If I bolted from the front door, they would see me. I ran down the corridor, and found a passage leading to what were the kitchen quarters on the other side of the house. I found a door, but it was barred. I flung the bar back, and emerged into a walled yard. Beyond it I saw the trees of an orchard. I was over that wall in double quick time, and sprinting through the orchard. A thorn hedge enclosed it, and I saw a gate in the hedge and a meadow beyond it. Not till I had got through that gate did I stop to look back, peering through the thorn hedge. I saw nothing but the orchard trees and the back of the white house, but I could hear those heathen giving tongue like a pack in full cry. I did not think they had seen me. The house and possible plunder were causing all this ululation.

I turned again and ran, and as I ran I remembered that Pellias must have run as I was running. The dastard! But, he, at least, had taken one blow, and here was I running like a hare! But, damn it, I could not have fought a whole boat-load of those savages even if I had possessed all the prestige of an Achilles. Legs, not arms, were the members of a wise virtue.

I ran until I had gained the shelter of a grove of yews, and
then I leaned panting against a tree, and looked back.

I could see no sign of the Saxons, though I could hear them
shouting, and since their voices were less sharp, I gathered
that they were in the great house, rummaging for plunder or
for food. Well, they would not get much of either, which
might not make them any less savage and dangerous, and my
considered impulse was to put more space between us. I
worked through the grove of yews, meaning to strike the
track again at a safe distance from the villa. I came to a field
of young wheat, and trotting along the hedge, reached some
open grassland dotted with trees. I could see the thatched
roof in the distance but no marauders. I took to the open and
ran for the heath and the woods, and in a little while I came
upon the trackway. I was not chased, and so could infer that
I had not been seen.

Well, what next? Obviously, it was my business to get back
to Honey Valley and warn Aurelius and his people. I was
feeling pretty tired now, but I raised a trot, and kept it up
steadily through that wild country. My new shoes had begun
to chafe me, and I was glad when I saw the Downs rising
against the sunset. It was a strange and fiery sunset, and
somehow sinister and prophetic. Twilight was falling when
I reached the ridge. I turned, stood and looked back.

I saw something burning in the distance, a knot of yellow
flame, or petals of fire licking at and lighting up a cloud of
smoke. I understood its significance. Those savages, finding
neither food, plunder, men to slay or women to ravish, had
set fire to the white house.

I turned, and crossing the dark Ridgeway, went down into
that dim and silent valley.

CHAPTER SEVEN

𝒜ᴛ ᴡᴀs very dark in the valley. The suddenness of the nightfall was such that had I not found the sunken lane before the afterglow had faded, I should have been lost. Moreover, the darkness and the silence had a strange effect upon me. They seemed to bring me up against the mystery of things, and to translate the essential self in me into the past, and to withdraw it from what I knew as the present. This velvet blackness, and the bosky foliage, and the smell of the woods, and this utter silence! I was not listening for trains or cars, or for any twentieth-century sound. I was a more elemental creature who had escaped death by the narrowest of margins; I was in wild, dark country, listening, every fibre of me taut. I remember pausing under a great shaggy holly, and putting to myself that catastrophic question: Was I dead or alive? Was I, in fact, Pellias, and that other world the illusion? Had I, a Roman Briton, dreamed a fantastic dream of grotesque machines, of contraptions that flew in the air, of men in queer clothes, of a monstrous world that was, as yet, unborn?

Also, I was oppressed by a sense of tragedy, by a feeling that I was involved in happenings that were beyond my control. I was at the mercy of nature, nature as it expressed itself bloodily in the urge to kill. Had I not felt that urge? But in the darkness and the silence of this lane I was the hunted creature, not the hunter. I gripped my spear. Yet I could not help thinking how history reproduced itself. In that modern world we young folk had felt ourselves living under the edge of a catastrophe, of a sky black with menace, of roaring planes and death raining upon the nice order of our little lives. Nothing had seemed calculable. All life was soured by that eternal "If." "We will try Scotland for our holiday, if—" or "If the war doesn't come—" Always, sensationalism, headlines, the nine o'clock news on the wireless. A.R.P. Fear, hatred, worry! That babbling little beast Goebbels! Russia. Chaos hanging over one by a thread! How like was the pattern in this island world into which I had been translated. Beauty, order, peace, crops and herds, farmsteads, orchards, and into it spilling this savagery, this wolf spirit, slaying, destroying, fouling. Was the higher order always to fall before the lower? Was the planned violence of Totalitarianism any better than the savagery of these other Teutons? Did the wheel always turn and find itself crushing our dreams in muck and blood? I felt suddenly drawn to that old man in the valley down yonder whose white head was confronting the same tragedy. I could divine his love of order, his cultured humanism, his civilized artistry, all threatened by this savagery, this rush of wild men who came to destroy all that he and his forbears had created. He had no machine-guns with which to counter them. Their silly, slashing swords were more potent than all his philosophy. And in such a tragedy was not the humane and cultured spirit at a horrible disadvantage? There might be nothing but blood and tears.

I was nearing the bottom of the valley, and its silence and darkness troubled me. Surely there should be lights here, or had Honey Valley experienced a sudden exodus like that which I had watched a few hours ago? Had the Saxons come and left blood and a great silence behind them? That horror shocked me. I seemed to see Meona looking out from the portico of the temple on Farley Heath, or driving her white horses in the chariot, and I was torn by compassion and anger. Arrogant she might be, turbulent and impetuous and proud, but the thought of her being savaged by those brutes moved me to sudden primitive nausea. Yes, I was very much man. Her scorn had scourged me, but as I groped my way down that tunnel of a lane I realized that her sleek but vibrant youth had scourged me in other ways. If I was ready to fight for anything I was ready to fight for the tormenting tenderness of this black and white Roman girl. This may sound very blah and boyish, but I gather that some supercilious and epigrammatic negation in trousers has no great social value when throats are cut and women are ravished, and houses go up in flames.

I passed the farm where the dog had barked at me, and it was lightless and silent, and its silence quickened my forebodings. My feet were hurting me rather badly, but I broke into a trot, for the lane became less of a black tunnel as it approached the bottom of the valley. But what if the Saxons were down yonder? I came to the valley road, and stopped to listen, leaning on my spear. The only sound I could hear was the stream making a faint, moist pother among the water-weeds. I could see no lights. Well, caution was the thing, though I was feeling strung-up, and almost eager for violence. I suppose some solitary sentry might feel as I did, when in the darkness and the silence, some unseen yet sensed danger got upon his nerves. I stalked slowly down the road, holding my spear ready, eyes and ears on the alert. I passed a dim, lightless, voiceless cottage, and then another. I began to think that the place had been abandoned.

I crept on, and then I saw a light ahead of me, a mere chink of light. It was where the house of Aurelius should stand. The wooded hills seemed ready to roll in like great waves and engulf the valley. The white walls of the house became visible in the darkness. I reached the high wall of the enclosure. Now, I could hear a queer, murmuring sound that was not the sound made by running water. What was it? I flattened myself against the wall and listened. It was like the sound of many people whispering together, a kind of startled crepusculation such as a wood makes when a little breeze ruffles the leaves in the silence of the night. Somehow, it suggested fear, horror, human shudderings. I crept further along the wall, and found myself at the courtyard gate. It was shut and barred.

The queer murmuring had ceased. There was silence, a stark, listening silence. Had I been heard? Was that courtyard full of people who were listening for any sound that might betray the stealthy approach of an enemy? I stood by the gate, holding my breath. I must have been standing there for fully a minute when another sound broke the stillness, the sudden whimpering of a very small child, a whimpering that enlarged itself into a vigorous howling. I heard a woman's voice trying to still and soothe the child.

This little human hullaballoo brought me back to solid earth. I hammered on the gate and shouted.

"Hallo, there, hallo."

A man's voice answered me.

"Who's there?"

"Pellias."

They opened the gate, but only a crack, and the point of a spear showed as well as a dim face.

"Alone?"

"Yes. Who should I be with?"

They opened the gate and pulled me in. I heard the gate slammed behind me, and the bar banged into place. Two men were holding me. Another shoved his face close up against mine. He had a foul breath. These fellows seemed to have the jitters.

"Is it you, you white-livered rat?"

"You're talking."

"Yah, in such devil's darkness one can't see a face."

I was resenting being held, and the contemptuous roughness of their welcome.

"Bring a lantern if you doubt it. Why all this fear?"

That angered them.

"Fear! You are a pretty one to talk of fear."

There was the sound of someone spitting.

"If it is the spunkless pup, let us put him out again. Pellias brings bad luck."

I lost my temper, and I shook them off.

"Where is my lord? I have news for him."

"Good news, I guess!"

"Yes. Take me to my lord."

They tried to crowd round me, but I pricked one of them with my spear, and he cursed me.

"God rot you."

"Well, mend your manners."

But they did seem to realize that I was somehow man, and not to be jostled as they pleased, and I think they were in such a state of nerves that any show of spirit impressed them. I walked forward from the gate, but I had not taken three steps before I trod on something, a leg. The owner winced, and a woman's voice shrilled at me. Must I go stepping on people? Then, in the dim light, I discovered that the court-yard was full of people, lying and squatting, dark lumps of humanity huddled about the water cistern. Refugees? Had the whole village taken shelter for the night behind these walls? It was so.

I picked my way up to the great house, the men followed me. A man was sitting on the loggia steps with a spear across his knees. He was dozing, but he woke up with a gasp and a start when I touched him with the butt of my spear.

"Who's that? Hold off."

How jumpy all these people were! I saw the whites of his eyes shining. His face looked vaguely bleached and haggard in the darkness.

"It's brave Pellias come in," said a voice.

I turned on the voice.

"You mend your manners. I wish to speak, at once, with my lord."

The man with the spear was unsteady on his feet, and seemed to be drunk with weariness, but he laughed, and strangely enough his laughter made me recognize him.

"Festus."

"Yes, Festus, my lad. We seem to be treading on thorns here. I'll take you in. Come."

The house was as dark as the courtyard, and I began to understand this darkness, for, to be without lights was to share the darkness of the valley, and to mask and cloak your-self against beasts that were on the prowl. I saw a slit of light at the end of the corridor, a V-shaped slit between the folds of the curtains. Our footsteps seemed to echo in this silent, breathless house. It was Festus who drew back the curtain.

"Pellias, master."

I heard a voice say: "Let Pellias enter."

I felt Festus's hand upon my shoulders, and it was a comradely hand. Festus was good for such a crisis, a man who could raise a laugh in the face of it, though he was ready to fall asleep on his feet. I stepped into the summer-room, and he let the curtain drop behind me. This great room seemed all shadows. A solitary light was burning, a small oil lamp set on a bracket in the recess where the household gods had their sanctuary. Aurelius was sitting in his chair, facing the figures of his gods. His hair stood out like a white fringe. I saw Meona half crouching on a window-seat by one of the lattices that was not shuttered up against the night. Her eyes looked like black hollows in a mask of ivory.

Aurelius did not turn his head or move.

"So, you have come back, my son."

I knew that Meona was watching me and those huge dark eyes of hers bothered me. The trouble with the modern mind is that it can never shed its self-scrutiny, or cease from wondering how it may shape in the world of the self-conscious. I stood up straight, with the butt of my spear on the ground, and my two hands gripping the handle just below the head. Was I adopting the pose of the Roman sentinel keeping his post while Vesuvius rained death upon Pompeii?

"I have news, lord."

The old man did not seem to hear me. He might have been deaf, or deaf to the mere empty sound of my voice, or so sunk in profound thought that nothing I could say would rouse him. After all, what was I? A ghost out of the future, and maybe he was afraid of this ghost. I stood and waited, feeling Meona's eyes watching me. The lamp-flame flickered, and the faces of the gods seemed to pull grimaces.

I heard a voice crying in the night: "There is death in the land." It was a woman's voice, shrill and abrupt with anguish. The still night shuddered. I felt myself stiffen, and looking at Meona I saw her sitting rigid, her hands gripping the edge of the seat. The weight of her body seemed to be carried by those two tense white arms.

Her voice came in a whisper that was almost a hiss.

"Is there nothing, no vengeance, no strength in the land?"

I stood and stared at her and the man in me was fiercely moved by that sound that seemed drawn from her like a jet of blood. But Aurelius had come out of his stupor. He rose slowly from his chair, saluted his gods and turned to face me. Never had I seen a man so aged in so short a time. His face had fallen in; he looked shrunken; his whole body was tremulous with the tremblings of sudden senility.

"We have seen death, my son."

I suppose my face was vacant, for he looked at me steadfastly for a second or two, and then made a sign to his daughter.

"I would speak with Pellias alone."

But she came swiftly across the room, and putting her arm about him, raised her face to me defiantly.

"I can bear what men can bear."

"You have borne enough, child."

"I will not leave you."

She must have felt his old tremblings and been wounded by them. She seemed to press her young body against his, and buttress him with the fierce, slim pillar of her body. Her face had changed. It seemed to me a different face, so different that I could not help staring at it. Her mouth looked bigger, her lips fuller, and the oval of its shape broader from cheekbone to cheekbone. The dark eyes were not flashing pebbles, but more like dewy, luscious fruit. I would have said that her face had a sudden, mysterious ripeness, that mature richness which comes of deep emotion.

Even her voice and her words were different.

"We, we are young, Pellias. We should be able to dare and to fight."

Something seemed to happen to me in those three seconds. She was speaking to me as to an equal, as man, as one who had blood in him and courage. She was alive, vibrant and passionate, and I too was alive. I felt a kind of singing in my ears, and my heart beat hard and fast.

I said: "Something has happened. All those people out yonder."

She nodded at me, and then inclined her head towards her father's chair. I understood her. I turned the chair so that Aurelius could sit in it without facing that little flickering lamp and the vague and inconstant faces of his twilight gods. Both his gods and his world were chaos, and he was a very old man. She made him sit in his chair, and standing behind it, and leaning over the carved back, she let a hand rest upon his head.

She said: "Be silent, Father," and to me: "I will tell you."

Her gentleness both surprised and won me, for her young compassion was so contrasted with her pride, and with my memory of the young women of my time who appeared to regard old men, and fathers in particular, as tiresome and superfluous old fools. Parents should be seen but not heard. I saw that Aurelius's eyes had closed themselves. He lay back and listened, while her fingers played softly with his hair.

"It was to Collis Alba that we drove. Three miles from the place, where the wooden bridge carries the Regnum road over the river, we met—these people."

She paused, and stared at the wall behind me, as though compelling herself to confront some horror.

"Women and children, and old men. Aquila had sent them away. He and his men had thought to hold the villa and beat off those savages. They had been seen on the hills by his scouts. We drove on. We had crossed the bridge when we saw smoke rising. Again, we drove on, Festus riding ahead. In a little while Festus came back to us. He was very white and grim. He would have stopped us. But one must see, one must know, one must not shirk things. We came to Collis Alba. It was burning. The courtyard gates were broken. Again, Festus would have stayed us there. We," and she faltered for a moment, bit her lips, and went on: "Dead men and blood, and Aquila's head planted in a pot of flowers by the cistern. Death, and silence and flames. We came away."

Her hand rested motionless upon the old man's head. She stared beyond me at the wall, as though her eyes were still full of all that horror. Then, she gave a little jerk of the head and shoulders, and seemed to come back to life, and to a confrontation of the tragic things that threatened all of us.

"One must think, think, decide."

She looked at me as though even Pellias the coward might have some significance on such a night as this. I felt that she was tortured, torn, distracted. Should this house and the valley and its good life be abandoned, or should we dare to stay and fight it out?

I said: "I too have seen those savages. They set the white house over the hills on fire. The people had fled."

Her eyes gleamed out at me.

"Constantine's house! Ye gods! Are the wretches every-where?"

I saw the old man's eyes open.

"Raiding parties. How many were there of them, my son?"

"Perhaps fifty."

"Wolf packs. Ah, for a single cohort of trained men. That may be our undoing. We are not ready. We are attacked and beaten in detail. There cannot be so many of those fellows, but they are fighting men."

I was leaning heavily on my spear.

"Are there no soldiers in Britain?"

He gave me a quick, warning look.

"Pontius of Pontes has raised a body of horse. If only we and the Aquilas and such men as Constantine could have joined strength."

"Can we not rouse the country?"

He straightened in his chair.

"Someone to lead, someone with courage and a voice. But what now? Do we go or stay?"

My eyes met Meona's, and I was a new man.

"Let us send the women and children away, and stand. Let someone ride and gather people to us. If someone stands we shall be a rallying point. Surely we could hold this house?"

My lord looked at me steadfastly.

"That is how a man should speak, my son. The women and children shall go. But who shall be our torch-bearer?"

I saw Meona's face blaze.

"Why not I? Surely, men will listen to a woman, or be shamed. I will go."

"The hazard is too great."

"We must dare it. I'll drive to Pontes. I'll—"

Her eyes were on me, and I was man.

"Give me leave to go, too, lord. Let Festus and the others hold this house. We must get help."

I saw Meona smile at me, and her smile was an enigma. Did she think I was still a coward, and being brave in flight! I changed my mind suddenly.

"No, let Festus go. I will stay."

There was silence for a moment. Her great black eyes were studying me.

"No, Festus shall stay. I will take Pellias with me."

CHAPTER EIGHT

I OFTEN wonder whether she thought it better to take the coward with her than to leave a coward behind.

We called Festus into the room and spoke to him of our plans. He had brought his own people in from the farm, a young wife, two children and his labourers, and weary though he was, he fired up when we spoke of holding the valley, even of gathering such power as we could and of driving these German swine back into Kent. There were some twenty able-bodied men to defend the house and courtyard and the flock of fugitives, and if there were no arms for all, scythe blades fixed on poles, and bills and axes could make good play in desperate hands.

That was all that the night could do for us. Festus had posted his watches, and we who had work to do next day, went to our beds. My body was weary, but my brain was alight. I seemed to have come alive in this other world, and my old self was growing dim. I was to drive out with Meona in her chariot. I was to be her shield-bearer and man-at-arms. The night was a new, strange dream to me, yet presently I fell asleep.

I woke very early to the gradual greyness of the dawn. I heard the birds break into song. It was a marvellous volume of sound in that deep, green valley, exultant, clamorous, as though the trees themselves were singing. I lay for a while and listened to that dawn-song, and my heart exulted in me. If this was a world of tragedy and of tears, I had been re-born in it, to fall in love, and to be wounded by its perfume and its wildness.

I got up and washed myself and dressed, for we had decided to start very early, and strike the road over Farley Heath, which linked up Stane Street with the London, Staines, Silchester highway. I give the English names, which convicts me of perpetrating the strangest of anachronisms. It would be a long detour by the Guildford gap, but since the savages had spread into the Wey valley, we dared not take the track I had followed yesterday. There was a small mirror in my room, and I was looking at my unshaved face and wondering whether Aurelius's man would come and shave me, when I heard footsteps in the corridor. In the days that were to come I was to forget a bearded chin in a world of swift happenings and desperate adventure.

It was Aurelius's gentleman's gentleman, but he brought into my room more than a new suavity, a bowl of hot water, olive soap, a towel and a razor. He carried in a set of harness, helmet, breastplate, greaves and a shield. A sword in a red leather scabbard lay in the hollow of the breastplate, with a belt buckled to it. He laid all this warlike gear on my bed.

"With my lord's compliments, sir."

So, I had become "sir" to him! I picked up the sword, and drew it out of its scabbard. It was a shortish sword, like the old stabbing swords used in the legions, but it looked a useful weapon, and I remembered reading somewhere that this curt,

stiff blade, had out-fought the long, clumsy, slashing swords of
the Gauls.

"Is this Niger's work?"

He stood waiting to shave me.

"No, sir, it is my master's own sword, as is the harness. He
has grown too old for such gear."

The war-harness of Aurelius Superbus! Well, well! But
had he not told me that no provincial had been suffered to
bear arms? I could suppose that the more notable folk had
been privileged in that respect or that this harness had been
ceremonial dress worn on some state occasions. I sat down on
a stool, and the man lathered and shaved me, and while he
was busy I wondered how I should shape as a fighting man.
My blood was up, and tingling. I was to wear harness, and
drive with Meona behind her two white horses.

When the barbering business was over, the man offered to
help me arm. The breastplate had to be buckled on, greaves
fastened, sword belt slung. He appeared to understand the
process better than I did, though I checked him when he
buckled me up too tight. It was rather like being fitted by
one's tailor, but with a suavity that would send in no bill.
Ought one to tip the fellow? But I had no money save the
coins I had found in Pellias's wallet, and I was utterly ignorant
of their value. If I gave him one I might be presenting him
with a farthing or a pound! I refrained. I was beginning to
feel that I was a fighting man, and he a mere lackey born to
serve me.

There are many shades of feeling which are so delicately
coloured, and so evanescent, that it is difficult to put them
into words. I had Welsh and Roman blood in me, and if the
average Saxon is not a very subtle person, and no creature of
moonlight and mystery, I was somewhat English in my

simplicity. England would have produced no Freud, and I had often marvelled at the intricate psychological analysis developed by some continental novelist when describing a simple case of lust or of cowardice. A page may be devoted to the woman's person, how her flat hard breasts or her stringy passionate thighs provoked the hero to almost insane raptures. I was no hero, and if I had been transfigured into the sudden lover, I was without lust, as the intellectuals appear to understand it. But I did feel that strange colour had come into my life, and that I could sing of things as some of the old Welsh sang of them. There was a swagger in me, a happy, dramatic lilt in the rhythm of life that seemed inevitable and much less self-conscious than the posturings of a more sophisticated age. Life was its own justification. It was made to be lived, not observed and catalogued and criticized like a set of statistics. All that one did and said and felt was more vivid, more dramatic. It might have suggested melodrama to my twentieth-century self, but that self was to grow hazed and sleepy, and to cease from pulling the petals off the rose. I lived. So must men have lived in less drab, reach-me-down days when the world was wilder, and the dark woods held both death and mystery.

Things and the feel of them, action and its emotion; they put to the sword all theories of living, even as these savages were tearing the Roman Peace to tatters. I imagine violence to be one of life's necessities, a thunderclap that wakes us from the lassitude of peace and plenty. When a civilization becomes too fat and greasy, blood has to be let. Perhaps that is what these Germans were teaching us, the philosophy of force. Unfortunately, or perhaps fortunately, the pen is not always mightier than the sword. I wanted to show myself in harness, as the new Pellias who was man, and not a poor, scared, decadent lout. With my helmet in the hollow of my left arm, and my scabbard clapping against my thigh, I walked out into the corridor, and along it to the vestibule and loggia. I saw the crowd in the courtyard, and a fire burning, and an iron cauldron slung above the flames on an iron tripod. A woman was giving suck to a child. Two fellows were washing themselves in the stone cistern, which seemed to me a piece of impertinence. I stood on the steps of the portico in my new harness, with the sun shining down over the green hill, and the valley still full of a kind of cobweb light. There had been a heavy dew. The stones of the courtyard were wet with it.

The analysts would have described me as being very much in the shop-window, a tailor's gentleman-dummy advertising the latest in battle-suitings, but I was to escape more and more from a cheap and cramping self-consciousness. One has not much time for self-conscious posings in the thick of a rough rugger match, or when the other fellow's gloves are stinging one. My blood was to be hot blood, not educated milk. As I stood there in the early sunlight, watching the crowd in the courtyard, the two men who were washing themselves discovered my presence. Both of them had followed Gerontius to disaster, and both of them had been witnesses of the same cowardice. I suppose my new splendour peeved them. They made mocking faces at me and became rudely ironical.

One of them spat into the water-cistern.

"There's spunk for the coward!"

"Fine feathers, brother, fine feathers, but that cock won't fight."

Women and children began to stare at me. Someone laughed, and the laugh was more than an insult. I laid my helmet on a pillar of the stairway wall. I walked down to the

water-cistern and the two men. They had jeering faces. One
of them had the eyes of a fish, and red hair. They stood and
smirked at me, but when I got close to them Master Red Head
began to blink. I swung my right fist, and caught him cleanly
on the jaw, and he went down backwards. The other fellow
snatched at a knife that he had in his girdle, but before he
could draw his sting I had floored him also. Those blows felt
good. I stood over the two, with my hand on my sword. I
had knocked out Red Head, and he lay limp and sprawling.
The other fellow crouched, and glowered at me, but he kept
his hand from his knife.

I said: "Fellows like you should mind your faces," and I
turned about and left them, and in the courtyard there was
silence.

Young fighting-cock that I felt myself to be, I was startled
when I saw Meona standing in the portico. She had seen me
smite those two lewd fellows, and they were her father's
men not mine, but I kept my chin up and I looked her straight
in the face, though, God knows, the wild, proud loveliness
of her had begun to frighten me. I am not much use at
describing women and their ways, but if I was a big simpleton like John Ridd I could adopt his motto of "Never Be
Ridden." Anyway, it was a good bluff when a girl's face
made you feel like a flapper in love with her first film star.
Meona had a frown on her forehead. She had a falcon's head,
and her eyes were like two little daggers of dark steel.

"Why did you strike those men?"

I stood and smiled at her.

"For the good of their souls, and the mending of their
manners."

She seemed to be considering me and my new, braced-back
pride. Her lips looked dry and thin and pale. Never had I

seen lips change so quickly. Almost, I could hear her saying
to me: "Do proud feathers make brave birds? You were less
bold with the barbarians." If that was in her mind, the tinge
of scorn that hung about her mouth and nostrils was valid.
But I was not going to wilt before her, or throw my arms away
in this battle of tempers.

She looked past me at the crowd in the courtyard. It was a
silent crowd. It watched and listened. A child began to wail,
and the mother crooned to it as though such whimpering was
unseemly. I think many things must have happened to Meona
in those few seconds. She was as swift and as quick in reflecting a crisis or a mood in her mind-mirror as she was in
handling her horses. She could turn in the air like a hawk.

"Insolence may have two faces, but that which is high may
strike at that which is low."

I do not suppose that they understood her words, but her
manner of uttering them was significant. She looked at me
again, with her head held high.

"It is time we broke fast. We have things to do."

She turned and swept me in with her as though the draught
of her serene young skirt drew me into the house after her.
She had used that wild word—"We," and it was strange how
wild a significance it had for me. I might be man to her if I
could strike with the sword as I had struck with my fist.

Aurelius was waiting for us in the summer-room. He had
a roll of parchment on his knees, and he spread it on the
table, for half the table served for the meal we had to eat,
milk, bread, eggs, and honey. I noticed that the lamp in the
shrine was unlit, and the faces of the gods were dim. The
old man looked me over from head to foot as I stood before
him, and maybe he found me comforting to his eyes, for I

was in a striding mood after chastening those two men.

"You carry it well, my son."

I thanked him for the harness and the sword, and for the honour he had done me. I was feeling like one of Shakespeare's heroes. I could utter brave, resonant words, and they did not sound like claptrap.

"May I wear it as it should be worn, sir?"

I felt Meona watching me like a young falcon. How should I shape on the wing, and in the face of peril? That was the question.

Aurelius smiled. He was less the old and bewildered man on this sunny morning.

"Let us look at the map, Pellias."

His hands held it spread upon the table, and bending over it I was astonished by the amount of detail in this map. It covered the Kentish borders, the Thames, Surrey, half Berkshire, and the northern edge of Hants. Londinium, Pontes and Valleva were marked upon it, and also a number of townlets and villages whose Latin names were a blank to me. The forest areas were coloured green, great wild spaces like the sandstone ridge and the Weald, and the heathlands round Bagshot. Surrey was dotted with little diagrammatic designs which represented country houses, and Aurelius's finger pointed from one to the other, while in a low voice he deciphered the details. Romano-British Surrey, it appeared, was a pleasant land of great estates where nobles and gentlemen farmed, and hunted and lived an Arcadian life, with perhaps, a town house in Corinium or Calleva. London was there with its shops, its physicians, its lawyers and its bankers. The picture was so modern, and so comfortably Victorian, a world of horses, dogs, gardens, farms and orchards that I gaped over it. Both Calleva and Londinium were shown encircled with towers and walls, but otherwise the thing might have been a large estate-map.

Meona had gone to look to her horses, and Aurelius, glancing up at me, laid a hand on my arm.

"How is it with you, my son?"

There was a wise benignity about him that touched me.

"I feel—man, sir, in this harness."

"I am trusting you. Maybe the gods had a hand in this. You see how our country lies. Londinium has its walls, so has Calleva. If we lose our land to those savages, we shall be refugees within those walls."

"Is there no one to help us?"

He produced another map which he had kept between his knees, and when he spread it I saw that it charted all the island south of the Great Wall. He laid his finger on a red crown that lay, so far as I could judge, in the Wiltshire country, south-east of Corinium.

"That is my brother's house. He has sons and much strength. If Calleva and Londinium will not help us, we will send our groans into the west. My brother, Pellias, is wise in war. He has fought in Gaul and on the Rhine, and on the Great Wall. Such a man as he is should lead and bind the country together. With an island in arms we could beat back the Irish and the Picts, and drive these blond beasts into the sea."

I seemed to be listening to some old story, a dim and tragic epic out of the past. So, there were other Aurelii in Roman Britain, and those Arthurian names were sounding in my ears, Aurelius, Ambrosius, Uther, Arthur, Guinevere, Geraint, Modred, Galahad, Tristan and Iseult. Had I been translated into Mallory? Was I, perhaps, to ride in arms like one of

Arthur's men, that Romano-British Arturus, with one of the Aurelian clan? I asked my old lord questions. Was the island now ruled by a number of nobles who were tribal chieftains, men of old Celtic stock who had been Romanized? He said that it was so. The family of Cunedda held north Wales. The Aurelii ruled in the south and middle west. There were Silurian lords in south Wales. All the country north of the Trent was more or less desolate, as the Great Wall had been overrun. Then there were the cities and towns, *municipia* and *coloniæ,* like Colchester, Verulam, Ratæ, Corinium, Venta, Calleva, and Viriconium. They had governments of their own, city councils and officials. The problem appeared to demand the alliance of the petty nobles with the towns, under the leadership of some man of power and prestige.

But the day's purpose and its hazards were our matters of the moment. We were to take two armed and mounted men with us, and I was to drive with Meona in the chariot. I was glad of this, as I was not too sure of my horsemanship, though I had done some riding as a boy. Meona knew the ways. We were to carry a letter to Pontius of Pontes, explain our perilous position to him, and try to persuade him to come to our help with such force as he could muster. If he were to prove unhelpful we were to return to the Honey Valley, and Aurelius would then reconsider our situation. We might decide to stay and defend the manor, meanwhile, sending an appeal for help to Calleva and to Aurelius Ambrosius in Wiltshire. I gathered that this other Aurelius had a strong place at what might have been Sorbiodunum. I questioned my lord about London. Surely, the most powerful and populous city in the island should be able to help us?

Aurelius gave me a look of kindly tolerance. I was very young!

"Shopkeepers and tradesmen, my son. Not very valorous people. They have their walls and their towers. Such folk are apt to believe what they wish to believe, that the storm will pass, blow off a few country roofs, and leave them unscathed. A city is egoist."

"But won't the fools realize that if the island is over-run piecemeal, they will suffer in the end?"

"Fools may see their fate too late, Pellias. So long as food comes down the river to Londinium, they may remain fat and comfortable within their walls."

"Why not cut off their food-supply?"

The old man laughed, and shrugged his shoulders.

"An idea, my son, an idea! The barbarians may do it for us."

Then Meona came back into the room, wearing her green Phrygian cap, and a long greenish frock that buttoned down the front, and was shaped to the figure. It reminded me of modern riding-kit. She carried a pair of red leather gloves, and a dagger at her girdle. Little did I guess that that bodkin was to be our salvation. We sat down to breakfast. Festus, I heard, was out scouting on the Downs, watching the ways from Collis Alba and the Thames valley.

We were near the end of the meal when I heard the chariot and horses in the courtyard. Meona and I looked at each other across the table, and I could divine the question behind those eyes: "What manner of man will you be if danger comes?" Well, she should see! Never, in my innocence, had I felt more sure of myself.

Aurelius went with us to watch us sally. The two mounted men were in the saddle, and both of them were strangers to me. Their names were Ferox and Marcus. The crowd in the courtyard stood back, and touched their foreheads to Aurelius.

I saw that there was a spear in the chariot, and a bow and a sheaf of arrows. An automatic pistol would have been more to my liking! Meona went and spoke to the horses and rubbed their noses. She sprang in and I followed, and she whirled us out of the gate and into the village street. The crowd poured out to wave us away.

She spoke to the man Ferox who was riding on our right. "Ride ahead, watch."

He saluted her and pricked up his horse, but before he left us I saw his face for a moment. Ferox his name might be, but his face was not the face of a man who liked the adventure. That was an unpleasant fact that I had yet to digest. The blond beasts had put the fear of death into these Britons.

All this country was, in its main contours, so infinitely familiar to me that the reality of this other consciousness was almost poignantly incredible. The road was a mere trackway following the valley, with the green surge of the hills just as I knew it. There was no Chilworth, but two or three cottages or farm-houses, and they seemed to be deserted. The flat stretch of open country between Chilworth and Shalford was like a park, set with great trees, and here cattle were grazing. Wonersh would be behind us. Contemplation was not encouraged, for Meona drove like Jehu, and the springless carriage bumped and rolled, and I wondered how she kept her feet. I stole glances at this young, dark Boadicea. Did she know what fear was? If she loved, would she love like a young tigress, or was there a capacity for tenderness in her that was as strong as her courage? And then something happened. We were nearing a big, open wood of oaks and beeches when I saw Ferox halt his horse, sit staring, and then come galloping back to us. I saw by his face that he had the wind up.

"There are men in the wood."

Meona stopped her horses. She looked hard at Ferox, and I imagine she understood his trouble.

"Swine, perhaps!"

"No, lady, men. I saw them moving among the trees."

I glanced at Marcus, and he too had a pinched look. I reached for the spear, stood up, and scanned the shadows amid those distant tree-trunks. I could see nothing.

"Stay here. I will go and explore."

I remember the quick look Meona gave me.

"Take Ferox's horse."

"No, I'll go on foot. Stay here."

My recklessness, or whatever it was, did not satisfy her, though it may have pleased her. She whipped up her horses, and so suddenly that I was jerked back and sat down abruptly on the seat. She looked at me and laughed, for this summary jostling of my dignity had peeved me. Almost she seemed to say: "My lad, what a sensitive face you have! You do give your hand away." Actually, what she said was: "We will drive up closer to those trees. You can go in and look. If the savages are there in numbers, you must run. I will wait with the horses to pick you up." Ferox and Marcus were riding behind us, and I heard them indulging in what one would describe as mutinous back-chat. Their mistress was a wild young cat. I twisted round on the seat, took a look at their silly faces, and cursed them.

Again I heard Meona laugh, though this might be no laughing adventure. She whirled us up towards the wood, which I was scanning with peculiar interest. I could see nothing but the trunks of the great trees and the blooms within, and scattered patches of sunlight, and the brown of last year's leaves. Meona turned and stopped the horses about seventy yards from the wood, so that she would be facing in the right direction if we had to gallop for it.

"Good luck."

How modern that sounded! I got down and stalked towards the trees. The place seemed utterly silent, a great canopy of young greenness carried upon a thousand grey-green pillars. My head jerked to and fro as I advanced, holding my spear at the ready. Mystery, dark and secret perils! I was not conscious of fear, but of a feeling of brittle and extraordinary excitement. I was on my toes. I passed the first trees, and stood looking, listening. And then I saw something moving, dim shapes. I heard a squeal, gruntings. Pigs! I walked on, and found a little glade opening before me, and in it a herd of swine, with two lads in smocks sitting on a dead tree-trunk, playing some game together. So, Meona had been right. I waved to the swineherds, faced about, and walked out of the wood, with the spear on my shoulder. Meona was standing, watching. I waved to her and laughed.

"Swine."

I saw her turn and speak to Ferox and Marcus, and though I could not catch what she said, I gathered by their sulky, shamed faces, that her tongue had scourged them.

"Just two lads and some pigs."

She looked down at me steadfastly and with a kind of intense, searching seriousness, and then she smiled.

"It might have been other swine."

We drove on.

CHAPTER NINE

We crossed the Wey by a timber bridge somewhere near where the Pilgrim's Way must have crossed it. Our valley track had joined itself to the Farley road which linked up Stane Street with the great west highway. There was a village here in the narrow valley, an inn for travellers with a posting-house attached to it, a shop or two, cottages, a smithy. The people had not fled, and as the chariot rumbled over the wooden bridge they came out into the street and crowded round us. The inn-keeper and posting-master, a very fat man with a cheerful countenance, came out and saluted Meona.

"What news, my lady?"

He smiled at me, so I presumed I was supposed to know him, and I smiled back. I was standing up beside Meona, for it would have been unmannerly to sit while she was standing.

"Watch your bridge, Paulus."

"Is there much danger, lady?"

"Constantine's house has gone up in flames, and Collis Alba has been sacked, and its men slaughtered."

There was a kind of moaning sound from the little crowd.

"Should we burn down the bridge?"

"Not on your life," said she, "it may be needed. Set a guard and watch. We are going to Pontes to get help."

We drove on, leaving that little, dismayed crowd of villagers behind us, and I had my doubts about the safety of that bridge, and whether we should find it standing when we returned. Our road took us over the Hog's Back, and I thought of Compton, that most exquisite of villages with its perfect church, and the Watts Gallery, and the green spaces with their poplars and the willows. Compton and its setting had always felt to me like Tennyson and the Fair Maid of Astolat, and here was I looking back into the valley where Compton was not. No Charterhouse towers, no great red smudge to mark Guildford! Northwards, I saw the plain with its soft undulations spreading towards the Thames. It was a blue day, with diaphanous distances. Instinctively I looked for that red gobbet of gentility—Woking, and realized that Woking lay somewhere in the future. Was I sorry? Not much.

There were scattered farms and wheatfields along the foot of the Downs. Pasture and woodland followed, until we struck the heather country, a sandy waste that would have caused Cobbett to curse. Meona kept her white horses at a rattling trot, and I wondered at their staying power. She had ordered Ferox and Marcus to ride in front, and I saw their heads keep turning right and left. These two men were still very windy. We must have passed close to what were to be Ottershaw and Chertsey. This seemed to be fat, cattle country, with poplars and willows and great stretches of grass. I saw cows grazing. The road was banked up beyond Chertsey, and marked here and there with posts, and I supposed that it might be flooded in winter, as is the wretched modern road. I missed that remarkable collection of home-made shacks and bungalows, pathetic improvisations inspired by progress. And so, we came to Pontes with its great timber bridge, and I saw its pantiled roofs and orchards, and one proud white house standing apart with gardens going down to the river. There were swans on the river. That surprised me. But why should there not be swans?

Several barges lay near the bridge, and a boat laden with vegetables and corn-sacks was drifting downstream, with a man leaning upon a long oar and steering. The bridge was guarded. That is to say wooden trestles had been placed across it, and several very amateurish-looking soldiers were swaggering about, and shouting to the bargees on the bank below. Bargee language has always carried a fine flavour, and I gathered that these fellows were cursing the bridge's guardians, and the barbarians, and everything that could be cursed. Apparently Pontius of Pontes had some authority over the bridge, and he had given orders that no barges were to pass down the river because of the Saxons. Also, I was to discover that he was in the thick of a squabble with the citizens of Londinium, and if he stopped their food-barges the laugh would be his.

So busy were the bridge's guardians in returning the blackguardisms of the bargees that they did not pay much attention to us until Meona cracked her whip at them. "Wake up, you foul-mouthed fools." That was what the whip seemed to say. The sergeant in charge of the guard, persuaded to take notice, saluted our chariot and ordered the trestles to be moved.

"Pardon, lady."

Meona drove on into Pontes, and the sergeant resumed his slanging-match with the fellows below.

It was obvious, at a glance, that Pontes was feeling the draught of the day's danger. This was the first Romano-

British town that I had seen, and it straggled along the main road in haphazard fashion, and appeared to be a perfect example of early ribbon development. We drove into a triangular Place which was in a state of confusion. Farm carts, wagons and carriages were parked here. Dust, dogs, children, tired cross women, horses being watered and fed, an universal hubbub. I saw a large caravanserai and posting-house, and in its loggia people were sitting at tables, much as one might have seen them outside a modern road-house. In fact, in the garden, which appeared to be sacred to the gentry, I saw two or three large red umbrellas in the centre of a lawn, green tables, and two girls in white smocks waiting upon the people round the tables. A little temple occupied one corner of the Place, with pollarded limes shading its portico, and on the portico steps fugitives were strung out like sparrows on a fence. Meona had to drive slowly through this agitated crowd. One fat fellow, drinking from a jug, was jostled by the off-horse. The liquor was splashed out of the jug, and down his chin and tunic, and he turned a furious red face, and cursed. I looked at Meona. Her nostrils were pinched with scorn. The fellow might have been a blow-fly for all the notice that she took of him. This dismayed and sweating rabble did not move her to compassion. If the Saxons crossed the bridge these people would be cattle to be slaughtered.

We got clear of the crowd and turned down a lane which led to the big white house by the river. I saw a row of horses tethered to a fence in the lane, and a number of men in harness squatting with their backs to the wall opposite. Home-made cavalry. The off-wheel of the chariot passed so close to their feet that some of them jerked up their legs, and looked at us blackly. Not very promising material—this. I began to feel that Pontes was not a place likely to provide us with much succour. We came to a gate-house with more armed men lounging about. Meona took the chariot through the archway, and I saw the long white house with its pantiled roof and portico, and the garden going down to the river. A brick wall gave a terrace effect, and there were steps leading to the water. A gaily-painted boat lay moored there. A couple of peacocks were sunning themselves on the wall.

Lying on a wattle couch, I saw a very large, black and white young man in a saffron-coloured tunic. When I say that he was young I include in that class those who persist in posing as young-fellah-my-lads at the age of forty. He reminded me of what one would describe as a smart cad-about-town. A servant was in the act of handing him a silver cup on a pewter salver. Two or three other servants were in the background, and a morose, hawk-faced person in harness was striding up and down and casting such looks of unrestrained scorn and disrelish upon Sir Pontius, that I was attracted by the fierce person's air of seething impatience.

We left the chariot and walked across the grass towards the gentleman who was sunning himself like one of his peacocks. He had taken the cup from the servant, and I saw that he wore gold bangles, and that his flabby fingers were crusted with rings; but directly he saw Meona he lifted his legs off the couch, and with an air of suave languor, got on his feet. He smiled, and his smile had a sallow and sleepy insolence. He bowed to my mistress, but even his politeness was ironic and smeary.

"Hail, daughter of Aurelius. Hail, lovely lady!"

I was standing behind Meona, and I wondered how she would react to this supercilious, flashy cad who seemed to stink of scent and sex-appeal. I saw her standing slim and straight, like some young cypress; she was holding her whip crossways across her thighs.

"Greetings, Pontius. I bring you a message from my father."

He ogled her.

"Take my couch, charming one. Wine for the lady. Be seated, child."

Child, indeed! He was like a great white slug to which a yellow flower petal was adhering. He did not look at me, and I supposed I liked him even less for that. The fierce person with the burnt-brick face had ceased from raging up and down, and was watching us and listening.

But Meona remained standing with the whip held across her thighs. Her neck and hands looked tense. I was expecting her to sting the fellow, but she was of finer mettle than I was.

"My lord, my father asks for your help. The Saxons are bringing death to our valleys."

I was watching Pontius, and leaning upon my spear. I could have presented him with a monocle and watched him tuck it into his eye.

"Ah, these savages! My dear, do drink. Be seated. You must be exhausted after this excursion."

The servant had brought another cup of wine, and my lord waved him forward.

"Serve the lady, fellow, serve the lady."

Meona stood very still.

"I ask for your answer, my lord, not for wine."

His great flabby face grew superciliously indulgent.

"Dear lady, why this impatience? Be seated. Yes, I agree, all this barbaric business is very boring. If you will permit me—"

I saw her head give a little jerk; her hands were clenched.

"People are being slaughtered, my lord, and houses plundered and given to the flames. My father is holding the manor, but we need help. You have men here—"

He shrugged, drank, and wiped his lips with the back of a be-ringed hand.

"Oh, a few. Homely levies. But, dear lady, my duty here is to hold the bridge. And the river, dear lady. We do not want these hairy fellows—"

Meona's voice seemed to fly suddenly like some fierce bird into his face.

"I see. You sit and drink wine. You think yourself safer on this side of the river."

My lord might be flabby, but he had a thick, white skin, and infinite complacency.

"Tut-tut, temper, my dear, temper. You do not do justice to my responsibilities. Let me suggest—"

"I suggest that you are a coward, my lord."

It was here that the fierce person came into the picture. I imagine that he had been trying to sting this mass of sex and superciliousness into action, and had failed. He came and stood half-way between Meona and the Lord of Pontes. His eyes were glittering and his lips were like the edge of a sword.

He said: "Our friend here, lady, is no fighting man. I do not think you will persuade him to leave his bath and his unguent bottles."

I am afraid I laughed, and my lord of Pontes gave me the look one might give a giggling waiter.

"Ha, dear old Robur here likes to talk the hero-stuff. You must forgive him."

Said Meona: "I forgive any man courage, however great a fool he be. But Robur is no fool. I leave you the fat and the folly, my lord. If I have come all these miles to see—a capon—"

I think that touched him. He, the pride of Phallus, an emasculated cock! I saw a fierce smirk on the face of old Robur. If he chuckled, it was a noiseless sound.

"*Verbum sap.* Lady, I can command a few men. They are gathered at my manor over the hills. I could be with your father before nightfall."

She walked deliberately up to Robur and kissed him upon the forehead.

"My friend, I salute you. You know the ways. Stay, I will leave my two men with you."

He smiled at her.

"Why not wait for us?"

"My father waits for news. No, I will go. My horses are fast."

Sir Pontius had strolled off to the river wall, and was stroking the head and neck of one of his tame peacocks.

"Cross your Rubicon, Robur. You fire-eaters must be singed, I suppose. I have more subtlety."

Meona might not have heard him. She turned and looked me in the face.

"Let us water and feed and rest the horses. Then, we will dare our fat friend's Rubicon. Robur, my friend, I salute you."

Robur laughed, a hard, dry, comforting laugh.

"Tell Aurelius I will be with him before nightfall."

When we pulled up at the posting-house a groom came to take the horses, but Meona would not trust the watering and feeding of her beloved Whites to a stranger. She drove into the stable yard, and saw that both water and corn were clean, and rubbed the beasts' noses and talked to them. That they loved her was just nature, and I, who was man, had begun to offer up my soul to this quick-tongued, passionate, masterful girl. She could do things, she was thorough. Kind, in the easy sense she might not be, but it has been my experience that a facile kindness is the virtue of fools. There are other and fiercer kindnesses. A gate led from the yard into the garden, and I followed Meona, feeling suddenly posed by a preposterous problem. If she sat down at one of those tables, was I to stand behind her chair while my lady broke bread and drank? And if she bade me sit with her who was to pay? I had those Roman coins in the pocket of the linen knickers they had given me, but I did not know their value.

There was a vacant table under a lime tree, and Meona took it. I could remember river-days when I had sat on a lawn with Lucy, but the face of Lucy had grown strangely dim. I stood and waited while Meona gave her order to one of the white-smocked girls. She ordered meat and a salad, bread, and a honey-drink. I felt damnably awkward, not knowing what to do.

I said: "Shall I wait with the horses?"

She gave me a quick, upward look over her shoulder.

"Is not my bodyguard to eat?"

She pointed to the other stool, and I sat down.

We could see the river and the placid greenness of the poplars and the willows, and the swans afloat. It all seemed very peaceful, in spite of the armed men on the bridge and the pother and confusion in the town. Yet, over yonder Death was abroad and I could remember sitting in my garden and thinking how strange and incredible it was that war might blow up over the sea, and aeroplanes drop death upon all the peaceful things I knew. Was this life, the eternal recurrence of man's violent urges, his instinct for power, his passion to conquer and possess? I felt that Meona did not wish to talk. Her face had a young, bleak severity, and her eyes were turned inward upon tragic thoughts. God knows, she had enough to brood upon, that great house in the valley, her father and all those people waiting upon disaster. We might return, if we returned, to find that the Saxons had been there before us and left smoke, flames, corpses, and a great silence.

The tragic hazard was so much more hers than mine, and I think that as we sat there I divined in her the fine, passionate stuff that was too deep and rich for any confessional. This girl's spirit was like a white flame burning steadily on the edge of the darkness. You would not understand its fierceness or its temper until it touched you. So unlike was she to anything I had known in my conventional world that I sat in silence, and wondered, and felt myself joined to her like some legendary hero. I suppose man and the earth have their heroic moments, and react to them and reveal them differently. My world might go to meet death in some muddy place with a "Cheerio" and a fag stuck in the corner of a casual mouth. The Greeks of Homer were otherwise, so were the men of Marathon, and the Normans at Senlac, and the Elizabethans in their ships against Spain. More spacious, more impetuous, more colourful days those, when a man might almost declaim in blank verse, and not be accused of posing. Perhaps the ancients did not pose. Life was in their blood, inevitable, hot and adequate. Meona was no dark flower tucked consciously into a vase. There was something poignantly elemental about her that made the man in me feel that I wore a sword.

A string of carts creaked over the bridge, followed by a little mob of men, women and children. A drove of cattle followed. Straws in the wind! I was aware of Meona watching them darkly. There were little spicules of light in her eyes. Almost I could hear her saying: "These, poor, panic-stricken fools! All the world is running away. Ye Gods, have we no pride or courage?" I was conscious of a pang of pity. She looked so young, so brittle and passionate in her protest against this break-up of her world.

She may have divined what I was feeling, for she looked me suddenly in the face, and I was to come to know those sudden glances of hers that went deep and swiftly like the thrust of a sword. I expect I was a puzzle to her, and well I might be. She had brought with her on this adventure a potential coward, and I could not have looked as white-faced as my ghost-self should have looked. I was feeling anything but a coward, for my blood was growing hot in her service.

She asked me a sudden question.

"Do you see which way all those people travel?"

"From the south."

She was frowning at the bridge.

"I think I would break down that bridge or burn it. As for my lord Pontius— What would you do with such a fellow?"

"Cast him in the river."

She flared, her nostrils dilating.

"I would hang him on the bridge after I had broken it. I would take such a man as Robur, and send torches and trumpets through the whole island, and preach shame to those who would not stand and fight. But our time is past."

She rose, and taking two or three coins from the little wallet that she wore, tossed them carelessly upon the table. It was a stately little gesture, and I could suppose that such trifles were to her of no account. The reckoning and largesse were satisfied, and you went upon your way, and when I came to consider it I could see in that one gesture the serenity of an aristocratic world. No little slip of paper was brought to such a creature as Meona, and three pennies were not slid under a plate.

She rose, and passing towards the gate, was curtseyed to by the girl who had served us. My lady had paid our reckoning, and the amount thereof needed no question-mark. Life before the coming of those wild men from over the sea had been spacious and easy for these patricians, and perhaps they would die as they had lived, if fate so willed it. Meona's scorn caused me to believe that Pontius of Pontes was no national symbol, but some oily upstart, or an urban highbrow whose very spunk was mere supercilious slime.

When we drove out of the posting-house yard we found Pontes even more a place of congested panic than when we had entered it. Meona had to drive slowly through the crowd, missing legs and feet and cows and bundles by inches. It was a querulous, bewildered mob in which infants squawled and women chattered. I glanced at the men, these peasant fellows, and they looked to me stout enough to stand and fight were they properly trained and led, but they had been rushed into this mass-panic by one of those primitive impulses which carry a whole country-side in flight over rivers and mountains. So, had the thing happened in my day in Abyssinia, Spain and China. I could suppose that these peasants had no weapons save their sickles and their flails and their axes. Had those in authority failed them? Were the British gentry all like Pontius of Pontes? These men had run away to save their women, their children and their cattle, and if such an exodus was not halted, I could see it ending, as it ended in history, in the wilds of Cornwall, Wales, and the sea.

That, perhaps, was the strangest part of my dream-adventure, its duality, in that I was supposed to know how the play ended while playing my part as an actor in it. I knew the end, but what I did not know, nor have our historians ever been agreed upon the point, was how long the play lasted. Did the Romano-British civilization crumble to death in the course of a few years, or were Aurelius Ambrosius and Uther and Arthur more than legendary figures, heroes who caught the sea-wolves by the throat and held them off for a hundred years or more? I could not say. But what I can swear is that as I drove out of Pontius with Aurelius's daughter I was no fatalist, no mere mummer in a predestined play. I was man, conscious of bitter happenings and of great hazards, and passionately concerned to play my part in them. I was no mere partisan, but the partner in peril of this dark-eyed girl whose loveliness was crowned with courage. Academic history could go to hell so far as I was concerned. I was living life, not scribbling about it in some donnish study. That was all I knew, and all that I needed to know. I was a live figure in a mysterious, moving tapestry.

The mystery of it all still moves me to an exquisite anguish. Mystery! We drove back over the bridge past the dumb faces of Pontius's guards. I got the impression that these men were not willing supers in this passion-play, and that they were creatures of secret shame. Here was a girl driving back against the tide of panic to confront the terror from which the whole country-side was fleeing. I was very conscious of her courage, and of my pride in sharing it. Maybe I looked at those men with irony and a flicker of rallying scorn. They would not meet my eyes. They were dumb and sullen, and yet I had the feeling that had Meona challenged them to action, some of them would have followed us. But Meona drove through and past them as though they were poor cattle, and turning my head for a last look at Pontes and the house of my lord Pontius, I saw a yellow shape lounging against the river wall, with a strutting peacock on either side of it. He was feeding the swans.

Again we took the road across the river meadows between the willows and the poplars, but only one party of fugitives did we meet, with their cattle, and their household goods piled on their wagons. Some of their lumbering carts were drawn by oxen, and Meona had to give them the road and take our chariot on to the grass. I shall never forget the faces of these people, and their kind of dusty vacancy. Mouths hung open; their very eyes seemed to show more of the whites than was normal, the glistening, staring eyes of terror.

One very old man mounted on a donkey shrilled at us and waved his stick.

"You be going the wrong way, lady."

No, she was going the right way for Britain, and she told him so, and his senile voice shrilled at us in a creaking quaver.

"Nay, they do say these savages have got them horses, and a man can't run against horses, hee-hee."

We let them pass and then drew back on to the road.

But, if what the old fellow had said was true, and it might very well be true, then our journey home might well be hazardous. Mounted men might follow the roads, and not break across wild country. Moreover, what was there to stop them, with the whole country-side flying in panic? We had lost our outriders, and I was moved to question Meona's wisdom in leaving Ferox and Marcus with Robur. They might not be very valorous fellows but they had eyes.

She gave me one of those quick, deep looks of hers.

"Do you quail, Pellias?"

I flashed back at her: "No, but I might fear for you. Three men may be better than one in a tight corner. And they could have scouted for us."

She looked at me so steadfastly that I had to remind her that the chariot might get ditched.

"Is that so, my friend?"

But I think she was beginning to discover that I had a temper, and that I might be of other mettle than I had seemed.

This river country had a loveliness of its own, with the fields cloth of gold, and the white-thorns in flower, but it suggested to me the sadness of a wide-eyed resignation. Its people had fled, and resignation was not our torch. I was feeling a little wild, as though I had drunk of the cup which Isoult and Tristan had shared. Life had a bitter-sweet tang to it; everything was more rich and mysterious and colourful, but it was no mere drugged dream. I felt my muscles taut and my head utterly clear. My blood was up. I was enjoying this danger.

So, we came to the wilder country, and it pleased me with its great woods, and bosky thickets, its wastes of heather, and that adventurous sky. The hills seemed higher, the valleys deeper. I saw wild creatures, deer, swine, and in one black wood a large, fierce dog-like creature that might have been a wolf. My head kept moving like the head of a ship's look-out at sea. The sun was in strength, and began to shine slantwise across us, and it was easier to pick up details on our left than on our right. Meona kept the horses at an easy trot, and I realized that she was sparing them so that we might have speed and staying-power in hand should we need it.

The strangest thing of all was the emptiness of this country, its supreme silence. We too were silent, until we saw the chalk ridge ahead of us, and the same thought must have come to both of us. What lay beyond it? I noticed how pale

Meona's lips were, and as though suspense had tightened them and drained them of blood.

"What shall we find, my friend?"

I tried to reassure her, for I could feel even her courage wincing. I may have said a lot of silly things, that to be forewarned was to be forearmed, that the Saxons could not surprise the manor, and that there were men enough there to hold the house. I reminded her that Robur would be with us before night fell, and though she listened to me I felt that she was filled with an increasing dread. The road climbed the Downs slantwise, and Meona walked her horses up the hill. She pulled up on the summit, and we stood side by side in the chariot, looking for any sign of life or of danger. Particularly did I look for smoke in the valleys amid the crumple of hills, but I could see no smoke that might mean that the raiders had been at work there.

"It is all so very peaceful."

Her words were like a sigh, and they touched me.

"So it may be. All this panic may be nothing."

"It is hard to believe, I mean, that such things should happen. Well, let us go down and see."

Almost, I could feel her steel herself to the last and most hazardous and most revealing part of our journey. It was not physical fear that troubled her, but that suspended anguish of the soul. She walked the horses down into the valley, and when the road levelled out, put them at a trot. We were nearing the Wey and the bridge and that little cluster of cottages in the valley. There was the same silence here, the same feeling of emptiness, and I knew that both of us were hungry for some human sound, even a dog's barking. I felt myself alone in a deserted country.

A turn of the road showed us the hamlet and its narrow

street. The sun shone upon it, but even before we drove into the little place I had divined its emptiness. And empty it was, doors hanging open, the people gone. I saw no living thing there, nothing that suggested life save some fresh horse-droppings in the middle of the road.

Meona pulled up. She looked white and shocked.

"But which way have they gone? We should have met them."

I suggested that they might have gone to join her people in Honey Valley, but she shook her head.

"No, they have taken to the woods."

Even the woods above us seemed sinister, hiding, perhaps, men who watched and waited like wild beasts for the ambushing of their prey. Meona, with a last look at this deserted place, drove on towards the bridge. Should we find it broken? But the bridge had not been touched; the people had fled and left it defenceless. We looked into each other's eyes, as we drove over the bridge, and the timber echoed to the horses' hoofs and the rumbling of the wheels.

"What shall we find?" her eyes asked me.

I remember feeling my sword, to see that it was loose in the sheath, for I seemed to sense death ahead of us.

CHAPTER TEN

It all happened so suddenly that even now it is difficult for me to describe our ambuscado. I suppose that when one is set upon by a couple of savage beasts and one is fighting for one's life, the business is a wild and bloody blur, a primitive squall that does not adjust itself to the recordings of subtle details. We were about half a mile from the bridge across the Wey, and skirting a thicket of white-thorns that grew close to the track when the savages rushed out at us. There were three of them, rough, hairy-looking brutes with bulging blue eyes. They were close on us, and I do know that my first thought was that unless I did something dramatic Meona would be at their mercy. It was not courage but a mad impulse that made me leap out of the chariot with my shield on my arm and my spear ready. The fellows were barking like wild dogs, and their cries frightened the horses. They stampeded, and though Meona told me afterwards that she tried to hold them, they galloped two hundred yards or more before she managed to get control and bring them about.

It has been said that a raw recruit is at his best in his first fight, and certainly I was raw enough, but I was fighting-mad. I remember realizing that these Saxons were much smaller men than I was, and feeling surprised by the fact. They came at me as though they thought me easy game, and then, the tallest of the three shouted something, and the others laughed and held their rush. It was no sporting spirit, I imagine, that persuaded them to leave the settling of me to their captain, and I had no time for such delicacies. The savage came at me like a Highlander charging with a claymore, his shield held to cover his body. He had a nasty, red, beefy face, and long yellow teeth which showed between snarling lips. I knew at once that I wanted to kill him. And my luck was in. I held my spear like a javelin, with my shield up, and as he came charging in, I jabbed at him and saw the spear head slide over the top of his big buckler and catch him in the throat. I swung all my weight into it, and gave the spear shaft a vicious twist. The whole business astonished me, the way his angry eyes suddenly grew blind, the spurting blood, the realization that I had got my man.

He went down and my spear went with him, and the other two rushed at me like mad dogs. This was to be no sporting affair, and never on the football field have I moved more limberly, and dodged and swerved to cheat a tackler. I am pretty quick on my feet, and I had to get my sword out. One of the Saxons, a man with a pug-dog face, had two swings at me with a kind of battle axe, and one blow just brushed my shoulder. My wits were as glib now as my feet. I did what they must have thought to be a bunk, and I sprinted for fifty yards, and looking back over my shoulder, saw that the pug-faced fellow had out-run his comrade. This was my chance, and I flashed round, and caught him as he blundered into me.

He had time only to get in a cramped half blow, and it bounced off my helmet and gashed my cheek, and I dug my sword into his belly. But he was not done for; he dropped his axe and clawed me, snarling like a wounded dog. And before I could throw him off, the other fellow was on me and tackling me from behind.

We went down in a three-headed maul. Pug-face was under me, and I dug for his throat, but the other fellow's arm came over my eyes, and I felt metal on my neck. I kicked and heaved to throw him off, while I finished off the man under me, but the other fellow hung on and straddled me, and was preparing, I gather, to cut my throat. We were all panting, and straining, and Pug-face was gurgling and twitching under me. My shield was hampering my left arm, and the fellow on my back was not discouraged by an elbow-jab in the ribs. I was mad, even though I felt that my number was called, and that I should have my throat slit in two seconds. Then, something happened. I heard the man above me rip out a sharp cry; his body seemed to stiffen above me, and then squirm and relax. I heaved him off and struggled up, and saw Meona with that little dagger in her hand.

But my blood was still up. I was feeling grim, and I made sure with my sword that those two Saxons would fight no more. Then I stood and panted, and looked at Meona, and she at me. The two white horses were close to us, and one of them was nosing the grass.

This was a different Meona. She was dead white, with a blaze in her eyes, and the blood on that bodkin of hers was much more red than her lips.

"Madman, why did you leap from the chariot?"

Good God, was I to face her anger after effacing those two

Saxons? The ways of women are beyond all reason!

I panted at her, for my chest was still heaving, and my heart going at a gallop.

"Well, to fight. Would you have had me run away?"

She looked at me and at those dead men and at her dagger, and then she dropped it on the grass. I can only describe what happened to her face as a kind of melting, or as though it had changed from raw fruit to a sudden bitter-sweet ripeness.

"You have blood on your face."

That must have been obvious. The gash on my cheek was not deep, but it was oozing blood over my chin, and dropping on to my breastplate. I put up my hand, touched the warm wetness, stared at my hand.

"Nothing much."

But she came to me quickly, and taking my face between her hands, looked at the wound.

"My friend, this must be seen to. We have only another mile or two to go."

Her hands, eyes and voice thrilled me, but I saw her eyes go to the woods.

"There may be others. Quick."

I was feeling reckless and exultant. I knew that the adventure was mine, and that I was its master.

"Get into the chariot, Meona. Be ready. There are some nice trophies here. Arms may be useful."

I bespoiled the dead men of their arms, shields, swords, an axe, daggers, and tumbled them into the chariot, and going back to the first man to recover my spear, I found that he was alive. He had plucked the spear head out of his throat and was clutching the staff. I wrested the thing out of his hands and putting the point into his left eye, jammed the blade home into his brain. My bloody, ruthless temper astonished me. Had I reverted, or was this just life in the raw? I took his shield and sword, and returning, bundled them into the chariot at Meona's feet. Here was a mixed bag of spoil, and I exulted over it. Would they call me a coward now? I climbed in beside Meona. The horses were cropping the grass, with their heads well down, and I remember the smell of the May flower drifting to us.

Meona did not pull at once on the reins, though she knew that any loitering might be hazardous. I felt her eyes upon my face, searching eyes, deep with a questioning scrutiny.

"You have ceased to bleed."

"It is nothing much."

Her next words came in a whisper that might have been the reflection of her thoughts.

"Three men—and you alone."

I think I must have laughed, for there was a savage and monstrous joy in me.

"I was fortunate. I had to run and be clever."

"But the first man."

Had she seen, looked back while she was struggling with the horses?

"Oh yes, I had a lucky thrust at him."

"Yes."

I understood that she wanted me to go on.

"My spear got caught when he went down. I had to dodge the others until I could get my sword out. I stabbed the second fellow, and then had the third on my back. You saved my life, you know."

She pulled suddenly on the reins, and spoke to the horses.

"They ran away with me."

"But you came back. That was brave."

"Brave!"

She reached for her whip and gave the whites the lash as though protesting against my praise. Her hand must have been heavier than usual, for the horses broke into a gallop, and we went heaving and bumping along the track, and suddenly I felt dizzy and sat down on the seat.

"Did you think I would not come back?"

I put my hand to my face, for it was beginning to hurt.

"I had not much time to think about anything. It was like being attacked by three wild beasts."

Her voice rang out.

"But you fought them, and slew them."

"Two."

I think she winced. The stabbing of that man had shaken her more than she knew, and I too was feeling shaken now that the business was over. I suppose men feel like that after a rage-storm and savage slaying. My knees were knocking together.

Her sudden cry moved me.

"Oh, let us go home, let us go home."

Fear had come back to her, black, tumultuous fear. I guessed that she was dreading that there might be no home.

The sun was well in the west and shining down the valley, and never have I seen any country look more lovely and more peaceful. The light seemed to stroke the grassy hill-sides and leave them velvet; the young green of the beech trees was very brilliant, and the great old yews looked like puffs of black smoke. A trail of dust lay behind us, for Meona was still galloping her horses, and I could see foam flecking from their bits. Great white clouds sailed across the hills in a sky of infinite blueness, and though my head was beginning to ache, there was a great joy in me. I could have tossed my arms and sung.

I was aware of Meona leaning back and pulling on the reins, and then I saw what she had seen, the sunlight shining upon harness and weapons. There were men in the road ahead of us just by the waters of a mere. It was a breathless moment for us, and then Meona waved her whip. She had the eyes of a falcon.

"Festus."

Festus it was, with three other men who had come to scout for us and bring us in. Those three Saxons must have broken away from the main pack and gone hunting on their own. Festus was mounted, and he cantered to meet us, the footmen running at his horse's heels.

He brandished his spear, and looked at Meona, and then at my bloody face.

"You have had fighting, lady."

She had pulled the horses up. She was very calm now.

"Yes, we have had fighting, Festus."

"Where are Ferox and Marcus? Dead?"

"No, we left them at Pontes to guide those who will help us. Look in the chariot, Festus, look."

He looked, and so did the other men, and I shall never forget their blank, fuddled faces.

"Saxon's arms, lady."

"Yes."

"But there are three shields."

Yes, three shields, Festus. It happened only a little while ago. They ambushed us, and all three are dead. That is how Pellias got his wound."

All four of them were looking at me now, and not at the trophies.

"Pellias slew the three of them?"

"He fought three and slew three."

The men gaped at me. I wanted to confess how she had saved me, but I felt her elbow pressing against my side.

Festus tossed his spear, and smiled at me.

"That is great fighting. Honour to you, brother."

We drove on, with Festus riding beside us, and the footmen trotting behind the chariot. From Festus we learned that they had seen nothing of the savages in the valley, but our adventure proved that they must have been very near. He told us that they had been busy all day strengthening the manor, blocking up unwanted doorways and windows, and putting up palisades, and bringing in stores of food. Even the hypocaust chambers had been cleaned out and half filled with flour and grain. The sheep and cattle had been driven up to an old earthwork in the high hills and hidden there, save those that had been slaughtered or had been kept in the cow-house and byres. Niger the Smith had been at work at his forge all day, beating out spears and swords. Honey Valley could muster about thirty men fit to bear arms. There were two old soldiers among them, and these veterans had been drilling the peasants.

I could see that Festus was looking lovingly at one of those Saxon swords, and I bent down and picked up the one that had belonged to the chief. I spoke to Meona.

"Shall we give Festus this?"

"It is yours to give."

"No, not mine, Meona."

"Then—ours. Give it to him, if it pleases you."

I passed the sword to Festus just as we reached the village, but he smiled at me, and shook his head.

"That shall be a pledge between us, brother, but not yet.

Let it lie there. Such trophies should cheer the hearts of the lads of the village."

At the Manor people had been watching for us, and I heard shouting, and saw men and women crowding out of the gate, though the guards on duty were trying to keep them back. Hands waved. I heard a voice cry: "Our lady is safe! Tell the master!" We drove into the courtyard through a little mob, and the gates were shut behind us. Aurelius Superbus was in the portico, sitting in his state chair. I saw the sun shining on his white head. The suspense was over for him.

Festus seemed to have appointed himself the day's herald. Meona had stepped out of the chariot and gone to embrace her father, but I remained where I was, feeling like a prize calf at a show. Festus had raised his arm, and was speaking to the crowd.

"Look into the chariot, people, and look into Pellias's bloody face."

They crowded round, peering and jostling each other. The little pile of trophies astonished them. They looked at me, at Festus, and at each other.

"Pellias's prize. Three Saxons slain and spoiled! How is that for an omen?"

I could see that they were a little incredulous, especially those men who had watched my ghost-brother turn tail in battle. They murmured; was this a jest? And where was Ferox and Marcus?

"I am telling you, people. Pellias fought and slew three Saxons. Ask our lady, if you do not believe me. Ferox and Marcus are at Pontes, and help is coming."

The crowd murmured. Some of the men began to handle the dead Saxons' gear.

A voice said: "He must have gone mad."

I was feeling rather a fool, but Meona came and rescued me. The people gave way before her, and she spoke to them.

"Festus speaks the truth. Three of the savages attacked us, and Pellias slew them. Come, my friend, your wound must be seen to."

But I did not get out of the chariot. I was lifted out of it by the shouting men, and carried on the shoulders of two of them to the portico steps where my lord sat waiting. His face and hair were lit up by the sun. He stretched out a hand to me, and I wondered what he must be thinking of this other Pellias, this futurist ghost.

"Thanks, my son, thanks."

I bent and put my lips to the signet on his hand, and he laid the other hand upon my head.

"Go, get your wound washed and dressed. Such men as you will be precious to us."

Festus had dismounted, and the white horses were brought to the steps of the portico so that Aurelius might see the trophies, and I was telling him that the best of the swords had been promised to Festus when Meona touched my arm.

"Go. Pollux is here to serve you. That wound must be cleansed."

Those were orders, but it was a sweet tyranny that she exercised, and I followed Pollux who was waiting for me. He took me to the bath-chamber, and in the bath-chamber was kept what one would describe as the house's first-aid cabinet. A woman brought warm water in a basin, and Pollux made me sit on a stool while he dealt with me. He was excessively affable and suave, and it was obvious that I had become a hero. He employed a swab of stuff that looked like dried sphagnum moistened in water to wash my clotted face and chin, but he used a sweet oil on the wound itself, and finished off with some unguent that smelt of herbs.

I asked him if the wound needed stitches.

"No, sir. I can draw the edges together with plaster."

His fingers were as deft as his manners, and when he had finished with me he showed me my face in a mirror, and I saw one half of my countenance decorated with criss-crosses of plaster in the shape of a star.

A servant came to us with a message.

"My lord will speak with you when Pollux has finished."

I got up from the stool, but Pollux restrained me.

"Sit awhile, sir, until the plaster has set. Then, your hands, too."

I looked at my hands. There was dried blood on them, and I had not noticed it before. Pollux washed my hands for me and anointed them with oil, and then, as though he could not do enough for me, he drew off my shoes and washed my feet.

The servant waited, and I asked him a question.

"Where shall I find my lord?"

"In the garden, sir."

"Go and tell my lord that I am coming."

CHAPTER ELEVEN

$\mathscr{I}$ FOUND my lord alone in the garden, sitting in the arbor of yews with the evening sunlight shining upon him. His hands rested upon his stick, and it seemed to me that his face had recovered its jocund freshness. His daughter was alive; help was coming, and the manor had not been attacked. Sufficient for the day was the hazard thereof.

He surveyed me with a contemplative smile. His eyes had a quality that I never remember discovering in any other eyes, I believe they were blue, but they could look black, both dark and brilliant like bright stones set in a mask. And yet the simile of a polished stone does not quite convey my meaning, for their very darkness and their lustre had the shadowy softness that one sees in a deep pool of clear water.

"Well, my son, you have broken a superstition."

For the moment I did not catch his meaning, though I knew that he and I shared a secret that would have confounded the wisest of the wise.

"Or an illusion, sir."

"In two senses. Make sure that we are alone."

He pointed with his stick, and I saw that two rough timber stages had been erected in the angles of the high wall, where sentinels could stand and watch the woods. One of these look-outs was held by my red-headed friend whom I had cuffed for insolence; the other was empty. The sentry-post was twenty yards or more from the seat, and I did not think the fellow would hear much of what we said. I told my lord that one of the posts was occupied.

"Who is on duty?"

"A man with red hair, sir. I do not know his name."

"Ah, Polus, a stupid oaf. Just a belly, my son. He would not understand us."

He motioned me to sit on the seat beside him, and closing his eyes and letting the sun warm his face he began to speak to me of our mysterious and mutual conspiracy.

"How did it happen, Pellias?"

I told him, and keeping his eyes closed, he seemed to drink in the warmth and the significance of my adventure.

"The sun, and a young man's strength are comforting to the old, my son. Tell me, in your world, had you ever fought in this fashion?"

"Never."

"Well, it seems to have been a happy initiation."

I laughed.

"I have played rough games, sir, but this was a different game. There was a sudden rage in me."

"The Furor Britannicus! Were you afraid?"

"No. That is to say, there was a moment of fear, but it was—"

I hesitated and he opened his eyes and looked at me.

"For someone else?"

I nodded.

"Well, that is as it should be. My daughter is very precious to me, my son."

"I know, sir. Did she tell you that she saved my life?"

"Yes."

"Her courage was greater than mine. The courage that can turn frightened horses and come back—"

He closed his eyes again.

"Tradition, breed. But, come, tell me, how does this world shape to you, or rather, how do you shape to it? Is the ghost alive?"

I had had a feeling that he would ask me this question, and I was ready to answer it, for it was the supreme question that had begun to challenge me.

"I think I am more man than ghost, sir."

"This life is blood, not vapour, eh?"

"Yes, you put it perfectly. It is most strange, but that other life seems to be growing dim, and this life becoming vivid. Is it credible to you, master?"

He pondered for a while, and whatever his secret thoughts might have been, he humoured the mystery.

"Things happen, Pellias, and the wisest of us cannot explain them. If you are to be of our world, and of it, then there may be a fate upon you, and I might hail it as good."

"How, sir?"

He opened his eyes, and did not close them again.

"Listen, I said that you had broken an obsession. What do I mean by that? Why—this. It has become a kind of superstition with us that a British man is not the equal in combat of these barbarians from over the sea. There was a time when our cities were not walled, but times changed. We were raided on both sides from over the sea. We had our Count of the Saxon Shore, the great fortresses such as Anderida, and the Fleet. That sufficed us in the main, save for one or two disastrous plunderings, until Rome had to leave us to our

own resources. Gaul has been overrun, but its ordered life
still holds. Their new men are less savage than these Jutes
and Saxons. Kent has fallen to the savages; there have been
landings in the north. More and more of these barbarians
arrive with their women and children. They would conquer
the island. We have lost battles to them. Our people leave
their homes and fly. Our men say: 'We cannot face these wild
beasts.' Why should they not be faced? Our peasants and
our gentry are not women. Only the man and men are
needed. We ask for our hero. And you, my son, have lit a
torch to-day. You have fought, not one but three of these
savages, and slain them. That is the trumpet-call that stir will
the bowels of my people."

Was I listening to some Wagnerian opera, or rather to the
voice of Merlin? I suppose much of Shakespeare would
sound like ornate clap-trap in the Stock Exchange or at a
meeting of the General Medical Council. Was I, a member
of the English bourgeoisie, to be chosen as a Romano-Celtic
hero or a young David who would lead Judah against the
Philistines? Yet, this was not mere rhetoric. Men had more
sense of drama in those earlier days, more feeling for the
pageantry of life and death; and their emotions and the expressing of them had more gesture and colour. The Ghost in
Hamlet has never failed to give me shivers down my spine,
and a feeling that back of all things lies mystery, be it of terror
or of tears. How would John Gielgud have reacted to such a
fate as mine? Would he have strolled about with a teacup,
bleating epigrammatic negations, or would he have drawn a
sword, and with the white and flashing face of a fighting-man
called the great adventure his? I have no doubt about that.
I felt a kind of turbulence in my belly. My ears seemed to
sing. I could spread my shoulders, and throw back my head.

"If that is to be my fate, master, I will grasp it."

He looked at me long and steadily.

"Then, you shall lead my people, Pellias. You shall be our Dux, my son, and may the Gods be with you."

I asked that I might be alone for an hour, and Aurelius left me alone in the garden. I had felt moved to ask him of the new religion. Where was Christ in Britain? Was Christianity a city cult, the creed of slaves? What of Joseph of Arimathea, of Constantine and Helena, and the Holy Grail? Even the name of Honey Valley sounded pagan, and its people were *pagani,* peasants who kept the old festivals. Not that I was troubled about the business, only puzzled. For me the sentimental Victorian Christ was as dead as Solomon, or rather he had withdrawn and become like Zeus or Aphrodite, a symbol expressing the eternal mystery of things. Well, I was in a pagan world, and I did not think of the Saxons as heathen but more as I would have thought of German airmen spilling death and horror and human dirt over the loveliness of an ordered richness. I walked up and down the garden, and there was an exultation in my mood. Did I dare to take up this splendid venture? I did dare. Maybe my flesh was proud and my blood a little arrogant.

I heard a voice addressing me, the voice of Red Head.

"Be it true that you slew three Saxons?"

I looked up at him.

"Quite true."

"Lordy, you must have been drunk!"

He leered at me, and I spiflicated him.

"Turn your face to the woods, you dog, and watch. That is your business."

He tittered at me.

"Tee-hee, we be head in air these days."

I was close to the wooden staging, and I caught his ankle and brought him down like a squawking hen.

"Get out," I said. "I'll take your watch. You are not fit to be trusted with the lives of your betters."

I had hurt him, and he limped off, muttering and rubbing his shoulder, but I have never liked or trusted that sort of red-headed man, with evil slits of eyes in a boiled-veal face. I mounted the staging of the sentry-post, and leaning upon the wall, looked out upon all the loveliness of that valley with the setting sun shining upon it. It was one of those miraculous moments when super-sensuous things seem very near, and the objective world a beautiful painting upon glass. One had but to penetrate that crystal screen to find oneself in some other dimension, where time and light and space are different, and the spirit floats in a new freedom. I felt strangely fey, and in feeling thus I seemed to divine a like feyness in my master. Had I come to him as some dreamer from the other world, the genius of our fate, and was he sufficiently credulous to be infinitely wise? Are those who have faith in super-human intervention the only beings who are supremely wise?

I was so deep in contemplating my world of White Magic that I neither heard nor saw her in the garden.

"Pellias."

I came out of my dream, and saw her standing below me, and again she was different to my eyes. She looked slighter, more fragile, and her eyes were dark velvet.

"What are you doing?"

"Thinking. And I should be watching."

"Let me stand there with you."

She put out her hands, and I helped her up. The platform of the look-out was no more than a yard square, and we were very close together and leaning upon the wall. She had come from the bath, and her body smelt of some sweet perfume, but in my super-sensuous mood she smelt of paradise. She put her face between her hands and gazed, and I could divine in her a melancholy, the shadow of the death we had escaped, and of the dead we had on our souls.

The sun was low, and the shadow of the wooded hill crept over us. I felt her shiver.

"Do men die utterly, my friend, or do their ghosts walk?"

I said: "I think the spirit must survive?"

Her face looked wounded.

"Poor ghosts, poor shadows. I have made a ghost. And yet—"

I wanted to touch her, to comfort this other Meona who was woman.

"But for you I should have been a poor, pale ghost."

Again she shivered.

"Are men born to blood and death?"

"We slay that we may not be devoured."

"Yes, yes, but we women, who should bear children? Like throwing good bread into the sea. I am troubled, my friend, I am troubled."

I dared to touch her hand, and she did not flinch from me, and then I found myself uttering a platitude about a war to end war. How one humbugs oneself with words, or allows a Hitler to do it for one. There can be no end to war so long as man has a belly and sex, and that instinct for power, especially so when he is feeling inferior. The old Romans did not have to shout and swagger and sweat in an attempt to convince the rest of the world that they were marvellous fellows. But what had this to do with Meona? She had been so innocent in her fierceness and her courage, and yet, when she had found real blood upon her hands, she had been shocked by it. She was dove as well as falcon, and my love was glad that she should be so.

She stood gazing up into the woods.

"Trees can be so friendly, Pellias. They do not kill."

"But they can smother and dwarf small things. Those beech trees suffer no rivals."

She nodded.

"So, it is our fate here to fight. Did you feel afraid, Pellias, when those men leapt out at us?"

"I felt afraid—for you."

That I, as her father's man, should have no right to utter such words, was evident, but she did not seem to resent them. Moreover, I was no longer Pellias the coward, but a fighting-man and captain, and perhaps the new young hero in me was evident to her. I had significance for women, when a man's job is to take the sword and thrust it into the belly of an implacable and cruel enemy.

The sun was below the hills, and the light was beginning to fail, and in the silence of the valley we could hear voices and the sound of horses' hoofs, and the tramp of men. We looked at each other.

"It is Robur."

"We must welcome him."

I jumped down, and put up my hands to help her, but she smiled at me in a strange way, and I knew that she did not wish to be touched. I did not feel that she had rebuffed me. Her elusiveness was far, far more subtle than that.

"More men, my friend, more strength."

We passed down the garden and through the house to the portico. Aurelius was there, leaning upon his stick. The gates were opened, and Robur rode in, and I saw in the road

behind him a whole press of mounted men. The afterglow
shone upon their harness. Robur brought his horse through
the crowd in the courtyard, and his fierce red face was jocund.
He saluted my lord.

"We have done better than I thought, sir. I have purloined
thirty of Pontius's cavalry."

His white teeth flashed in his brick-red face.

"Purloin is a good word, sir, but the fellows were fed up
with Master Pontius. They chose to come with me."

Aurelius smiled upon Robur.

"How many men have you, my friend?"

"Some forty horse and twenty foot."

"That is a brave succour. Why, sir, we have a small army
in the making! Well, we can feed and lodge you at a pinch.
And may the gods be with us."

Old Robur swung himself off his horse, and stretched his
legs.

"I am a little old and stiff, my lord, but not too stiff for a
fight. We have left our prize eunuch at Pontes. That is Pontius's trouble, sir, he cannot make up his mind whether he is
man or woman."

We laughed. Robur was good for one's courage.

"Let us go in and eat and drink, my friend," said Aurelius,
"and then we will talk. Pellias, find Festus, and bring him in
with you. The fighting men shall hold council together."

CHAPTER TWELVE

THE western window of the summer-room was lit by the afterglow, and Meona went to sit in the window-seat while we men gathered round the table. Robur sat on my lord's right hand, I on his left, with Festus next to me. Gildas, my lord's secretary, came shuffling in, to stand, tablets in hand, behind Aurelius's chair. I did not like Gildas. He had a smooth, suave, sallow face, and one of those mean little puckered-up mouths that make a man look superior and supercilious. His eyes were small, like his mouth, eyes that never seemed to move in his head, and yet gave you the impression of seeing everything, like the bright black eyes of a rat. Meat and drink were brought to us, but Meona took her meat and drink in the window-seat. A servant had set a small table by her knee, and she was like a figure in a frieze, dark and aloof against the saffron sky.

That which is most vivid to me is the memory of her lovely little head seen in profile against the afterglow. There was a new strangeness in its perfect contours, the curve of the forehead, the shadow of the brows, the haughty little nose, the soft lines of the lips and chin. The set of her head was just as lovely, and the sudden transit from the midnight of her hair to the exquisite shapeliness of her neck. I was conscious of a sudden, sharp anguish as I sat and gazed at her. She seemed to me to be so incredibly lovely and aloof, so unattainable, so poignantly apart from me, and what was I but a ghost, and she a creature of some other world. I suppose love, tragic love, takes one in this way, but the supreme anguish and exaltation of it were new to me. I felt that death must be near, because she was so lovely, and because of the strange anguish she caused me. I could not believe, somehow, that we had ever been so close as we had been on that look-out in the garden. She seemed part of the afterglow, an immaterial, legendary creature, yet immeasurably alive. It wounded me to look at her.

But I seemed to become conscious of some other scrutiny. I might be gazing at Meona, but other eyes were upon me, and not with blind adoration. I glanced up and sideways and found Gildas watching me. In common parlance one has heard of eyes being like gimlets, but Gildas's eyes were like corkscrews extracting my secret. I imagine that it was not a very obdurate cork. A mere touch of the thumb would have sent it to the ceiling. I saw a little disapproving, oily smirk smear itself across that sallow face. It became cold and prim and anonymous. Gildas stood with his hands folded over his tablets, gazing into space. Perhaps he had realized that I was not a safe man to be observed in that way. I was not. I was a fighting man, and pert, peering scribblers were not creatures to be humoured.

Gildas and the servants had been dismissed, and Aurelius was speaking to us. His voice seemed part of the twilight. I saw a bat go fluttering across the pale slip of sky outside the window. Meona's hair was black as jet, her face a cameo in ivory.

"My friends," he said, "has any one of you a plan?"

Robur and I looked at each other across the table. I saw his teeth white and smiling in the dusk. His tongue came out and moistened a terse, dry lip.

"Sir, let us hear what the hot blood has to say."

He nodded his head at me.

"Hot blood and old head, but let the blood sing first. Then, I may put a cap on it."

Aurelius turned to me, and his hair was like a halo. A moment ago I had nothing to say, but words seemed to come into my mouth, and with them word-pictures welled up into my consciousness. I might have been inspired.

"Lord, I would not wait for the Saxons to bring war to us. I would carry it to them."

"Speak your mind, my son."

"I take it, lord, that we have no strong body of these people near us. We have to deal with raiding parties. Moreover, these savages must think that the country-side is theirs for the taking, and that there is no one to counter them. The surprise can be of our choosing. Let us go out and fall upon them."

I was looking at Meona, and I saw her head turn full face to me. Her eyes were dark hollows, but I seemed to divine a swift flash in them.

"And the women and children, my son?"

"I would send them away, lord, to safer country. We can hold this place as a rallying point, and use all our strength to strike."

I felt Festus's hand upon my shoulder.

"Good for you, brother, good for you."

Aurelius turned to Robur, and I saw old Robur's profile in the twilight, the eagle nose, the tight lips, the hard round forehead. Then, those lips parted and spoke like the lips of a shadow-head.

"Pellias is our oracle. Let us send the women and children away, and fight for this island."

There was a movement, and Meona came to stand behind her father's chair. She stood there for a moment, very still and straight, and I felt her eyes upon me.

"Pellias has spoken as a man should speak. Let the women go."

She had her hands upon her father's shoulders, and he took one of them in his, and drew it down.

"You, child, shall be in charge of the women."

I was watching her face, and thinking how mysterious one face could be. Also, I was stabbed by the thought that I had spoken words that were recoiling upon themselves. Let the women go, and Meona would go with them! Good God, did I want her to stay in this most perilous place, so that I might see her day by day, even though my looking upon her brought me anguish? God forgive me, I both wanted her to stay with us, and to go.

The room was growing dark, and her silence seemed part of the darkness. I saw her bend, and lay her cheek against her father's head. She spoke, and her voice had a whispering hollowness.

"No, I shall stay."

Aurelius smiled. He put up a hand and clasped her head.

"Oh, no, you won't, my dear. We shall want no such hostages to fate."

"I will stay," said she.

I saw the caressing movement of the old man's hand. It

was as though he had to deal with a passionate and high-spirited child.

"Let the council of war decide. It is our right to choose, as men, men who have to face reality."

His eyes were on Robur, and there was no shilly-shallying about Robur. His words were dry and pertinent.

"The lady must go, sir. We shall have enough hazard without such a treasure-chest to guard."

I felt Festus make a quick movement.

"I disagree, lord. Such courage and such a presence would make any falterer brave."

Aurelius turned to me, and I heard my voice uttering words that seemed to come of themselves.

"Your daughter must go."

I felt her eyes upon me, great, tragic, mysterious eyes in a dim, white face. She seemed about to speak, but her father spoke before her.

"Two against one. And I make the third, and approve the verdict. All women must go."

I do not know why I did the thing I did. There was a kind of madness in it, the madness of a man who should be husbanding his strength and sleeping, but whose spirit will not let him rest. We had posted our guards and made all secure for the night, and given orders for the wagons and horses to be ready at dawn. Our first sally was to be something of an adventure in search of supplies, for, with a hundred men to feed, stores were necessary. We were to raid the deserted homesteads, and each man was to ride home with a sheep or a sack of corn across his horse. I had taken off my harness, but I could not rest. The anguish of this sudden love was too sharp in me. I wandered out into the courtyard and made the guards open the gate for me, and my new prestige was such that they did not question my orders. I told them that I was going to climb the hills, and look north and south to see if any place had been fired by our enemies.

It was a superb night, still and sweet, and ablaze with stars. I could hear the stream running. The darkness was a gentle darkness, and when one's eyes were used to it, the earth seemed to be lit by astral light. Objects were quite plain to me. I crossed the brook by a footbridge, and climbed to that little stretch of open land, grass and arable, that ran between the woods and the water. It was like a gently sloping terrace, and in my other world, in the other Albury that I knew, this sweep of wheat and of grass hanging on the hill-side between the high woods and the lush green valley, had always seemed to me particularly strange and lovely.

The path led up through an orchard, and each tree was a distinct and shadowy shape. The sky above the high woods blazed stars. There was not a sound to be heard save the fall of the water at the mill-weir down below. I have never known a night more still, with a velvety black stillness that we moderns do not understand. I suppose there may have been nature sounds that were unfamiliar to me, and so passed unregistered, the prowlings and scufflings of creatures of the night, badgers and pole-cats and weasels. Owls would be on the wing, but the night's wings were noiseless. I found a beech tree, and sitting down on a great clawed root, let my head and shoulders rest against the trunk.

I cannot have been there more than half a minute when I heard a little sound in the darkness below me, and so small and vague was it that I could not decide upon its cause. I sat and listened. The sound suggested something moving in the grass, a wild thing on the prowl, and then a certain rhythm in it became apparent. Swish-swish. There was a pause between each sibilant stroke, which, in the utter stillness of the night, was like a hand smoothing out silk. I understood. Feet were brushing through the grass. Who was it? Had I been followed? I stood up and held my breath, under the black vault of the great tree.

Then, I was able to distinguish a shape. It had moved, but now it was motionless. The swish-swish of the caressed grasses had ceased. I felt my heart beating. Even before I challenged that vague figure, a premonition stabbed me.

"Who's that?"

"Meona."

Had I not known it, somehow?

"Ye gods, you should not be here!"

I must have blurted out the words rather fiercely, and I heard her give back a little laugh that seemed to mock me.

"Are you afraid, Pellias?"

I believe that I have always been rather a fool about women, I mean, in my attitude to them, that of the dear simpleton whose directness glances off a woman's more oblique moods. I have failed to remember that a woman may be a creature of vanity, and that the love-game may be fancy-dress to her. Lucy was not like that, and I suppose that is why she married me. She was a completely sincere person, so wise and candid, and such good friends with herself that she never played tricks with you. I doubt whether it ever occurred to Lucy that a man could be a cad.

I said: "You should not be here, but inside those walls."

She countered me: "And you?"

I felt like telling her to go back by the way she had come,

and that if she did not go I would pick her up and carry her. One has heard so much in these modern days of enlightened feminism and its revolt against the male in man, but I am afraid my feeling about it is that there is an elemental sensuousness in every woman that reacts to man's strength and forcefulness. She may pretend to despise it, and to be nauseated by it, but the organic reality is there. I hesitated, and she came nearer, and stood so near that I could have touched her.

"And you, my friend, what are you doing here?"

I told her that I had felt restless.

"Is that the prerogative of man? The men at the gate told me."

Her pausing was like a challenge.

"What did they tell you?"

"That you were going up to the hills to look for any sign of fire."

I said: "And so I am. If I see any place burning in the distance, I shall know where our enemies may be found. And now, you will go back."

She answered me calmly.

"No, I am coming with you."

She may have been woman, and the child of her own colouring, a dark flower, intense, elusive, incalculable in her moods and vanities, and sometimes strangely cruel, but she was never a coward, or one who gave you a little cold moral snub when your heart was hungry. I think I was to love her for her lovely courage more than for anything else. She did not wilt, or become cold mutton, and even if she wounded you, it was a passionate stab, and not a school-marm's rap over the knuckles.

I said: "Are you mad?"

Her retort was instant: "Why should I not be as mad as any man?"

I think both of us must have been mad on that exquisite night. I told her I was unarmed, and I asked her to let me go back and buckle on my sword, but she stood and looked at the stars, and made a kind of singing murmur as women will when they are happy. I had known Lucy make just such a little song to herself when we had danced together as lovers.

She said: "Will the wolves eat us, or the terrible savages catch us? These woods are as secret as death, and I know the way."

Her words left me voiceless. She had the strange and most rare gift of giving back in words something that had an elemental rightness, the poetry of passion. She had no little blank phrases, those conventional cliches that shock one into realizing how shallow is the feeling behind them. Had she said to me: "Well, really!" or, "Get on with it," or "Sez you," I should not have known the exquisite anguish of loving her, for, in that way she was destined to be loved.

She led the way along the edge of the wood until we came to a cleft in the high foliage. The path was like a narrow, winding passage between towering trees. I saw the strip of sky and the stars. It seemed even more still here, though our feet made a rustling amid last year's dead leaves. Yet the path was wide enough for us to walk side by side, and suddenly I felt her hand slip round my arm. For a second or two I went rigid. The exquisite shock of feeling that soft hand and wrist resting there seemed to make me dumb and blind.

Then I must have realized that she trusted me, and I think I was never happier in my life, though I could not find anything to say to her, nor did she say anything to me. We climbed the hill-side, linked together, through the strange gloom of the great wood, with the strip of starlit sky above us. The silence was our silence, mysterious and immeasurably sweet.

The trees ended suddenly. There was no gradual thinning of the trunks. They ran like a great palisade along the shoulder of the hill. The downs were above us. They might have been part of the sky, save that they had no stippling of stars. The path went on, it must have been a very old trackway, for the turf was sleek and firm, and kept short by rabbits. There was rough tussock grass on either side of it, still showing grey and hoary under the stars. Scattered yews and thorns and wayfaring trees peopled the slopes, and for a moment these dim nature-shapes troubled me. I stiffened; my head went up. How was one to tell a bush from some enemy-man?

I felt Meona's hand press my arm.

"They are friends, Pellias. I know them all."

I said: "That may be so, but I am mad to let you come up here."

She gave a little laugh.

"Well, we are both mad. It is good to be mad when the stars are shining. Blood should be blood, not sour milk."

We went on up the path towards the long brow where the Ridgeway ran as it must have run for centuries, and suddenly she asked me that question.

"Why did you give your choice against my staying?"

There was only one answer to that, and I gave it her.

"Because you are precious."

"And what if I refuse to go?"

"That would hurt some of us, your father. In a bloody business like this—"

"Do women have no share? Do men think so? How you love to feel masterful!"

"My dear, it is not only that. We fear for what we—"

The word was nearly out of my mouth, but I smothered it, which was, I suppose, foolish. So few people understand one's reticences, the things one leaves unsaid, but I think she must have known what was in my heart. Her hand remained crooked over my arm, and we stood side by side on the dark hill-side, looking over a mysterious world that seemed infinite. There were no lights anywhere, save in the sky where the stars shone. Strange streaks of mist out across the hill-tops, and some of the valleys were pocketed with vapour. Hurtwood, Hascombe, Hazlemere and Hindhead were vague outlines. I thought of them by their modern names, and was struck by the silly reflection that they all began with H. I remembered that I must have stood near here with Lucy, looking at the same landscape, though how different was the material scene. There should be scattered lights pricking the darkness, perhaps the noise of a train running in the valley, the stridor of cars accelerating up the steep hill to Newland's Corner. But here was an almost primeval stillness. Those pools of mist might have been water, and we, two survivors of a dead world, landed from some Ark on this hill-top, while the flood still lay in the valleys.

I heard her speak to me.

"Do you see anything, Pellias?"

"Everything and nothing."

"No burning homesteads?"

"Not one."

A little, vagrant breeze blew along the ridge, and made a sudden sibilant sound of unrest in the grass and bushes. The night seemed to shiver. I wanted to put my arm round her, but did not dare to.

"Time to go back."

I felt that fear was abroad, and that the wind had been like the wings of death passing over us, and she must have felt as I did.

"Yes. The world is different, Pellias. How different! A little while ago there was no fear here."

The same impulse seemed to move us, and, as though stepping out together to the first note of some mysterious tune, we turned and went down the hill towards the fenced darkness of the woods. I was thinking of the to-morrow and of her leaving the valley with the women and children, and that I might not see her again. What if this dream passed, and I found myself back in a world where one caught the 8.55 to Town each morning, wearing tame clothes and a bowler hat? Did I want that to happen? There would be no Meona in that world, no hazards and mystery and adventure, unless that foul beast Hitler and the cold and sneering Ribbentrop let the German mad-dog loose on Europe. For the first time I realized that I wanted this dream to last. But was it a dream, or reality, and that other world the dream?

We were deep among the trees, and she must have felt the depth of my self-questioning. It occurred to me to wonder whether she had divined anything strange in me, as her father had done. Had that other Pellias—? But that was unthinkable. And yet! We came suddenly out on to the hill-side, and she paused there, and I, with her.

She did not ask me what my thoughts were. She let her hand slip from my arm, and I knew that she was going to leave me where she had found me, but she stood for a moment, looking down into the valley as though its darkened mood was hers.

"How things change! Even you, my friend."

So, I too was different, not the Pellias of a week ago, but a man who had fought for her, and who owed his life to her. Was it just that?

I said: "There are reasons why we change," and felt that I had said a silly, banal thing. Should I ever be able to tell her the truth, or would she divine it? Moreover, I might never see her again, after to-morrow. I might be snuffed out in some obscure scuffle with these savages. I wanted to tell her certain things, and I could not do so.

"Good night, my friend."

I was mute. I watched her pass down the hill, and become a dim shape that melted into the darkness. Again I heard the sound of the grass caressing her feet. Then, there was silence, utter silence. I sat down under the great beech tree, and fell to marvelling at the blessed hour we had spent together.

If it had given me nothing else, it had given me the conviction that she trusted me.

CHAPTER THIRTEEN

❧

*I*T HAS been recorded somewhere that the Roman soldiers stationed in Britain used to scourge themselves with nettles in order to feel warm in this dismal island, but I cannot remember noticing any marked difference between the climate of those days, and the weather that I knew. Even the familiar word "Unsettled" did not always apply to this particular summer. This island can have its serene and golden moods, and that seemed to be nature's mood during this tragic year. True, there were elusive moments, sudden passionate thundery tears, wet sparkling days when the trees dripped and flashed after a storm, but I can remember none of those long, grey interludes, the dreariness and the drizzle of a sanctimonious sky.

The morning when the women left us was a perfect morning. The birds sang me up, and I saw the early sunlight shining upon the trees of the great wood through which Meona and I had wandered together. I felt a kind of anguish as I thought of her. I put on my harness, for I and thirty men were to convoy the women and children as far as the bridge across the Wey near Guildford. Beyond the river they should be reasonably safe, and ten of our mounted men were to ride with them as far as Calleva. From Calleva they would travel on to Aurelius Ambrosius's country near Sabiodunum, and Meona carried a letter to her uncle, explaining how desperate things were with us, and asking for help.

The first person I met in the great corridor was Festus. He had a grimly cheerful face, the kind of face one blesses God for at such a time. The "Drearies," though they may have every reason for looking glum and may be utterly right in their prognostications, merely cause one to blaspheme. Give me a David in a tight corner, and no puling Jeremiah with a face like a sick sheep.

"Hail, brother," said Festus, buckling a strap. "I am going up to look at the country."

I went out with him into the crowded courtyard where the women and children were making a plaintive murmuring like a flock of sheep about to take the road. There were bleatings and baaings, and Festus grimaced at me. We should be better without these poor, scared creatures. Men were getting the wagons ready, and harnessing up the horses. I saw Meona's chariot down by the gate, and a man was polishing its woodwork and its wheels. Well, that was the right spirit. I was sentimental about that chariot.

Festus's horse was waiting for him. He swung into the saddle, took his spear from the servant, pulled a face at me, and shouted at the old cripple to open the gate.

"Nothing like a good glimpse of the morning, brother."

I saluted him, and he rode out, a gaillard, martial figure, and the old cripple hurried to close the gate behind him. In the orchard Robur's men had lit a fire and were grooming horses, and cleaning arms and harness, and their voices had a cheerful sound. I looked at the limpid blue sky and thought how useful a scouting aeroplane would have been to us, and how terrifying to our enemies. They would have thought that some winged god had taken the air against them. I should like to have turned a machine-gun on those savages, or bombed them, almost as much as it would have pleased me to get Hitler & Co. in a corner and blow the whole black-guardly crew to blazes.

Germans!

I remembered that I was supposed to be a hybrid Briton, half Welsh, half Norman.

I strolled across the courtyard, so very conscious of being a stranger among these people whose faces and names should have been familiar to me. Some of the women curtsied to me, and looked at me with wondering eyes. I, Pellias the coward, had become Pellias the little hero, the slayer of Saxons. I may have been almost as interesting as a film-star to these women. Even the children stood and stared at me as though I were Samson or King David, and one small thing toddled up and fingered the scabbard of my sword. I bent down and picked the child up and held him at arm's length, and he chuckled at me. Did this crowd expect me to walk the stage and utter sententious words like some Roman hero?

All that I could say was: "May God be good to you, small one."

I set the child down, and became aware of the faces of all these women, poignant, troubled faces. Some of them raised their hands to me.

"Pellias, save us."

"May the Sacred Mother watch over your head."

I walked slowly back to the portico steps feeling fiercely self-conscious, like a shy lad in some village pageant. I believe I folded my arms, and hugged a dignity that was very unsure of itself in this strange drama. The strong, silent man! Was there ever such a person, or could one see one's self as the simple folk saw one? There is no pose that can be adequate unless emotion lights up the mirror.

I made my exit from that stage, and walking along the cool, dim corridor, entered the summer-room. I was in a fever to meet Meona, and Meona was not there. I saw my lord Aurelius sitting by the window, being shaved, while Gildas stood waiting beside his master's chair. There was something so homely and reassuring about my old lord's lathered face that I wanted to laugh, and felt the better for it. Gildas had his tablets folded between his hands, looking like some sleek, sly, sanctimonious neuter-cat. He smirked at me, and later I was to discover the reason for that smirk; Gildas was to go with the women in attendance upon Meona; Gildas would be out of the fighting.

Aurelius raised a hand. The barber held his stroke, and a voice from the lathered face admonished me.

"Greetings, Pellias. Salute the gods, my son."

I think I blushed. I was strange to the ritual, and forgetting in my love for the daughter the secret I shared with the father. I turned and walked to the *lararium*. The little lamp was burning there, and I raised my right arm, and bowed my head before those images. After all, they did symbolize to me the mystery and the strangeness of things, man's feeling that there must be some God behind his hand-made gods. And I could utter a prayer. "May no harm come to her beloved head. May I have courage."

I still was standing there when I felt her presence in the room. That was the curious thing about my love, I always seemed to know when she was near. I turned, and looked at her, but she did not look at me. I might not have been in the room, and all that had passed between us in the woods and upon the Downs no more than an amorous fool's illusion. She walked to the window-seat, and sitting down, watched the crowd and the preparations in the courtyard. She was wearing her green riding-frock and that little Phrygian cap. Her face had a set pallor, a dark fixity of gaze that seemed to go beyond the concrete things of the moment. Her aloofness wounded me. I did not and could not understand it, and I stood there with my back to the Household Gods feeling hurt and bewildered. I happened to glance at Gildas and found the suave beast watching me with a smug satisfaction that was on the edge of simpering. So, the fellow was wise as to my condition. That stung me. I walked out of the summer-room and into the courtyard, and assumed that I was somewhat responsible for the loading and horsing of the wagons. I did not know much about such matters, and that made me all the angrier.

Robur came into the yard, rubbing a polished chin that had just been razored. His quick eyes saw me.

"Hail, my friend. The pride of the morning to you."

He looked at me consideringly, and his white teeth gleamed in his brick red face.

"Ha, in a fighting mood, what?"

I was, and I said so, and he laughed and came and clapped me on the shoulder.

"Good, my lad, good. We will drink blood together."

I was glad of Robur, for he suited my angry temper, and we strolled out together into the deserted village. It was not quite deserted, for Niger the Smith was at work at his forge, beating out spear heads. We looked in on Niger. He was stripped to the waist, and his chest was like a bearskin, and his face shone with sweat. A big, hefty wench of sixteen or so, his daughter, was working the bellows for him, her smock rolled up to her knees, and open over her bosom.

Robur smiled at the smith.

"Hail, Vulcan. Good luck to your hammer."

Robur spat into the fire.

"May this iron kill."

But Robur had his gentle side. We strolled along by the stream through all the greenness and scent of that May morning, and a kind of shimmer came into Robur's eyes. He looked at the hills and the woods and meadows as though he loved them, which he did, for he told me so.

"This is a good land, my lad. It is worth fighting for."

But I am afraid I was thinking of Meona and her strange unfriendliness, and that cold and lovely profile of hers seen against the sunlit window. Was it not possible to love a woman as old Robur loved this country, with a secret feeling for the essential mystery of things and their inherent loveliness? Or was I all wrong, an old-fashioned romanticist, dreaming dreams that were not of this world? Were the hard young realists wiser than I? I remembered the words of a hard-bitten naval officer who used to travel with me in the train. "My lad, because a wench has the face of an angel, it doesn't mean she hasn't got the soul of a slut." What would the young realists have said to me? That women did not ask for the highfalutin stuff. It might be all right as champagne, but that after the champagne they expected you to get busy and tumble them. I suppose I have always been rather a nice, romantic ass, believing a pretty woman to be a rather transcendental creature, which—perhaps—she isn't. Moreover, I imagine that Lucy had spoilt me, in that she was clean, and candid and comprehending, so absolutely without pettiness and all feline tricks. The face of Lucy appeared to me as

Robur and I walked back by the stream towards Aurelius's manor. I was flung back suddenly into my own and other life. I felt desolated, miserable, once more a ghost blown passionately hither and thither in a gusty world of tragic provocations.

Robur's men were grooming their horses in the orchard, and some of them stopped to stare at me as we passed. So, the tale had spread, and I was the village hero, the slayer of dragons. I was not feeling at all heroic at the moment. We passed on in to the courtyard, and a servant standing on the portico steps, came down to tell us that the morning meal was ready. I let Robur lead the way, and took cover behind him. We found Aurelius eating bread and honey, and dictating a letter to Gildas. Meona was still in the window-seat, and was being served there.

Robur saluted Aurelius and I sat down at the far end of the table, and fell upon my food like a man who had a train to catch. There was fish, and cold boiled eggs, bread, honey and small beer. I had no great stomach for the meal, but I stuffed the food away as though eating was the one and only thing that mattered. I did not look at Meona. Aurelius finished his dictation, and he and Robur began to talk about the invasion, and how the gentry of the west might be rallied to counter it. They spoke of places and people that were strange to me, and I was feeling an alien, a poor ghost cramming food that it did not desire. I kept my eyes to myself. I wanted to get this romantic business over, and go out with men to fight. I felt both savage and miserable, but fear was not in me.

I was aware of Meona rising and standing behind her father's chair. I was stuffing down bread and honey, and I made it appear that that was the only activity that interested me. I heard her say: "Give me the letter. I will go out and see that all is ready." Aurelius said something about Gildas carrying the letter in his wallet, but she would not have it so. I think Aurelius gave her the letter, and she passed behind me, and went out of the room. Her footsteps seemed soundless, not like those footsteps that had swept through the sibilant grasses.

Aurelius was asking for Festus, and I told him that Festus had taken his horse and gone up to the hills to spy out the land. Robur had his beer-mug in his hand, and was gazing down into it like an old woman conning fortunes from tea-leaves. But Robur was no old woman.

"This may help us, sir, if it has been left behind in the homesteads."

I did not get his meaning at the moment, but Aurelius was quicker than I.

"The German habit, my friend."

"Yes, sir, they can be sodden swine, and lie late, snoring when the sun is up. And that is a hint from the gods."

He looked at me.

"The earlier the deed, the better the promise. If I were friend Pellias I would get my convoy and its escort on the road while the swine may be sleeping off some orgy."

I stood up, and faced Aurelius.

"It is sound counsel, lord. Have I orders to take the road?"

"Yes, my son, but I have changed my mind as to the length of your journey. You and your men will see my daughter and the women to Calleva. They will be safe for the night within the city walls, and from Calleva they can send a message to my brother. You will lodge there for the night, and then rejoin us."

Was I glad or sorry? Emotions, like motives, are apt to be mixed.

"Then, I go at once, sir."

"Yes, my son, waste no time."

I saluted Aurelius, smiled at Robur, and with Gildas at my heels, went out into the courtyard.

Meona was there, standing on the stone steps of the water-cistern, and giving orders as though she and not I was in command of the convoy. The white horses had been hitched to her chariot and the wagons were laden, and our escort ready to mount. A groom held the horse that had been assigned to me, and I'll confess that I looked at the beast a little anxiously, for as a modern I was not much of a man in the saddle. And was this body my own, or the body of brother Pellias? If it were his, and the spirit mine, then, perhaps I might not fear for my horsemanship.

Meona saw me, and raised the whip she held.

"Get your men mounted, Pellias. We are ready."

So, she was giving me orders, and it did not please me, no, not at all. The wagons were at their horse's heads, and my fellows did not wait for my orders. My lady's voice had been sufficient. I walked up to my horse. He was a black beast, lean and fidgety, and with an angry, furtive eye. I thought: "I am going to have trouble with you, my lad."

I got on his back successfully, and headed him for the gate. I shouted to my men: "Half of you ride ahead with me. Half follow the wagons." My shout seemed to upset the beast. He shied, and nearly threw me, and then bolted out of the gate, and took me off at a canter. Luckily he went in the right direction, and I was mainly concerned in keeping my seat. But the beast's temper and the mess he was making of my dignity roused the devil in me. If he could be savage, so could I. I looked back for a second, and saw my troopers filing out of the gate. Then came Meona's chariot. My horse was going like blazes, and I let him have his head for a moment until we were round a curve of the road and out of sight of those who followed. Then, we had our battle. I held on to the crupper with one hand, and beat him about the head with my fist. He reared and nearly had me off, but I went on smashing him about the eyes. He backed, twisted, swerved forward, but I managed to stick on. I cuffed him, and cursed him savagely, and winding the reins round my left wrist, got a pull on his jaw. How long this damned scuffle lasted I do not know, but, suddenly, he seemed to accept me and the situation. He calmed down. He deigned to walk, though he was trembling and sweating. His abrupt docility might be as treacherous as his temper, but I spoke to him gently and began to stroke and pat his neck. As a matter of fact I never had any more trouble with him. We had had our argument, and he accepted me as master.

We had left the manor and the village far behind us. The road swung to the south-west, and I saw ahead of me a grove of old yew trees and beyond them the gleam of water. A smother of flowering thorns hid the stream, and the smell of them and the sight of those dark yews was like the sudden lifting of a curtain. Here was the place where Meona and I had had our adventure with the Saxons. We had sent out men to bury them, and I saw three brown mounds beside the road. My horse and I were within twenty yards of the graves when I heard the sound of hoofs and the rattle of wheels behind me. I pulled up and looking back saw Meona and her white horses coming at a fast trot, and behind her rode a dozen of our mounted men. Gildas was with her in the chariot, and I was not feeling friendly towards Aurelius's secretary.

I waited for Meona and her chariot, and as she drew near I saw that Gildas was sniggering. Well, if my supercilious scribbler's sense of humour was rather like that of some acidu-lated little critic, I would find something more robust where-with to counter it. I worked up a smile, and patted the neck of my horse.

"Pegasus and I had a little difference of opinion, but we have agreed now not to quarrel."

Meona's eyes were very black. There were times when they lost their lustre, when she was frightened, and sometimes when she was angry.

"Why did you leave us?"

Surely she understood? I laughed, and I looked hard at Gildas, and suddenly he became drop-eyed and demure.

"Firstly, because Pegasus ran away with me. Secondly, because he was running in the right direction, and I wanted to see that the road was clear. Shall we wait for the wagons?"

I saw her glance at those three graves, and her face seemed to grow pinched and thin. Her white horses were flicking their tails and nosing each other. My men set their horses in a little half circle behind the chariot. I watched their faces, and not one of them betrayed any sign of a Gildas snigger. I do not know what made me do the thing I did. I dis-mounted, led my horse aside to one of the yew trees, twisted off a small branch, and going to the three graves, laid a twig of yew on each of them. Then, I saluted the graves.

"There lie three fighting men. Let us not forget it."

The wagons came up with us. There were four of them, great clumsy things like boats on wheels. We were still in wooded country, and as I rode on ahead of our convoy I realized how easy it would be for the Saxons to ambuscade us. I was trying to make up my mind as to how one should meet such an attack. Form a screen round the wagons and charge the beasts if one had time? And then I remembered that the country opened out towards the Wey, and was like parkland stippled with trees, and but for an occasional wood, cover was less threatening.

My advance-guard were riding some twenty yards behind me, and I called up the man whom I had christened to myself the Sergeant-Major. He was a little, thick, ugly fellow with a bull's throat, and arms and legs like bolsters, but he was all muscle, not fat. I liked the look of his swarthy, humorous pug. His name was Ursus, and it suited him.

"Ursus," said I, "if these savages should break out of the woods on us, I mean to charge them. Let us take the fight to them, and so give the women and children a chance to scatter and hide. How does it strike you?"

Ursus grinned at me, and when he grinned his broad nose spread itself between deep creases.

"Yes, let us ride at them, Captain."

"Will your men play their part?"

"Sure, sir," said he, "if you and I show the way, they will follow."

I smiled at Ursus, and told him to go and warn his troopers that we should charge the enemy if he showed himself. I was taking my authority with great seriousness, especially so now that I and my horse were of one mind, but I was worried about Meona. I could not understand her moodiness, and I was feeling sore and brittle over her aloofness. Why had she suffered me to come so near to her, and then had withdrawn herself as though she had discovered in me something that repelled her? Had she fallen to some emotional impulse, recovered from it, pricked up her pride and her sensitive nostrils, and decided that I stank like a groom?

I pulled up and off the road, let Ursus and his men go by, and waited for the white horses of Meona. She was leading the string of wagons, sitting on the painted, leather-covered seat, and Gildas was walking beside the left-hand wheel. I was glad that she had extruded Master Gildas, for I had words to speak to my lady, words that might not please her. If I was the fighting man in charge of these people, I was going to give my orders and have them obeyed.

I saluted her as she drew level with me.

"May I speak with your ladyship?"

She gave me one of those black, straight glances, and turning her head, bade Gildas drop behind. I put my horse beside the chariot, and looking down the road, spoke to her as the trusted servant of her father. I said that I held myself responsible for her and for the women and children, and that if any marauding band of Saxons fell on us, I and my troopers were going to charge them. Meanwhile, my orders were that she was to gallop her horses for the nearest cover, and that the women and children were to scatter and hide while we did our best to cut the throats of the Germans.

She too looked straight ahead of her down the road.

"So, you give me orders, Pellias."

"I do."

"Do you think I shall obey them?"

If we were going to quarrel I decided that it was best to be thorough.

"I am in charge, and you will obey me."

I saw her face flash round. She bent forward and gathered the spear from the basket-sheath on the splash-board.

"I shall not obey you. I shall gallop my horses at the barbarians and charge with you."

I was feeling hot about the ears, and I tried irony.

"Like a veritable Boadicea! Let me suggest that you would be a nuisance to us."

She caught me up instantly.

"As I was yonder, the other day."

In a sense, she had me, and both my wounds of face and heart were feeling raw. I glanced back to see how near Gildas was to us, and found that he had climbed up into the first wagon. Probably, he had fastidious feet!

I said: "That favour was mutual, so we may forget it, I ask you not to hinder me, but to remember how heavy a burden lies on my shoulders."

She gave me an upward look, and it seemed less fierce.

"You are growing masterful, my man."

"If I am man, would you have me otherwise? I am no tame cat like Gildas."

She did not answer me at once, but she slipped the spear back into its holder.

"I will think on it, my friend."

"Ponder the last two words," I said, and rode on to join Ursus at the head of the men.

But no mischance befell us, and it must have been about eight o'clock in the morning when we reached the bridge across the Wey. I was beginning to judge the time by the sun, for though there was a sun-dial at the manor, and also a water-clock, my time-world was to be that of the sun and the moon and the stars. We found the hamlet beyond the bridge just as we had left it three days ago, silent and deserted. One's interest in crude details may be fatuous and fantastic, but I looked for the pile of horse-droppings in the road; it was there, and the only change was that it was stale and cold. Even the sparrows appeared to have abandoned the place. We did collect one live thing, a miserable dog that came fawning out of a yard, and was taken up into Meona's chariot. So, she could be compassionate to a homeless dog, if unmerciful to me!

I was feeling bitter and haughty, and taking my dignity with supreme seriousness. Almost, I was regretting that we had not clashed with the savages from over the sea, and that I had no chance to let my anger loose, and dig my spear into some German belly. One of my men was carrying my spear for me, like a medieval squire, and appeared quite proud of being my armour-bearer. He was a lean, dark lad named Morgan.

We climbed the Hog's Back, with the horses labouring at the creaking wagons, and half-way up the hill I ordered the women to get out and walk. They were quite ready to humour me, and I gathered from their cheerful chatter and the way they looked at me that they considered me some fellow. I was Pellias, Dux and Fighting Man. We did not take the road to Pontes, but followed the chalk ridge, and in retrospect, or forespect, I saw cars parked on the grass and people picnicking there. And I saw the same blue hills in the west, diaphanous and strange, and I knew that beyond them lay Calleva.

CHAPTER FOURTEEN

I MUST confess that I was excited by the thought of seeing this Roman town. I happened to know the Silchester of my day, the isolated church and farm, the grass-grown amphitheatre, that grey flint city-wall running its mysterious circuit and clasping those broad fields of wheat. The wall that I knew was ivy-smothered and tufted with bushes and young trees, but the wall I saw as we crossed the plateau towards the east gate, was black and clean and vivid. We had covered some twenty-five miles, and the wagon horses were very weary, and I saw Calleva against the evening sky, clear cut and strange, and moving me to inexplainable emotion.

Had I been here before? Had I any prescience that could prove it and the inward significance of this dream adventure? I saw the east gate ahead of us, battlemented and towered, and with its twin black mouths of entry. I saw the stuccoed walls of the houses coloured cream and rose and yellow, the red pantiled roofs, the green trees in the gardens. I saw the roof of the basilica shining like a great sheet of old gold, and near it a little figure posed on a column. I cannot say why, but there flashed into my consciousness a picture of a shop

169

that sold wine, with earthenware jars and drinking vessels, and a fat, swarthy woman filling a pannikin. Behind the shop rose a temple, with deep shadows under its portico. There were a couple of town-guards at the gate, and I saw one or two watchers on the wall. The gates were shut at sunset, but the men let us through, and we clattered and rumbled through the gate-tunnels into the town. I was riding ahead, and suddenly I saw my wine-shop, and the stone counter and the earthenware jars, and behind it rose the temple. Even the plump, dark woman was there, serving out drinks to a couple of soldiers.

I was a little dazed by the strangeness of the thing. My spirit gaped. Why, of all things, should I remember this? And what significance for me had that swarthy Hebe who sold wine? Had she been my mother or my mistress or my soul-mate? She did not look a soulful person, judging by her large and sensuous mouth and her jocund hips. I think I went on riding in a state of obfuscation up East Street, but the rumbling wheels of Meona's chariot recovered me.

I pulled aside to where some lime-trees shaded a little Place. Meona was standing in her chariot, looking black-browed and tired, and pinched about the nostrils.

"Have you forgotten the way?"

How was I to remember it? Nor did I know whither we were bound? So, why should she be peevish with me?

"Whither would my lady go? To an inn?"

Almost her eyes said: "Fool, have your wits left you?" Our convoy had halted, and people stared at us. More fugitives! I was to discover that Calleva was full of those who had fled from the German terror. Gildas came running up, and his waddle made me think of the running of a woman.

"Gildas, our leader has forgotten."

Gildas gave me a sneering look. It seemed to say: "Bumpkins get lost in town."

"Your uncle's house, lady?"

"Of course."

So, Aurelius Ambrosius had a town-house in Calleva, and our objective had been so obvious that it had not been mentioned to me.

"West Street, Master Pellias," said Gildas, as though speaking to a poodle, "past the Forum and over the cross-roads."

I rode on.

Calleva fascinated me, so much so that I forgot Meona's petulance. Maybe, she was born to be passionate and petulant by turns, and there should be other obsessions in a man's life besides the lure of sex. Calleva was completely Roman in its atmosphere and lay-out, its streets and alleys crossing each other at right angles, and plotting it into insulæ. The roadway was paved with cobbles, and very clean. We passed shops, villas, some set in their own gardens and shut in by high walls. Most of the shops were shut at this hour. There were fewer people in the streets than I expected, and the population of this Romano-British town was more sophisticated and dressy than the countryfolk of Honey Valley. I saw young men with their heads curled, and I was reminded of some of the exquisites among our London playboys. I looked for Calleva's Christian church, the one authentic thing of its kind in Roman Britain. I did not see it. Instead, and for the provocation of the philosophers, I may say I saw a particular sign semi-erect over a doorway, and a couple of oiled gentlemen waiting to be admitted to the shrine of Eros. How Pompeian! The phallic emblem was in more evidence than the Cross.

There was provocation in that symbol. It suggested to me that my attitude towards romance might be, not out of date, but too previous. Pagan we moderns may be, but we are still permeated with the Christian ethos, and sentimental illusions about love. Shades of Galahad, and Joseph of Arimathea, but had my feeling about Meona been too much Tennyson? Did this young tigress despise a man who behaved like an aerie fairy hero? Was one's sensitive approach inadequate? As a fighting man and a lover I did not make sense. But we were approaching the forum and the basilica, Calleva's heart, and though we passed it on the northern side I had an oblique view through the colonnade of the crowd that filled the forum. It was a colourful crowd, in its semi-Roman dress, suggesting both British woad and Tyrian purple. Some orator appeared to be making a speech from the rostrum, though the declaiming voice came to me blurred by the grinding of our wheels and the clatter of horses' hoofs. What was the orator's subject? Was he preaching a crusade against the invading Teuton, or delivering a Hitler howl because the city council had put a penny on the rates? But I forgot the voice and the listening crowd in seeing Gildas go scuffling ahead, holding up his skirts like a woman. We were passing the northern façade of the basilica and I saw a broadish street running towards the setting sun. It seemed to be a more sumptuous street, both in its atmosphere and its houses. Here were mansions and gardens, and I saw Gildas stop before a great gate in a high wall, and put his hand to an iron bell-pull. We had reached the town house of my lord's noble brother.

I and my horse arrived outside the gate at the moment one leaf of it was opened, and a porter put out his head and surveyed us. We must have astonished him, for, after hearing a few words from Gildas, he disappeared like a cuckoo into a clock. Meona had walked her white horses up to the gate, and our wagons and troopers filled the roadway.

"Whither has the fool flown?"

If she was feeling tired and petulant, so was I, in a particular place. I was not hardened to the saddle, and I was feeling damned sore.

Gildas was Agag to her.

"My lord is away on his estate, but the Lady Priscilla is here. The porter has gone for her."

I saw Meona's lips tighten. My aunt! If that was her inward exclamation, it was to be justified. I heard voices in the fore-court suggestive of the pother in a chicken-run after the laying of an egg. My Lady Priscilla appeared at the gate, and instantly I christened her Medusa. She was a lean, tetchy, tall woman in the late forties, with a snake's head of hair all crimped up and stuffed with bodkins. She had a mean mouth, a long, undulating nose, and small beady brown eyes. She threw up her hands when she saw us.

"Bless my soul, what is all this?"

I saw scorn and dislike on Meona's face. I think she said that there was war in Britain even if Aunt Priscilla had not heard of it. The women and children had been sent away in order that the men might be free to fight, also, the more fortunate people who lived behind walls might be expected to exercise compassion. These women and children needed food and shelter for the night, and on the morrow they would continue their journey into Wiltshire.

Medusa looked at us with her nose in the air.

"Impossible. And all these men and horses."

"My dear aunt, the porticos and corridors would do for the night, and we have some food with us."

"I won't have all this dirt brought into the house. The women can come into the courtyard, but no further. As for all these men, they must go to the inns."

She looked at me with her beady eyes.

"Who is that got up like a soldier? Oh, Pellias, the steward's son."

So she knew me, and I was supposed to be familiar with her aristocratic person! Presumably she had been a guest at my lord's manor, and she may have reproved me as a small boy for having a snotty nose or dirty knees. Evidently, I was not even small beer to Medusa. Meanwhile she stood in the gateway and kept us out, and I could see Meona's fingers playing with the handle of her whip. Her quick temper was boiling up in the presence of this congested and obstructive spinster.

"We are all very weary, Aunt."

"Tired! Who is tired? I am tired. I have spent the whole day visiting the poor and the sick."

My God, was Aunt Medusa a Christian! Even our small children in the wagons seemed to protest. One or two had begun to cry and very noisily so, and the black looks their mothers gave the lady were indicative. I saw Meona's tired face go very white. Her lips looked bloodless and compressed.

"Mind, Aunt, my horses are vicious."

She touched them suddenly with her whip, and the two beasts shot forward towards the gate. Her aunt, throwing up her hands, with a face of alarm and indignation, withdrew with undignified haste into the porter's lodge, and Meona thundered in. I could not help laughing rather grimly, and Aunt Medusa saw my mocking face. Her little black eyes pinned the offence upon me. I had made an enemy, but who cared?

My men had dismounted, and I ordered them to draw to

the side of the road, and let the wagons in. Aunt Medusa
had followed her niece, and I heard her shrill voice scolding
and calling for servants. I was asking myself whether I should
let my troopers follow the wagons into the courtyard when
the question was decided for me by half a dozen menservants
who came running across the court, and who banged the
gates to and barred them. So, that was that! Aunt Medusa
did not intend to house a licentious soldiery who might de-
bauch her wenches! I looked at Ursus, and he grinned at me.

"Better luck elsewhere, Captain. Good wine instead of
vinegar."

Ursus was a philosopher, and a sound fellow, and I agreed
with him. Did he know of a good inn where we could lodge?
He said there was a caravanserai near the Baths, and that if
that was full he knew of another place. I told my men to
mount, and with a glance at those forbidding gates, and with
Ursus beside me we clattered back towards the Forum. The
promise of a bath was pleasant, also, the application of some
soothing unguent to my chafed backside. We turned right
into South Street along the back of the Basilica, and I could
hear the voice of the orator still baying the moon.

Said Ursus to me: "The lady is a bitch, Captain, bred on
skimmed milk, and sour at that. If you should feel like having
a wench, I know a place."

I smiled at Ursus.

"I think I would prefer a bed, my friend, solus."

Ursus twinkled at me.

"As you please, Captain. But I always sleep better for a
little exercise."

We found our inn. It was in South Street, and not far
from the Temple of Mars. It had been full of refugees, whom,

the City Council not being very welcoming, had passed on to other patrons in the west. I think that was part of Britain's tragedy, the selfishness of the towns, and their commercial short-sightedness. I gather that the struggle against the Saxons was carried on the shoulders of the country gentry and the peasants, while the towns peddled safety-first behind their walls, and died of gradual inanition. The innkeeper accepted us. He said that he had had a glut of women and children, and he preferred men who were men and could drink and spend money. That was the immediate problem that faced me. Who was to pay for the night's billeting? I had those odd coins in my wallet, but I was pretty sure that they would not foot the bill. Should I adopt a lordly attitude, and tell the innkeeper to charge our lodging and keep to Aurelius Superbus?

He was an urbane fellow, this hotelier. He found me a room to myself overlooking the garden, and he put my troopers into the men's dormitory. He addressed me as captain. When I suggested that I needed a bath, he offered to send a lad with me to show me the way to the Thermæ. I sat down in the loggia to drink a cup of wine, and it was here that Gildas found me; he had been sent by Meona in search of us.

Gildas had a wallet on him. It appeared that the secretary was both banker and accountant. Possibly, a gentleman was not supposed to vex himself about the settling of bills. He had become more politely familiar to me, had Gildas, but it was the suavity of the cur that would bite if it dared.

"My lord bade me settle all bills, Pellias."

I did not like his succulent mateyness any better than his sneers, and I snubbed him.

"Dux, Gildas, if you please. Yes, go and see the innkeeper,

and arrange for a night's stay. I have other things to think of."

He squirmed. Maybe he had decided that I was destined to be a more important person than he had foreseen, and that as a diplomat it would be wise to cultivate me. Also, I gather that it is a mistake in psychology to treat a human rat otherwise than as a rat.

"At your service, Dux."

And then he produced a leather bag, and with a wheedling lilting look suggested that some petty cash might be welcome to me. It would be. As a captain of horse I had a part to play, servants to fee, drinks to pay for.

"Thanks, Gildas. Put it on the table. I will account to my lord."

"It could be unofficial, Captain."

"Thanks, no. Charge it against me. And my respects to your mistress. Tell her that I and the men shall leave as soon as the gates are open in the morning."

Gildas bobbed his head at me, counted out some pieces of silver, and made a neat little pile on the table, and I began to reflect that there are subtle ways of conveying one's meaning both to sycophants and difficult young women.

The boy guided me to the Thermæ. They lay beyond the Temple of Mars, and if anything was needed to convince me how much more clean and civilized Roman Britain was than the beer and belly culture of the Anglo-Saxon period, these Baths of Calleva did so. They were neither Buxton nor Bath, nor sacred to the sick and the doting. The main building stood in a fine courtyard surrounded by a cloister, and its flint and tile walls and rust-red roof had a depth of colour that was very pleasing. There was a garden, and alleys planted with lime trees, and a playing-ground, and a library and lounge. The boy left me at the porter's lodge where I was given a little bone plaque. In the courtyard two young men were boxing, with a small crowd watching them. Two girls, wandering round arm in arm, gave me challenging, jocund glances. I saw old gentlemen sitting in the sun and wagging their chins at each other. The whole ritual of the Thermæ was revealed to me by a genial little man in a kind of white bath-robe. I was stripped, my clothes hung in a niche; I had my plunge and was sweated and scraped with a strigil; and massaged and rubbed with oil. My attendant chattered like a barber, and his conversation might have been a broadcast of the latest news. He did not appear to be worried by the fact that a pack of savages were burning and butchering less than thirty miles away. If he symbolized the insularity of a place like Calleva, his cheerful complacency was appalling. His opinion seemed to be: "Oh, these broils have happened before. Just a plague of wasps, sir. They will pass."

I had a desire to see the Christian church. The porter at the lodge gave me my directions, and passing through an alley I came upon Ursus and some of my men preparing to enter a house that was dedicated to the oldest of the professions. Ursus grinned at me. Apparently, it was not necessary to be shy and self-conscious when engaged upon so natural an adventure. Moreover, the house had its sign for anyone to see. It hid neither vice nor virtue under a bushel.

I strolled on, and presently found myself upon an open space shut off by posts and rails, and in the centre stood a minute building, with a porch, and a stone *labrum* in front of the porch. So, this was Christ's house! I entered it, and was astonished, for the little church seemed incapable of holding more than fifty people. It had a red-tiled floor, and an altar table, and narrow, round-headed windows. I saw a solitary figure kneeling in a corner. It was very dark and dim here, and remembering Calleva's pagan temples, I marvelled. Had history been rewritten and edited to harmonize with the pomp and power of a priesthood? Most probably it had.

But this dim and sad little building changed my mood. I felt again a stranger in a strange world, a living ghost shot through with sudden anguish. No one would understand my real language nor the things of which I might speak, and now that I had trailed my curiosity round Calleva, a sense of desolation returned to me. Even this Roman girl whom I had begun to love seemed alien. My whole tempo and temperament were of another world. I am afraid the fighting-man was a poor creature in me at the moment; I was no more than a frightened and homesick child, with all my human ties severed by exile. There was an oak bench just inside the door, and I sat down on it, with my elbows on my knees, and my head between my hands. Oh God, would this dream-state endure for ever? I beat my two fists against my head, as though I could knock the present back into the future. I felt almost as frightened as I had been in the beginning. My bowels yearned, and my stomach fell down within me.

I heard the sound of footsteps, but I did not look up. The footsteps paused beside the bench. A voice spoke to me.

"Peace be with you, my son."

I looked down and to one side, and saw a pair of very brown feet in brown sandals. My impression was that they were old feet. Then, I raised my head and glanced up, and saw an old man standing beside me. He had white hair, and a luminous face that seemed to shine out at me in that dim place. It was a very gentle face, like the face of some old countryman, serene and without guile. He carried a long staff in his right hand.

"Peace be with you, my son."

I imagine that I must have been looking pretty miserable, for he laid his hand on my head as he might have laid it on the head of a child.

"Have you come to find Christ?"

The question was asked with such simplicity and with such gentleness that I felt that I had to try and answer it. That I was not being buttonholed by some pious busybody made the challenge more instant. How was I to answer such a question, confess that I belonged to a world that had lost Christ, and so had fallen to the cynical beastliness and opportune brutality of a Hitler and a Stalin? This old saint belonged to a world that was finding Christ, not losing him. I stood up. I looked into the old man's eyes.

"I have lost—that which you have, Father."

He smiled at me.

"Has the man lost what the child possessed?"

I could answer him that it was so. My mother had been one of those happy souls born with a capacity for faith, and as a child I had been taught to believe.

"That which is lost can be found, my son."

If that were true our poor, bewildered, dictator-ridden world might yet be rescued. Somehow, my two worlds seemed to run together. These German savages had to be fought, then and now, and Christ and the Cross rediscovered and revalued in place of the grim, treacherous, cunning face of Stalin.

I said: "Do many people follow Christ in Calleva?"

"More and more. The old order changeth. You are a stranger here, my son."

I told him that I had come to Calleva in charge of the escort that had guarded our women and children, and that I was going back to fight the barbarians. His face seemed to cloud over, but the shadows passed from it very quickly, and looking up at one of the windows through which a ray of sunlight was slanting, he smiled at it.

"Behold, the light, my son. Love alone can cure the ills of poor humanity. Until Christ and the Cross go to these barbarians, there will be no peace, only hatred and fear and death."

How could I disillusion him? His faith was so serene and gentle. How could I tell him that for nearly two thousand years Christ would be preached, and the world end in Stalin and Hitler? Would he answer me that the true Christ had not been remembered, and that men would salve their consciences by worshipping a caricature? And would he not be right? I did not know what to say to him.

He was looking at me with infinite kindness, and I felt that there was no smug self-complacency in his compassion.

"Have faith, my son."

Suddenly he took my hand, and led me up to the altar table, and made me kneel down with him. I saw that the red tiles had been worn by the friction of many feet. He closed his eyes, and still holding my hand, was silent in prayer. And the strange thing was, I felt comforted as though through him some mysterious assuagement had come to me.

"Have faith, my son. Do not be afraid."

He had opened his eyes, and was looking into my face.

"Cast out fear, and go in peace."

That I should ever kiss an old man's hand would have

seemed to me the height or the depth of absurdity, but I did kiss the old saint's hand.

"Thank you, Father. You have comforted me."

I left him kneeling there, went out from that dim place into the sunset, and met—Meona.

CHAPTER FIFTEEN

𝒮HE had her back to the sunset, and I had my face to the light. The glare of it was in my eyes. She must have seen me come out of the church, and if we were to share the unexpectedness of each other, she had me at a disadvantage. In fact, with the glare in my eyes I might have walked past her if she had not spoken to me.

"Has the slaves' god caught you?"

If she spoke with irony her voice gave me the impression that I was not the only victim. It was not the voice of the young autocrat, but the voice of woman, the voice I had heard in the dark woods and on the hills. It had strange implications, a kind of Cassandra sadness, a tinge of self-scorn, a self-questioning unrest. I got the sun out of my eyes so that she was both near to me and far away.

I said: "Is Christ the God of slaves?"

But her moment of irony appeared to have passed. She walked to the stone *labrum,* and bending over it, looked into the dark water. It was a mirror, and she stared into it like a crystal-gazer; her eyes made me think that her mood was as dark as the water. I joined her by the *labrum,* and saw her face reflected in that liquid mirror. "Bend down to the water, Melisande, bend down." She seemed to me a figure of tragedy.

Suddenly, her face expressed impatience.

"Nothing, nothing."

I saw her put out a hand and deliberately ruffle the water.

"How one can hate one's own face!"

Her petulance touched me. There was a childishness in it that made me forget her harshness. Surely, love can be the most selfish and exacting of all the passions! Man expects it to shine upon him, even in the thick of disaster, and whatever a woman's mood may be, and even if her heart is breaking. I began to understand that this passionate and impulsive creature was shaken and torn by dreads and loyalties and loves that had left me cold and uncomprehending.

I said: "I have been in a black mood, Meona. It has passed. Forgive me."

She looked at me quickly.

"And I, too, Pellias. We can forgive each other. All this horror hurts me. I am brave and a coward in one breath."

I leaned beside her on the *labrum,* and she looked intently into my face.

"You look happy. Why?"

"I am not happy, unless— But a little while ago I felt that my blood had turned to water. I went into that church, and an old saint came and spoke to me. A Christian."

She sighed.

"Ah, that would be Pelagius. He is Calleva's papa. I have felt tempted, my friend—"

"Towards this slave's credo?"

She winced.

"Why use my words against me? I was feeling bitter. Why

should we suffer these things, these burnings and horrors? Is man nothing but a beast?"

"These Germans are beasts. They have not been civilized."

"And what would Pelagius do?"

"Carry the Cross to them."

She gave a little, anguished laugh.

"And have his throat cut! Does that help us?"

It did not, and again I was confronted by the likeness of her world and mine. We were up against the German beast, and all the effrontery and falseness of an arrogant and cynical ideology. Had one sent a Pelagius to Hitler, would he have saved Austria or Bohemia? Hardly. He would have been treated to a Hitler howl; they would have bundled him into a concentration camp, and martyred him there. Starvation, and boots, and rubber truncheons.

"They bring the sword to us, and the sword is our only answer. That is the truth, Meona."

She breathed in deeply.

"I know. There is no escape. We must go through with it to the end."

She turned away from the *labrum*, thrusting herself off from it with her hands, and I could divine in that gesture a passionate protest against that which was and might be. How could I help her, I, who knew the end of the story, and that her Britain was doomed to be over-run by these savages? But the end was not yet. Did not Arthur blaze out in legendary lore, and might there not be one splendid interlude before the explicit? This girl might not live to see her people driven into Wales and Cornwall, and across the sea to Armorica. She might die before the curtain was rung down upon an epic sunset. And I? Might I not have a share in this great episode? Arthur and Guinevere, Tristan and Isoult, Pellias and Meona!

I walked with her back past the forum and basilica, and into West Street, but she did not stop at the gate of her uncle's house. She said: "I want to see the sky, and the fading country, and the stars coming out. Don't leave me." As if I could leave her now that I had begun to understand! To-morrow I should have to leave her. We walked on together, and the west gate and the wall rose very black against the flaming sky. I saw her lips move. She said: "Even the sky burns. Will everything burn? Is it an omen?" I put my arm round her, and she did not shrink from me.

"No, it lights us a torch, Meona."

A stairway beside the gate led to the battlements, and we climbed the stone steps and stood looking out over the parapet towards the west.

She said: "I shall go that way to-morrow."

I thought of the Wiltshire country as I knew it, Sarum and Amesbury, Stonehenge and Avebury, the great tranquil grassy hills, the barrows, the villages snug in the deep valleys where water ran. It was shepherd's country, and I always thought of it as a green sea of grassland under a sky big with sailing clouds. Why did one's fancy always travel west, to Glastonbury and Avalon and Tintagel, or the Welsh mountains? Why did the east always seem flat and commercial and prosaic? Was it in my blood? Meona's arm was touching mine, and a kind of grey-blue twilight was settling like water over the fields and woods. I felt very near to her, nearer than I had ever felt before.

Did she know Old Sarum, and Stonehenge and Silbury Hill, the great circle at Avebury, and the Kennet Long Barrow? They would be as primeval to her as they were to me.

I said: "It comforts me, Meona, to think that there will be no peril over yonder."

She did not answer me for a moment.

"There is no peace in running away."

My dreams were divided. I both wished her out of danger, and I wished to be near her, but I did manage to transcend my possessive self, and to tell her that we men would be happier now that we were free to fight without the fear of our women and children being slaughtered behind our backs. She listened to me in silence, a silence that struck me as unconsenting. She was not made for a passive part, or to sit placidly at home while tragic things were happening.

"I shall come back."

I tried to reason with her, but her pale face was set and stubborn, and my sentimental platitudes were useless.

"I shall come back," she said, "with the arms and the men. My uncle's country is a country full of those who ride on horses. Proud, fierce men, Pellias, not like these townsmen."

I wondered whether Aurelius Ambrosius, her uncle, would see the hazards as she did, or would suffer a girl in a chariot to drive with him and his horsemen. It was more likely that he would leave her with Aunt Medusa, and forbid any Boadicea adventures.

She said: "I can shoot with the bow. You should know that, my friend. You have seen me bring down a buck in our woods."

"Yes."

I had to lie to her, and to pretend to be that other Pellias, and in some ways I was beginning to hate my brother ghost. He was always gliding in and haunting me, and condemning me to contradict that which he had been. Meanwhile, it was growing dark, and though this darkness and her presence were very near to me, I could not forget Aunt Medusa and her congested, acid face.

"Won't your good aunt be worrying?"

I don't think I have ever said a more banal thing, and she laughed at it.

"Let her wonder. What are death and desire to Aunt Priscilla? This is a man's world to-day. I envy you, Pellias."

"I envy myself."

"And how?"

"In that I shall be fighting for all that is precious to me and to you."

I saw her hands moving. She seemed to be drawing something from a finger.

"I have a lucky stone here. I should like you to have it, my friend. Hold out your hand."

I did so, and she tried slipping the ring on to my third finger, but the ring was too small.

"Ah, a man's hand. Let us try the little finger."

The ring accepted my little finger, and I kissed the ring, and then I kissed her hand.

"All that I can give is yours, Meona."

She put her other hand on my head.

"May the gods keep you, my dear."

That was all that was said between us, but I walked back with her to the great house in West Street, feeling that if a thousand Gorgons rushed out at me I could laugh at their serpent-spitting heads. For that was how the joy of her blessing took me. I wanted to laugh, with a tender, reckless exultation. She and old Pelagius had set me on my road, sacred and profane love, call it what you please. There can be joy in the thought of dying when such wine is in one's blood, and as I walked beside her, the trite saying seemed true. I did not feel the stones under my feet.

At the gate, with a planet shining over her head, I dared to let the words loose that my lips had fumbled over.

"Meona, if I should die, in your cause, I shall die happy."

She gave me her hand and I kissed it.

"Speak not of dying, Pellias."

"Lovely Meona. Forgive me. I cannot help saying these things."

She was silent, holding my hand, and looking in my face.

"Live, my dear, live."

"Be careful. You will make a coward of me."

"Oh, no."

"The fear of never seeing you again."

She said: "I feel, in my heart, that you will see me again."

We more sophisticated moderns are not too appreciative of love scenes, and our attitude to them is apt to be that of irreverent small boys and cynical little wenches in the cinema's sixpenny seats; for love, unless it is just rank sex and the rubbing together of cow-faces, is a delicate and fastidious affair. I imagine that we moderns lived such little, constricted lives that romantic passion was beyond us, and so appeared melodramatic and insincere. Perhaps, great love is born only in tragedy, under strange moons, and perilous, sanguinary sunsets. It is a thing of mystery, of hazard and adventure, stung and wounded with the anguish of doubts and dreads and thwarted yearnings. It is an exquisite madness, like that of Tristan and Isoult, and this madness was mine on that starry night.

I wandered about Calleva streets, into the Forum, and up the stairway to the terrace above the line of shops. The dark city was patched with light, little streaks and pools of it. I heard music coming from some tavern or wine-shop, the

music of flutes and harps. How strange was all this! I looked
to the west, and I looked to the east, and in the east I thought
that I could distinguish a faint glow in the sky as of something burning. I watched it, only to realize that it was the
moon coming up.

Moon, silver moon, moonlight and sweet madness!

I found my way to the Christian church, and stood by the
labrum, and looked into the water that had mirrored Meona's
face. I dabbled my hand in it. Moods, moods! Thank God,
now I understood her and the pangs she was suffering. Had
I touched her hand with my lips? I had. And she had
touched my adoring head.

I did not even remember that I had not supped. My body
was indeed a wraith. It seemed to drift like vapour. I must
have wandered about Calleva till nearly midnight, and all I
heard was a dog baying the moon. Lights were out, and
music and voices stilled. I lost myself twice, and my inn
looked dark and shut up when I found it. Other footsteps
were coming to meet me along the empty street, and by the
light of the moon I saw a solid, stocky figure rolling a little
unsteadily along the footwalk. It was Ursus. He drew up,
hiccoughed, and recognized me.

"Hail, Captain."

I gathered that Ursus was full of wine, and the leer of
pagan love.

"Ursus, you seem happy."

He chuckled and belched.

"Ha, ha, Captain, hunting your own kind, what!"

So, he thought I had been out wenching on my own!

"The moon is my goddess, Ursus."

"Tra-la," said he, "a little cold, Captain, for my taste. I
like 'em like the sun in August, moist and hot and round."

I did not see Meona again, for I had given orders that we should start our homeward journey an hour after sunrise. Unencumbered by the wagons a couple of hours' riding should find us back in Honey Valley before our friends, the German swine, had begun their day's rootings. That was to be my experience in this British war, that these men from over the sea were sluggish risers, big in the belly and heavy in the head. At least one glorious slaughter that we made of them was due to our catching them wallowing after an orgy.

I did not see Meona, but I had my horse out and rode to the Aurelian house in West Street. The porter was not up, but I hammered on the gate with the butt of my spear, and he came out to me, yawning and peevish.

"My respects to your lady. Tell her we have gone."

He gaped at me.

"Now, Captain?"

"No, you fool, at some decent hour."

"What lady may you be meaning, sir?"

Which lady, indeed! As if I should have troubled to leave a vale on Aunt Medusa!

I still was very sore, which was not at all romantic, and reminiscent of one's rowing days, but I had other things to think of, whether Ursus would be fit for duty after his celebration, and whether the town gates would be open at so early an hour. I need not have worried about Ursus. He was one of those jocund, thick set, vigorous devils whom no amount of fatigue or dissipation can submerge, and when I reached the inn I found the men saddling up in the courtyard before breaking fast. Ursus saluted me. He had a merry eye, and a stomach that was indomitable. I had not yet seen Ursus angry, but when he did flame up he became like a furious Spanish bull.

We broke our fast, and filed out of the inn yard about the time that Calleva's shopkeepers were taking down their shutters. I saw a squad of men collecting the town refuse, and emptying it into a rude, barrel-shaped tumbril. It was a perfect morning, dew drenched after the clear, cool night. There was a guard on duty at the gate, and its arch was a great black mouth full of the morning sunlight. I rode out, with Ursus beside me, and we saw the distant Surrey hills like silver smoke.

When we left the gravelly plateau upon which Calleva stood, we struck clay country, a country of oaks. It was forest land, set with occasional clearings of fields and farmsteads. The Saxon terror had not troubled this sylvan scene. I saw a farmer driving a couple of oxen and a harrow over a field of young wheat. Cattle were pastured in the fields, and here and there a meadow was down for hay. We had covered six or seven miles when the country began to change its temper. There were stretches of heathland and birch woods, and clumps of Scotch fir. Ursus, who was riding beside me, asked me a favour. He had a brother, a farmer, who farmed land that lay a little way off the road about five miles further east, and Ursus suggested that he would like to see his brother. Also, we could rest and water our horses here, and his brother would feed both us and the horses.

I did not see any objection to Ursus's plan. The farm lay less than a mile from the road, and we should have to halt somewhere.

"We are rather a large party for your brother to welcome."

Ursus reassured me. His brother was a man of substance, with hams hung in his kitchen, and a granary full of grain, he had a bakehouse of his own, and a cellar that was not to be be despised. Also, Ursus assured me, his brother ate oysters.

"Oysters!"

"Yes, Captain. They come from the coast opposite Vectis. There is an oyster service twice a week."

I remembered the fame of the British oysters, and that numberless Roman sites surrendered dumps of oyster shells, but the fact that there should be a delivery of oysters in these country districts intrigued me. Here was a land on the edge of a catastrophe, and oysters were still carted up from the coast and distributed like fish from Billingsgate.

This country was so familiar in its dress that I might have been riding across a Surrey golf-course, with the fairway flowing between heather and pines. The gorse had ceased flowering, but patches of broom were brilliant against the blue of the sky. There were sheets of wild hyacinths amid the rust of last year's bracken. Ursus declared that this was devil's country, fit only for foxes and outlaws, and that his brother's farm was on fatter land where wheat grew well and cows gave good milk. The day had warmed up, and I was feeling less saddle-sore, perhaps because a portion of my anatomy was accepting fate and eschewing peevishness. The country was wild and lovely, as wild and lovely as Meona. I let myself dream dreams, while listening to Ursus's growling chatter and the rattle of our horses' hoofs.

We came to a green way turning north, marked by a white wooden post. The green way led us down into a little valley. I could see a pool shining, and placid trees, and among them the redness of roofs. Ursus pointed with his spear. That was his brother's house.

I do not think any of us expected to see the dreadful thing that waited for us. We rode past a little wood, and nothing but a meadow separated us from the farmstead. A stout, high timber fence enclosed the garden and the house, and against the fence I saw a number of people standing. It was all very serene and still, but it struck me as strange that the whole household should be paraded there, as though they were expecting us. The figures were of different heights and shapes, men, women, children.

I glanced at Ursus, and saw that he was puzzled and frowning.

"How did they know?" said he.

And then, suddenly, he uttered a fierce cry, and clapped his heels to his horse, and went off at a canter. I followed him. Certainly, there was something very strange about those figures lining the fence. And then I divined the horror of the thing. All those people were dead. The Germans had been here.

I shall never forget that sight. Men, women and children, all had had their throats cut. They were drenched in blood, and their poor faces expressed every sort of anguish. Some heads lolled with the whites of the eyes showing. Mouths were agape. One man hung there grinning, his eyes set in a harsh stare. Those devils had found a long rope, and had lashed all the poor wretches to the fence, and then slaughtered them. I could not bring myself to look at the women and children.

Ursus was off his horse. I saw him staggering about with his arms over his eyes, making no sound whatever. I too got off my horse, and saw the faces of the men behind me. They were the white, grim faces of men in whom a cold and relentless rage was gathering.

I turned again to Ursus. He was on his knees and being sick like a dog. The vomit was in his black beard. I saw his strong body heaving.

Nausea attacked me. I too wanted to be sick, but something stronger than nausea gripped me, a blazing anger against the brutes who had done this thing, and laughed over it, and called it a German joke. I spoke to the men, and my own voice shocked me.

"Get off your horses. There is work to do."

I do not think that it occurred to any of us that the devils who had made this slaughter might be lurking about the place. I ordered a third of the men to hold the horses, while the rest of us rescued the poor dead. I drew my sword and went and cut one end of the rope. It had been looped through the rough slats of the fence, and when it slackened, those bodies toppled or crumpled forward like a row of pitiful dolls.

Ursus was on his feet now. With his arms above his head he seemed to twist like a man on a rope, but it was emotion that was throttling him. I saw his teeth and his vomit white in his beard. His lips snarled. He looked at me, and did not seem to see me. He walked to the row of bodies, stared, and then, bending down, turned one over. It was his brother's body. With strange deliberation he rolled one of the children over, and stared, bull-eyed, at the pitiable little corpse. All this time he had been silent. It was a dreadful silence. Suddenly, he threw his arms up, fists clenched.

"You gods hear me. For each of these poor dead, I swear three Germans shall die, and not easily. I swear it."

There was a growl from the men, and hearing it, I knew that there was born in us all a ruthlessness that would be cold and without mercy. Ursus had drawn his sword. He kissed the blade, and held it aloft.

"You shall drink blood, my love, much blood."

I was looking at those poor prone bodies and thinking, with a stab of horror, that such a thing might have happened to Meona. Terror, outrage, death!

But there was work to be done, and that—quickly. I was

in a fever lest some such horror should have fallen upon those in Honey Valley. We went and found spades and mattocks and dug a long grave in front of that fatal fence, and laid the bodies in it. Ursus, who had grown silent again, insisted upon handling the bodies of his brother and his brother's wife and their children. His face looked black and pinched, but he uttered no sound.

When we had covered up the bodies we stood for half a minute in silence, and then we mounted our horses and turned back to the main road. Yet, even here we were to be given a last proof of German beastliness. A poor horse, painfully neighing, hobbled out from among some trees. It had had its belly slit with a sword, and its bowels were hanging out.

We pulled up, and I sent two of my men to put an end to the poor beast's anguish.

They came back, looking white about the gills, but hard of eye. Without a word we rode on.

CHAPTER SIXTEEN

The day was still young when we came to the bridge across the Wey, and saw the Downs sleek and peaceful in the sunlight. That was the strangest thing of all about this human horror. Nature remained the same in all her beauty, as though ignoring man's beastliness. Those splendid trees and sun-kissed hills and secret valleys did not vex themselves over our violence. The birds sang, the flowers bloomed; the sun, the moon and the stars were as ever. I know that nature is red of claw, the nature of tooth and talon, but the tiger kills to eat, while man has made of killing a science. He can slay with a ruthless, cold precision, especially so in these latter days. If science teaches us that everything is force, and that man should function like the protons and electrons, then I can imagine a hypothetical God saying: "You fools, in your little arrogance you have misread my meaning. Destroy each other. You, as an experiment, are not worth while."

I was feeling on edge after the morning's horror, and desperately afraid that we might find that the manor had been attacked, and its people slaughtered. It may seem strange, but I had developed an affection for the place, even as I had loved Albury and its valley. Also, it was so associated with Meona that it had a glamour for me that was irrevocable. After crossing the bridge we quickened our pace, for this would be the most hazardous part of our journey, and I think the men shared my eagerness to know the worst. If Honey Valley had been over-run then we should be a forlorn few in the midst of desolation, with our enemy between us and Calleva and Pontes. I kept my eyes skinned as we cantered along the narrow track under the Downs. We passed the three graves of the dead Saxons, and I regretted the yew branches I had planted upon them. This was no chivalrous, honourable war, but a fight to the death with unclean beasts.

I was glancing at those graves when I heard Ursus give a shout; my chin jerked round, and I felt my muscles tighten. Were we to fight at last, and take our revenge for the blood and the anguish of those poor dead? I saw three horsemen trotting towards us. They were our people, old Robur and two of his troopers.

I sang out to him, for I was still unsure of the manor's fate. "Is all well?"

"All's well."

I blessed his hard old face. We should be strong enough now to try a stroke against these slaughterers of women and children.

Aurelius met us at the courtyard gate. It seemed to me that he had aged even in a night, for it must have been a night of supreme suspense for him. Festus and his riders had brought in nothing but bad news. The whole country-side between the Weald and the Thames lay desolate, and even if the homesteads and the hamlets had not been ravaged, the people had fled from them. Aurelius leaned heavily upon his staff, and his shoulders were bowed. His old eyes had lost their peculiar brilliancy, and seemed filmed over with sleep-lessness and sorrow.

Ursus had been growling out his grim story to Robur, and before we had reached the manor I had charged Ursus to keep the bad news from the old man, and I was glad that I had done so. I saluted him, and dismounted, and left my horse with Morgan.

"I am glad to see your face, my son."

I told him that all was well, and that Meona and the women were on their way to his brother's place.

"Give me your arm, Pellias. I seem to have grown feeble."

He leaned upon me as we crossed the courtyard to the house, and I saw that they had been busy in our absence. The wall had been strengthened with baulks of timber and a stag-ing built against it for archers and spearmen. Windows had been boarded up. But the south window of the summer-room had not been obscured. The morning sunlight was streaming in upon a bowl of flowers that had been set upon the table. I saw that the curtain had been drawn across the *lararium,* and the faces of the gods were hidden, as though my lord's faith in them had failed him.

He bade me close the door, and sitting down in his oak chair, he looked at me with infinite sadness.

"How does it end, my son?"

His question scared me. Did he wish me, a ghost out of the future, to speak words that might be fatal to all hope? If so, what should I tell him? Should I pretend that a gradual blindness had effaced my knowledge of the present-past? I hesitated, and suddenly his old face grew grim.

"The truth, my son. Am I to fear it?"

He rapped on the floor with his staff. His eyes had recovered their lustre. They made me think of Meona's eyes, and I felt myself swept by a gust of compassion. Why should I tell the truth, as history recorded it? Was there not that dim, legendary period in the life of the island, concerning which learned gentlemen wrote books with the apparent purpose of proving the other fellow to be wrong? Why not assume that the Ambrosii and Arthur were to give Britain a hundred and fifty years of heroic happenings? Aurelius would be dead. Even Meona would be dust before these barbarians made of England a land of beer and belly. It would be a dirty, unwashed, oafish island until the clean Danes and the stark Normans rubbed some soap and civilization into it.

I said: "Lord, I will tell you what our legends relate."

He caught me up.

"Legends, my son? Give me more than legend."

His courage challenged me and gave me the courage to lie to him. I said that our learned men wrote of a certain Aurelius Ambrosius who gathered the fighting men of the island together, and with his sons drove the barbarians back into the sea. I did not speak of Vortigern and his sons, for, judging by legend, Vortigern had been a sinister person, an uncheerful cad. I confessed that history had it that Aurelius Ambrosius lost his life in the struggle, but that his son and a certain hero named Arturus, carried Britain to victory. My lord sat forward, leaning on his staff, his eyes fixed upon me with unflinching steadfastness, and I, with arms folded, stood to justify my rendering of the story.

"So, my son, according to your books, my brother has to die?"

I bent my head to him.

"But his son carries our cause to victory. Yes, my nephew is the true son of his father, a strong and lovely lad. But who is this Arturus of whom you speak?"

"A British dux and hero, lord, who served Ambrosius and Britain. We read that he drove the Picts and the Scots back into Caledonia, and the Saxons into the sea. A band of splendid knights followed him. So, the omens of our books are good."

He was silent for a while, his eyes still fixed upon my face.

"I wish to believe you, my son. I will believe you. And under what God does all this happen?"

"Under Christ, lord, and the sign of the Cross."

He frowned.

"Is that so? Well, what must be—must be. My gods have veiled their faces."

I was glad when we heard footsteps and the clang of harness in the corridor. The door opened and Festus and Robur came in to us. Festus was flushed and sweating, and his eyes shone, for Festus had been on one of his gallops along the Downs, and he had news, urgent news.

Festus had seen the Saxons on the march. They were following the Downs on their way back to the main body which had remained on the Kentish borders, carrying their plunder with them in wagons taken from the Surrey homesteads. Festus believed that this was the raiding party that had put such fear into our people, and that its purpose had been to terrorize the country so that when the main body moved westwards they should find the land lying desolate and waiting to be possessed. Festus said that the Saxons were marching with utter carelessness, straggling along the ridge with their wagons and horses strung out for a quarter of a mile. No doubt they believed that they had so swept the country-

side that there was no one to give them battle. Festus, knowing all the ways, had shadowed the savages until he had seen
them halt to rest their cattle and to eat. With flashing eyes he
swore that the gods had given us our chance to ambuscade the
raiders and put them to the slaughter. He estimated that the
Saxons did not number more than a hundred men, and that
we should be their equal in numbers and have the advantage
of surprise.

I looked at Aurelius. His eyes were roaming darkly round
the room. I looked at Robur, and saw that he was smiling. I
thought of Ursus and the horror of the morning. No doubt
these were the devils who had roped those peasants to the
fence, and cut their throats, and I felt my blood hot in me.

I said to Festus: "Have we time to waylay them?"

He said that we had if we marched out at once. He knew
the very place for such an ambuscade, where the Ridgeway ran
between thick woods.

I looked again at Aurelius.

"Let us go, lord."

"Yes, go, my friends, and the gods be with you."

Old Robur had been keeping his men ready for some such
alarum, and when I went out into the courtyard and saw my
men unsaddling I remembered that we had ridden twenty-
five miles. Would the horses do it? But when Ursus got the
news from me, he was like a man mad with joy. He went
about waving his arms and shouting to the men. We could
muster about fifty horse and about the same number of footmen, and I was detailing ten men to stay behind and hold
the house, when Aurelius Superbus appeared in the portico.
In very truth he had become the old Roman. No longer was
he bowed down, but he stood there like some white-haired
Jupiter, his staff held aloft, a man exalted.

"Go, all of you, I and the gods will guard this house."

I urged him to let some men stay, but he would have none of it. He would close the gates after us, and sit in the sun, and wait, and meditate upon life's mysteries.

"No, my son, take every man you have, and the gods be with you."

We marched out, and I let Festus lead, for Festus knew the ways. The foot-soldiers hung on to our horses, and we followed the valley road eastwards for half a mile and then began to climb the hills by a bridle-track that was hidden in a smother of yew trees. It reminded me of that steep way that led up from the Silent Pool through the yews to the ridge above.

I have often wondered how the reactions of the civilized man and the savage differ in their relation to fear. I had heard older men describe crude physical fear and its unloveliness as they had experienced it in the trenches. You shook and shivered, but you endured. In the beastliness of modern war the imagination paints a picture of your headless corpse, or of you lying torn and disembowelled in the mud, or of you being sent back to your familiar world with only half a face. I can understand the nausea and the horror of such fear, but in this adventure I was not conscious of fear, only of a tense excitement. This was no foul gas and bomb business, but a tussle, man to man, with one's blood up, and savage beastliness to avenge. I had a feeling that most of our men felt as I did. Ursus was licking his lips, and there was a redness in his eyes. Old Robur's brick-red face wore a grim smirk. Festus was whistling.

I had been thinking out a plan of action, and I put it to Robur. We should divide our horse and foot, hiding both bodies in the woods on either side of the Ridgeway. The mounted men would be to the east, and when the Saxons were within fifty yards of us, we should dash out and charge them. One could assume that our charge would take them by surprise, and put them in disorder. Then, our footmen, sallying out on either side, could fall on the fellows whom we had not speared.

Robur listened and agreed. He thought the plan a good one.

When we were nearing the brow, Festus left us and rode ahead. He had the eyes of a hawk, had Festus, and he knew every path and trackway. I halted our force among some beech trees on the top of the ridge, and I gave the men our plan of action. We sat on our horses and waited, nor had we long to wait. I saw Festus coming at a gallop. He had the news we needed. The Saxons were less than half a mile away, straggling along the ridge, and obviously not suspecting danger.

I rode forward and placed our footmen under cover, with orders not to show themselves, nor to attack until our charge had got home. Robur had put our cavalry under cover in an open beech wood that was screened by yews and thorns. The may flower was still out, and whenever the smell of it reaches me now I think of those vivid moments on the chalk hills when we waited for the coming of our enemies. We were all mounted, save Festus, who was crouching among the branches of one of the yews, watching the Ridgeway.

We heard the voices of the Saxons before we saw them, and a wheel of one of their wagons needed greasing, for it was squeaking like a thing in pain. I heard laughter and then a burst of song, like some ale-house giving tongue. I would have described it as a bellyful of bawling, for these Saxons did not sing as the Welsh sing, with that strange yearning after vague beauty. I gather that they were singing of beef and beer and blood, and somehow those bawling voices enraged me. I was watching Festus, and I saw him slip back from the yews, and make a sign to us. He ran to his horse and mounted and took his spear from the man who held it.

"Now, brothers, now."

We rode out of the wood, swept round the yews and the thorn trees and saw our quarry. The head of the Saxon column was less than a hundred yards from us; it was made up of about twenty men, half of whom were mounted. The wagons were close behind them, loaded up with plunder. A number of the Saxons were asleep or lounging in the wagons, and I saw a crowd of them trailing behind. I remember, as I worked my horse up to a gallop, that some historical wiseacre had written that no cavalry charge was made at a gallop. So much for the expert. We went in at a gallop, because we wanted to close with the wretches while their surprise was complete. Also, I believe that we were in a fury to get at them, and perhaps, for some of us, it was the fury of fear.

In such a moment one perceives and remembers vivid details coloured by some supreme emotion. Mine was hatred, the hatred of the dark, vivid Celt for the blond and boorish Nordic, so-called. I remember the figure of their leader, a barrel of a man with a red beard and a mop of flaming hair under his steel cap. I remember the way his bulging blue eyes stared, while he bawled to his fellows, and struggled to get his sword out. His round shield was hung at his back, and he had no time to order it. Moreover his horse grew restive, and as I made for him it shied sideways so that his rider's unshielded flank was exposed to me. I drove at him and caught him in the ribs, and felt the spear-head bore its way in. My horse crashed against his, and man and beast went over, and my spear went with them.

Also, I very nearly went over my horse's head, and had to right myself and get at my sword. I might have been easy game for one of the fellows, but Robur, Festus and Ursus had charged past me, and I was hemmed in by our shouting troopers. I saw Robur pin a man through the throat, and Festus with his spear in another's belly. We crashed through their advance guard to be met by the men who were leaping helter-skelter from the wagons. We may have surprised them, but they were ready to fight for their lives. Our horses carried us on, over and through them, leaving half of them on the ground. We were past the wagons and ready to deal with their rear-guard. I turned my head for a moment, and saw our footmen pouring out of the woods to finish the business we had begun.

It was when we rode down upon their rear-guard that I realized that half of them had had more liquor than they could carry. They had been drinking hard during their mid-day halt, and these fuddled beasts fell to us easily. A scattered few ran for the woods, and we lost them, for I got my men about and rode back to help our footmen end the slaughter. And slaughter it was. No mercy was shown or asked for. I saw Ursus get off his horse and blaze into the scrimmage like a mad black bull. A big Saxon closed with him, but Ursus threw him, straddled the fellow, and drove his sword into his throat. I caught a long savage who was running, and stuck him between the shoulders. In five minutes it was all over. My men left no live men there, but slew the wounded as they would have slain dangerous wild beasts.

Ursus, with hands and face all red, walked around gloating and scanning the dead.

"We have poured out blood," said he, "for those poor ghosts."

Meanwhile, the wagon-horses stood there with strange placidity, switching their tails, and some of them cropping the grass. We stripped our enemies of their harness, took their arms, and piled them on the wagons. We had lost but three men killed, and half a dozen were wounded, and these we placed on the wagons.

Festus rode up to me, laughing.

"Hail, Captain, you led us well. Shall we bury these swine?"

"No, leave them," said I, "as a warning to others who may come this way."

Some of our footmen took charge of the wagons. We had to turn them and make for a track that would take us down into the valley. I remember the wheel of a wagon lurching over the dead body of a Saxon, and the way the body jerked up for a second as though the thing had life in it. Ursus was the last to go. He wandered around looking at the dead, and exulting over the vengeance we had taken.

CHAPTER SEVENTEEN

AURELIUS was wiser than we were. I have heard it said that many old men grow cruel, and that when their powers begin to fail they discover that life passes them by, and a starved self-expression turns to venom. I think I had read somewhere that the most avid and pitiless spectators at the gladiatorial shows were the women and the old men. It was they who turned their thumbs down, and cried: "Kill! Kill!" I remember the picture that I saw when I rode my horse through the courtyard gate. Aurelius Superbus had had his chair carried out and placed below the portico steps, and he was sitting there in the sunlight with such an air of serenity that one might have thought that we were harvesters coming home, bringing in the peaceful sheaves.

I had ridden on ahead to bring him the news, and I dismounted and left my horse by the stone cistern. I gather that my lord could tell by my face that all had gone well with us. Moreover, I could hear the creaking and lumbering of the captured wagons in the lane, and the triumphant voices of our men.

"So, the gods have been kind to us, my son."

I told him that we had surprised and overthrown our enemies, and left scores of them dead on the grass of the Ridgeway, and that only a few of the Saxons had escaped us. I saw him smile, close his eyes and raise his arms as though blessing me. His face had a wonderful serenity.

"You are not wounded, my son?"

"No, lord."

"And our men?"

"Three dead and some six hurt."

He rose and stood leaning on his staff as our people poured into the courtyard. He was a figure of such singular dignity that when Ursus came swaggering to him and threw at his feet a severed head, I was shocked. Ursus was all blood and sweat. I had not seen him possess himself of that head, and he had carried it wrapped up in a Saxon cloak. I looked at the bloody thing as it came to rest after toppling over like some monstrous turnip, and recognized the bulging blue eyes and the flaming hair of the German chief whom I had spitted. I saw Aurelius look at that bloody head with a sudden frown of disgust. His face seemed to go cold and austere. And then he looked at Ursus, bloody and gloating, and I understood that he felt as I did about this barbaric business. Clean, cool killing may be a righteous affair, but blood-smeared exultation can nauseate.

He pointed his staff at the head.

"My friend, the gods made that somewhat in the likeness of man. Take it and bury it."

Poor Ursus looked as blank as a boy who has been reproved by a beloved master.

"Yes, lord, but—"

"Take it and bury it."

I watched Ursus pick up the head by its hair, and then I

went and stood close to the old man and told him how Ursus had found his brother butchered, and that his blood-rage was understandable.

Aurelius laid a hand upon my shoulder.

"Does mere blood wash out blood? Tell me, Pellias, have the dead been buried?"

"No, lord. We left them lying there."

"Even the dead should have dignity. Let them be buried. Death can be ugly. It is better under the green turf, than fouling it. Let the dead heathen be buried."

There were other wisdoms in his counsel, for if the dead were left lying there, and more of our enemies passed that way, they might conclude that those who had slain their kindred had come up from the valley. Also, as my lord had said, it was unbecoming that so sweet a place as the Ridgeway should be fouled by all that corruption. So, when our men had been fed and rested, and my lord had spoken to them in praise of their valour, I took thirty of them, well-armed, and went up to the Downs to bury the dead. It was no easy matter to dig a trench in the hard chalk, but we dug it below the brow of the hill behind some thorns, where it would be hidden, and my fellows dragged the bodies down by the heels and tumbled them into the shallow grave. I sat at a little distance and watched them, for I found that my stomach was more queasy than the stomachs of these peasants. They joked over the business, for they were feeling mighty pleased with themselves and the day's doings. The chalk was spaded back into a long mound, and I made them replace the soil and the turfs, so that the grave should green over.

I began to feel very weary, and ready for sleep, and my horse was as tired as I was. When we returned to the manor I went in and lay down on my bed, and in spite of the day's grim happenings, I was asleep in two minutes. I seemed to drop into it like a man falling into still, deep water. I had gone to my bed clothed, supperless and unwashed, and I must have slept for twelve hours, for when I woke the sun was rising in the east instead of setting in the west, and the birds were at their matins.

I felt hungry and thirsty and stiff, as stiff as I used to feel after the first rugger match of the season. Gosh, for some early tea and bread and butter, and then a bath and a pipe! Someone was standing in my doorway. I was not in the white house at Weybridge, but in a Romano-British villa, and my lord's barber-servant was smiling at me with his pink pig's face.

"I trust that you are rested, sir. My lord bade me not disturb you last night. The bath is ready."

I scrambled up and shook my head as though to toss the present out of the past.

"A bath. Splendid. I need one. What's the time?"

"An hour after sun-up, sir."

They were early risers, these people, and he used the American phrase for sunrise! How queer!

"My lord's compliments and he will wait breakfast for you. Shall I shave you, sir, when you have bathed?"

I felt my chin.

"Yes, I think you had better shave me."

When I had bathed the fellow scraped me with a bronze strigil, rubbed me with oil, and applied a soothing unguent to my chafed skin. I felt in fine fettle after it, but none too eager for more saddle-work. My posterior needed a rest, and it was to have it. My lord and I broke our fast together. The tireless Festus was out scouting, and old Robur was lying late in bed. Moreover, a Saxon's sword had dented the shoulder piece of his cuirass, and Robur was resting a sore shoulder.

My lord was in a serene mood. The look of pinched and crumpled senility had left him. The way he spoke to me and looked at me were as pleasant to me as the bread and honey.

"I have a desire," said he, "to go up to the temple and look at the world. You will come with me. We will go alone."

I asked him if I might walk and stretch my legs after two days in the saddle. Also, I asked him if he thought it safe for the two of us to go alone, for I had not forgotten that some of the Germans had escaped us. I said that I would go armed, but was it wise for our chief to run such risks?

His eyes had recovered their brightness.

He said: "At the end of one's life, my son, one should not be too careful. As for you, I should not accuse you of that vice. I have a desire to sit in the portico of the temple which was built long ago by my ancestors, and to look at this British land."

I said that I would go with him anywhere. And then I asked him to explain a thing that had puzzled me. Where was the priest who served the temple?

He smiled at me.

"I—am that priest."

So, in that Romano-British world he was squire and parson in one. Well, that was good philosophy. Who should be wiser than he as to the temporal and spiritual needs of his people? I felt that he wanted to give thanks for what had happened yesterday, though to what god he would address himself was beyond me.

We set out together about ten of the clock, to judge by the sun, my lord riding a stout little old horse, a grey, who had been in his service fifteen years. I carried spear and sword, though I left my breastplate and helmet behind, and wore a wadded coat which my lord had ordered his man to find for me. There was something biblical about our pilgrimage, Aurelius looking like some Italian picture of Moses, and I— young Israel—marching at his side. We climbed the opposite hill by the deep track which I and Meona had followed on the first day of my dream. We came to the woods, cool beech-woods to begin with, solemn and still, and my lord's mood was like these woods. His little horse padded along solemnly, and I left him in peace. Heather and fir woods followed, and now that the sun was warming the earth I could smell the pines. Then the sky opened before us, and I saw Farley Heath and Hurtwood, and the little white temple with its red roof standing alone in that green and empty landscape.

My lord stopped his horse by some furze bushes, and sat at gaze. I was wondering why they had built the temple there, and not on the hill above Honey Valley, and I asked him the reason for it.

"It was for the service of those travellers who came and went in the old days."

"Travellers?"

"Yes, soldiers, merchants, pilgrims. You see, my son, those who came up from Regnum and the sea might wish to pass westwards to Calleva and Corinium. London was not everybody's bourn. We used to have a little guest-house there, a traveller's rest, but in these emptier days, few people come that way, and the rest-house was pulled down."

We moved on and down into the next valley, and up the long heathery slope towards the temple. Young bracken was opening its crooks, and looking back I could see the line of the Downs, and almost mark the spot where we had buried the Saxons. So, we came to the sacred place, and I helped the old man off his horse, and was looking for something to which to tether the beast when my lord told me to loop the bridle round one of the portico pillars.

"God is not so easily offended in these days."

His words had a touch of such jocund cynicism that I began to wonder whether he and I were not very near to each other in our attitude to the Eternal Mystery. He told me to take the saddle cover and spread it on the steps for him. I did so and he sat down.

"Have you seen the inside of the sanctuary, Pellias?"

"No, sir."

"Go and look. The doors are always open."

I walked round to the south and entered the little *cella,* and all that I saw there was a lump of rough stone on a fluted pedestal. I had expected a statue, and here was nature in the rough.

I returned to where my lord was sitting gazing towards the Downs.

"Well, my son, what of our god?"

"Is it a symbol, sir?"

He retorted with a question of his own.

"In your future days, Pellias, how did you see your god? As a glorified man, a large and muscular person with gilded hair?"

I hesitated.

"I don't think we saw him. Or rather, we had ceased to see him. Though certain simple souls with a capacity for faith—"

Almost I could hear him laughing gentle inward laughter.

"Yes, the simple souls! Blessed innocents. A statue of Mars used to stand on that pedestal for the benefit of the legionaries who passed this way. I had it removed, and I put that stone in its place."

"But your people, sir, the simple souls?"

"They believe it to be a sacred stone, my son. It is supposed to be endowed with magic. It will heal wounds, cure sickness, make women fertile."

So my intuition had not misled me. The educated gentleman of those days confronted the Great Mystery much as we did, though they were happier perhaps in not being the slaves of a mechanical obsession. They had their Attilas just as we had our Hitlers, whom the devout believed to be the Spirit of Evil sent to chasten poor humanity. But what of my lord's *lararium* and his household gods? What of Pelagius and his Christ?

I said: "Let me not be impertinent, but, sir, you keep your household gods."

He looked up at me with gentle irony.

"One must not offend against the faith of the simple. I believe, my son, that man is made to believe. Tragedy arrives when he believes in nothing. Even those Germans believe in a butcherly sort of beast in a bloody ape whom they call the Hammer, or Thunder, or something. The thing has the head of a sheep, but what would you!"

I sat down on the grass at his feet.

"In our future days, lord, some of our wise men retained their faith."

"In what?"

"Well, in the sensing of a Presence. Nothing could prove it. All we can say is, with profound humility, that our poor wits must have limitations, and that the mystery is there. We have to take the leap and transcend our senses, and believe that there is some super-sense that can feel that Otherness, and be convinced of it."

He spread his hands to the sun as though warming them at a fire.

"It seems, my son, that you and I are very near each other. Yet, the strange fact that you are both here and there seems to suggest—"

He paused, smiled, and looked at me.

"Other dimensions."

"What word is that?"

I tried to talk Ouspensky to him, using the Euclidian idea, and I found that he understood me, though he phrased it differently.

"A world above a world," he said, "a cube within a cube, a kind of crystal shell which reflects. Yes, and sometimes we seem to see the other side of the mirror. Then, even your wise men are not so much cleverer than ours."

I laughed at his gentle raillery.

"They can be so clever that one cannot understand them."

"Ah, that kind of affectation. To appear wise because of the multitude and the length of one's words! In my old age I have come to know that the profundities are simple. Simply because we do not know! In serene simplicity one ceases from being a hypocrite. But I would hear more of your world, my son."

Sitting there with the spacious sky before me, and the dim Downs that were beginning to be hazed with heat I told him something of our world, of its motor cars and aeroplanes, and bombs and guns and gases, its wireless and cinematograph, our brilliant cities and our shabby slums, our great factory towns, our multitude of mechanical gadgets, and our restless boredom. I do not know how much of it he believed, but he listened to me in silence, his face strangely serene.

"It seems to me that your world, my friend, is never still. Have you time to look and think, as we look at those hills?"

I said that I did not believe our world saw very deeply into anything. It could not even see its own streets for the traffic. It tore through the country and tore back again. I saw him smiling at me.

"And you have not found peace."

"I think we have lost both peace of mind, and God."

He was silent, and then he said: "May it not be, Pellias, that God grows weary sometimes of fool-man? We become smug in our little complacencies, in our little clevernesses. Or we begin quarrelling with each other over pieces of the earth when there is more earth than we need. I think that if I were God I should become very bored with man."

"In the sacred book of the Jews he did become weary of man, and drowned all of him save for a chosen few."

"Always the chosen few, my friend! Maybe God likes man savage, and to watch him fighting and crucifying. We had grown soft and comfortable in this island, and God may have sent us these hairy, butcherly fellows to stir up our virility!"

His irony piqued me.

"It will be the same in the future, and so far as Britain is concerned the German tribes will again be the gadflies led by a little strutting fellow with blob eyes and a smudge of a moustache. A cosmic business, perhaps, initiated by the unknown God!"

"A form of education, Pellias, that seems perennial! Well, here is this lovely landscape, and growth, and the fruits of the earth, and a hundred mysteries, yet man must spend himself in acquiring the thing called power, and in cutting throats. What would you do about it?"

I answered him promptly.

"I would try to cut the throats of the throat-cutters."

I looked at his splendid head and could not help comparing it with the block-headed noddle of some muscular oaf who exemplified crude force, and nothing else. He and my pacifist friend Pelagius were spiritual cousins, yet not completely so in practice. I could not see that the world was ripe for Pelagius and his ideals. Pelagius would have been a League of Nations enthusiast, but the world was still very young, and I have heard dear old Gilbert Murray use the word young in gentle irony. But irony does not alter things, or endow a crass egoist like Hitler with a sense of humour, or restrain louts who are all breeched backside and bum-head, from goose-stepping over our flower-beds.

My lord was smiling.

"Yes, my son, I think we shall have to try and cut throats. It may be poor artistry, but in a butchers' world one cannot always be the sheep."

He rose, and turning, walked into the temple, and I followed him. He laid his hand on the rough stone.

"That should be a symbol. Surely, creative man should be able to carve the shapeless mass into beauty? Well, well, we must return to those men of action, Festus and Robur, and consult as to the cutting of throats!"

As I walked back beside his horse he would rein in now and again, and pointing at the familiar hills, ask me if I knew them in my other world. I gave him our names for them, Leith Hill, Holmbury, Hurtwood, Hascombe, Hazlemere, Hindhead. He frowned over them, and I wondered whether I had exposed my lie and my editing of history by giving him names that suggested an alien future. But that was not so. I think he was still profoundly perplexed by the problem of my double self, and could not make up his mind whether I was what I said I was, or the genuine Pellias whom some god had visited with visionary madness. But, obviously, his interest in me was practical. I was proving myself a useful man of my hands, and a leader of men. One thing I did fear, that he might ask me to produce one of the useful lethal weapons of my time for use against these savages. Could I and Niger the Smith turn out a primitive cannon or machine-gun? We could not, though I might have managed powder. The only thing I could think of was an armoured chariot to serve as a tank, but when I reflected upon it I realized that swiftness and mobility and the quick, merciless blow were what we needed, fierce mounted men who could surprise and ride down these marauding bands.

I said so to Aurelius.

"That, my son," he answered, "is good counsel. When Rome last freed us from these vermin she sent us cavalry who hunted and slew them."

The valley gave us peaceful sounds, the lowing of cattle and the bleating of sheep, the sound of running water and the monologue of the mill. The miller was grinding flour. I heard Niger the Smith hammering away in his forge, and I thought how foreign all these country sounds were to my world of speed and explosives. As Jeans has written, the mechanical mind has misread and made a mess of nature, and though Sir James sets up the mathematician as the interpreter, I would, with all respect to him, also retain the artist. Let man play at making beautiful things, and in the making of them discover beautiful behaviour. Let it be shame to us that any super-bully should boast of bloody and corrupt hands. True, my friend Niger might be hammering weapons of war, but such things were being forced upon us. And yet, I must confess, I was finding a sharp joy in fighting, when my heart and my soul were in the business. I suppose that dictators are like pestilences, sent to stir up our wits and to temper us to the upward struggle.

We came upon old Robur sitting on a rail above the millpool and watching the water sliding under the wheel. He had his shoulder bandaged, and his arm in a sling. He rose and joined us, looking so much like Julius Cæsar that his Roman ancestry was palpable.

"Well, my friend," said Aurelius, "Pellias and I have been discussing the philosophy of cutting throats. The question is, how to proceed with it. Where is our good Festus?"

"Out on the hills with his riders."

"The man is a veritable falcon. How would you order things, Robur?"

"Seek out the enemy wherever he is, sir, and destroy him."

"An admirable plan, provided we have the strength."

"We must raise the whole country, sir."

"Yes, my friend, nothing else will save us. I should receive word from my brother to-day or to-morrow. Meanwhile I have a desire to visit Londinium and Verulam, and speak to those townsmen."

Robur looked fierce.

"I would not count too much on the alley-dwellers, sir. They are not the stuff that will turn a sword. Give me the men from the west."

"Have patience, my friend. I have a feeling that they will not fail us."

CHAPTER EIGHTEEN

𝒯HE indefatigable Festus, that human centaur, came back with the tidings that he and his men had ridden close to the Kentish borders, and had not come in contact with any of the enemy. It seemed that our surmise was correct, and that the strong plundering party which we had destroyed in the battle of the Ridgeway had been responsible for all the burnings and terror in our Surrey valleys. But Festus did return with a rumour that he had picked up from an old shepherd who had remained loyal to his sheep, and whom Festus had found defying fate and Nordic frenzies on the north side of the Downs. The shepherd had said that he had seen a large body of the Saxons on the march in the valley below him, as though making for the Thames. The shepherd had believed that the invaders were marching on London.

And Aurelius Superbus was proposing to ride to London! No one tried to dissuade him, for I think all of us realized that this was no time for caution. A fine recklessness might serve us better than Fabian tactics, if we were to make head against this peril. To sit at home and pull long faces, while waiting for a selfish world to sacrifice itself for distant neighbours would not set the courage of our men mounting. Tragedy might be in the air, but the tragic mask, black-eyed and hollow of mouth, can be less cheering than a face full of laughter.

My lord said: "Shall we be deterred by these savages? No, my friend, we will go to Londinium."

I am bound to confess that I was very keen to see Roman London. I told him so, and he decided to take me with him, but he gave me some wise counsel as to keeping my mouth shut. I could play the part of the simple, uneloquent soldier. His would be the task of venting his eloquence upon the mayor and the city council, to persuade them to combine in some mutual plan of action against the invaders.

We decided to cross the Thames at Pontes, and approach Londinium by the great west road. If the Saxons were across the river we should soon hear of them. Our party consisted of Aurelius, myself, and six of our best men, including Ursus, all well mounted. Our horses were fast enough to give the Saxons the slip, were we to blunder into one of their raiding parties. We should hear at Pontes whether the river was open, or whether any of the Saxon ships had come prowling up it.

My lord might be old in years, but he was a young man in the saddle, for he had been bred in a world of hunting and of horses. We saddled up soon after dawn, and were at Pontes by eight of the clock. Pontes was not the bustling place it had been on the day that Meona and I had visited it. The Place was empty, the caravanserai shut up, and there were no barges moored by the bridge. Nor was there any guard there. Pontes had the air of a place that was semi-desolate and swept by a north-east wind. It had a brittle, shivering atmosphere, though the sun shone hot on the houses. Many of them were shuttered, for their owners had fled. An old beggar was sitting on the steps of the Corn Exchange, and to him Aurelius addressed himself.

"Is my lord Pontius in residence?"

"No, master," said the beggar. "They do say that he has gone to be cured of the rheumatics at Bath."

"Ah, and of other ills, also, no doubt," said my lord with a dry laugh.

"You see, master, they all be so afeared of the Saxons."

"Have you had the Saxons here?"

"No, lord. You see, I be that lame that I'm thinking I be more comfortable sitting here than taking the road."

Aurelius tossed him a coin.

"You are a wise fellow. Are any boats passing down the river?"

"Thank-ee, lord. No, there be no boats. They do say that the Saxon ships have come up past London."

We rode on.

"Only the lame do not run," said Aurelius with irony. "My lord Pontius has set them an example. He is very brave in subduing the women."

I have always thought the flat country north of the Thames some of the ugliest in England, and this Roman road traversed it as though it was of the same opinion, and wished to pass as quickly as possible through this dreariness of gravel and of clay. A fine road, banked and ditched and paved, it made me think of a French highway, save that it had no avenues of planes or poplars. There were swampy places spreading from the river and the road became a causeway some five feet above the reeds and rushes. Shepperton and Hampton were mere names, though, as the road swung away to the north-east I could see high ground that suggested Kingston Hill and Richmond. We passed a few shabby-looking farms and market-gardens, and there were orchards about what must have been Twickenham; also, we overtook a few country folk on the road, and carts taking vegetables to London, but these people looked on us blankly when my lord questioned them about the Saxons. The panic at Pontes did not appear to have spread over this dreary, Middlesex flat. Even the peasants had flat faces, and looked too stupid to react to any stimulus other than a kick.

I was bored with this country, and no doubt my description of it might be reminiscent of the deadly modern ugliness round Walton and Chertsey. I wanted Roman London, and the strange, bitter tang that attaches even to the London of all time. Almost I expected to see the dome of St. Paul's and the towers of Westminster. We passed across a ragged heath, and saw more swamps on our right, and then I caught the sun shining on a cluster of buildings crowded together on a low hill. A grey wall clasped the little city, and the pantiled roofs rose above it with regimented precision. Almost it suggested a modern building estate, hundreds of little cardboard villas crowded together in anonymous obscurity. I saw only one big building rising above that angular choppy sea of red and brown roofs. It might have been a modern super-cinema, or a Woolworth stores. I gathered that it was London's basilica. So, this was London, the city of merchants, and the bourn of all the ships that sailed the sea!

Romano-British London had its West End. I had seen the city on its hill, clasped by the casket of its wall, but outside the wall and strung along a shallow valley were villas and gardens, veritable gentlemen's residences sacred to the richer merchants. I saw the river, and some single-masted ships lying moored close in to the Middlesex bank, and a wooden bridge. There was something queer about the bridge; one of the central spans seemed lacking, and I realized that this gap was artificial. Aurelius also noticed it, and I saw him smile that serene yet ironic smile.

"No Horatii in London, my friend."

Moreover, these plutocratic villas had a desolate look, shutters closed, courtyards and gardens empty. The city merchants had taken refuge within the walls, and on the walls themselves I could see armed men patrolling. We crossed a stream which I took to be the Fleet river, and came to the West Gate, Ludgate, half-way up the hill. The gates were shut, and the men up above on the two turrets looked over and down at us as though they occupied the grand-stand, and we were a gang of race-course thieves who were more welcome off the course than on it.

There was some delay in the opening of the gate, and I could see that my lord's temper was rising. The man in charge of the gate's guard was a saucy fellow, and barred us out with his spear held crosswise, while he asked for our credentials. London appeared to be a suspicious and unfriendly place, and very concerned as to its own security.

Said my lord with extreme politeness: "My name is Aurelius Superbus, and I am lord of the lands beyond the chalk hills. I have come to consult with your præfect and the city council."

The fellow let us through, but in passing him Ursus leaned sideways and chucked the gentleman under the chin.

"Feeling a little windy, brother! We are fighting men, not civvies dressed up as soldiers."

We rode up the hill, with a row of narrow-fronted houses on one side, and tall warehouses on the other. The road was paved, and there were side-walks, and these paths were crowded with people who hung about in groups and chattered like frightened monkeys. Even Romano-British London was a city of noise. Women hung out of upper windows and talked to other women across the way. Children scurried about. No one seemed to be doing any work. There were small mobs outside the wine-shops. I saw a couple of men who looked like sailors staggering down the road, bawling, with their arms round each other. They came blundering into my horse, and I put out a foot and heaved them off, and they both fell down in the gutter. I got sulky looks from the crowd for that, and I caught Ursus grinning in his beard. Obviously, London had the wind up, and was sulky and scared, and in no temper to go out and fight the heathen.

Then, in what appeared to be a principal street, one might have called it Cheapside, we met a person of palpable importance being carried along in a litter. He was a very fat man with a fiery face, and Aurelius was known to him, for the litter stopped, and our fat friend swung two large legs to the ground, and stood fawning beside my lord's horse. I learned later that he was London's principal wine importer, and that my lord was a notable patron. His tunic was of red silk, his cloak of purple, and he wore a gold chain round his neck with some sort of badge of office dangling from it.

"My humble welcome to my lord. Is there any service Pomponius can render?"

"Pomponius" was exquisite. So was his little red beard, and his leery, greedy eyes, and the way his hands washed themselves.

"I am here to see your præfect and your council."

"They are in session, sir, in constant session, talking, talking, talking."

"Indeed! Is that so?" said my lord, and I saw that he looked upon Pomponius as having spittle in his beard, "and of what do they talk?"

Pomponius flung up his hands.

"Of what, sir? Why, the Saxon peril. Two of their ships came into the Pool yesterday. We broke the bridge and manned the walls. A bold front, sir. The wretches departed. But, of course, you, my lord, in the peaceful country are not vexed by such terrors."

Aurelius disillusioned him.

"No, we too have our alarums. Farmsteads and manors have been burnt, people slaughtered. And we have fought, and not unsuccessfully with these savages. My friend Pellias, here, could tell you a story."

Pomponius gaped at me.

"Your servant, sir. Incredible. Revolting. My business is in the pot. And you come, my lord—?"

"To see if we in the country, and you in London can join forces against the Saxons."

Again Pomponius threw up his hands.

"I fear you reap the wind, sir. Talk, talk, talk, and nothing done. I assure you we are smothering in officialdom. I have been in the council-room since the morning, and believe me, no one would listen. They all talk, my lord, and no one listens. It is nothing but a gabble-house."

I could see that Aurelius had had enough of the wine-merchant and wished to be rid of him.

"I will go to the basilica, and see if they will listen to me. My thanks to you, Pomponius."

"Are you lodging here, sir?"

"Probably."

"May I presume to put my poor house at your service? You

know it, my lord. I assure you I shall be greatly honoured."

My lord thanked him.

"I would see, first, how your council shapes to my plan. May I leave the courtesy open?"

"Assuredly, sir, assuredly. I will hasten home and warn my good Cornelia. All shall be prepared. May I ask, my lord, if you like vinegar with your oysters?"

Aurelius smiled like a god with a secret sense of humour.

"Without vinegar, I think, my friend."

"And a little Bordeaux wine? Aha, I can serve my lord with a wine that has a bouquet and a flavour that are—unique."

So, there were snobs in Roman Britain, and Pomponius did not match his wine; he was not a vintage port! My lord rode on, and Pomponius stood bowing and washing his hands beside his litter. The street brought us to the Forum and the basilica, which I had a feeling should be called the Mansion House. I expected mayoral robes and a posy of city fathers, and I was not to be disappointed. Meanwhile, the Forum was chock-a-block with people, all waiting, I suppose, upon the deliberations of their elders. It was a smelly crowd, much less clean and more cosmopolitan than that of Calleva, nor would I have accused it of good manners. I saw strange foreign faces here, with expressions of greed and fear. Moreover, the crowd had caught Mr. Polonius's impatience, and was arguing and shouting and calling for the city fathers to come forth and make a declaration from the rostrum. This crowd craved news, as all crowds crave it, and had begun to grumble and grow bitter and sarcastic, and frothy with rumour.

There were a dozen fellows in livery at the top of the basilica steps, keeping the crowd back with red and white staves. We had a solid mass between us and those solemn and sacred steps, and this human barrier showed no disposition to favour us. Ursus pushed his horse forward and shouted.

"Way for my Lord Aurelius."

His horse trod on somebody, and several lewd fellows turned and cursed us.

"Here, keep your hoofs off me, my buck."

"Who the Hades is Aurelius?"

My lord showed himself capable of dealing with these roughs. He sat and smiled upon them, and raising a hand, spoke.

"Gentlemen, please permit me to pass. I have urgent business with your council. Are we not all concerned in facing this peril that threatens town and country?"

I have heard it said that a great gentleman will always remain benign even when obstructed by louts and fools, and my lord's dignity was such that these gentlemen of the market-place gave way before him, and opened us a channel to the basilica steps. Here the chief of the municipal lackeys met us, and having some experience of men of mark, was very polite to my lord. The council was in secret session, but he would convey to them my lord's message. And would my lord dismount and wait in the great hall? The notables were assembled in the council chamber.

Aurelius bade me accompany him. We passed up the steps and found ourselves in the basilica's main hall. It was a splendid chamber with two rows of pillars, a barrel roof with a coffered ceiling painted in blue and gold, and tall windows glazed with bull's-eye glass. Treillaged screens covered with gilding partly shut off the apse of the curia. A series of fine bronze doors opened from the back of the hall, and when our chief-lackey opened one of them a splurge of voices came to us and went echoing up to the hollow roof. My lord looked at me and smiled. Babel seemed loose in the city's council-chamber.

We stood on a fine mosaic floor, and my lord pointed to the figure in the centre panel. It portrayed Jupiter seated upon a cloud, a thunderbolt in one hand, and what looked like a bag of gold in the other.

"Most symbolical and apposite, my son. Thunder and lightning, or hard cash. Which will our worthies choose?"

I laughed.

"History has it, sir, that business men will always try to buy off the barbarians!"

"And if the barbarians possess any wisdom they will know that both gold and sheep's-heads can be had for the taking."

The bronze door had closed, damping down all those civic voices, and when again it swung open the burble refilled the hall. I heard a snarling voice declaiming: "Think of the poor, think of the women and children, think of the men who labour." The angry ringing of a hand-bell suggested that the chairman was attempting to bring this orator to order. My lord gave me a shrewd, ironic look.

"London's Cleon, no doubt. Such occasions as this are the demagogue's opportunity."

I translated Cleon into Hitler, that supernatural liar and self-constituted crony of God.

The gentleman with the staff approached us.

"The council will hear you, my lord."

How very magnanimous of them! Aurelius beckoned me to follow him, and we ascended the steps and entered the council chamber. It was insufferably stuffy, and did not indicate that these city worthies used their baths. There were about twenty councillors seated on state chairs. Their president or præfect occupied a more decorative chair on a low dais. He had a table before him, and a secretary at his elbow. I got the impression that all these hard-faced notables were in a state of fume, flurry and heat. Faces were shining with sweat, and again I remarked a number of Hebraic noses. There was silence when we entered. We were stared at. The gentleman with the bell, a large, black, turgid person, glared at me.

"The audience was granted to you, sir. Who is this soldier? The tradition of our council is that—"

My lord took him up.

"Indeed! Then we will not trespass upon your civic dignity. This soldier is the captain of our forces, such as they are. I pray you, gentlemen, excuse me."

He bowed, and turned towards the door, as though to leave the council chamber, but I imagine that certain of the city fathers were glad to behold something in a shape of a fighting-man, for there were sudden sharp protests. The turgid chairman with the large white kidney face grabbed his bell and jerked it angrily.

"Silence, please. These interruptions are insufferable."

A lean, sardonic man rose and lisped at him.

"May I suggest that all your tintinnabulation, sir, is equally exhausting, may I say, intolerant. I put it to the council that we wish to hear my Lord Aurelius, and we do not object to the presence of his dux."

Hands went up, and the sardonic councillor claimed a majority. The præfect put his bell away.

"You have my permission to address us, sir."

Aurelius bowed to him.

"Gentlemen, I come to propose that we of the country and you of the city should plan to join our forces against this very urgent peril. May I say that we are not without experience and that we have fought with some success. Only two days ago, my dux attacked, routed and put to the sword a raiding party of these savages. But, gentlemen, we are faced with more than mere raids. We have to confront invasion."

He paused, and I watched the faces of the city fathers, and they did not move me to great confidence.

Said a large, black and white councillor: "Doth the gentleman ask us to fight?"

Aurelius turned to him.

"I do, sir. And what is the alternative?"

Another voice said: "A little money'sh might perthwade the pirates to leave."

I wanted to shout "Rats," but the sardonic gentleman was on his feet. There was an element of courage in his thin lips and cold blue eyes. He twitted the assembly with cowardice, asserted that Londinium, with its population, had both the money and the men to wage war and successful war against the invaders. Had not the British served in the Roman legions? Londinium had a number of old soldiers who could drill and stiffen a levy of virile men. His acid eloquence was all to the point, but my impression was that these worthies would prefer to sit behind their walls and hope and wait for the storm to blow over.

When our sardonic friend had finished, babel broke out again, and I divined in my lord the sudden weariness of exasperation. He was an old man and frail, and not one of these fat and self-important fools had offered him a chair. I was losing patience, and I turned to the master of the lackeys and asked that my lord should be provided with a chair. But my lord waved it aside. The præfect was again active with that futile and busy bell, and when silence had returned, my lord was the first to speak.

"Gentlemen, I think we will leave you to your deliberations. I am an old man, and I have ridden far."

I could see that he was weary, and oppressed with a tired scorn for these babblers. The præfect rose and bowed to him.

"Perhaps it would be as well, sir. We have our own particular interests to consider. May I ask if you are remaining within the city?"

"For one night, Mr. Præfect, at the house of my friend Pomponius."

"Then, sir, we will communicate our decision to you."

We left them talking, remounted our horses, and riding through that sullen, anxious crowd, took our way to the house of Pomponius.

Said my lord to me: "That was a most illuminating experience, my son. Mark you, they have their particular interests to consider! I have no great wish to tarry in this city. These jackdaws will chatter, but they will not fight."

I felt full of compassion for him, for he was weary and disappointed.

CHAPTER NINETEEN

❧

𝓘 HAVE not much to relate concerning our night's stay in the house of Pomponius. Pomponius and his wife and daughter were all types, and thousands of them can be studied in our modern suburbs. The oysters and the wine were excellent, so was my bed, which Miss Flammula showed a readiness to share with me. Pomponius was all for drama, even in the cracking of an egg; his wife was large and remote and blonde, and excessively stupid. The daughter fell upon me as though I were a sale's bargain. I suppose we should have called her a bright young thing, much over-sexed, slangy and slim and flat chested, with long febrile legs which suggested ecstatic spasms and entwinements. She sat next me at dinner and kept nudging her knee against mine.

My lord, who was very weary, went to his bed after reading the communication that the city council sent to him by the hands of the præfect's secretary. "This is to inform your Excellency that the Council will resume its deliberations on the morrow." Aurelius showed the epistle to me with a whimsical and ironic nod of the head. We lingered at the table after he had gone. Our host ate enormously, and became sleepy. His wife had a capacity for oysters that fascinated me. I counted twenty-seven. Flammula drank more than was good for her, and became affectionate and a little tipsy.

Her mother, complaining of *flatus,* with the frankness of an American, said that she would take a doze and go to bed. Pomponius fell asleep and snored, his hands clasping his civic tummy. Flammula offered to show me the garden, and since I was rather curious to see how like the girl was to some of her modern sisters, I went with her.

Almost I could hear her saying: "How marvellous! You've fought and killed Germans. How marvellous of you!" And with her sinuous, soft body making contact with mine, she invited a supporting arm, and implied that nothing could be denied to such a hero. Flammula was sensual and romantic, with a tinge of red in her hair, but I could not help seeing the father in the daughter, and the likeness left me cold. The garden possessed an arbour with a couch and cushions, and Flammula posed herself. I should not have been surprised if she had asked me for the inevitable cigarette.

"Tell me all about it, you wonderful man."

But I was thinking of Meona. This body of youth might not provoke me, and I claim no virtue on that account, but it seemed to bring that other loveliness nearer to me, that passionate, dark girl with her Cassandra eyes. Well, if my lady wanted her hero, she should have him, but not in the flesh, and I am afraid I swaggered to her and romanced, while remaining blind to other insinuations. What Pomponius's daughter thought of me I do not care and I do not know. She should have damned me as a cold and conceited egoist, a kind of Narcissus in armour talking to his own reflection in a mirror and not to a young woman who wanted to be able to say:

"How terribly excited he is about me." Her father, who came yawning and belching into the garden, rescued the occasion from slipping between the sheets.

My memory of Roman London remains one of suburban banality. Was the Arthur Legend compatible with this little cosmos of commercialists? There were no Welsh singers here, no green glooms, and sunsets and mysterious dawns, no fine ecstasy even in tragic things, nothing but a number of saprophytic exploiters worried about their money and their merchandise. Well, and why not? Trade is a serious business, the modern sap that circulates in the products of our commercial glasshouse. Surely, the legend of the Apples of Gold had been spun by an economist. All that I know is that we left the house of Pomponius and the stereotyped streets of Londinium without regret and with no illusions. Pomponius washed his hands of us, but very politely so.

"Should my lord need his cellar restocking, I think I can charter transport."

I knew that Aurelius was not thinking of wine or oysters, but of the tragedy of burnt homesteads and cries of despair, and of world tragedies that sweep upon men through man, sneering, cold, supercilious beasts like Ribbentrop, or sadists like Attila and Stalin. I did not see the daughter again. My heart was hungry for Meona, and for woods and hills and villages, and even for hazardous and passionate happenings. I felt that fighting might be a more wholesome business than the making of money. Has any epic grown up round a monstrous consignment of cheese or of cocoa? Why did not Homer sing of pork and beans, and shiploads of stinking hides? I wonder. St. Francis may have been a dreaming fool, and the Crusaders a collection of colourful gangsters, but I was still a young man and hot in the head, and Meona's chariot with its white horses seemed to me to be a more splendid symbol than a lorry loaded with barrels of beer. Yes, I know all this may be called rhetorical nonsense, but I was a fighting-man, and in love.

God, Love and War; I believe that these have been man and nature's Trinity at any period of stress and of greatness in the human story. As I rode beside Aurelius across the uninspiring Middlesex flats towards Pontes, he spoke to me of these crises in the affairs of man which repeat themselves through the centuries. He confessed that he had not hoped much from London. Such a community did not breed the virtues that make for survival. When a man became afraid of his money-bags, he forfeited the one essential virtue, courage, that can protect the treasure from the spoilers. Luxury and ostentation could be the devil. A hard, strong, simple living peasantry might save its country in a crisis such as this, led by men of honour who could embrace the higher courage of self-sacrifice. He said that we should trust to the country gentlemen and the men of the farms and the marches, men hardened by toil and whose faces were not afraid of the weather. The simple virtues would save us, and nothing else. I could not help thinking how closely his words applied to an England that had grown soft and complacent and careless. My country of the future might need its purge, its struggle, its bitter days. In confronting its own barbarians, it might recover its soul.

I thought of the Swiss, and Holland in its struggle against Spain, and the England of Elizabeth and the Napoleonic phase. A certain fine ruthlessness seemed necessary, a simple hardihood. The little clever people who played pin and winkle with words and theories would be relegated to the Prig's

Corner. Highbrows who wrote laudatory articles on the hyena, and ran for their lives when the live beast appeared, would be given the job of emptying life's latrines, and after all, so far as literature is concerned, they seem to like that sort of job. The peasant and the soldier and the smith would be God's own gentlemen, not quite according to the Russian model, for the Russian seems to be a dirty beast. And so, we came to Pontes, and crossed the river and saw the Britain of Arthur and of Dreams, not Slough and its productive ugliness, but a poets' and a painters' and a peasants' world.

Was ever any district more appositely named than Slough? And our Industry had fastened on it as a predestined, commercial pig-sty. Yet Slough wallows on the edge of a loveliness that need never be destroyed.

There was nothing adventurous about our homeward journey. In fact it was so peaceful that the very peace had a tragic face. We rode through country that was desolate, and from which its folk had fled. Lovely it might be in its infinite and varied greenness, with the grass lushing up for hay and filling itself with the faces of flowers, but a haunted silence lay over the land. Birds were the only live things we saw and heard, and when a yaffle laughed at us, or a jay scolded I was moved to wonder what happened when such a country went back to nature. I thought of my history books, and then, divining the sadness in the heart of the old man beside me, I closed the book. Did it help me to remember that the cities of Britain crumbled into gradual ruin and desolation; that they became ghostly places which the barbarian avoided? There would be rude, remote homesteads scattered through the woodlands. Britain would become again a wilderness of woods and swamps peopled by a slow, lazy, unimaginative folk. Then,

Christ would come again to Britain, and a few devoted men would plan, and build and teach. The Danes and the Normans would chasten it, Flemings settle in the land, Jews bring their persistent cleverness, Huguenots teach it other things, and slowly that English breed would evolve, and Rome be forgotten. This world that haunted me would be rediscovered as fragments of brick and tile, buried mosaics, hoards of coins, worn down, toothless walls.

But, I must quicken my tempo, for these reflective interludes and sentimental digressions were to be like mere maidenly sighings in the world to which I was returning. We came down from the Hog's Back to the deserted hamlet and the bridge across the Wey. I saw armed men upon the bridge, and we pulled up sharply, not knowing for the moment whether they were friends or enemies. One small detail reassured me. The man who was sitting on his horse in the centre of the bridge had his arm in a white linen sling. It was Robur.

He too had recognized us, and he rode forward to meet us. I was to see many grim faces during the days that were to follow, but I think old Robur's face was the grimmest I remember. There was no smile in his eyes, and his mouth was a thin hard line. He raised an arm and saluted my master.

"I thought it best, lord, to meet you here."

I guessed that Robur had no good news to give us, and my lord must have been equally quick in reading that stark, lean face.

"You have been attacked, Robur?"

"No, not yet, sir."

"Well, let us hear the worst."

"It is not sweet wine, sir. Festus brought it in before noon. Our friends are on the march."

"So soon?"

"Yes, it would seem that their main body which had advanced on Londinium must have found the bridge broken and the gates shut. They turned about and came south on to the Ridge. What their plan may be, I do not know, to cross the river higher up and swing back on Londinium, or to try a forced march and their luck against Calleva."

"Are they in force?"

"Hundreds of them, sir. More must have landed in Kent. At the moment they are a dozen miles from us."

"If they pass along the Ridge they may see where their dead lie buried."

Robur moistened thin lips.

"If you remember, sir, some escaped from that slaughter. They may know of it. They may know even more than that, and turn aside to try and take their vengeance."

So the citizens of Londinium, instead of helping us, had by their careful selfishness turned the torrent upon us. They could sit in comparative safety behind their walls and their closed gates, with the river and its mud between them and the Saxons, who, like many wild tribes, trusted to a first savage rush and would recoil from fortifications. They would not sit down and lay siege to Londinium when the whole country lay open to them. There would be other ways of bringing Londinium to ruin, by encircling it and cutting off its food supply, until it fell like rotten fruit from a tree starved of sap.

We three quickened up our horses and rode on together, taking counsel as we went. The manor walls were not like city walls. We had not the strength to meet the main host of the heathen in the open. If we attempted to hold Honey Valley, and they poured down upon us, we might make a bloody and notable fight of it, but our extermination would not help the country. Unless we were reinforced quickly by

Aurelius Ambrosius and his power, we were like a sand-castle on the edge of the sea.

What was our choice to be? To hold the manor and dare the chance of our enemies passing by? Or to abandon Honey Valley and retreat upon Calleva and the help that might be coming to us from the West? There was yet another plan, and it was Aurelius who proposed it. We might abandon the valley temporarily, withdraw to some old hill fort or strong place which could be more easily defended, and send word to my lord's brother of the peril and the place we were in.

Robur acclaimed this plan.

"We must have eyes, sir, eyes. Sunk in a valley we cannot see. Some wooded hill-top."

"And what of water?"

"Yes, a spring or dew-pond."

It was my lord who thought of the temple on Farley Heath. The temple cellar itself was too small to give shelter to more than twenty men, but it would form a strong core for defence. Moreover, there was a bank about it that could be strengthened with brushwood and tree-trunks, and in the little valley on the south a spring fed a clean pool. We could hide the horses in the woods to the south of the temple, and the place would give us a spacious outlook along the Downs. Both Robur and I welcomed the idea, but there was no time to be lost if we wanted to occupy our eyrie before our enemies appeared upon the Downs. I suggested that we should fell young birch trees and pile them round the temple as camouflage. Also, our men could deepen the ditch and raise the vallum, and pile more trees and brushwood there so that our activities should be hidden by a green bank.

We galloped into Honey Valley and set our men to work, loading food on to the horses and collecting every sort of receptacle that would hold water. Every axe, spade and mattock in the village was requisitioned. Festus was sent up to the Black Down to watch the chalk hills. We knew that we should have to leave the manor-house to chance its fate, and that closed doors and shuttered windows would be useless, but we took all the food and forage we could gather. My lord was the last to leave the place, riding out through the open courtyard gates. I saw him look back, raise an arm and salute the place, and his farewell touched me.

We had reached the brow of the Black Down, and our leading files had disappeared into the beechwood when I heard one of the men in charge of a pack-horse give a shout. He was behind and below me, and had been having trouble with his horse. I saw that he was pointing across the valley, and my first thought was that he must have sighted the enemy moving along the Ridgeway. That was the last thing we wanted, and I turned my horse and rode down the hill to where the fellow was standing.

"What are you shouting about? Did you not hear our orders?"

His arm remained outstretched, and I realized that he was pointing down into the valley and not across it to the Downs.

"Look, Captain, look!"

And then I saw what he had seen, a loop of the road in the green hollow of the valley, and moving along it two white shapes with something that shone and glittered behind them. Meona's white horses and her chariot! Good God, what madness had brought her back to us at such a moment?

I told the man to take his horse on and get under cover, and to say nothing to my lord. I glanced again at the line of the Downs across the valley, and for a second I thought I saw movement there, vague shapes threading amid the yews and thorns. As a matter of fact a herd of deer must have come browsing along through the thickets, for when we did see our enemy there was no mistaking him for deer. I went down the hill at a pace that would have sent me over my horse's head had he made one false step. What had brought Meona back? Had she found help, and driven on recklessly and impetuously to bring the news to us?

Again I was the victim of mixed emotion, anger and a lover's exultation at the thought of seeing her, nor was I innocent of all sense of self-drama. I was her rescuer and her protector, and I even heard myself scolding her with tender fierceness for her recklessness. But I could not shed that modern virtue, the mirror of self knowledge, that distorting glass which chastens one's reflection with humour. I could laugh at myself. I could see a particular adventure, not as a piece of bombast and of swagger, a brass-band stunt, but as a job, and perhaps a nasty job, to be done coolly and efficiently, and without self-flattery. That is why we more ironic people find your simple creatures so exasperating. Being very little, they have a passion for appearing important. They mistake sulks and surliness for dignity. They object to any new thing because it is new and strange to them and challenges their ignorance and their vanity. They boil over with crude emotion, and wave little mock-heroic flags, and fling at you old frothy phrases in defence of a stock complacency. The plain citizen may be a useful fellow, but the arrogance of his ignorance may make him appear an awkward brute.

But what am I prating about? Here was I galloping along a country lane to intercept an impetuous young woman whose recklessness not only put her in great danger, but threatened the lives of us all. As I passed the manor mill I saw the white horses and chariot swing in through the open gates of the

courtyard. Meona did not see me, for I took the driver to be
Meona. Well, if she had surprised us, her own recklessness
would have its own reaction. The haze of dust raised by her
horses and her wheels was still hanging in the air when I rode
into the deserted courtyard. The white horses had their noses
in the water-cistern. I saw Meona standing on the steps of the
portico. Her back was turned to me, and I could divine her
wonder and dismay at finding this silence, this emptiness.

She heard the sound of my coming and turned, and her
little face had a blanched, wild loveliness. Her eyes stared at
me; her mouth hung open.

"Pellias! What has happened?"

I was off my horse, and blown between love and anger.

"Don't ask me questions. Into your chariot, and go back by
the way you came."

Her mouth closed. She was frowning. I suppose I must
have been rather hectoring in my haste.

"Do you give me orders?"

My temper rose to hers.

"I do. The Saxons are on the hills, hundreds of them. We
have abandoned this place, and are going up to the Temple.
But for God's sake get into that chariot, and drive back the
way you came."

She answered me with extraordinary calmness.

"Is my father well?"

"Quite well. But you can spare him this. Quick, into your
chariot. You can carry back the news to those who can help
us."

I remember the way she came down the portico steps, slowly
and deliberately. She never took her eyes off me, and I should
have known that she had never before been spoken to so
abruptly. She walked to the cistern where her two horses were

still holding their wet muzzles over the water. She caressed their noses.

"Why the temple, my friend?"

"Because," I said, "it is on high ground, and we can see over the country, and because it can be made more defensible than this rambling place."

She went on caressing her horses, and my impatience began to flare. It was like reasoning with a lovely but wilful child.

"Will you please go now."

She bent down, dipped her two hands in the water, and drank from them. She did this thrice, while I stood and fidgeted. I felt like picking her up and putting her into the chariot.

"Help is coming. I drove to tell you."

"Were they mad enough to let you go?"

She gave me a strange look.

"I did not ask them. I do not ask to do what I please to do. Aurelius Ambrosius is gathering his men. They may be here to-morrow, or the next day. Is not this silence strange?"

I lost my temper with her.

"Look here, you are not only risking your own life, but the lives of others. We have work to do up there before these savages can see what we are doing."

"What work?"

I could not say that she was sullen. Rather, there was a bitter sweetness in her obduracy.

"Building a breastwork, piling trees against the temple to blot it out, hiding the horses. Every minute is precious. Now, are you going, or—?"

"My horses are tired."

"Nonsense. Get across the river and you should be safe. Make for Calleva."

She gave me another queer, oblique look, stepped up into her chariot and gathered the reins. She did not say a word to me, and I thought that I had made her see reason. She turned her horses, and I mounted mine, and watched her take her horses out of the gate. I saw her raise her whip and beat them up.

But, instead of turning to the right and towards safety, she swung her horses to the left and towards the track leading up to the Black Down. I shouted at her, but it had no effect, and when I trotted out into the lane dust was flying from her chariot wheels.

CHAPTER TWENTY

I DO not know how far she had come that day, but her horses seemed less tired than Pegasus, and in spite of their having to pull her carriage they kept their lead along the lane. The chariot rolled and bounced along the rough road, fanning up a sheet of dust, and I wondered how Meona could keep her feet, for she drove standing. I was hot on her heels now, and hot in the head, for she had both fooled and flouted me, and I felt that I had made an ass of myself. It was not until she turned her horses up the track leading to the Black Down that I began to overhaul her. The drag of the chariot told on the steepish slope, and she hauled her horses in and made them walk.

I drew up beside her. I said: "You are more merciful to your beasts than to those who would think for you."

She looked straight over her horses' heads.

"Is it necessary for you to think for me? Who gave you that privilege?"

"This is a man's affair, my lady."

"How arrogant we have become! A little authority seems to have gone to your head."

247

Her sarcasm stung me.

"Do you think my lord your father will be pleased to see you at such a time?"

"Is there any reason why I should not see my father?"

"But, Meona—"

"Let me finish. Why should I not see my father, give him good tidings, and go upon my way? There is a road, my friend, past the temple, and it leads to Pontes and the West. Have you forgotten it?"

She had me, yet even when one is in love one may want to feel justified by circumstances. We had reached the brow of the hill, with the beechwood towering in front of us, and with some ostentation I turned my horse and pulled up. I told her that I wanted to watch the Downs for any sign of our enemies. Meanwhile, it behoved her to get her horses under the cover of the trees so that she should not betray us to the Saxon scouts. I added that white horses could be conspicuous.

Instead of humouring me she stopped her horses, and facing about, stood looking across the valley.

"Are you sure you are not imagining things?"

"Festus was not imagining things. Besides, other things have happened since you left us."

She was frowning and scanning the green ridge opposite.

"I can see some deer, my friend, but deer are harmless, save in autumn when the stags are bellowing. Perhaps your eyes are not as good as mine."

"I grant you every superiority."

"Thank you, Pellias. And what were the other happenings?"

"Can you, by any chance, see a long green mound on the ridge? I think it still shows some of the raw chalk."

"I can see something. What is it?"

"A grave."

She turned her head sharply.

"A grave! Have you been fighting again?"

"Well, yes. We ambuscaded the Saxon raiding-party that had been burning and slaughtering in our valleys."

She was looking at me now with fierce black eyes.

"Ha, and you overthrew them?"

"We buried some ninety dead bodies in that grave."

"Who led our people?"

"I had that honour."

She was smiling, as though exulting over that slaughter. She shook her hair, turned, gathered up the reins, and spoke to her horses. I let her go. I drew my horse into the shade of the beeches, and sat watching the Downs. I could see the little fawn shapes of the distant deer moving among the thorns and yews, but nothing else. The wind, such as it was, was coming from the south-west. If our enemies were near would those wild beasts be browsing so placidly? And then I saw a strange thing. A beast that seemed bigger than the others had wandered close to the Saxon grave. Suddenly, its head went up. It swung round and trotted off, and there was swift disorder among the herd. Was it that the deer had scented death and fled from some nameless terror, or had they been stampeded by the sight or scent of live men? I waited there under the trees for another five minutes, but the Downs showed me nothing. I took it that the deer had been frightened by the smell of death.

I rode into the wood. Half-way through it the track opened into a little clearing, and the great trees stood about it like the pillars of a peristyle. I could remember this place, and its sudden sunlight in the midst of the green glooms, and the pool in the centre of a cup of grass where the drip and shade of the beeches did not kill all other growth. The pool was a smother of water-crowfoot and looked as though snow had fallen on it. A spear of sunlight slanted down between the tops of two trees. Meona was kneeling by the pool on a little cushion of turf, and her two horses were nosing the grass. She did not seem to hear me, but might have been some Cassandra looking in a glass darkly. The droop of her shoulders and the lovely curve of her neck filled me with sudden compassion and anguish. How was it that women could look so douce and gentle and yet be so hard?

I stopped my horse on the edge of the clearing. She appeared so remote and mysterious that I vowed I would not go blundering in again upon her aloofness to be rebuffed. I saw her dabble her hand in the water, and push aside some of the white flowers of the water-weed. I saw bubbles rise to the surface. She watched them as though they had some secret meaning for her.

I sat very still.

How long was she going to keep me loitering here when there was so much to be done?

The white horses were nibbling the grass.

Suddenly, she sat back on her heels and looked at me, her hands resting on her knees.

"Can you see ghost-pictures in water, Pellias?"

"No," I said, "I cannot."

Her face had grown soft and shadowy. She looked into the deeps of the wood where the grey and crowded trunks of the trees dwindled into a kind of twilight. I saw her lips move. Then, in one swift movement she was on her feet, and walking away from the pool towards the place where the trackway left the clearing. Was she fey, sleep-walking, obsessed by something she had seen in the water?

I turned my horse and followed her.

"Meona, you have forgotten something."

"No."

She gave a kind of bird-cry and the two horses raised their heads, and like two creatures moved by the same instant impulse, trotted softly after her.

Her mood had changed. She was the most baffling and wayward of creatures, and her face had changed with her mood. It was a woodland face, or that is how I would describe it, a soft and shadowy mask, not a hard white profile, ice in the sunlight. I wondered what had changed her mood. Had she, like some Cassandra, seen sad and tragic things in that woodland pool? Could one believe in such magic? But, after all, this ghost-game of mine had translated me into the thick of such mysteries.

She walked through the wood, and I rode beside her two patient horses and her chariot. I, too, tried to be patient, and to follow her like those two white beasts. She might be wiser than I was, wiser than all of us, and somehow sensing that which was hidden from our mortal eyes. Not till we reached the open heathland and the sunlight did she come out of remoteness, and turn and speak to the horses as though they understood her better than I did.

She called them Castor and Pollux, and she rubbed both their noses so that there should be no jealousy between them. Meanwhile, I was looking across the valley to Farley Heath and the temple. I could see figures moving, and the white pillars and walls of the little building, and even while I was looking a green veil spread over the north-east corner of the temple. So, our people were wasting no time. They had begun to fell birch trees and pile them as a screen. Meona was still caressing her horses, and I am afraid a sudden puckishness

prompted me to keep her from looking towards
until the temple had been blotted from the landsc

I said: "How old are the Heavenly Twins?"

It was only when she looked at me queerly
what a silly question I had asked her.

"You should know, my friend. It was your
them."

My hypothetical, dead father, Gerontius! Anu ..
displayed proper grief for his violent end? Nor had I eve
entered the house that had been his.

I tried to laugh away the lapse.

"But are not Castor and Pollux timeless and immortal?"

Her face had lost its softness. She looked at me with a perplexed severity.

"Do not trifle. There is a strangeness about you, O son of
Gerontius."

I said: "Perhaps I have suffered much."

"Is that so? Have you yet crossed the threshold of your
father's house?"

"No."

"And why?"

"Sometimes one shirks certain memories."

Again her face softened. I have never seen a more mobile,
light and shadow face. She gave a last caress to the white
muzzles of her horses, walked to the back of the chariot,
stepped into it and gathered up the reins. I glanced at the
further hill, and saw that the temple had been blotted out, and
that the heath might have been the heath of my other world.
I wondered whether she would notice it. H
begun to move th

had been translated with me into the future?

Suddenly, I saw her pull on the reins. She held the horses in, and her startled eyes surveyed the further hill. I saw that she was frightened.

"Where is the temple?"

"Can you not see it?"

"No. But I see—"

"What if it had vanished?"

"Don't talk like that. It is dangerous to talk like that on these hills. There are strange spirits here."

So, she did believe in mysteries. But my heart went out to her and her frightened face.

"The temple is there, even though you cannot see it. Our men have been cutting down young trees and piling them round it. So, it will be no more visible to our enemies than it is to us."

I saw her draw her breath deeply.

"My friend, I think I should feel that I was in another world if the temple was not here."

Her simple words touched me. What if she knew that in my world there was no such temple, and that her world was just as strange to me as mine would have been to her?

But at last I had convinced her that time was precious, and that if I had been brusque with her it was because her safety was precious to me. Nor, I believe, does any woman resent masterfulness in a man when danger is in the air. She put her horses at a canter, as though to humour me, and I, realizing that the packhorse-man had obeyed my orders, and not confessed to my lord that Meona was in the valley, thought it kind to warn her.

"I am the only one who knows that you are here."

I saw her in profile, for the narrow way compelled her to keep her eyes upon her horses.

"How did you see me?"

"I had waited there above the valley to see whether our enemies were in sight."

"So, you think my father will be angry?"

"Well, I was angry."

She gave a little flick of the head that was characteristic of her, a kind of toss of her pride.

"Anger might be presumptuous. But my father will understand."

"Your recklessness!"

She flashed a momentary look at me.

"I do not like pedagogues. Pride is above prudence. We are noble people."

The simplicity of her sincerity was to me splendid. We moderns had lost that inevitableness.

"Yes, I grant you the courage."

"Does anything else matter when war is with us?"

We were climbing the long, gradual northern slope of the heath, and suddenly she turned her horses into another sandy track which skirted the lower slope. Her lips were smiling. I was about to ask her why she had changed direction. There must be some reason for it, and turning in the saddle I looked back, to find that the high woods on Black Heath hid the Downs. I glanced again at her, and her smile teased me.

"Are all women fools, my friend?"

She pointed with her whip.

"I know the ways. If you use your eyes you will see that my father and his people passed this way. Look at the sand."

The sandy surface was pocked with fresh hoof-marks and the patterns of men's sandals.

"You see?"

"The pedagogue accepts the whip."

"It is as well. This track goes round the hill under those woods. We can come by it to the temple. My white horses will not show on this green sea."

So, it was we who sprang a complete surprise upon our people, for we came up through the further woods to where our horses had been hidden. So well hidden were they that but for men's voices we should have passed them by. The astonished face of the first man who saw Meona and her white pair was a tribute to her unexpectedness, and also to what she symbolized. He was a Honey Valley man, and he stared at her as though the Genius Loci had descended upon this sacred hill to bless and hearten its people. He ran to us and bending low, kissed the hem of her garment as she stood in the chariot. Then he began to dance about and shout: "The Lady Meona is here, the Lady Meona is here."

They must have regarded her sudden coming as a good omen, and as a manifestation of the intervention of the gods and of fate. They crowded round, and made so much noise that I raised my arm to silence them, but I must confess that they took no notice of me at all. But when Meona put up her hand they were silent.

"Greetings, my children. I am here and I bring good news. Take my horses and care for them."

It amused me to hear her address these fellows as her children, for some of them were going grey in the head, but they crowded round the horses and chariot like a lot of eager boys, all scuffling and scrambling with each other to carry out her orders.

I may have acquired some sort of reputation as a fighting-man, but to these peasants I was no more than the steward's

son, when their lord's daughter swam like the moon into their
sky. It was not that I was piqued, but the incident did provoke
me to quote history, and to remind myself that in the Roman
culture even a freedman could become his master's friend
and deputy. Which, after all, was a foolish reflection,
for what permanence had I, a ghost-man, in this ancient
world? I got off my horse, and led him into the wood, decid-
ing that Meona would not need me in her meeting with her
father. Also, I seemed to become sorely conscious of my un-
reality. This was all a dream, and yet a terribly consecutive
and persistent dream. It was not like any experience I had
ever heard of, save in such fables as the Sleepers of Ephesus and
Rip Van Winkle. I remember twisting the bridle round my
fingers. It was good leather, and completely objective. So was
my horse's neck when I patted it. The trees were solid trees,
and so was the sandy soil under my feet. Where and what
was I? Could a congeries of electrons and protons spin backwards in the time scheme? I thought of the table beloved of
psychologists, the table of the senses, the table of other realities
or of no realities, and how the two tables might be imagined
occupying different situations here, now, and then. How one's
vision was clouded by one's senses! How little did man know
of the possibilities that might lie outside the ground-glass case
of his particular dimension! The mystery remained. Why did
we play like complacent children in a nursery, with the lights
on and the curtains drawn, and chant the new credo: "There
are no fairies. Everything we know and can know is here.
God is only a silly old gentleman in a white nightshirt." Why
do we not pull up the blind and look and wonder, even though
our poor little faces may be plugged up against dark glass?

I strolled further into the wood, for I was feeling a rather

pile of saddles, with Meona standing beside him. She did not look at me. She was frowning, and I gathered that words had passed between these two. One could see the Downs through the foliage of the birches. It was like standing just inside a wood and looking through a film of leaves at the landscape.

My lord turned to me.

"Pellias, my son, there are occasions when one speaks one's mind without covering the words with silk. Tell me, what would you do with a contumacious young woman who will not be advised?"

His voice was both angry and ironic, and he put me in a quandary, for Meona's face was not helpful.

"I should appeal to her good sense, sir."

At that my lord laughed.

"The philosophers have argued that the virtue has been denied to women. It would seem that you young things welcome danger. My daughter brings me news that my brother is sending strong succor to us, and that within the next few days he will join us in person. Meanwhile, we have this added challenge on our hands. What would you do with it?"

This was indeed a challenge to me! I was gazing through the green leaves at the Downs, and I saw there something that saved me from answering his question. I could see a stretch of the Ridgeway, and moving along it a thing that suggested a huge multi-colored snake. I did not even stop to answer Aurelius's question, but ran round the portico, and shouted to the men who were at work.

"Lie down, keep flat. The Saxons are on the Downs. They must not see you."

The men obeyed me, though one or two of them had a look at the distant ridge before throwing down mattock and spade.

Festus, who had been in charge of the men who were felling trees for a stockade, came striding through the heather, and I shouted to him, pointed, and signed to him to take cover. He went down in the heather, and I saw him crawl through it to the vallum, and lie there scanning the line of the chalk-hills.

I returned to the north side of the temple. Meona was leaning into the foliage of the piled trees, but my lord had not moved from his seat.

"So, they are there, Pellias. My eyes are too old for me to see them."

I went and stood by Meona, and together we watched the Saxon army crawling along the green ridge opposite. I grant it the honour of being dubbed an army, for in those days a thousand men was a formidable force in Britain. These barbarians loved colour, and the skin of that crawling snake seemed iridescent with many colours. It flashed and glistened. The head of the column was made up of horsemen, and no more than half a dozen wagons rolled along in the rear. I was conscious of a feeling of excitement, of fierce tension, but my head was as clear as the sky. Would our enemies discover the grave where their dead were buried, and if so would they turn aside in search of vengeance? And would they discover any revealing signs of our presence upon the temple heath?

I glanced for a moment at Meona. Her arms were spread, her hands gripping the trunks of two trees. Her face looked very white and set in the greenish light. Her lips were pale and pressed together. It was not the face of one who was afraid. Her eyes were the eyes of a fierce bird ready to strike.

I heard my lord's voice.

"Are they many, Pellias?"

"I should say a thousand, sir."

It v.
both Meona ...
of a Norman descript...
manning their breastworks a...
looked and sounded to the Normans lik...
dogs.

Meona's hand touched my arm and clasped it.

"Did you hear?"

Both of us believed that that faint yet grim ululation had sounded the doom of the great house in the valley. My lord too had heard it, and his old face seemed to grow haggard.

"Ye gods, I had forgotten! He must have left for Calleva this morning."

"Someone must be sent to warn him. Call Festus."

I went and called Festus who was still lying in the heather watching our enemies. Who was Maximus? I could suppose that Maximus was Ambrosius's son, and that he was leading those who were riding to succour us. My lord's anxiety was obvious. If Ambrosius's people rode blindly into danger, and disaster overtook them, the blame would be ours.

My lord did not waste a moment. Had Festus a horse that was fresh? He had. And did Meona know by which road Maximus and his men would be riding? Yes, he would come by the Calleva-Pontes road, as she had done, but he would turn off short of Pontes, and follow the by-road that crossed the Hogs Back and made for the bridge across the Wey. No doubt the Saxons were heading for that same bridge, and were marching to surprise either Pontes or Calleva.

Festus had his orders. He was to ride like the devil for the bridge across the Wey and make it before our enemy could seize it. He must meet young Maximus on the road and warn him, and counsel him to retreat upon Calleva and wait until his father should join him with his forces. Meanwhile, we would lie concealed on Farley Heath, and be ready to hold it as an advanced post. Festus should wait upon Aurelius Ambrosius, hear what he proposed to do, and then return to us. If Aurelius Ambrosius felt himself sufficiently strong to give battle to the Saxons, we might plan to join him, and perhaps, if fortune favoured us, attack our enemies in the rear.

I went with Festus to see him mounted, and to urge our men on to work upon the defences.

CHAPTER TWENTY-ONE

My LORD made no attempt to send Meona away. Maybe he thought her to be safer with us than storming about the country with her two white horses. Maybe, that during these bitter days, he was glad to have her with him. The sacred *cella* was theirs. We rigged a curtain made of blankets across the little chamber, and my lord occupied one half, Meona the other. Robur and I had a bivvy of branches and heather in the temple enclosure, and our men built themselves shelter of the same sort against the vallum. It seemed that we had solved our problem as completely as it could be solved with the data that were available. We posted our outposts and our watchers, and sat down to wait.

This active life seemed to reduce itself to its simple elements. Even as I describe it I am conscious of a sense of childishness. The complex and studied cleverness of my other self appeared to be going to sleep. One did not think of the smart or the clever thing to say; something was desired and had to be expressed, and one just expressed it. The only soul to whom I could talk intimately was to my lord, and I discovered that in

263

spotty arrogance, its raucous, bullying truculence.

"Need the young be like that?"

"Judge for yourself, my son. What is it that has driven us up here? The new, hairy, semi-savage youngness of a Germanic tribe."

How like were our two ages! Rome had grown old in creating an ordered system, and here were these young savages sweating to destroy it. Would it always be so? Need it be so? Shades of the League of Nations, could man never transcend a swaggering, tempestuous, blatant cad like Hitler?

Here was I, a man out of the future, and chosen to experience the most fantastic experiment in Time, and yet I could not see three days ahead of me. No, not even one day. I did not know how near the tragedy was to me, even though I was conscious of a curious restlessness, a kind of vague sweet anguish such as a spring day instils into one with its strange, vivid, bitter beauty. Is there anything more joyous and more poignant than a blackbird's song, when there is frost in the May air, and the sky has brittle and treacherous eyes? I felt haunted by something, I knew not what. Well, I was in love, disastrously in love. The stars sang, and their voices were the voices of tortured heroes. I was jealous, furiously jealous, even of old Robur and Meona's precious horses. She seemed to give more thought to them than she gave to me.

Peace reigned. We waited for Festus, and Festus did not come. We looked across at the serene hills which seemed to smile at our suspense and reproach us for it. Where was our danger? The hazard seemed to have passed us by, and we shared with the beasts and the birds an unvexed, manless world.

It was late on the afternoon on the second day when Meona

called to me. I was sitting on the grass in the sun, staring at nothing, and thinking of nothing in particular. Indeed, I was a throbbing vessel of emotion.

"Pellias, Pellias."

I started up, and went to her, and there was mystery in her manner. My lord was asleep on his couch in the temple *cella*. Old people seemed to be happy when they fall asleep.

"I have an adventure."

I felt that there was mischief in her mood, and I waited.

She said: "I have left my favourite hand-mirror in the house. I am going down there. Come with me."

My impulse was to tell her that she must do nothing of the kind, and that I would not humour such a silly hazard, but she must have read my face, and she laughed at me.

"If you are afraid I will go alone."

"You will not."

"Where is the danger? This land is an empty land. And I have a desire to see the great old house. It must be so unhappy, so perplexed."

Her words moved me, as all words that have a wildness of fancy must move one. Oh, for more such words, more strangeness, more mystery! We moderns seem to think in terms of horse-power; in cams and connecting rods, voltages, calories. The fairies have been eliminated, God liquidated, oh, wonderful world beloved of the Germans, when they have put a hoof on some small nation's soul! A great, empty house in a deserted valley! A ghost place! I knew now that I should go with her, and that we were like two children setting out to explore some mysterious and magic castle. Was her mirror of silver or of bronze? What did it matter? I buckled on my sword, which was lying on the grass beside me. I was becom-

I w...
In truth, I ...

exquisite muteness of my own self-questioning. What did this mood of hers mean for me? I had never known her like this, and I wanted to be alone for a moment with my wild hopes and fears. I am afraid I forgot all caution. I went leaping down into the valley. I felt like quicksilver. I came to a gate and a hedge, and I went over the gate like air. I can remember reading in some Greek history of hoplites leaping in the market-place of a city, and in the haphazard way in which one's thoughts interweave themselves I wondered how a fighting-match between Greek hoplites and German savages would have ended.

I came down through an orchard. It had a hedge and a gate flanking the lane. I admit that I became more cautious here, for any recklessness of mine might involve Meona in disaster. The only live things I saw were two hens dusting themselves in a dust patch beside the road. I followed the lane past the mill, keeping on the grass and close to the hedge, and stopping every twenty yards or so to listen. I saw a big bird floating overhead. It may have been a buzzard or an eagle, but it made me think of a scouting aeroplane. I could see the grey sweep of the courtyard wall. The silence was utter save for the voices of the birds. I slipped along the wall to the open gateway, peered round the pillar, and saw two white pigeons preening themselves upon the stone water-cistern. The great house looked just as we had left it, open-mouthed and wide-eyed, but I wanted to be sure that it hid no enemy. I reached for the chain of the porter's bell, and with one eye round the gate-pillar, set the bell pealing. Nothing happened. The great house gazed at me as though it considered my carefulness rather foolish.

I returned to find Meona where I had left her. She had kept her promise to me, but she had been startled by hearing the ringing of the courtyard bell. When I told her that I had rung it to test the emptiness of the place, and to make sure that no Germans who had been taking a long siesta would come blundering out, she threw back her head and laughed.

"You are very careful of things, Pellias."

"When they are very precious, yes."

She put out her hand to me, and I bent and kissed it, and I dared to keep hold of her hand, and she let it stay in mine. Were we then lovers? Was this but another mood of lovely childishness, or did the woman in her understand? We went down through the orchard together, and along the lane with its riotous sweet hedges rich with the richness of June. It was the lovely season of the year, and every June I think of the Albury valley as it looked and smelt on the day when Meona and I walked hand in hand along it.

When we came to the courtyard gate she let go of my hand and stood gazing at the house. Its serenity and stateliness seemed to deny the horror of its being fouled by a barbarian beastliness. I kept silent. I felt that her mood had, for the moment, become remote and visionary. The two pigeons were still on the water-cistern, and one of them was courting and cooing to the other. Oh, brave bird, good luck to you!

Meona's voice came to me in a strange, soft whisper.

"Let me go in alone, Pellias. Then I will call you."

I saw her cross to the water-cistern and speak to the birds, hold out her hands, and one pigeon settled on her wrist, the other on her shoulder. They fluttered off again when she reached the portico. I saw her pause there for a moment, watching the two white birds with a smile on her face. Was this an omen? Then she disappeared, and instantly, now that she was out of my sight, a fierce uneasiness seized me. What

paused, shivered, let go of my hand, and went s˙
door. She opened it almost with stealth, peere˙
peared, to reappear a moment later with a br
clasped to her bosom. There was a kind of angu˙
her hand pressed the thing to her body.

"Let us go. The house frightens me."

She caught my hand, and we went quick
those mysterious doors to the sunlight on
portico. One of the white birds was cooing
on the Black Down green and serene in the
utter peace seemed to possess the valley.

Meona drew a deep, sharp breath.

"Why was I afraid? There is nothing
ness. This house has never been empt

Suddenly, I felt her fingers tighten
discord had come to us down in the v
and so did I, for this sound seemed
sense of distant horror. We stood l˙
questioning, challenged. I saw he

"What is it, oh, what is it?"

And suddenly I understood.
the distant shouting of many ˙
death-struggle.

CHAPTER TWENTY-TWO

*T*HE wind, such as it was, blew from the south-west, and the distant, ominous clamour seemed to come from the same quarter. I felt Meona leaning against me, and I put my arm about her.

I heard her say: "It must be Maximus. They are greeting each other."

That is what she wished to think, but the wild and distant broil of voices was not that of men meeting in vociferous welcome. Maximus it might be, or Aurelius Ambrosius with all his strength in sudden battle with the barbarians. Or, it might be? Were the Saxons in retreat, or had some fresh horde of them come marching towards the west? Had they surprised our people at the temple? I did not know what to think, and for the moment the horror of that prospect paralysed me.

"Pellias."

She was looking up into my face with fear and a question in her eyes.

"It may be—"

"Oh, let us go, let us go."

A wild eagerness to see and know took possession of us both.

We left the white pigeons in possession of the courtyard, and running together along the lane, climbed through the orchard and fields to the Black Down. She was out of breath when we reached the beech wood, and once within its shade, she leaned for a moment, panting, against a tree. The pinched pallor of her lovely little face ravaged me as she stood there with mouth open and nostrils wide. I was listening, but the stillness was utter. That wild, battling clamour either had died away, or the great wood blanketed it. Her eyes watched my face.

"Can you hear anything?"

I shook my head, and she swayed away from the tree, and began to run, still holding the mirror in her hand. The air seemed heavier among these towering trees, and I could hear her panting. I ran by her side, and laid my hand gently upon her shoulder.

"Wait here, Meona, while I go on and look."

But she would have none of it.

"No, don't leave me, Pellias."

"Stay and get your breath."

"No, no."

I wanted to save her from rushing with those frightened eyes of hers upon some possible horror, but I realized that she could not bear to be left alone, and that she was wild to know what was happening. I saw the sky, and the trees thinning in front of us, and I caught her by the arm and held her back as we came toward the open heathland. I did not mean her to rush recklessly into danger, and betray herself. I do not think I had any thought of my own safety.

"Steady, my dear, steady. Make for that big tree over there."

She gave me a wounded look, but she obeyed. One big beech

r
d

trem-

"Maybe th_

think we ought to do,

way along the edge of the vall_y

with my lord and his people."

She closed her eyes for a moment.

"I do not believe that you believe, Pellias, that that is wh_
has happened."

Dear God, what was I to say to her? Very gently I kissed
her hair.

I made her lie down in the heather and fern beside me on
the edge of the wood, and from there we watched the opposite
hill. I was wondering what the devil to do, for, even if Aurelius and our people had escaped scatheless, Meona and I were
in a pretty perilous position. We had no horses, no food, no
shelter for the ni_h_   l our only chance seemed to be that
                          the woods and get across the Wey,
                          l the roads and trackways would be
                          · chin on my fists and watched the
                          about it. I am afraid that I was in
                          d not believe that our people had

escaped. The wild cries that had reached us in the valley had been the cries of men in combat. Again, I was puzzled by something I saw over there, little round objects bobbing up and down like coco-nuts stuck on sticks. Did these savages carry war-maces? It was damned unintelligent of me, but I did not divine what those objects were.

Meona was terribly restless, writhing with the anguish of suspense. Once, she got on her knees in the heather as though to see more clearly.

"I am going nearer. I must go."

I drew her down.

"Wait, my dear, wait. Do you think I am going to let you go to your death and worse? These Germans are wild beasts."

We must have been lying there for an hour when that which I had dared not hope for, happened. The barbarians were leaving the temple and its enclosure. A ragged mass of them began to stream along the hill-side, following the by-road towards the west. There must have been hundreds of them, and I suppose they were marching on to join their brothers who had come by way of the Chalk Ridge. What tragic fools we had been! I don't think it had occurred to any of us that more of these savages might take the road that linked up Stane Street with Pontes. We lay and watched our enemies pass down towards the valley, the gaudy colours of their cloaks and shields brilliant against the dark woods. We could hear them singing. And so they vanished from our sight into the early evening sunlight, and peace was upon the earth.

Peace! Meona was on her feet, and running through the heather. I caught her up and grasped her arm.

"No, my dear, I'm going up there."

"Let me go, Pellias."

"Not on my life. There may still be danger."

"Would you leave me alone here?"

"You can come half-way and hide, while I go on."

I think she realized that I was determined that she should not go with me, and I suspect that a part of her flinched from the thing we feared. We got down into a little valley, and followed it up towards the heath, and there I made her sit down under a solitary thorn tree while I went on. I crawled up through the heather like a hunter stalking deer, stopping now and again to raise my head and look. I could see no movement up yonder, hear nothing, and the silence scared me. What should I find? Crawling on I reached the edge of the fern and heather and saw the stretch of turf and the vallum and brushwood, and the roof and three pillars of the temple. I lay and listened. There was not a sound, and suddenly my very fear made me reckless. I wanted to get it over. I stood up, and with my sword ready, walked deliberately across the stretch of grass to the bank. I climbed it, and stood looking.

I have never known such cold horror as that which froze me. The place was a shambles, a chaos of corpses. They lay scattered, or tumbled upon each other in all kinds of dreadful attitudes. There was blood everywhere. But that was not the worst. I saw two spears stuck in the ground, and impaled upon them two horrible heads. I seemed to know those heads, in spite of the blood in their hair and upon their faces. One head had white hair. I was looking at the severed heads of Robur and my lord Aurelius.

Even while the horror of the thing was making me feel physically sick, I was able to thank the gods that Meona had not come with me. I remember turning and glancing back to make sure that she had not followed me. Yet, something stronger than myself was telling me what I had to do, in spite of my cold nausea and my impulse to turn and run. I could

ot deal with all these dead, but those two poor, dreadful heads
had to be rescued and hidden. Meona might yet insist upon
coming up to see her dead. I got down into that bloody enclosure, and stepping delicately, approached those terrible
symbols of defeat and victory. I could not bring myself to
look at them. I pulled the spears out of the ground, and keeping my eyes lowered, carried first one and then the other to
the ditch which our men had deepened. I laid them in the
ditch, and finding a spade, flung earth over them.

The whole place stank of blood, and I felt that if I stayed
there I should vomit. I was sweating, and yet I shivered and
was cold. I remembered our horses, and the men who were
guarding them, and a hope flickered in me that they might still
be lying hidden in the woods. I got out of the enclosure and
walked round it on the clean turf, and then ran for the woods
where I hoped to discover some live thing. It was in vain. I
found the glade, and it was empty. Meona's chariot and her
white horses had gone. I could only suppose that the men in
charge of the horses had fled when the bloody business had
started. Fugitives from the temple might have joined them.
All that I know was that Meona and I were alone with the
dead.

Good God, and I had to tell her!

What if she was determined to see the dead body of her
father?

And where was it, a hacked, and headless thing?

A mad rage began to burn in me, the rage of impotence.
I would like to have inflicted every sort of torture upon these
German beasts. I would have rushed at the chance of going
blood-mad against some not impossible odds, and of hacking
and killing even if I was to go down in the end. Never before
had I realized how flimsy are our conventional draperies, and

that we can be savage beasts, and all the more so when our sensitive souls have been splashed and shocked with blood.

The next thing I remember was Meona's face looking up at me from the heather. Why did she look at me like that? Was I horrible, a dreadful apparition? And then I realized that I must have carried on my countenance the stigmata of the horrors I had seen. There was no need for her to ask me questions.

Her face seemed to have gone very white and small, but the eyes were huge, and the mouth the mouth of one about to utter a cry, but whose spirit had been smitten with dumbness. I saw her looking at my hands, and then at my feet. I glanced at my hands. There were red smears on them, and my shoes had picked up the same dreadful stains. I saw her cover her face, and her kneeling figure was strangely and terribly still. Then, a shudder went through her. I heard her speak.

"Is my father among them?"

"All are dead."

I saw her shoulders shaking, and I wanted to comfort her, but I had a feeling that she did not want to be touched. The trembling passed. She seemed to go rigid and remote. Her hands dropped from her face, and uncovered her dry, dark eyes.

She said: "Come, I must see him."

This was the very thing I had dreaded. It was unthinkable that she should look upon all that slaughter. Thank heaven I had hidden that poor head! I could lie to her.

"You cannot see him, Meona. I have buried him."

She gave me a strange, wounded look, and rose from her knees.

"I must see him."

"No, my dear."

"You are lying to me, Pellias, out of kindness. You had not time to do all that."

I shook my head at her.

"I buried him in the ditch."

I do not know what tragic obstinacy possessed her, but she made as though to go up through the heather. The idea of her seeing all that horror terrified me. She should not go. I caught her, and gathering her in my arms, began to carry her towards the wood, but, for a moment, her passionate purpose fought against me. She struggled. She struck me in the face.

"Let me go, let me go."

I took her blows, and holding her against me, ploughed on through the heather towards the trees. Suddenly, her struggles ceased. She put her arms round my neck, and hid her face. She began to weep, and to weep most terribly.

"Forgive me, my friend."

I was scorched with tenderness by her tears.

"You are safe, Meona. That is how he would have wished it."

I carried her to the wood, and we sat down together under the great beech from which we had started. I had my back to the tree trunk, and I held her close to me with her head against my shoulder. She had ceased from weeping and her stillness was almost more tragic than her tears. Dear God, what an escape had been ours! I could not let myself think of what might have happened to her. I held her close and stroked her hands. I was trying to think of what I should do in this desperate dilemma. Here were we alone in a wilderness over-run by our enemies, without food, without shelter. I knew that my only hope was to get her to some place like

Calleva, and Calleva was twenty-five miles away. Moreover, those German swine might be at the gates of Calleva.

Or, should I try to make for London? Anyhow, action was the thing, action, and food of some sort. Dared we go down again to the house in the valley and try to rummage up food for the journey? It might take us two days, or longer, to reach Calleva, for we should have to avoid all roads and find our way across country. There was the river to be forded, for we could not risk the bridge.

I spoke to her at last.

"Meona, my duty is to carry you to some safe place. We shall have to go by foot."

Her head moved against my shoulder.

"Calleva, and your friends. We shall have to travel at night, and keep to the woods by day. And food?"

She said: "I am not hungry."

I let that pass.

"Have you the strength, Meona?"

She sat up and looked at me, and I saw that her spirit was rising like a new young flame.

"I shall have the strength. I have my purpose."

I understood her. She was thinking of vengeance, and so was I, for vengeance is sweet, whatever the dear old senti-mental gentlemen may say. I told her that I was going down to the valley to try and find some food. Yes, she would have to eat, for we should need our strength to outwit our enemies and to carry the news to those who might wipe out in blood this savage slaughter. She shuddered at the prospect of going down again into the valley, but I told her I would leave her on the hill-side and go down alone.

I did not go alone, for when it came to the point I did not

like leaving her, nor did she wish to be left.

"No, I will go with you, Pellias."

How bitter-sweet those words were to me after the ugly things I had seen! I took her hand, and with my sword drawn we went down into the valley. It was the same valley, with the sunlight shining more aslant it, peaceful and still, and yet how different for both of us! Of all those who knew it as the Honey Valley, Meona alone had survived. She was the young mistress and great lady of a dead place, and almost I was moved to think that the great house had known what was to happen, and that was why we had felt its silent, haunted terror.

In one of the orchards above the lane I became aware of the pressure of her fingers. She stood still, and I with her.

"Pellias."

"Meona."

"Swear to me one thing."

"What shall I swear?"

"That you will kill me, if needs be."

I understood her. A kind of horror of tenderness swept through me. I stood looking at her, and for the moment I was dumb. Could fate be so ruthless, that it would compel me to slay the thing I loved? I felt that I could not do it.

"Meona, life cannot be so merciless to us."

Her pale face grew fierce and passionate.

"Swear it, Pellias. What would my lot be?"

"Meona!"

"Swear it, by the gods and by your sword."

I bent my head, and taking my sword by the blade, kissed the crossed hilt.

"I swear it."

She laid a hand upon my head.

"That comforts me, that gives me courage."

I had sworn my oath, but, dear God, should I have the courage to honour it? Yet I too would be dead, slain in a last furious Berserker fight with those who had made me use my sword upon her.

CHAPTER TWENTY-THREE

So, WE did not leave each other, but like two lovers who have sworn a death-pact, we went down hand in hand into that dead valley. Yet, it was no more dead than we were confessed lovers, for though I loved her utterly, she was both near to me and remote. Moreover, there is such a virtue as chivalry, and to have plagued her with sex-stuff at such a time would have been blackguardly. My love was not of that sort, not fat Goering and his obese, mock-virgins, nor little scurrilous Goebbels chasing after other men's wives. Nor, as I said, was the valley dead. Nature carried on. The Tillingbourne had its own soft song to sing, and the birds were beginning vespers. The lovely greenness of the year was bitter-sweet, and somehow, now that we had sworn our pact, crude fear had left us. We dared fate and the unknown, and walking hand in hand along the lane, came to the courtyard gate.

More white pigeons were there, which was a happy omen. It crossed my mind that we might catch a brace of those birds and roast them, but I put the thought from me. We had had enough of blood. Let the creatures live and enjoy the sunlight.

286

I don't think it would have been in me to wring those white birds' necks.

As for food, life in Roman Britain was not tinned, and there was no Sainsbury round the corner, and in June the fruits of the earth are still immature in Nature's lap. No potatoes, no oranges, no bananas, no sardines! Meona led the way to the kitchen quarters and the cool dark dairy. We were to be more fortunate than I had hoped, for our hurried exodus had left some stores behind. Meona found a loaf of stale bread, a pot of olives, another pot of honey, and hanging from a beam were some dried fish and two smoked hams. It was the realist in me, and not the romantic, who exulted over that ham. I found a sack and stuffed both hams into it, also the bread, and Meona slipped the honey and the olives into a wallet we found hanging on the wall. Her pale, unsmiling face made this provision-business seem all the stranger, nor was there any hunger in either of us for the moment.

We left the sack and wallet in the vestibule, and Meona walked down the corridor to the summer-room. I did not know whether she wanted me to follow her, but she beckoned to me, and I went. That spacious and serene room saddened me. There was my lord's chair, and as I gazed at it I was conscious of a pang of desolation. The only creature who knew my secret or could know it, was dead. I saw Meona go to the *lararium* and draw the curtain across it. This was indeed the twilight of her gods. She also drew the curtains across the windows. I remember her passing down the corridor and closing all the doors.

"Is it the end, Pellias? Shall I ever come back here?"

"Of course you will come back."

I do not think she believed me. She bade me close the outer doors, and while I was doing it she went and shut the shutters of the summer-room. I heard birds singing, and the pigeons cooing. How little did Nature care for man's male madness! I had the sack over my shoulder, and Meona's wallet slung on the other side, and as I stood there the shadow of a cloud fell across the courtyard. Where were we to sleep? In the woods? Well, could I not find something with which to cover her?

She came back to me with silence in her eyes.

"Meona, can I find a coverlet or something?"

She looked at me vaguely.

"We shall have to sleep in the woods."

She gave me a nod of the head, and re-opening the doors, went in, to return with a coverlet and a cloak. I told her to fold them and lay them over the sack. Then we walked down to the gate, with the pigeons running round our feet. Meona stretched out a hand as though blessing them.

"Good-bye, my dears."

We closed the courtyard gates behind us, and crossing the lane to a cottage garden, made our way up it and through an orchard to a hayfield below the woods. A little breeze came up the valley and made the long grass run away from our feet. The whole field seemed to be in movement with its white daisies and its sorrel and looking at Meona I saw that her hair had blown loose upon her shoulders. I had not seen her very black hair free in the wind before, nor had I seen any hair like that in my modern world of crimped curls and little baldish foreheads. Somehow, it made her look like a lovely child, but that pale and poignant face was no child's face. Those eyes had seen death and disaster, and the end of happy things.

We reached the woods and edged along them, keeping to cover, for the woods were open and without coppice. We still had two or three hours of daylight, and I wondered if we could reach the Wey before night fell, and creeping down to it in the twilight, swim across. Could Meona swim? I asked her the question, and she shook her head, and that set me the problem of getting her across. She told me that there was a ford near the bridge, but I decided that we could dare neither bridge nor ford.

This woodland journey gave me an added sense of solitude. We might have been Adam and Eve in a primeval world, but even against this feeling was set the knowledge that at any moment we might come upon our enemies. Savages in these very English woods! I might have been playing the kind of game one played as a small boy, but this was a grim game fierce with reality. I was on the alert all the time, watching the tree trunks and the shadows and the elusive streaks of sunlight. I don't think any place can be more eerie than a wood when its green glooms may hide fear and death. Yes, this was a jungle game, and the stake the life of the creature whom I loved. I know that when we came to the more level and open country, I got the wind up rather badly, and made Meona sit down and rest while I crawled about scouting. I could see nothing of our dear friends, and I could assume that if they were pushing on to join their other body, they would be well ahead of us, and over the Wey.

I could see the road crossing the plain. Scattered trees and bushes gave one some cover, and in the west the wild and wooded hills and valleys north of Godalming welcomed us. I should like to have loitered here till twilight, but there was the river to be crossed, and it occurred to me that I might find something for Meona to cross in. I had visions of a British coracle. I went back to Meona, and put the chances to her, and found that she was all for action.

We made haste down into the broad valley which was like

parkland, and when we came to the road we dashed across it for a group of trees. As we had crossed the road its gravelly surface had suggested the passing of many feet. There was not a living creature to be seen. I asked Meona if she knew in which direction we should bear, and she stood a moment, looking under her hand, for the level sunlight was in our eyes.

She pointed.

"You see where the woods curve round, Pellias?"

"Yes."

"The river lies over there in those meadows."

We made for the line of woods towards which she had pointed. The ground shelved gently from them to the meadows, and the evening sunlight lay spread upon the grass. It was very blinding was this light, with the great yellow sun blazing at us just when I wanted to be so sure of the ground ahead of us. I thought I could see the gleam of water and the green tangle of the water-weeds along the banks, nor could I make out any sign of life. I must have been tired and irritable and over-wrought, for I cursed the sun, which was rank blasphemy.

"With this glare I cannot see."

I felt her touch my arm, and when I looked at her there was something in her eyes that moved me to self-shame.

"Wait, there is no hurry, Pellias."

There was a new and intimate quality in her voice, a little tang of tenderness.

"I feel so responsible."

"For the sun, my dear, and everything?"

"For you, and my promise."

Her fingers clasped my arm.

"Is it nothing to me that you should have to face so much

for my sake? There is no hurry. Let us sit here until the sun is below those hills."

"Forgive me," I said. "Maybe, what I feel, is fiercer than my patience."

"You have been very patient with me, Pellias."

Her words had for me the exquisite touch of a caress. I wanted to blurt out things to her, my love and how I would serve her in death and until death. I bent my head and kissed the hand that rested on my arm.

"Meona, I would give you anything I have, honour and strength and faith. Yes, be patient with me. We will wait here till the old sun goes down."

We sat in silence and close together under a tree until that yellow disc sank gradually behind the hills. The valley below us was brilliant with diffused light. I could see everything now, the colour, the detail against the blackening woods. There was the river, one loop of it, like a silver sickle. I could distinguish some black object projecting from the near bank like the trunk of a dead tree that had fallen into the water. Was it a tree or a boat? I stood up in my excitement and pointed it out to Meona.

"Are we in luck? What do you see there?"

She thought it was a dead tree, an old alder that had rotted and fallen into the river. There were other alders along the bank, but I still believed that providence might have blessed us with a boat. I told her to wait there while I went down and explored. A line of willows crossed the meadows along a ditch, and I followed the cover of these trees, and coming to the bank, found a grass path along the edge of it, one of those paths where the turf has been compressed by the comings and goings of men and beasts. The water was covered with a sheet of limpid light, and I saw the dark object projecting from the water-weeds. It was not a dead tree, but a clumsy boat, flat bottomed and snub-nosed. It was tied to a post, and there was a pole in it.

I got to the place and waved to Meona. The afterglow was full upon her, and she looked like some white and purple flower growing on the edge of the woods. She raised an arm, and I pointed to the willows, and she came running down under the droop of their graceful foliage, and in a minute she was with me.

"It is no dead tree," I said. "Someone must have used this as a ferry."

I helped her in, piled our gear on the back seat, for there was half an inch of water in the bottom of the boat. I bent down with my back to her to unknot the rope, and I became aware of those stains on my hands. God, I must get rid of them! I pretended to drop the rope into the water and fumbling at the knot, managed to wash away those bloody stains.

We must have crossed the Wey somewhere north of Godalming. There was a good deal of marshy ground on the other side of the river, and a narrow causeway traversed it. I did not like this causeway, for there was no cover, and in the very brilliant glare of the afterglow I knew that we could be seen by any prowling savage. I went first, carrying the sack and the coverlet, and I must have gone at a devil of a pace, and rather too fast for Meona, for, looking round, I saw distress on her face. She was growing weary.

"Sorry, Meona, this open country is dangerous."

But I slackened speed, and soon we were among meadows and willows and poplars. It was Compton country, but however lovely and peaceful it might be as the green grey dusk

flowed over it, I wanted the wilder hills and woods. We bore
to the left along an old track-way, and it brought us, as I had
hoped it would, to the high ground on the south. We must
have been near the site of Charterhouse. It was growing dark
now, and I sighted some old yews on the slope of a hill, and
I turned aside here, and dropped my sack on the grass.

"Shelter for the night, Meona."

She had been limping and she sat down on the grass.

"Footsore?"

She nodded, and my love felt very tender towards her.
There was a beech wood higher up the hill. The weather had
been dry, and I took the coverlet and filled it with dead beech
leaves and brought them back and spread them under a yew.
I went thrice for leaves before I had made a bed. She sat there
in the half darkness, aloof and silent, and yet I felt that she
was watching me. I took my sword and cut off some yew
boughs from another tree, and piled them into a bower under
the yew. That would give her double shelter, and what I
wanted her to feel, that the little refuge was wholly hers.

"That will keep the dew from you. I'll shake down under
one of these other trees."

I had spread the coverlet on the leaves.

"I'll stuff the wallet for you to make a pillow."

I saw her face as a little white streak. How silent she was!
Did she trust me? I saw her reach for the wallet and empty it
on the grass beside her.

"Give me the sack, Pellias."

I gave it to her, and she drew the little dagger from her
girdle.

"This is my service, my friend. Sit here by me. Even heroes
must eat."

I think I laughed self-consciously.

"No hero—this, but just—"

"Sit down by me. It comforts me to have you close."

Even in the midst of tragedy there can be humour, and when she drew one of those hams out of the sack, she did not know what to do with it. Her lap was no place for a ham, and her perplexity was so potent that I could have laughed had laughter been possible on such a day.

"Oh, Pellias!"

There was Cassandra pathos even in this dismay over a ham, and I took the thing from her and held it by the knuckle end while she cut slices, skewered them out with the point of her dagger and dropped them into my palm. I laid the ham on the grass beyond the yew boughs, and held out my hand for her to take her share. The bread was easier. It was in the form of a flat cake, and one just broke pieces off with one's fingers. We had begun the meal, sitting there side by side in the darkness, when I remembered that we had no water, and nothing to hold it if we had it, unless I used my helmet. Could she drink from so common a vessel? As for the honey, she soon solved that problem. She made me give her my bread and poking her dagger into the pot, skewered out honey and spread it on my bread for me.

I said: "I was a fool not to think of water."

She told me that she was not thirsty. I was, and I inferred that her need was like mine. Where could one find water on a dark and strange hill-side? Besides, she might want to wash her hands. The idea of washing reminded me that I had nothing to shave with, and that I should look a sloven until we died or reached Calleva.

She had finished her own bread and honey.

"I can find water, Pellias."

"You? How?"

"I have the feeling. What shall we put it in?"

"There is nothing but my helmet."

"Give me your helmet."

I gave it to her and she rose, and I made as though to rise too.

"No, stay here. I shall not go far."

I understood, and I obeyed her, though I did not like her wandering off alone in this dim light. I sat and listened, with my sword across my knees, ready to spring up and run to her if I heard her voice. I did not think that she would find water, but find it she did. She was back with me in less than three minutes, and holding out the helmet to me in her hands.

"Drink, Pellias."

I was astonished.

"You found it?"

"Yes, a little spring. I can divine water. It comes out of the hill-side. Drink."

"You first, if you can bear such a beaker."

"I have drunk. Drink, dear friend."

Her words must have put wine into that water. I half emptied the helmet, and then I put it aside upon the grass.

"Would you wash, Meona?"

"Presently."

She sat down beside me with her arms folded over her knees, and I, with her words still in my ears, could hardly dare to look at her even in the dim light, because I loved her so.

I remember filling the wallet with leaves, and giving it to her, and telling her that I was going to play sentinel for an hour or two. I adjured her to lie down and try and sleep, for we should have a long and rough journey on the morrow. She crept into the yew-bower, but she had forgotten the coverlet, and I passed it to her, and when she had spread it, I tucked it round her feet.

"But you have nothing, Pellias."

"I have the cloak, and I can collect some leaves."

And then, I left her, so that she could feel herself safe and secure in that green niche. I went to and fro between the yew grove and the beech wood, collecting cloakfuls of leaves, and I spread them under the yew tree next to hers. I moved about very quietly, and now and again I stood listening. The night was utterly still, with not a leaf moving, and the darkness had become intense. Also, it was growing cold, damned cold, and I walked up and down on the hill-side to try and warm myself, with the cloak over my shoulders.

I must have been listening for any sound from her green tent, and presently I heard something, a sound that went through and stabbed me. She was weeping. I heard her sobs, little spasms of woe which she seemed to be trying to stifle. I could not leave her to weep like that, alone in the darkness. I crept up to her shelter, and knelt down, and spoke to her.

"Meona, would to God I could help."

Her hand came out and touched me.

"Hold my hand, Pellias."

I knelt there, holding her hand and stroking it, and presently her weeping ceased. Her breathing grew quiet. I knew that she must be very weary, and I willed her to fall asleep. She did fall asleep. Her hand grew limp. I laid it down very gently, and taking the cloak from my shoulders, spread it over her. Then, I crept away, and went to my nest of leaves, and tried to burrow into it like a hare into its form. But it was damned cold that night, and I did not sleep very much, but my heart was warm in me and happy.

CHAPTER TWENTY-FOUR

❧

J woke very early, just when the sky was growing grey, and the birds were beginning to sing. There seemed to be birds all round us, and the whole hill-side throbbed with their singing. I was feeling stiff and cold, and like one of the Babes in the Wood whom the robins had covered with dead leaves. I scrambled out of my nest, and saw the valley below us filmed with mist, and a pale yellow glow where the sun was rising. I took a peep at Meona and saw that she was still asleep, curled up under the cloak, her hair flung about her. She looked like a child. But I wanted to get warm, and work the stiffness out of my limbs, and I ran to and fro along the hill-side until I felt thawed. Then I remembered the spring of water Meona had found, and the direction she had taken, and in a little while I discovered the spring, a green cleft that dribbled clear water into a small pool. I knelt down and looked at my untidy head and smudged chin in this nature's mirror. I dashed water over my head and face, and put my hair in some sort of order. Then I took off my shoes and washed my feet. They needed it after the foot-slogging of yesterday.

I remembered that Meona had finished the day limping. What could one do for such a chafe? Would a dock leaf be of any use? But, perhaps, she would know of something. I estimated that we had at least another twenty-five miles to cover before we could make Calleva, and that it might take us two days unless we came upon some homestead that was not deserted, and could hire horses and a guide. I was a little vague about the lie of the land, but I reckoned that if we went west, and bore up to the chalk hills about Basingstoke, we should find ourselves near the road that led from Winchester to Calleva. I was still muddling up my English and Romano-British place-names.

Before lying down to sleep I had packed our food into the sack and slung it over a yew bough where it would be safe from any creature prowling on the ground. I took the sack down and got out the provisions, using the sack as a rustic tablecloth. Meona was still sleeping, and I collected my helmet and refilled it at the spring, and carrying it back, put it ready for her. I was turning away, when I heard a little sound like a moan.

"Oh, oh, the pain of waking!"

How utterly helpless one can feel when the creature whom one loves is in anguish, be the pain physical or emotional. I turned and looked into the green cleft of the yew bower. She was sitting up, leaning back with her body supported by her arms, her face upturned, her throat showing. It was as though a sudden spasm of pain had been shot through her in that moment of returning consciousness. Almost, the reawakening anguish rocked her. Her eyes had a blind brightness. Even her clouding hair was tragic.

I was groping for something to say to her.

"There is water in the helmet, Meona."

She did not seem to hear me. Her eyes were set in a dead stare.

"Have I slept? How could I sleep!"

Her tense, immobile figure came suddenly to life. She was up and out of the shelter. She put her arms above her head with a kind of writhing movement. Her eyes had a sudden, strange brightness. She looked at the misty valley where the sun was making a golden haze; she looked at my helmet of water, at the food spread on the sack, but she did not look at me.

"Lest one should forget! How much have I to remember!"

They were dark words, and she spoke them darkly and with black passion, as though this lovely world and the dawn were ugly with hate and horror and blood. It rather shocked me until I saw again those gory, severed heads, and all the distortions and beastliness of that slaughter, and was stirred to nausea and to a sense of implacable wrath. Why should she not feel like that? Her young ruthlessness seemed to become part of my love.

I found the words I wanted.

"Let us eat and drink and be strong, for we have enemies to slay."

She looked at me with a flash of the eyes as though she loved me for sharing in her fierce young ruthlessness.

While we were breaking our fast, sitting on the grass with the sack spread between us, I remembered her chafed foot, and spoke of it. Could she manage to walk? Could anything be done? She would not allow that any such chafe existed. Of course she could walk. Her face had a young, white austerity. All the softness had gone from her mood, and I felt that she would walk to the ends of the earth if she could compass her revenge and give her dead their bloody recompense. There

was a swiftness in her temper. She was like a young hawk
eager to be on the wing, and when we had eaten she began
to pack the food into the sack. We would waste no time, even
on this most lovely morning, for, on Farley Heath the dead
waited to be avenged and buried.

She was in a very silent mood that morning, lips stiff, eyes
looking towards the horizon that might bring us to our friends
and avengers, those proud, fierce men out of the west. It was
she who set the pace. I was watching her, and she did not
limp, though I was sure that the chafed skin hurt her. Her
insurgent temper transcended pain. All was peace about us,
but I felt that her spirit was in turmoil. This island of ours is
noted for its foul weather, its grey and grudging temper, its
sudden inconsistencies, its winters in May and June, but during all my dream-life the weather was douce, serene and
lovely. Rain we did have, and thunder storms, but the rain
was the blessed manna that nature and growth desired.

We could see the Hog's Back in the north, and so long as
we had that great ridge to guide us I knew that we were
travelling as we should be, but when we came south of what
must have been Farnham, the lie of the land became much
more baffling. Meona had a stiff, pinched face, and I guessed
that she was in pain, though there was no limp to reveal its
origin. I knew that she would walk until there was blood in
her shoes. Also, the sun was well up, and the day growing hot.
I wanted to call a ten-minute halt every three or four miles,
and I did persuade her to rest now and again, but I knew that
her spirit was protesting.

How was her foot? Would she not let me look at it? She
would not. The country here was as strange to her as it was
to me, and we had to march by the sun, and the shadows it
cast. Then, we struck sand and heather, and the sandy tracks

we were compelled to follow were like the sea shore, and filled our shoes with grit. It was a wilderness of gorse and heather and birch trees and brambles. Sometimes a strip of turf helped us, but my own feet were getting sore, and now and again I saw Meona wince.

"Let's rest awhile."

We sat down under the shade of a birch tree, and Meona took off her shoes and emptied the sand out of them. I saw blood on her stockings.

I said: "Can't we bandage your feet?"

Her answer was that she would not be able to get into her shoes, and I could see that her feet were swollen. How she must have missed her two white horses! I divined her impatience, her anger against the frailties of the flesh, her ruthlessness towards herself.

"It is better to go on walking."

We walked on, but much more slowly. The only satisfaction to be gained from this heathy waste was the assurance of its emptiness and the absence of plundering enemies. There was nothing here for the swine to put their snouts into. As for our likelihood of striking an isolated farm-house in this wilderness, it did not seem probable, for it was country that Cobbett would have loved to curse. Also, it lacked water. We passed a brackish pool, and stopped to drink there, but it was so full of obvious life that, thirsty though we were, we could not bring ourselves to touch the water.

Meona had gone lame. No longer could she conceal nature's protest. Also, the sun was near the meridian, and I suggested a halt in the shade. One thing was spared us; Beelzebub had not yet got busy. We were in a small, shallow valley, shut in on every side, but the sand had given place to clay, and birch and heather to oak woods. This seemed more hopeful, and when we found a brook in the bottom of the valley, we threw ourselves down on the grass beside it.

I opened the sack, but Meona said she had no hunger. I did not scold her or worry her to eat. I bent over the bank, sluiced out my helmet and filled it, and carried it to her.

"Drink, Meona. I have a feeling that the gods are with us."

She drank, and like a thirsty flower, began to lift up her head. I borrowed her dagger, and cut bread for her and spread honey on it. She looked at it and me, and her face broke into a little smile. She was like a child to be tempted. I said that she must sleep for an hour in the shade, while I climbed the low ridge ahead of us to see if I could discover any sign of life. With a dark seriousness, she ate her bread and honey, and suddenly she said:

"My friend, you are being tried out and tested."

That touched me, and made me rather proud.

"It is not hard, Meona, for me to serve you."

"That is the wrong word, Pellias."

"Have you another?"

"Are we not fellow players in this tragedy?"

"Meona, I kiss your hands."

There seemed to be no danger here, and I spread the coverlet for her under an oak tree, and stuffed the wallet with leaves and put it under her head. Then I took my sword and helmet and followed the trackway towards the ridge. It spread out into a grassy bluff, and I could see rolling hills ahead, hills that had the indefinable, silvery patina of chalk. Hardy's Stoke Barehills should lie over yonder. I had been looking into the distance, but when I turned my eyes to the ground immediately below me I saw something that made me take cover behind a furze bush. I peered over its top. I saw a chequer of fields, and in the midst of them a small homestead with flint walls and a thatched roof. A wagon and horses were standing in the yard, also, cattle and sheep. Men and women were busy loading gear, and I could distinguish a couple of children sitting on an oak hutch in the wagon. The presence of children solved the problem for me. Here were country folk who had heard that the Saxon terror was abroad, and who were preparing to flee from it.

I came out from behind my furze bush, and ran down the hill, shouting to the people below, but their first reaction was far from welcoming. I had started an alarm, and I saw a man snatch up something which I realized was a bow, and other men picked up bills and axes. A woman scrambled into the wagon and spread herself like a protecting hen over the two children. I stopped, waved my arms, and shouted to these peasants that I was a friend. Strange, that I should be hailing them in Latin; equally strange was it that they understood me.

I saw the man with the bow lower his weapon, but the arrow was still on the string. He appeared to be the farmstead's master. He shouted to me to come nearer, and I walked down the grassy slope and into the little paddock in front of the house and yard. The men watched me, with their weapons still in their hands. They were farm labourers, dressed in short, coarse smocks, their legs swathed in what appeared to be bands of undressed hide.

The farmer hailed me. He was a big, black, husky fellow. "Halt, there. Who are you?"

I told him my name, and whence I came, and what had happened. I said that I had the daughter of Aurelius Superbus in my charge. That she was footsore and weary, and that we would pay for a seat in their wagon.

"Come nearer."

I walked down towards them, and they came to meet me.

watching me carefully as though I might turn out to be a
dangerous beast. I stopped when I was within five yards of
them, and pointing to my sword, which was in its scabbard,
smiled and asked them whether it was likely that I should
venture so near them if I spelt treachery. They had the common sense of countrymen, and they believed me.

"Where is the lady?"

"Over there by the brook. I left her to sleep. She has had
much to suffer."

"Go and fetch her," said the farmer, "and be quick about it,
for we have no time to waste."

I asked him if the Saxons had been seen in these parts, and
he pointed with his bow towards the north.

"They are about Calleva, so we hear."

"Calleva! Then, where are you bound for?"

"Vindomis."

"And where is that?"

He told me that it was on the great road from Calleva to
Sorbiodunum. He had a brother who farmed a farm near
Vindomis. The news was good. We should be travelling to-
wards the country of Aurelius Ambrosius.

I ran back over the hill, and coming down to the brook,
found that Meona had fallen asleep. It seemed a shame to
wake her, for sleep had passed a merciful hand over her face,
and given her back all her soft youth and loveliness. It made
me think of the face of a sleeping child. But my consolation
lay in the good news I had for her, and I knelt down and
touched her arm.

She woke, and started up on her elbow, her eyes wide and
tragic, her forehead all shadows. She looked ten years older,
and I made haste to reassure her.

"Good news, Meona. A farmer will take you in his wagon."

"Where?"

"To Vindomis. It lies towards your uncle's country. These people are going because of the Saxons."

I began to pack our belongings in the sack, and she helped me. I told her that the peasants had heard that the savages were all about Calleva. No doubt they were hoping to storm and sack that wealthy little town. We paddled through the brook and over the hill, and saw that the men had driven the cattle into the paddock, and that the farmer and his folk were ready to move off. Meona was limping badly, but her face had a young fierceness.

"The poor people. Why should the gods let us suffer these things?"

I said that, in the end, good might come of it.

"Yes," she said, "when these wild beasts have been hunted down and slain."

The farmer came forward to meet us, and he saluted Meona.

"Welcome, lady, these are hard times for all of us."

She answered him with simple dignity.

"We must seek to make them harder, my friend, for those who are merciless and our enemies."

Not till we had joined the peasants, and Meona was sitting in the wagon beside the housewife and her children did I realize that this wonderful and poignant pilgrimage of ours was at an end. I had been alone with Meona for all these unforgettable hours. I had been her comrade, and almost her lover.

Should I ever be alone with her again?

CHAPTER TWENTY-FIVE

ANY illusions I might cherish upon my social status began to crumble when Meona took her seat in the wagon. The housewife soon discovered that my lady was the niece of the most potent prince in Britain, nor need I accuse this peasant woman of being a snob because she began to make a fuss of Meona. A pillow was found for her to sit upon; the children were ordered to be quiet and to behave themselves, and not to worry the lady. It was just human kindness. The farmer had passed on my story to his wife, and to the good woman Meona was a beautiful and tragic figure who had suffered cruelly at the hands of these German beasts.

As for myself, I soon gathered that I was regarded as a superior sort of servant. I might be footsore, but I was expected to leg it, and not to ride in the wagon. No longer was I a little Dux, Honey Valley's captain, for, as a leader of fighting men I had no men left to lead. The farmer walked beside me, and was matey and talkative, and wanting to hear all I had to tell him of my lady's tragedy. What had my job been? I told him that I was the son of my dead lord's steward, and that my father also was dead.

"Ah, hard fortune," said he; "you have lost a comfortable job."

His condolences had so modern a sound that almost they changed me from a romantic into a realist. I was tired, and my feet were damned sore, and I was fed up with walking. And why did not Meona suggest that I might be given a lift in the wagon? The farmer and I were heading the retreat; the wagon lumbered behind us, followed by the cattle and the labourers. One fellow on a pony was sent on ahead to top every hill we approached, and keep a look out for any sign of our enemies.

I had begun to limp, and my farmer friend noticed it.

"Not much used to footing it, I reckon."

So, I suppose he would have classed me as a pampered super-menial whose feet were more accustomed to mosaic pavements than trackways and cloddy fields.

I said that we must have covered twenty miles or more in the last twenty-four hours, and that sand had a way of getting into these damned shoes.

He looked at my shoes.

"Ah, gentleman's shoes. You haven't been brought up hardy. Borrowed your father's horse, may be. I've done a bit of soldiering and I could march my twenty miles, and not know I had been on my feet."

I am sure that in his rough way he was being kind, but his assumption that I was, in modern parlance, a gilded playboy, exasperated me. I wanted to tell him of my exploits, but I suspected that he would not have believed me. Also, it would have sounded so like silly swagger. And then he said a thing that sobered me.

"You can't ride in the wagon with the lady, but I have an old plough-horse behind who doesn't mind a man on his back.

You can have a lift on him if you feel like it."

I accepted the offer, partly because I wanted to escape from his friendly loquacity, and to think my own thoughts. We stopped and let the wagon pass us, and I climbed up on Dobbin, who tolerated me with resignation. I looked into the wagon, and saw that Meona had fallen asleep again with her head against the housewife's shoulder. Poor kid, she was tired out. Maybe I had not been forgotten, and the hope comforted me.

For I needed comfort. It is extraordinary how another person's candid opinion of the beloved self can shock one and depress one's mood, especially so if the critic is an underling. I was no Sir Pellias to this farmer, but a gentleman's gentleman, a tame fellow who had tender feet. I know that it is ridiculous that I should have been both angered and depressed by his palpable pity, a good-natured pity that was subtly indiscreet, but his assumption that I was a pretty water-fly persuaded me to look the future in the face, and to discover it to be an unflattering prospect. What was my future? I had ceased to be a person, unless Meona should choose to be kind to me. These princely gentlemen from the west would regard me as the steward's son, a faithful fellow no doubt, but no comrade in arms, no brother, and most certainly no lover. I should be not quite a gentleman, but something a little better than a servant. I should be classed with that grinning, supercilious scribbler, Gildas. Most certainly I should not be welcomed as a hero. These Aurelii might indeed ask me awkward questions. How was it that I had happened to be absent when the Germans had surprised and slaughtered our people? Gildas might damn me as a fellow who was prone to run away. No doubt I was tired and irritable, but this feeling of future humiliation fell upon me like a fog, and seemed to blot out all the pride and the loveliness and the wounded sweetness of the last few hours.

Nothing can be more futile than self-pity, and if I needed a flick of fortune's whip, it was to be given to me more kindly than I deserved. Wishing to be alone, I had ridden on ahead on my old cart-horse, only to find myself cheek by jowl by the lad who was scouting for us. He had pulled up his pony on the round top of a grassy hill, and was staring north-westwards under his hand. I asked him what he was looking at, and he pointed.

"Smoke, brother."

I was not his brother and I was not feeling fraternal to any human creature, but when I looked in the direction he indicated I could distinguish a distant column of smoke. It rose from behind some trees, and had a black and oily look, a dark flower spreading out above a sinuous stem. It reminded me of the conventional picture of Vesuvius in eruption. It was much too considerable to be the product of a chimney, and it had not the shape of a heath fire. I did not like the look of it, nor did my farm lad. He turned his pony, and leaving me on the hill, went cantering back to tell what he had seen to his master.

One of the wheels of the wagon had developed an ugly squeak, and it was the cessation of this sound that warned me that our party had halted. I had been watching that smoke, and looking back I saw Meona and the farmer's wife standing up in the wagon. Our cattle had overflowed on to the grass beside the track, and the drovers were rounding them up. The farmer was running towards me like a great big blundering steer.

He joined me on the hill-top, his chest heaving.

"What's amiss? My lad says he has seen smoke."

I am afraid I was laconic with my downright friend.

"Yes. There it is."

I could see that he did not like the look of that smoke. He rubbed his hairy chin, and his eyes were anxious.

"That's not peaceful smoke."

"No," said I. "I have seen such smoke before."

"Where?" he snapped.

"In our country, when the Germans had set a homestead alight."

He rubbed his chin still harder.

"Our road goes that way. What if the swine are there? We can't risk it."

I put on a casual voice, and a blasé manner.

"That should be easy. If you will risk this old rocking-horse of yours I will ride on and see what is happening."

I saw his jaw drop and his eyes bulge.

"All by yourself?"

"Of course. I am a fighting man, my friend, not a farmer."

He gobbled over my retort, and I left him gobbling, and urged Dobbin down the hill at a ponderous trot. I heard the farmer shouting after me. "Hi, that's my best horse. Hi, come back, master." I let him shout, and went pounding on into the valley, feeling reckless and as cocky as a boy who is out to prove his courage. I would show these clod-hoppers what manner of man I was. Also, I was honouring the old soldiers' text: "When you are feeling down about things, do something."

I drew my sword, and rode on like St. George to confront and slay some hypothetical dragon. I had no fear. I was so much and so hopelessly in love, that provided my courage shone in the eyes of my lady, I felt that I should be happy. I was beginning to realize that I had no flashing symbol to carry, save my courage. Either I was to be Pellias the hero, or Pellias the steward's son.

I came to another grassy hill and rode over it, and saw below me in the valley buildings burning. The smoke was rolling up in the still air and spreading out into a dark canopy. I could see flames like serpent heads darting here and there. The place was more than a homestead. I judged it to be a considerable mansion, with outbuildings, an orchard and gardens. It lay in a kind of park embossed with splendid trees. But not a sign of life could I see, neither man nor beast.

Had the people set fire to the great house before abandoning it, or had some malicious slave or peasant put a torch to it after it had been deserted by its owners? I could not say, but I took my hazard in my hands and rode down close to the place. I saw no one. There was something very strange and tragic about this blazing and lonely house. What its secret was I do not know, nor did I discover any sign of our enemies. I rode right round it and made sure of my facts before turning Dobbin back towards the hill.

When I topped this rise I saw two figures like little dark statues set on the green swell of the further hill. As my lumbering old horse brought me nearer to them and they became more than mere silhouettes against the sky-line, I recognized the farmer's bulk, and Meona's white and purple tunic and cloak. Dobbin was beginning to roar, and I let him walk up the hill. When I was within a hundred paces or so of the ridge the farmer started down to meet me. I heard Meona's voice sharp and sudden, and the fellow stopped like a bull that has been roped by the horns. He turned about, slouched back up the hill, and I saw him bend down and kiss the hem of Meona's cloak.

What had she said to him? I could infer that she had

spoken to this boor as the daughter of Aurelius Superbus, and that he had come like a dog to her feet. So her spirit was on the wing, and had ceased to droop. She waited for me on the hill-top, while the farmer disappeared over the sky-line like a cloud-shadow that has become superfluous upon the high places of a notable pride.

I got off my horse when I was within ten yards of the hill-top. Meona's stillness puzzled me; so did her eyes. She looked like a young queen whose orders had been flouted.

I said: "There is a house burning over yonder. I rode round it, but found no living thing."

Her question came like a dart thrown at a board.

"Why did you go alone?"

Why should she be angry with me because I had thought of her safety and that of these peasants?

"There was danger, and I wanted to make sure."

"I have told that coward that he should have gone with you."

She was not being fair to the farmer, and I explained that I had given him no chance of accompanying me. Moreover, if we had found enemies over yonder I should have been able to ride back and warn them, whereas that ponderous fellow, left to foot it, might have been overtaken and slain. But she was in a flashing temper, and my logic might have been swansdown.

"You take too much upon yourself, Pellias."

My temper rose to hers.

"I take that which I choose to call my duty."

It was a silly, sententious retort, for what I had done was to please my own recklessness and to satisfy my own vanity. I must have appeared to her like a petulant, passionate boy, and she may have understood my malady, for her face softened, and her eyes ceased to flash.

"You should have spared me that fear, my friend. Yes, I was angry. One is not angry over nothing."

In metaphor I was at her feet, and instantly so.

"I would not have you in any more peril, Meona."

"Nor I—you, even in rashness."

I had let go of my horse, and I went to her, and bending, kissed her hand.

"One can be a fool, even in one's pride."

"Folly may be finer than too much caution. But what if you had not come back?"

"You would have known that it would mean death to go further."

"Thank you," said she, "for so melancholy a warning. But you say you found a burning house and nothing else?"

"Yes. How it came to be burning heaven alone knows. Its people may have set it alight before leaving."

She frowned over that.

"Is it likely? No, malice, Pellias. A grudge had to be consumed. But can we go on?"

"I think so. I will ride ahead, and watch."

"You will do nothing of the kind," said she. "Have you forgotten your promise to me?"

I had.

"Meona, let it rest."

"It was a sacred promise. You will stay at my side. You will not leave me."

Again I kissed her hand, and my heart felt big in me, but my Hodge of a horse, who appeared to have become bored and was cropping the grass, let out a sudden mocking and vibrant neighing. I could not help laughing.

"Horse-sense, Meona! Out of the mouths of babes and sucklings!"

But she did not laugh with me.

"Call to those people and let us go."

My heart was big in me; my mood of self-pity had passed. Why had she been angry with me? Was it because I had forgotten my promise, or was I more to her than Pellias the steward's son? I did not dare to answer that question, and her reproaches had taken the silly, selfish conceit out of me. When the wagon and cattle came up with us, she stood aside and made a sign to me. I was to let these peasants pass, and we would follow them at our leisure.

"You shall not walk," said I.

She gave a flick of the head.

"My knight is fond of giving orders."

"No, but I give you my horse."

"Is it yours to give?"

"It is mine to lend. He has a good broad back, and is quiet, and you can hold on to his mane."

She looked at the beast and she looked at me.

"Where shall I find a mounting-block?"

"May I lift you up, Meona?"

She nodded, and I picked her up and placed her on the horse's back, and as I did so her hand brushed my face.

"Why should you walk, Pellias? You are as footsore as I am."

"A happy heart goes all the way. I could walk to the ends of the earth."

"Hyperbole, my friend, but I will not quarrel with it!"

The wise men tell us that when a woman becomes God's

partisan, or the inspired angel of some crusade she will take and use all men and things and creatures to feed the flame of a splendid fanaticism. And I, walking beside the horse of this fierce and passionate St. Joan, was simple enough to dream of her as a man dreams of woman. I did not ask myself whether she chose to tolerate my tenderness, and could show a moment's play of fancy when my love for her blazed out. Silent she might be on that long journey, sitting and gazing dark-eyed and dark-browed upon this pleasant land. My devotion believed itself to be sensitive and comprehending. She carried a great grief with her, and I allowed her her young austerity and her aloofness, not looking too often in her face, or vexing her with words. How little did I divine the implacable and inspired purpose that was coming to fierce fruition behind the veil of her almost mystic loveliness. I walked beside her horse, and dreamed. She too must have been dreaming, but not as I was dreaming. Maybe, she saw the skies opened and a tempestuous, fiery vengeance descending upon the brute beast man who had outraged all that she loved.

So the day passed. The smoke from the burning homestead was far behind us, and no alarms troubled us as I marched beside her horse, feeling neither weary of leg nor sore of foot. It was as though her spirit entered into me and carried me on, the servant of a dear and passionate illusion. It was late in the day when we came to a rich deep valley with a lake in its green trough, and a great white house set on the side of a hill. There were high woods all about it, and when Meona saw the place, her face lit up. She knew it.

"That is the house of Geraint. We are safe."

Who this Geraint or Gerontius was I did not know, but one thing was certain, this valley was no valley of death. I saw tents pitched on the hill-side, and horse-lines, and sheaves of stacked spears. Between the great house and the mere were a score or more of wagons, and people camping about them, with fires lit and children playing around. A fenced paddock was packed with cattle. Obviously, this green valley had become a place of refuge for many of those who had fled from the Saxon terror, and also a rallying ground for armed men. Our farmer let out a bellow when he saw all this.

"Look, Mother! The gods be praised. Here is a safe pound for beasts and men."

We were preparing to descend into the valley when half a dozen horsemen came out from a clump of trees on the ridge, and challenged us. They were led by a comely, dark young man in gilded harness with an eagle on his helmet. Who were we, and what was our business? Meona answered him, and the young man swung off his horse and came to salute her.

"Is all well with your people?"

I stood there watching and listening, and feeling suddenly jealous of this comely lad who was plainly a person. Meona told him her news, and I saw his face darken. I heard her speak my name, and the young man looked at me, and then came striding towards me. He held out his hand.

"Welcome, brother."

My hand went out to him, and so did my good will, for he had one of these clear, clean, friendly faces that challenge all that is fearless and frank in one.

"I am Geraint, the son of Geraint."

"And I am Pellias."

We looked into each other's eyes and were friends.

CHAPTER TWENTY-SIX

IN THIS great house I was to experience nothing but courtesy and kindness. My lord Geraint the elder was a very old man, ninety years or more, and though his legs had failed him, and his servants had to carry him about the gardens and estate in a kind of open sedan chair, his head was very much alive. He had a great mane of white hair, and never have I seen a more splendid-looking patriarch, nor a man with more gentle manners. It was the son who first saw to my needs, for Meona had gone straight to the women's quarters, and the younger Geraint's kindness to me made me believe that my lady had spoken of me as a man of prowess and of courage.

"What would you, my friend?"

I laughed, and fingered my chin.

"A shave, sir, and a bath."

I was barbered and bathed, and God knows, I needed these ministrations, and while I was being strigilled and oiled on a marble couch, young Geraint sat on a stool and talked to me. There was a naturalness about all this business that took away my shyness. I understood that in this spacious, comely world the cult of the body was as much valued as the cult of the mind. Moreover, it was a country culture, yet utterly without boorishness. My lord had travelled much, to Rome, Athens and Byzantium. He had a notable library, and a gallery of pictures. As for the younger Geraint, he had studied at some famous house in Southern Gaul, a monastic house I imagine, for these gentlemen were Christians.

I had to tell him all about the Aurelian tragedy, and of our battles with the Germans. He heard me quite calmly, though I could divine a deep blaze of horror and anger at the back of his dark eyes. I gathered that he was not a blind hater, or compounded of that urgent yet stark fierceness that goes to the making of a great captain or a fanatic. He made me think of an English public school boy, say Winchester and Balliol, to whom such cads as Hitler and Stalin would remain somewhat incomprehensible. Such barbarism had to be countered, but coolly and with dignity, as one treads upon a noisome, evil thing. I believe Geraint would always have referred to Old Nasty as Herr Hitler, even though his scorn for the bragging beast was abysmal.

His father was of a different temper, even at the age of ninety. My lord Geraint had been a notable fighting man and leader of men in days of earlier confusions when the Island had been vexed by the barbarians, and Rome had helped to rescue it. When I had been barbered and washed, the son took me to the father who was seated in his carrying-chair on the terrace. This terrace might have been Elizabethan, or even St. George's Hill! It was paved with stone, and its balustrade was set with vases. There was a garden house and a little formal pool with lilies in it. The loggia, which opened upon the terrace, had vines, roses, and wild clematis climbing up its pillars. The view was superb, hill upon hill, valley upon valley.

I stood before the patriarch to answer his questions, but he pointed to an oak stool, and bade me sit. The son had left us alone together.

I was to tell him everything that had happened. Very old he might be, but I divined in him a greater capacity for rich anger and for a noble disgust than existed in the son. He could say the most scathing things in a deep and gentle voice, and like my dead master his vision was spacious. He spoke of world movements, of storms and stresses in the human fate, of the eternal and vainglorious savage in man. These louts from over the sea who came to plunder and rape and slay! The egregious, horrid arrogance of spotty youth! A Christian he might be, but a Christian of the crusading temper. He would have had no use for Conscientious Cowards, the little clever people who deem themselves so precious that no sacrifice should be asked of them. Meona must have seen him and spoken to him of me, for he dwelt upon my combats.

"I gather that you are a stout fellow, Pellias, and I, an old man, salute you."

I countered his praise by saying that the courage of a great gentleman was precious, and that the old should not be afraid of speaking frank, bold words to the young.

That seemed to amuse him, and his great dark eyes smouldered.

"Ha, my son, no one can be quite so wise and infallible as a young man fresh from college! I like your modesty. But we will not be modest with these savages. There is a time for ruthlessness."

Then he told me that he had mustered all his tenants, and that on the morrow the Aurelii would join us with all their power. This was challenging news to me. The Germans, as my farmer friend had heard, were all about Calleva, raiding and plundering, and we were to march against them.

"How will that suit your temper, Pellias?"

"Very well, sir."

So far, so good. My self-pity and the doubts of a few hours ago became small and cowardly now that I had experienced the courtesy of these great gentlemen. I had been accepted by them for what I was, and for what I wished to be, but would the Aurelii accept me in the same spirit? I do not know why, but I had a feeling that I should find Meona's kinsmen haughty people who might treat me as an underling, and the thought of being treated as such before Meona was not a humiliation that I could stomach. Moreover, they would come into the valley with panoply and power, and I, the lone survivor of that slaughter, might be surrounded with suspicion. How had it come about that I had been alone with Meona at that moment? Would they not regard me as a forward fellow, impertinently trailing a woman's skirts when I should have been visiting my outposts? The thing worried me.

I must have been tired and touchy and temperamental that day. We supped in the state-room, and I was admitted to my lord Geraint's table with sundry of his gentlemen and his soldier-tenants. Meona sat on his right, the young Geraint opposite her. I saw him looking at her with frank admiration, and how could I quarrel with so natural a reaction, and yet I felt petulant and jealous.

I was the only man at my lord's table who had met the Germans in battle, and when the wine had warmed us, my lord and his gentlemen questioned me as to how the barbarians fought. What were their tactics? Was there any soldierly subtlety in their strategy? How did our people compare with them, man for man?

I felt rather self-conscious about answering some of these questions. Strange, how one's English prejudices haunted me even in this ghost body. One should not boast and swagger, or exhibit oneself, even though there may be an immoderate niceness in all this modesty. But, as in our modern world, one left the part of Bombastes Furioso to Hitler.

I said that there did not appear to be much subtlety in the Saxon's methods. They used shock-tactics, and attacked like wild beasts in a howling pack whenever the chance offered. I told how we had ambuscaded them, and that it might be easy to bait a trap for them.

They listened to me with seriousness and respect.

"Yes," said my lord. "I gather there is no great cunning in their strategy. But you have fought, man to man, with them, and you are alive. Are they so terrible?"

I was wondering how to answer this question without appearing boastful, when Meona answered it for me.

"I was there when Pellias fought with three of them, and slew them all."

"Yes, gentlemen, but—"

She shook her head at me. I was not to tell them that her little dagger and her courage had saved my life.

Whether I was over-tired or over-worried or too much in love, the fact remains that I was consumed by a burning restlessness. My room was on the first floor, with its window opening on the terrace. I understand that the Romano-British country houses were supposed to be like glorified bungalows, but the house of Geraint was of two storeys. An older house had been burnt during one of the earlier periods of turmoil, and the present mansion had been built by Geraint some fifty years ago. I had a bed with a feather mattress and pillow, but sleep would not come near me. The night was very warm and still, and I put on my tunic and stood at the window. The camp fires were still alight, like flowers burning in the darkness, but a great silence covered the valley. I knew that our patrols were out on the hills, for two of my lord's gentlemen had left the supper-table to go on duty.

The room oppressed me. I wanted to be out under the stars, and I went barefooted along the gallery and down the stairs to the paved and pillared hall. The great door stood open like a mouth breathing softly in its sleep. A servant was curled up on a mat beside it. The man rose and challenged me, but when I gave him my name, he saluted and let me pass.

I had expected to be alone on the terrace under the stars, but someone else was there. I saw a white figure drifting to and fro on noiseless feet. There was something mothlike and restless and fluttering about this figure, and then, the lover in me seemed to divine its fated flame. It was Meona who was walking here as sleepless and as troubled as I.

I stood very still. What right had I to intrude upon her sorrow, for I could imagine that her grieving was more bitter now that she was safe and in this peaceful place. Even its spacious peace must remind her of that other house in a green valley, a ghost house, forlorn and empty. Perhaps I was too sensitive about my love, and too ready to shirk its poignant issues, for the thing can be too full of anguish when it is rebuffed and thwarted. As I said, I stood very still, wondering whether I could slip along the terrace and away into the night without her being aware of my presence, but I saw her drift towards me, and then stand still.

"Is it you, Pellias?"

"It is I."

"Can you not sleep?"

"No, Meona."

So, she had known me in the darkness even as I had known her, and a secret exultation stirred in me. Were we so sensitive to each other that some more subtle awareness linked us in a mysterious sympathy? Did my love float to her like a gentle ghost, and haunt her with the knowledge of my inevitable nearness?

"Does my presence trouble you, Meona?"

"No. Come and stand here with me, my friend."

She was looking down into the dark valley and at the camp fires burning there, and as I stood there beside her, her white figure was unreasonably still. It had lost its mothlike, vapoury quality, and made me think of white marble, rigid and brittle.

She said to me: "They come to-morrow."

"Your people."

"The avengers."

She spoke in a fierce, hard whisper.

"You see those fires, Pellias. I see nothing but those fires, like red eyes and bloody swords, our swords. No, my friend, there is no gentleness in me. There can be no such feeling, no quiet breathing until we have made an end of the evil thing."

Her passion astonished me. It was so concentrated, so cold, so still.

"I shall go with you all."

"You, Meona?"

"Of course. My eyes are dry for the blood of those wild beasts. And you, my friend?"

In that moment I think I understood her and all that she expected of me. Her passionate ruthlessness smothered all gentler urges. We men were to her the winged death, the avengers, the slayers, and that might be the only use she had for us.

I said: "Geraint will be with us, and he—"

She flashed out in the darkness with sudden scorn:

"Geraint! A pretty boy. He has not the soul of his father. Such men are not for the slaying that I ask for, for which my dead cry out. Men should be fierce, and strong and relentless at such a time. It is upon you and your like that I count."

There was a quality in her passion that both shocked and devoured me. If mine had been a mere pretty passion, I think that it ceased to be such. The elemental urge in her moved me, as some of Wagner's music has moved me. She was like one of those epic women, the Brunhilds, the Iseults, or Lear's daughters. No pert or simpering parlour miss was she, but Nature, passionate and strange and tragic, with the wind and the thunder and the sea-lash in her soul. If ever a man was intoxicated by emotion, I was that man.

I spread my arms to her.

"Count me your avenger, Meona."

She came close, took my face between her hands, and as though consecrating me, kissed my forehead.

CHAPTER TWENTY-SEVEN

ℐNDEED, though I knew it not, she was the dark and fatal goddess of my world, sending me either to Elysium or to Hades. She had involved me in her hate, consecrated me to it, bade me come to her splashed with the blood of her enemies. So, I have held that hate can be a good and lovely thing, perhaps because I loved this creature who could be so splendid in her anger, and who understood that hatred may be a sacred flame burning away the cankers and the suppurating sores of sentiment. We babble about love, and of forgiving everything that we understand; and how the Stalins of this world must laugh at us! For how much do we understand? And how often may Nature be fooling us. The kiss of Judas may be more potent and natural than the blessing of Christ, and assuredly, in these later days the Judas kiss is life's sign and seal. We dear, nice, awfully decent fellows with our B.B.C. voices have lost that primeval virtue, the sacred wrath that will not rest until the evil thing is dead.

Shall I ever forget how the Aurelii and their people came to us? Six dusty horsemen rode down into the valley three hours after dawn, to herald the coming of their host. There was a clamour and a crowding in our camp. Some of our captains were going out to meet the British, and young Geraint went with them, but I stayed behind upon the terrace with Meona and my lord Geraint the elder, watching for the flash of sunlight upon spears. They came dancing over the green hill opposite between the high barriers of two woods, a young forest of spears, of helmets and of painted shields. The horses were of all colours, black and roan, white and chestnut. Trumpets brayed. I saw a great banner of gold with a red dragon upon it, and I felt as though I had slipped back into Mallory. So, Arthur and his knights must have ridden over these British hills, splendid in their strength and splendour.

I looked at Meona, and her face was proud and exultant.

"Are they not lovely, Pellias?"

They were. This great concourse of horsemen poured down the hill like a moving garden, and the points of steel were like glittering drops of dew. Here, indeed, was the old glamour of war, the splendour of the fighting man, no anonymous scuffle in the mud with steel splinters ripping up chests and bellies. The sight fascinated me. I saw a body of "Foot" following the "Horse," and after them came archers. The whole valley was in an uproar, trumpets blowing, soldiers and refugees running to watch and welcome the avengers. Horses neighed as though smelling the coming battle. I looked at old Geraint, and saw his eyes ablaze. His face seemed to have shed twenty of its years. His hands were grasping the arms of his chair.

He spoke to the bearers who stood behind him.

"Lift me up that I may see."

They stepped between the poles, and raised their lord

shoulder-high. His white head caught the sunlight, and made me remember that other white and tragic head. I saw him raise his right arm.

"Hail, pride and power of Britain! Hail, O Red Dragon!"

I looked again at Meona. She seemed to stand there remote and dreaming, smiling like a girl upon her lover.

If love can be instant, I think that hate can be even more so.

I was standing with Meona beside my lord's chair when young Geraint and Aurelius Maximus came up the flight of steps leading to the terrace. A score or so of gentlemen and captains followed them, fierce, proud, stalwart men with plumes or horse-hair in their helmets. The young Geraint was a comely fellow, but when I set eyes on Maximus, Ambrosius's son, I knew him to be the handsomest male thing I had seen ever. And I loathed him. He stood well over six feet, and wore gilded armour over a purple tunic, and high boots of red leather laced with green silk laces. He was a blond Briton, with eyes of blatant blue, and a fleece of curly hair. There was all the splendour of the perfect animal about him, a sleepy arrogance, a lion-like complacency. He came up the steps like a young god climbing Olympus. But do gods swagger? He saluted Geraint the elder, and then I saw those blatant blue eyes of his set in a stare. He was looking at Meona.

I knew at once and with the intuition of my hatred, that her dark loveliness inflamed him, and that instantly he had marked her as his. He was the sort of man whose complacency is so complete that he will pick up life's chalice and drain it, as though the gods had dedicated it to him and to him alone. He was not a man who smiled. When emotion moved him he stared the harder. I knew what his voice would be like even before I heard it. It was throaty and rich, and could produce a kind of insolent playfulness. The whole world was a groom to him.

His manners were flamboyant. He my-lorded this old man, and bent his head over Meona's hand.

"Greetings, sweet cousin; you have grown more beautiful even since we met."

I watched Meona. Her smile had gone, and there was a little frown on her forehead.

"This country needs you, Maximus."

"The man and the hour, hey! We'll teach these savages a lesson."

Geraint's eyes seemed to have sunk back into his head.

"Your father will join us, Maximus?"

"Papa is becoming an old man, sir. I carry the Red Dragon for him. Strange, but he has great faith in me."

Egregious, super-confident beast! My feeling was that old Geraint was not pleased. Maximus might possess all the splendour of manhood, and be a virile, striding creature, a bustling Mars, but the supreme wisdom was not in him.

Meona remembered me.

"Maximus, this is Pellias, who led my father's people."

I don't think Maximus troubled to look at me.

"Ha, Pellias, my man. Yes, we have a fellow with us named Festus who spoke of you. A drake without the ducks!"

Let me swear that I had hated him before he fobbed me off with a poor joke, but I was human enough to hate him all the more for it.

"The pleasure is mutual, Max, I assure you."

This time he did give me a blue glare. Max, indeed! But ever afterwards I thought of him as Max. The name stuck to him like grease-paint.

"May we come in, sir, and drink? My gentlemen are thirsty."

Old Geraint was a courtier, but I am convinced that he liked Ambrosius's son as little as I did.

"All my house is at your service."

"Thanks, sir. Come, sweet cousin, and crush the grape for me. Look into the cup and it will be sweet."

Meona smiled upon him. After all he was a magnificent creature and the symbol of her vengeance, but I did not understand the essence of the secret self behind her smile.

I went in search of Festus. I had forgotten Festus, and the evil news I had to tell him. Poor Festus, he had lost a brother and many friends, and a good over-lord. I found him among Maximus's men, attending to his horse, for I believe that Festus would have groomed and fed his horse before touching food himself, had he been starving. His humorous, hard face lit up when he saw me.

"What, you, brother!"

I was sorry to take the shine from his face. Poor Festus, his homestead might be in ashes and his whole world in ruin, and for a moment or two he stared at me as though he did not believe me.

"My lord slain!"

I nodded.

"And Robur?"

"Yes. I think a few escaped, but I do not know how many."

I saw the sudden, sinister question in his eyes. How did I happen to be here? How had I saved my life? Had I reverted to the part of Pellias the coward? I told him the truth, and quickly.

"Yes," said he, "our lady gave us the slip. That's true. So you owe your life, brother, to a mad wench's recklessness. But, by the gods, we have debts to pay."

He was himself again, grim and lean, though his smile was crooked.

"How many are there of these swine?"

I said that I might number them at a thousand and a half, but that I could not be sure. And how many men had Maximus brought with him?

"Seven hundred horsemen, brother, and perhaps five hundred foot-soldiers and three score bowmen."

"Geraint has mustered three hundred. The odds should be even."

"The odds are with us," said Festus, "for we have the blood-rage in us."

Courage is so relative a virtue that I could not help wondering how true Festus's words would prove. One may be a coward in the confronting of danger, and a stout fellow when in the thick of it, and again a trembling, puling boy when the bloody business is over. I think I would ascribe to hate and to a lust for revenge, especially when revenge appears sacred, supreme value as stimuli in the day of battle. That is as nature would have it, blood-pressure and tails both up, and the lust to kill a rage in the belly. A cold, calm, ruthless ferocity may be equally potent, and I speak as a man with experience. In my own case my courage, such as it was, had a more gaillard quality, for I was in love, and she whom I loved asked for trophies.

It was after the midday meal that the Geraints, Maximus, and the captains held a council of war, and I was suffered to sit at the lower end of the council table. Old Geraint spoke to us of the great issue, and I was aware of Maximus becoming impatient, and pulling at his blond moustachios. His blue eyes said: "Must we listen to this old babbler?" And surely enough he interrupted the old man with a brusqueness that was brutal.

"Gentlemen, I think the issue is to march on these savages and destroy them."

I was watching old Geraint's face. It betrayed neither impatience nor resentment. His dignity never blinked an eyelid. He looked at those other men about the table, and smiled, and went on speaking.

"Gentlemen, I may boast of some experience in war. I am an old man, and to the old, cunning is a key to unlock good fortune. I would say to you: 'Let us be cunning in our business. Let us so plan it that we shall have the advantage with us. Blind valour may be a good horse, but wise valour is a better one.' "

A man can show impatience and scorn even by the way he sits in a chair, and though Maximus let the old man finish, he was like a bad-tempered king of beasts clawing the bars and switching his tail.

"Good, sir, good, but as I was saying, this is an affair of arms and of men, fighting, not talking."

Then young Geraint flashed at him across the table.

"I, for one, wish to listen to my father. Because you have brought more power with you, Maximus, that does not mean that you carry all the wisdom."

Young Geraint's face was ablaze. This splendid swaggerer exasperated him, and we were brothers in that respect. I looked round the table. I saw two rows of rather grim faces. One veteran was chewing his beard, and I got the impression that these fighting-men were with the Geraints and not with Maximus.

Maximus looked across with sleepy insolence at young Geraint.

"Are you, too, all for caution?"

The fierce old man who was biting his beard, broke in on this clash of tempers. He had a deep, hoarse voice that was like the wind in a chimney, and it seemed to come in gusts.

"I listen to men who know. My lord Geraint has been in battle, and so have I. Is there any young man here who can say the same?"

I met old Geraint's eyes. Something seemed to have amused him. He smiled at me.

"Gentlemen, that is a pertinent question. We have one friend here who has been in battle, Pellias, yonder. Let us hear you, Pellias."

All eyes were turned on me, and I had a horrid feeling that I ought to get on my feet and make a speech. I hesitated. Then, I stood up and saluted Geraint the elder.

"Sir, I would say that you have spoken wise words. These Germans fight like wild beasts, and for wild beasts one can set a trap. We set such a trap on the hills above our valley, and caught our prey."

I heard Maximus's throaty voice.

"Yes, my friend, and history has it that on the next occasion you were not the fox but the rabbit."

I am afraid I lost my temper. I laid my hand on my sword, and was about to tell Maximus that I would meet him in some quiet place, when the biter of beards banged the table.

"The lad speaks right."

He spat his words at Maximus.

"The Aurelii are great people, my lord, and your father is a man of wisdom, but, if his pup—"

For the moment I thought there was going to be turmoil,

but my lord Geraint raised a hand and spoke with a level calmness that held us all.

"Gentlemen, let us vote on the issue. Shall we be cunning or reckless? Let those who would use cunning put up their hands."

The whole vote went against Maximus; my lord smiled, and we got down to business. A big man with a red beard proposed that we should send out a scouting party towards Calleva, see how the land lay and our enemies were posted, and then frame our plans. It was agreed to. And then, I was moved to volunteer for the adventure, if Festus would go with me. Maximus sat sulky and silent, pulling his blond moustachios, his attitude suggesting that so surreptitious and foxy a plan was beneath his magnificence.

My lord asked me a question.

"Is Festus wise as to the ways?"

"No man more so, sir."

"Then, go, both of you. We will hold our force here until you return."

I was glad to go. I cannot give any reason for the feeling that possessed me, that this other world had become strangely sad and sinister. It may have been that the reaction was upon me, a lover's hopeless mood, and that the coming of Maximus had put me out of humour with romance. I went and found Festus, sitting on the grass with his beloved horse beside him, a figure of melancholy and meditation. The sinews of his soul were slack, but when I told him of the adventure that had been assigned to us he was on his feet like a boy. Would he go with me? By the gods, he would! He blessed me for choosing him.

Young Geraint had promised me harness and a horse. I was

becoming a hardier horseman both as to buttocks and self-confidence. Geraint took me into the great house, and to a room that would have been known as the gun-room in an English country-house. Here were bows and hunting-spears, and six suits of harness hanging on the wall. Geraint bade me choose, and I chose a plain black breastplate with shoulder pieces, arm guards, and greaves.

"You are modest, Pellias; not like our friend Maximus."

I laughed and said that Maximus might be a rainbow, in that he came out after the storm was over, and Geraint laughed with me. He had one of those lovely natures which cannot sulk.

"Good wit, Pellias. I have a suspicion that so splendid a creature will not soil himself in battle. You had better take this spear."

I thanked him, and we went out into the great corridor where a servant was waiting with a leather wallet full of food. These Geraints were notable people. They could remember the little things as well as the big ones, and Festus and I were to be grateful for that wallet.

I had not expected to see Meona. I will confess that I was suffering from one of those attacks of anguish when one fears and avoids the thing one loves. How she would look and speak mattered to me too bitterly. Yet, I was to see her, and a little flame of jealousy was to blaze up in me. She was walking on the terrace with her cousin, looking like a slim dark cypress beside a flaunting young oak in the gold mail of May.

How one is fooled by emotion! I gather that jealousy can make of man the most awkward and boorish of beasts, but her being with Maximus angered me, though I had no right or reason to be angered. I should have crossed the terrace and gone down the steps to where Festus and the horses were waiting without taking leave of her, had she not seen me and called to me.

"Pellias, where are you going?"

Did it matter to her where I was going or what might happen to me upon the adventure? In my silly, cynical, jealous mood I was ready to throw away all that I had cherished. Love makes one such a petulant child. But when she left Maximus and came to me, for I had paused at the top of the steps, my foolish passionate self swung round like a wind-vane, and my love was at her feet.

I said: "Have you not heard?"

She glanced at my harness and my spear, and the look that came into her eyes filled me with sudden exultation.

"No."

"We have held a council of war. Festus and I have offered to ride out and find the enemy."

"You two, alone?"

"It is to discover how best we may attack them."

It seemed to me that these words of mine both wounded and challenged her. She stood looking at me, and her eyes were deep and still. Almost they caressed me. Then, I saw her eyes harden. There was sudden anger in them.

"Why did not Maximus tell me?"

I shrugged, and something in me laughed.

"It is against his wisdom that we go, Meona."

"Wisdom!"

She turned sharply and looked at Maximus who was standing like a gilded statue ignoring poor mortal man. Had she divined the hollowness of that splendid shell?

Her eyes came back to me, and the other light returned to them.

"I will come with you to your horse."

We went down the steps together, and half-way down them she paused and looked up at me.

"Do not forget all that I have asked of you."

"There are things one never forgets, Meona."

"Nor I. Do not be too reckless, O my dear."

A moment ago I had been absurdly churlish, and now I was as absurdly happy, if such happiness can be absurd. Festus was waiting for us, and it seemed to me that he was watching us with a secret and whimsical smile. He saluted Meona, and I saw his smile die away.

"Festus, it is good to see a familiar face."

That was all that she could say to him. The horror of it all had suddenly come back to her, and I knew that she was greatly shaken. As for Festus, he said never a word, but stooping, raised the hem of her skirt and kissed it, and I could have kissed Festus for that simple gesture.

We mounted, saluted her, and rode away, and when I turned in the saddle as we were passing the mere, I saw that she was still standing there. I raised my arm, and saw hers rise in answer.

CHAPTER TWENTY-EIGHT

❧

WE TOOK the road to Calleva.

If Meona's words remained in my ears, they did not move me to caution. Recklessness! If any man ever felt royally and joyously reckless it was I on that day in June.

I was content to leave the guidance in Festus's care, nor did he hold long to the road, but took to the chalk hills where we trotted on sweet turf, and saw all the country spread before us. It was a most perfect day, the distances hazed in blue greyness, the sun giving a lambent polish to the hills, the spacious valleys full of mystery. If we could see all that lay about us, we could also be seen, but that troubled Festus not at all. He seemed to possess that intuitive sensing of nature, which we moderns have lost, and to know by the wind and the sun and the shadows how and where a journey should be plotted. I should have said that he could smell the wind like a stag, and his eyes saw things that I should never have noticed.

I asked him if these hills ran all the way to Calleva, and he grinned at me.

"Yes, brother, right into the market-place."

337

I said that I had forgotten the lie of the land, and I asked him what his plan was.

"How is Calleva called, brother? The city in the woods. So, you see, when needs be, we come down off the sky-line and run like foxes. Moreover, if our friends are lying about Calleva, we shall hear of them before we run our noses up against the city wall."

"Shall we enter the city?"

"I think not, brother. Rumour has it that the raiders have sat down before the place. Maybe they have tried to surprise it and have failed. Calleva has good walls, and scaling ladders will be needed. If we find our friends making ladders, we shall be wiser than we are now."

Rumour, rumour, rumour; rumour and surprises. We were to get our surprise, and it was other than we expected. We were just passing a clump of beech trees on a hog-backed hill, when Festus pulled his horse aside with a jerk, and so sharply that he blundered into me.

"Under the trees, brother, quick."

I saw him stoop and dive with his horse under the beech boughs, and I followed.

"What's in the wind?"

"Did you not see them?"

"No. What?"

"Men on horses just coming over the sky-line and on to this hill."

I suppose I had been dreaming of the things a man in love may dream of, but now I saw what Festus had seen, the shapes of men and the heads of horses. They were some three hundred yards from us, and rising above the lip of the hill like ships out of the sea. Were they enemies or friends? I had come to expect bright, crude colours in the German make-up, and these figures were not brightly coloured, but tinted a grey-ish brown, a peasant mixture. I was watching the leading horsemen when I heard Festus cry out:

"Ye gods, look. The white horses!"

He was pointing with his spear towards a kind of plateau below the ridge, and I saw two white horses with their heads bobbing up and down, and a chariot behind them. There were two men in the chariot. Either these were Meona's horses, or their ghosts.

"Our people, Festus?"

He was screwing up his eyes.

"Hold back, brother. I am not sure yet. But look at that fellow on the black horse, the one with something white wound round his throat. If that isn't Ursus, by the shape of him!"

Ursus it was, and then I realized that these were our people who had escaped from the slaughter on Farley Heath, the men who had been in charge of the horses picketed in the woods. We rode out from under the trees, shouting and waving to them, but for a moment or two they were scared of us, and I saw the driver of the chariot pull the white horses round as though to make a bolt for it down the slope of the hill. Festus shouted to them, calling Ursus by name, and then they recognized us, and the danger of their running away in panic was past. We cantered up to them, and they gave us a feeble little cheer, for they were in a sorry state, half starved and frightened. Ursus looked deathly. He had had a spear thrust into his throat, but had managed to break away from the slaughter and escape to the horse-lines in the wood. There was a wounded man curled up in the bottom of the chariot. This wreckage had been drifting about the country for days, experiencing all sorts of terrors and privations. They had attempted to make Calleva, only to blunder upon a small German raiding party, and in a running fight: they had lost three men.. Again I had to meet glances of suspicion, and to explain how I had missed the tragedy, and then given myself to the saving of Meona. We told them to hold in along the hills for the Geraint valley, and assured the poor devils that they were out of danger.

But what could they tell us about our enemies? Not much. They had picked up some scraps of rumour from one or two frightened peasants who had taken to the hills, and rumour had it that the Germans were encamped about Calleva, and were raiding and plundering the whole country-side. We wished them luck, and watched them hobble off on their fagged horses, and I thought how glad Meona would be to see her two "Whites" again. Little did I think that those horses and her gay chariot would carry me to the dark edge of that sea from which there is no return.

Well, Festus and I rode on, until we came down from the hills into wooded country. It was more difficult going here, and we had to be very much alert, for we were not many miles from Calleva. We were travelling north-east, and I remember passing a burnt-out homestead whose blackened rafters were still smoking, and the tragic reek of it seemed to stick in my nostrils. Festus was looking very grim. I was astonished by the sureness with which he threaded this blind country. It was forest, wild country patched with open woods, and shaggy with gorse and heather. Festus's method was to slip from wood to wood like a bird in and out of cover, and before breaking from each wood we sat on our horses and watched and waited until we were sure that the open ground ahead of us could be crossed in safety.

It was Festus who spotted smoke rising above a wood that capped a low hill on the north-east, not half a mile from where we had pulled in among a smother of gnarled old thorns. That smoke flew us a danger signal and buckling our bridles round the trunks of two thorns, we scouted forward on foot towards the hill and its cap of trees. There was plenty of rough cover, and it did not take us long to gain the wood. It was an open wood of hundred year old oaks, and slipping from tree to tree we made our way through it.

Then, I saw Calleva, framed like a picture in a gold and green frame. It hung slightly below us on its plateau, somehow both mysterious and distinct in the sunlight, its chequers of red pantiles angled about the gilded roof of the basilica. There was no smoke rising from Calleva. The air about it seemed brilliant and clear. I could see men upon the walls, diminutive figures that glittered when they moved. The south gate was shut. The place looked strangely peaceful.

I felt Festus nudge me.

"There is your smoke, brother."

He was pointing to the meadows west of the town, and I saw a thing that seemed to me incredible. The whole German host was camped there, with fires burning and wagons parked with an insolent and serene carelessness, as though mocking the city and daring the men of Calleva to show their noses outside the walls. There were hundreds of the fellows strolling about, or lying asleep, or drinking. One saw them as clots of colour on a green cloth. They had taken the precaution of keeping one body of men under arms, and this company was marching up and down about a furlong from the city wall, and amusing itself by shouting and waving its weapons at the watchers on the battlements.

I said to Festus: "What the devil are they playing at? Have they taken the town?"

"No, brother, or those fires would be inside the walls. I take it to be swagger, a cat and mouse game. They are telling Calleva in dumb show that they can cut its throat just when they please."

"Exercising dumb frightfulness!"

He laughed grimly.

"Yes. The longer they keep Calleva dangling on the rope, the more terror the town will be in. That is how I read the picture. The snake and the bird, brother."

It was just the beastly sort of game that the Germans love. Meanwhile, my attention was focused on what appeared to be a large green tent in the middle of the camp. I took it to be a kind of huge arbour built of branches, and a thing that resembled a coloured snake had its head poked into the green mound of leaves, and this sinuous thing was a long queue of men waiting for food or drink.

I pointed it out to Festus.

"What do you make of that? The regimental cookhouse?"

"No smoke, brother!"

"That's true. Maybe they keep their bloody god in there, and they are forming up for service."

Festus laughed, but it was not pleasant laughter.

"No, love, brother, I should say. Germania's travelling brothel."

Both his laughter and his terse words shocked me. If that was so, then those savages had collected a little herd of British girls. To be outraged in that brothel might have been Meona's fate. I gnawed my fist and thought of the promise I had made her.

I think my hatred gave me my inspiration. I know it came to me quite suddenly as I lay watching the Saxon camp and the city. These Germans, in their arrogance, were as colossally square-headed as their descendants, and all those of us who have not been quickened with brighter blood. The beasts, in playing this game of frightfulness and reducing Calleva to terror by keeping it in suspense, were exposing themselves to the riposte of a surprise. Judging by the way we had been able to approach the place, they had no scouts or patrols out, and were so sure of the efficacy of the Furor Teutonicus, that they were taking no precautions against an attack.

"We have them, Festus."

I told him my plan. If we could slip half our force into Calleva by the east gate under cover of the night, rally the courage of the townsmen, and be ready to make a sortie, the rest of our people could march up the great west road and offer the Germans battle. Probably they would rush at the British like a bull at a red flag, leaving only a small body to watch Calleva. We should be ready, hidden by the walls, to sally out and take the Germans in the rear. We should have to arrange a signal with our people, so as to be able to time our sally rightly.

Festus let out an oath.

"By the gods, brother, that is a rare plan. Let us take it back and our news to Maximus and the Geraints."

I lay prone, with my chin on my crossed wrists, thinking.

"Wait, Festus. We shall have to slip somebody into Calleva and warn them, someone who is well known to the people."

"I am that," said Festus; "a sister of mine is married to one of the councillors. I will take on that job, if you can find your way back."

"But how will you get into the city?"

"Take to the woods and come at it by the east gate. If I ride hard for the gate they will have time to let me in, even though they may be as frightened as mice."

"How shall we know that you have managed it?"

"That should be easy. You see the flagpole on the roof of the basilica. We will hoist a flag there, or even a white sheet, if needs be."

"Good. Supposing we say that our people shall be in the woods to-morrow night? We shall have to have a password for you at the gate."

"Something lucky, brother."

"White Horses. Holy Gemini!"

"Yes, they are fortunate beasts."

We made our way back to the thorn thicket and our horses, and there Festus embraced me like a Frenchman.

"Good luck, brother, and may the gods be with us."

I suppose a man's natural vanity persuades him that any construct or conception of his own will command immediate and enthusiastic acceptance, just because it is his. Critics may be admirable and necessary, but they are negative people, and negation inspires no love. Swiftness was necessary if we were to seize our chance, and when I had ridden a couple of miles over open country, I took a risk and turned north, knowing that I should strike the high road. I did, and never have I travelled along a more deserted highway. I met nothing but the Roman milestones. The road had grass verges, and I cantered and trotted along a verge, to spare my horse's hoofs. I reckoned that I had covered about ten miles when I came to an oak post with a sign and a pointing arrow. "To The White Valley." It looked so English and modern, even in its Latinity, that I was reminded of the St. George's Hill estate, and the white posts that guide you to middle-class mansions.

The grass track wandered up and down through secret valleys and beech-smothered woods to the great house of Geraint. It brought me to the gates, and inside them I saw a queer, stone, circular building, open to the sky in the centre, with a pent roof covering in the outer part of the circle, where chariots and carriages and farm-carts were housed. This too was "St. George's Hill," save that it held no motor cars. Also, the scene I witnessed was no twentieth-century tableau. Meona's chariot stood under the open sky. The white horses had been unhitched from it, and Meona herself was caressing the beasts while two grooms rubbed them down.

How rare is beauty in a woman, and how strange that it should be so rare when every woman desires it! Almost as rare is beauty of spirit, and when I speak of beauty of spirit I am thinking of those exquisite, temperamental shades that are as wounding as the colours of azaleas. The average woman is such porridge. I know that even when I had been separated from Meona for a few short hours, and saw her again, her loveliness had a newness that filled me with anguish. For, not only is it amazing that so few women should be beautiful, but equally amazing is it that the majority should be so ugly. Oh, those white flannel faces, those primped mouths and pinched noses and spectacles! Those silly voices! I confess that for the best part of a minute I sat on my horse and watched Meona caressing those beloved horses of hers. Fortunate beasts, holy Gemini.

She must have become conscious of being watched, for, God knows, I was looking at her as a starved man might look at Canaan, for she turned her head and saw me. Her face and pose had been full of gentleness towards her horses, but when she saw me her face seemed to grow hard and fierce. It was all white edge, like a lamp flame seen somehow like a wave running with the wind, or a swirl of dead leaves in March.

"Pellias! Tidings?"

Her pale lips were hungry, and I had a feeling that I, as man, was not man, but a vehicle, a mere torch-bearer, an adventitious flame.

"Yes, and they are urgent."

"Good news?"

"It can be and should be splendid."

"Tell me."

Her eyes had a kind of brittle brightness, and as I told her what I and Festus had seen, and what my plan was, her face grew almost tender. And how strange was this tenderness to me, when I was one who might bring her bloody heads on some superhuman charger. She loved me for that news. Her face flamed with an exultant, lambent radiance. She caught me by the arm, and her voice was breathless.

"We have them! Geraint and Maximus must know. Oh yes, instantly."

She swept me along with her, through my lord's formal garden and up the white steps to the terrace. She was up them like fire, and indeed, the burning stage was set for us. Geraint the elder sat in his carrying-chair, watching his son and Maximus and sundry gentlemen playing a game that was, God forgive me, very much like pitch and toss. The scene made me think of Drake and his captains playing at bowls while waiting for the Spaniards.

"Gentlemen, tidings."

Maximus had just tossed a coin with a lordly and languid

smoothness, but it lighted on its edge and rolled, as though fate-willed, to Meona's feet. She picked it up, and cried out to us that the head upon it was an omen, the head of Mars. I think that all these men were stricken by the white face of her, even old Geraint, for she was a dark Bellona with storm and tragedy in her hair.

"My lord, Pellias has news."

They looked at me. Maximus was tossing another coin up and down, and catching it deftly upon the back of his hand. That is what he thought of me! My lord Geraint bent his head. "Let us hear you, Pellias." So I told them what Festus and I had seen, and with Meona watching me, I was like a man carried above myself. Almost, I harangued them. I spoke of my plan of action, and of how we could fool the Germans and catch them in front and rear. I watched old Geraint's face, and I saw by his eyes that he was with me, but it was Maximus who, still tossing his coin, smudged out my nice picture with a sneering and supercilious hand.

"Do we behold both Hannibal and Cæsar in the son of my uncle's steward?"

He looked at me over his shoulder with a sleepy scorn that put me in my place as a ranter. Who was the lord and leader here? Not I. I know that I went hot about the ears, but if I could find nothing to say, Meona said things that could not have come from my lips.

"My cousin," said she, "I would rather listen to the man who has dared danger than to his Excellency who plays with pennies."

That may have been rhetoric, but it set Maximus aflare.

"What do women know of war? I think, sweet cousin—"

She gave Maximus one look, and turned to Geraint.

"My lord, I have a right to speak, for I have suffered things that my cousin does not understand. If he has not the courage—"

And Maximus laughed, which was fatuous of him, for her hand went to her dagger.

"Fool, do you giggle like a girl? Had you one spark of daring in you, you would be in the saddle."

It was young Geraint who went and stood by her, and put his arm about her shoulders.

"I am with Pellias and Meona. What say you, Father?"

I think all of us turned to the old man and waited upon his words as though he were Nestor. He sat for a moment with closed eyes, and when he opened them, he did not look at Maximus, but at his son and Meona.

"I am with those who dare. What say you to that, Maximus?"

Maximus blustered. That sort of egoist seems to erupt in froth when his high and mightiness is questioned. Shut himself up in Calleva, not he, and wait for the other party to take the shock! That was an ingenious piece of poltroonery. If Master Hannibal Pellias chose— But old Geraint's white eyebrows were bristling, and like the old Nestor that he was, he caught Maximus with his own bombast.

"I take it, then, that yau, Maximus, are ready to lead your men against our enemies?"

A toss of the head from Maximus.

"Very good. My son, you and Pellias will lead our own people. The subtler blow shall be yours. If you can enter Calleva secretly to-night, and be ready to sally with such of the townsmen who are not women, Maximus may deign to attack soon after dawn. What say you, gentlemen?"

The verdict was with us. Only Maximus stood and

pshawed and pulled his moustachios, and said he would consider it. I think we were all very sick of him, but if we gave him sardonic looks, Meona gave him words.

"My cousin, maybe, the Aurelii may prefer to follow me instead of you. I am for Calleva."

The fierce fellow with the red beard let out a sound that was half laugh, half growl.

"The girl has the spunk! Hail, lady, we who may die salute thee."

CHAPTER TWENTY-NINE

ALL this had been so actual and rather ridiculous that I felt that we had been playing melodrama, or like public school boys fitted out with beards and buskins, over-acting a Greek play. True tragedy can have so vague and delicate an umbra that one may blunder oafishly into the glare of the limelight. I had been the ranting hero, Maximus a kind of Bombastes Furioso, and Meona the stage heroine, with these gentlemen in costume serving as chorus. Something very strange seemed to happen to me upon that sunlit terrace. Two selves might have been struggling in me for mastery, and my consciousness was a blur in which past, present and future were intermingled like the colours in a slowly revolving wheel. I think I was staring at Maximus. He was posed there on a pedestal of magnificent sulkiness, and still tossing that coin up and down. Where had I seen him before? I remembered the particular captain of a particular footer team whom we had played regularly twice a season, and it had always been my lot to find myself in conflict, both temperamentally and physically, with that blond stallion of a fellow. Often he had tackled me ferociously, or robbed me of the ball.

Then, one of my distraught selves seemed to dominate the conflict, and to break away like a swimmer shooting into the light after a dive into deep water.

I heard a voice, like a voice off-stage, Meona's voice. She was calling me.

"Pellias, Pellias."

Suddenly, everything was both very bright yet very dark about me. The woods were a deeper green, the sky a more brilliant blue, and yet the effect had the splendour of that moment when twilight comes. I was in a strangely vivid world in which all my senses seemed to be more quick and passionate and sensitive. I had a feeling of lightness, and Meona's voice was calling.

I was running down the steps of the terrace. I found myself in a grassy walk between a high yew hedge and a long flower border. The flowers were pansies and sweet-Williams and I remember thinking how queer it was that these old cottage plants should be growing in a Romano-British garden.

The vista ended in a great green arch of clipped yews, and here Meona was waiting for me. She was in white, and in that dark hollow she looked like a poised statue. Never had she been so vivid to me, and yet more intangible and remote. I had the feeling of experiencing a vision.

I seemed to be floating along the grass towards her. She stood very still, and her eyes had a dark blaze in them. I saw her lips move.

She said: "My horses are tired, but they must serve me."

Something about her bewildered me. I do not think I quite grasped the implication of her words, for I asked her a stupid question.

"Why should they be in harness again, Meona?"

"I am coming with you to Calleva."

My feeling of confusion seemed to pass. I was conscious of only one reaction, a passionate protest against her risking herself in so reckless a venture.

"But you cannot come with us."

She did not move, but looked steadfastly into my eyes.

"I am coming. I shall go with you, Pellias, into the battle."

This was not melodrama, but blank tragedy. I realized that my love for her was no rush of selfish, splurging sex. We were together in all time, united in some mysterious relationship, even in the heart of history. Whether that which I did was due to lack of control, or to a supreme variant of the same virtue, I do not know, but I put my hands suddenly upon her shoulders, and looked straight into her face.

"You cannot come, Meona. You are too precious for that."

Her face was like white light to me, yet so lovely that it seemed for a moment to blur my senses. I must have been shaking with the fierceness of my feelings, for she said to me: "Do not tremble so, for me, Pellias, or I might tremble for you."

How do these things happen? I was so profoundly moved, so full of wonder, that my head went down, and I felt her hands clasp themselves about my neck. She drew my head down until my forehead rested between her breasts, and so we stood, quite still and in silence, with that voiceless confession flooding over us like the supernatural radiance of a sacrament.

I said: "O my beloved, you must not do this thing."

She was far stronger than I was, for I was shaken by the intensity of my emotion, but she stood like some slim young tree against which my bowed head rested.

"Should a woman have less courage than a man?"

"Meona, it is not your courage, but your precious self."

"Do you fear that the Saxons might take me? I should not live for that. Besides, it is we who are going to win this battle, you and I, my dear, together. Will your arm fail you if I am at your side?"

Her greater courage wounded me. I raised my head and looked at her.

"Never, in all the world, was such a love as this!"

Steadfastly, and with a shining serenity, she gave me look for look.

"Never, Pellias, never."

What do I remember next? That I was riding over a high hill with the sun at my back, and all the splendour of the sunset flung like a great yellow cloak over the country. I was riding beside Meona's chariot, and on her dark head was set a little helmet. Young Geraint and his three hundred rode behind us, with their spears aslant, and harness jangling. I felt high above the world, and high of heart and head, for, it seemed to me that we two were part of History, Pellias and Meona! Would poets sing of us and of our love in the dim days that were to come?

Infinite danger there might be, and death in the blue grey dusk, but there was a strange smoothness about all these happenings, as though they had happened before, and having worn a track in time, repeated themselves with mysterious inevitableness. When we drew nearer to Calleva, young Geraint sent out his scouts, but I remained beside Meona's chariot, for nothing would have made me leave her. My dark oath held. The sheeted sunlight began to furl itself as the dusk came out of the east, and on the last spur of the hills Festus himself met us with two of Geraint's scouts.

"All is well, brother, all is well."

A stout fellow was Festus, shrewd and strong, a good man to have by one in a tight corner. He had been lying in the heather, watching for us on the hills.

Meona bade him come up into her chariot, and as we rode down to the forest country, Festus gave us the news. Calleva was waiting for us; two hundred armed men were to sleep that night in the forum and the basilica, and charge with us when we made our sally at dawn. The Germans were preparing to sacrifice to their Belly God, as Festus put it, for watchers on the walls had seen them spitting oxen over their fires, and unloading barrels from a captured wagon. It would be a sluggish and a baleful dawn for them. Festus believed that our foes were feasting before storming Calleva on the morrow.

The sweet dusk in the woods, and Meona's face becoming dim. Shadows that faded and merged into a universal greyness. Great trees reaching over us. The smell and the chill of the dew-fall. Two guides from Calleva met us where several woodland ways joined in a star, and Festus dismounted and walked with them. They were taking us by a track that looped its way in a curve to the south-east, and would bring us back to the city and its eastern gate. We had warned our men to be silent. No one spoke, and scabbards were held so that they should not strike against greaves or harness.

I rode as close as I could to the chariot. I could see the heads of the white horses rocking up and down against the dark woods. Trees, trees, trees, and the smell of the woodland. Stars were out, and dusting the sky above the tree-tops. The silence was supreme, and our moving horses seemed to make no more sound than that of a river gently flowing. I could see a tawny glow in the sky towards the north. The German camp-fires. To-morrow we would charge over their ashes.

I bent down in the saddle and spoke in a whisper to Meona. "Oh, unforgettable night! Look at the stars, beloved."

I saw her dim face upturned as though to receive the kisses of the stars.

"Are you happy, Pellias?"

"I did not know that life could hold such happiness as this."

"Nor I."

"Meona, I love you."

More light, more stars, fewer trees. We came upon Festus and the two guides waiting for us. I saw one of them point with his spear. Across the dark plain Calleva showed as a walled blackness with a light shining here and there, and over and beyond it the German camp-fires glowed. Oh, dark city of fate! We turned eastwards across the plain, moving silently like a long, black, stealthy snake. Calleva seemed to rise out of the earth. I could distinguish the high roof of the basilica. From the distance came the sound of singing, a faint, blatant, drunken bawling. The Germans were stuffing their bellies. To-morrow we should slit those bellies!

Nearer and nearer we came. I could see the gate looming up, black and solid. One of our guides had trotted on ahead. Those in the city were taking no chances and without the password, the gate would not open to us. I heard voices, the sound of a beam being withdrawn, the creaking of hinges. Now, we were under the shadow of the gateway. I saw its arch lit up by the glow of the fires beyond the city. Meona's chariot rumbled through. We rode in like a long file of ghost horsemen, and up the street towards the forum. Our horses' hoofs made a clattering on the cobbles, but the Germans over yonder were bawling so boisterously that I was sure that there was not much likelihood of their hearing the music of our cavalry.

A group of the city fathers was waiting for us at the gate of the forum. There were no lights save the lights in one of the rooms opening from the peristyle. Geraint and I were off our horses and saluting these solemn worthies, who, I realized, were in a devil of a panic, and mighty glad to see us. Yes, our horses could be stabled for the night in the forum, and straw had been laid for the men on the floor of the basilica. I could almost feel these city fathers quaking to the kind of terror-making tom-tom music the Germans were producing over yonder.

"I see you have a chariot with you, sir," said a bearded old gentleman who carried some sort of staff of office.

Need I explain Meona to him? She had pulled up her horses inside the forum gate, and I supposed that Meona would go to her uncle's house, and be ministered to by Aunt Medusa. I told the councillor that, for the sake of her safety, we had brought the daughter of Aurelius Superbus with us into the city, and that her aunt would lodge her.

"I can give you a bed, sir," said he.

I thanked him, and told him that I should keep watch most of the night, and that if I wanted an hour's sleep I would lie down with our men in the straw.

Moreover, so welcome were we to Calleva, that the city had prepared a meal for our men, and laid it in the great council chamber, where lamps and torches were burning. I left Geraint to see to his men, and went to speak with Meona. It was very dark out there in the street, and what surprised me was the emptiness of the place, though I discovered later that the folk of Calleva had been told to keep to their houses.

"Meona."

She said to me in a strange, soft voice: "My horses are tired. Where can I feed and stall them?"

"Why, at your uncle's house. You can sleep there."

"I shall not sleep, Pellias."

It was as though a sudden great sadness had fallen upon her now that we had accomplished that which we had set out to do. I leaned over the wheel and touched her.

"But you must sleep, Meona."

She found my hand and held it.

"Do you crave for sleep, Pellias?"

"No. Everything in me is too live and wakeful."

"So it is with me. Come, we will put my horses in my uncle's stable. And then—" she paused, "then, let us go up on to the walls. To-night— I have a feeling for the open sky and the stars."

CHAPTER THIRTY

❧

I REMEMBER that we walked as lovers down the dark and empty street to the west gate of Calleva. The parapet of the wall cut like a black girdle across the sky. The glow of the German fires put out the stars, and all that drunken clamour seemed so near to us that it splashed over the city wall like scud from a savage sea. What if these barbarians were exercising a characteristic cunning, and were staging an orgy before springing a surprise attack upon the city? Such a trick would be in keeping with the German idea of strategy. Your Teuton will subscribe to any set of rules, and then break them and fool you, and think himself a deuced clever fellow for doing so. I saw that there were guards upon the walls, a dark figure showing its head and shoulders against the glow every ten yards or so, and looking like ornamental vases spaced along a terrace. But these men would be too few to deal with a sudden rush and the planting of scaling ladders against the wall. I felt worried about the danger we were in. It seemed to me that half our men should be posted on the walls, and the rest of them ready to double up and reinforce us.

A flanking stairway led us up to the battlements. No sentry

challenged us, for I think they were too intent upon watching what we saw. There must have been at least a dozen great fires burning, and about each one of them our enemies were clotted in clamour and confusion. Some sprawled on the ground, others stood swaying and jolting at the hips, drinking-horns raised, the firelight flickering on their faces. The nearest fire must have been little more than a hundred yards from us, and well within bowshot, and its very nearness suggested the insolent contempt in which our enemies held Calleva. Or was this all camouflage? Were all those fantastic and barbaric figures fooling us with their crude celebrations? I stood and watched them as one might have watched a mob of dangerous wild-beasts in a bear-pit. It made me think of the descriptions of the Saxon scene before the Battle of Senlac. Stupid, bellowing, arrogant swine! The modern Nazi may be equally arrogant, but I am convinced that he would have been more evil and dangerous in his cunning. For some minutes I watched those coloured figures posturing and surging about the fire, while trying to decide whether this was stage-effect, barbaric decor, or indubitable sottishness.

If my silence was sufficiently grim I was to realize that it was not so ruthless and implacable as the stillness of the girl beside me. She was standing a little apart, her hands resting on the parapet, her face pale towards the distant firelight, her eyes like two dark pits. So still and rigid did she look that she might have been in a trance, but I knew that no dream-state possessed her. It was consummate and pitiless hatred that stared out of those dark pits of consciousness at these uproarious wretches who had killed her father and brought ruin and death to the country that she loved.

I saw her lips move, and the sound that came from them was no more than a fateful whisper.

"They are ours, Pellias; they will be ours, for the slaying."

The good people tell us that hatred is an evil thing, but what of the hatred that gives the spirit wings against the powers of evil? I am afraid I have no use for the nice, tepid people, or that milk and water maiden-auntishness which primly reproves all colour and passion. How would the dear old gentlemen who write sentimental letters to *The Times* upon loving one's enemy and being gentle with him, have dealt with those violent animals over yonder? I felt that I loved Meona in her passion and her hatred. It had the loveliness of a wild sunset, a kind of splendid rightness. Why should she not hate this evil thing? Why should she not yearn to slay it?

The strangest part of it was that she seemed utterly without fear. Here were we upon this city wall, within a hundred paces of all that potential beastliness, and she was not afraid. I think she must have been fey, and forewarned of the fate of those bawling, boisterous fighting-men, and so sure of the inevitableness of her vengeance that she could look ruthlessly and calmly upon the picture. We moderns would call it a case of precognition, but when I, who was much less confident than she was, spoke of bringing some of our men up to the wall, she forbade it.

"Let them eat and sleep, Pellias, so shall they be more ready for to-morrow's reaping."

I was astonished at her calmness.

"Are you so sure, Meona?"

"So sure."

She turned to me and put her hand in mine.

"I pray only for one thing, the dawn, when we shall hear the trumpets of my people, and that gate will open, and we shall go out to take our vengeance."

Did she mean to go with us?

I said: "You can watch from this wall."

Almost, she seemed to laugh, and to stand close and caress me. She must have known what was in my heart.

"How strong you are, Pellias, and yet how some things make you tremble."

"You will not come with us?"

"Nothing can stop me."

I stood with my arm about her, thinking how I could prevent her doing this wild thing. What if I hid her horses, or took the wheels off her chariot? Incontestably she was fey. She seemed to read my thoughts.

"No, Pellias, no cunning will serve. You and I shall go out together."

"Pellias and Meona."

"It is our fate."

I tried to persuade her to go and get some sleep, but she would not be persuaded. This wall was her watch-tower and she would remain upon it until the day began to break. I knew that I should not sleep. The peril was too near to us, and the problem of our savage enemy's cunning too challenging. Meona might be fey, but I was taking no chances with that clotted mass of cruelty so near.

The captain of the guard, making his rounds, bore down on us out of the darkness like an actor entering from the wings. We might think ourselves the stars upon the stage, but this gentleman challenged us. He had a couple of spear men with him. Who were we and what were we doing upon the city wall? His peremptoriness was, I imagine, largely inspired by fright, for that florid, turbulent tableau over yonder could not be soothing to civic nerves, and the captain of the guard was a silversmith in civil life. I was about to answer him, when Meona took up his challenge.

"You should know me, Master Argenteus."

He peered at her, and then became utterly polite.

"Surely, it is the Lady Meona?"

He had served the Aurelii, sold them silver plate, girdles, pins, buckles and the like, and his suavity became the suavity of the shopman. No, assuredly, no explanations were needed. The gentry had ridden in to save the city and to disperse all this savage nastiness. What, we were remaining on the wall all night? But, surely, her ladyship would choose to rest in a comfortable bed? No? Well, was there anything that he could do, send us some food and wine? Our notable and excellent company was so reassuring! I took Mr. Argenteus aside, and spoke to him, and all the time that I was speaking I realized that he could not keep his eyes from those fires and figures. The horrid sight fascinated him.

"Certainly, sir, certainly. I will do all that you desire."

He sent a couple of his men down into the darkness, and they returned carrying a truss of straw, and I cut the band with my sword and spread the straw under the shelter of the parapet.

"If you will not leave the wall, Meona, lie down and sleep."

The night was growing cold, and though she had a cloak with her I had none. We came near to quarrelling over that cloak. She accepted her couch of straw, and I took her cloak and was for spreading it over her, when she bade me keep it. I was to put it over my shoulders while I kept watch. I told her that I should walk up and down and so keep warm, and I think we haggled for half a minute over that cloak. At last she accepted it, and as I bent down to tuck it round her, she put her arm about my head and kissed me on the forehead.

"Wake me if I sleep. I mean that I would take my turn at watching. Promise."

I promised, though I had no intention of keeping that promise very strictly. And sleep she did, as though calmed and consoled by her belief in the inevitableness of her vengeance. She was sleeping when Mr. Argenteus's man appeared with a beaker of wine and some bread and cooked meat on a pewter salver. I assumed it to be of the baser metal, for, even in so hazardous a crisis good property has to be cherished. I drank some of the wine and ate some of the food, and then placed the beaker and the salver under the parapet, knowing that Meona might be glad of them when she woke.

I marched up and down, making my sentry-turns at a little distance from her so that she should not be disturbed, and I took the trouble to warn the nearest guards that this particular section of the wall was mine. The night air grew cold, but I had those pagan fires to warm my wits, and that boo-hoo chorus to cheer me. Assuredly, this German beer-festival was authentic. I saw some of the beasts staggering about, and dancing together with clumsy, oleaginous movements. Many of them were asleep about the fires. One thing did much to reassure me. I saw a party of some dozen men detach itself from the great circle of light, and move towards the city. They halted about fifty yards from the wall, and I heard an order given. This was the night picket posted, almost contemptuously, to ensure that the doomed and frightened town should not molest the slumbers of these German swine.

If I had promised myself that Meona would sleep the night through, I was wrong. The fires were dying down, the drunken voices becoming smothered, and I had walked softly to the place where she was lying. I was suffused with an exquisite tenderness. Here lay she whom I loved more than life, peacefully asleep, secure in her faith in me, while I watched for her. It was so dark now that I did not see that her eyes were open.

"Pellias."

"Did I wake you?"

"No. But it is my turn to watch."

She sat up, throwing back the cloak, and making a rustling in the dry straw. I remembered the wine and meat, and I picked up the pewter platter and the wine-jug, and kneeling, served her.

"Drink and eat, O my beloved."

Did a still, small voice in me complete the quotation? "For, to-morrow, we die." Death was the last thing that was in my thoughts, her death or mine. I knelt beside her while she ate and drank, and even put the beaker to my lips when she willed me to.

"It is very silent, Pellias."

"The beasts sleep," said I, "and the fires die down."

"Was I not right?"

"Utterly right, Meona. And to-morrow—"

"They will sleep that other sleep, and you and I shall ride our horses and look upon the dead."

When she had finished she rose and stood beside me by the parapet. The fires were mere heaps of glowing ash, and the figures piled about them shrouded in a prophetic darkness. Almost, I fancied that I could hear the whole herd snoring. A great stillness lay upon the city. Not a light showed. I looked for the picket that had been posted to watch the western gate, and they too had scorned all possible peril. I could see them huddled together in a knot of slumber, like corpses thrown together on the ground.

Meona touched me.

"Lie down and sleep, Pellias."

"But I am not sleepy, Meona."

"Do as I bid you. It is my turn to watch."

"I will, if you will take the cloak. The night is cold."

"Do you wish it?"

"I wish you everything, O beloved."

She took the cloak and wrapped it round her, and I lay down in the straw.

I cannot say that it was a warm and comfortable bed, but my love had slept here, and it was sacred. Also, I must have been more tired than I knew, for when the strain of watching was relaxed, sleep fell upon me suddenly and profoundly. One moment I was looking at the stars, the next, all consciousness was blotted out. There was no feyness in me, no awareness of that which lay behind the mirror of the senses. It was to be my last sleep in this— But that is pulling the fruit before it is ripe to fall.

I woke to find Meona bending over me. The night was both with us and not with us, for a gradual greyness was bringing colour back into the world. I saw the stars, and Meona's face, mysterious and dim, and the clouding of her hair.

"It is time, Pellias."

I felt life leap in me. I was up and standing beside her. We held hands, and turned to look upon the German camp, with the gradual dawn stealing up behind us. There was a great stillness, and then a cock crowed somewhere, and a twittering of birds began in a garden below the wall. I heard a horse neigh exultantly, and to me it was like the sound of a trumpet. I could see no movement anywhere about the dead camp-fires. Our enemies were still asleep, and I felt that God had delivered them into our hands.

CHAPTER THIRTY-ONE

❧ ☙

The belly of a cloud caught the upward light and took fire as we hastened to the Forum. I could feel the city stirring, and in the Forum we found our men armed and harnessing their horses. The levies of Calleva had gathered in the street west of the basilica, and I could hear a deep and restless murmur coming from them. Young Geraint and Festus were standing together by the base of the great column.

Said Geraint: "We had lost you, Pellias."

I told him that I had spent the night upon the wall, watching our enemies, and that the swine were still sodden with sleep.

Geraint was full of young impatience. Would Maximus keep his word, and should we hear his trumpets sounding as the sun came up? Festus had offered to ride out and make contact with Maximus, and we were still debating the point when we heard the galloping of horses in the street. We turned to the forum gate, and then it was that I missed Meona, and I guessed that she had gone back to her uncle's house for her white horses and her chariot.

I was conscious of acute suspense like a tight belt about my loins. What did the sound of those galloping horses presage? News? And would it be good or bad? The light was spreading, and outside the forum gate we saw three warriors dismounting. One of them was old Red Beard, and when I recognized his grim, boar's face, I seemed to know that all was well.

He came striding in to us.

"The stage is set, gentlemen."

Young Geraint started forward and embraced him.

"Maximus is there?"

"Most surely there, my lord. We thought it wise that you should be warned and ready. When the sun rises above the city wall you will hear Maximus's trumpets."

"And we charge," said I.

Red Beard smiled at me.

"No. Hold your hot blood in for a space. Let our enemies scramble into action, and rush to meet Maximus. He will be on them before they can get into good order. Someone must be on the wall, watching, and all your men should be ready at the gate. Then, when these swine have their snouts stuck against British spears, charge out and take them in the rear."

There was no time to be lost, for the gilded roof of the basilica was brightening to the dawn. As for the watch upon the wall, I thought old Red Beard was the man for it, for he was of a cool and ruthless temper, and would not launch our sally either prematurely or too late. Moreover, I wanted to find Meona. I took Geraint aside and told him of her purpose, and instead of looking shocked, his eyes blazed.

"Ye gods, she shall be our eagle."

Meanwhile, Geraint's horsemen were filing out into the

street, and we mounted and joined them. At the crossroads the captains of the Calleva town-levy were waiting for us, with their spearmen packed in the roadway. It may have been the effect of the dawn-light, but I thought these fellows' faces looked as white as paper, and I wondered how they would shape in the bloody business that was before us. I glanced at Geraint, and I saw him frowning and looking fierce. These townsmen impressed him no more favourably than they did me.

"White as a lot of girls."

I said that many men went that colour before an attack, and that, at all events, they would be behind us, and might give a good account of themselves if our charge went home.

"Yes," said Geraint, "I guess they will wait to see how the wind blows, and when the business is over no one will boast more valiantly than they."

We were passing down West Street when I saw Meona, and my heart seemed to drop a beat. She had brought her horses out into the roadway, and was standing up in the chariot like a slim statue of Bellona. If any creature could be said to be inspired and exalted it was she. Her hair streamed down from under her little helmet; she had a shield on her arm, and a spear in her right hand. She raised her spear and saluted us as we walked our horses up the street.

I rode forward, and she turned her horses towards the gate. I said: "You cannot go out alone in that chariot, Meona," and she gave me a steadfast look and smiled. Yes, her exaltation would not be reasoned with or be put down. She spoke to her horses, and they broke into a trot, and then I realized what her purpose was. The West Gate loomed up over us. There were men stationed there to drop the bar and fling open the gates, and Meona drove her horses into the tunnel of the gateway so that we could not pass her. She had made herself, as it were, the white spearhead of our sally, and I had a feeling that she was the winged genius of our Fortune.

I managed to edge my horse in beside her chariot.

"Must you be so splendidly mad, O my beloved?"

Her face was radiant and serene. Never have I seen a more happy face.

"I am victory, Pellias."

The inevitableness of her courage was beyond dispute.

But I backed my horse out of the gateway and spoke to young Geraint. I said that Meona was god-inspired and that no words of ours would stay her. All that we could do would be to ride on either side of her chariot with a score of picked men about us to form a sort of human ploughshare, a wedge of fighting men to spear a way around her. Geraint took up the challenge. I gather that he had got his best men in the van, and he turned his horse and spoke to the leading files. They were to mass round the chariot, follow it and envelope it, and guard it as though it held a sacred standard.

Old Red Beard was up on the wall, and we were to wait upon his signal, but my impatience was such that I could not leave the business to other eyes. The sun was up, and shining almost horizontally upon the cobbles of the street and making them look like silver. Colour had come back into the world, and the eyes of the morning were growing blue. I dismounted, and leaving my horse with one of Geraint's men, I ran up the stone steps leading to the battlements. Old Red Beard was there, his jowl stuck over the wall like the snout of a boar, and there was a grim grin on his face.

"Ha, Pellias, the hot blood is restless! Take a look at our German friends."

I looked, and I gathered that his grim smirk was justified.

The Saxon camp was oozing into sluggish life. Men were yawning and stretching themselves. Others still lay sleeping. Some of the fires were being relit, and two fellows were slinging a cauldron over one of them. I saw one large, barbaric person in a sky blue tunic sitting astride a saddle and combing his golden locks. So, the Spartans combed their hair before Thermopylæ, but this would be a less heroic business.

Old Red Beard chortled.

"Observe the gentleman combing his hair! A rather superfluous task, sir. Those locks will soon be bloody."

He sniffed and bit at his beard, and looking at the rising sun, said gruffly that it was time for me to return down yonder, and wait for the sound of Maximus's trumpets. I'll confess that I was a little loath to go, for, as the Americans might have put it, I should have been tickled to death watching the confusion in that camp when the trumpets sounded, and a thousand horse and foot came charging out of the woods. How those swine would grunt and gallop, and scramble for their weapons! There was an exultant ruthlessness in me that was more prophetic than I knew, the cold and implacable rage that was to inspire Britain against Nazi Germany.

I returned to the street, remounted my horse, and edged him in beside Meona's chariot.

I said: "The sun is up, and many of the beasts are still sleeping."

Her pale face seemed to have the sharpness of a new moon.

"I wait for the trumpets, Pellias. I wait, I wait!"

There is the old cliché that minutes can lengthen into hours, and if Time too is relative, our waiting there in the darkness of the gate was to be a memory that remains for me symbolical. I was a man in a dream, a child in the womb of time, and then the trumpets would sound and the wounded dawn cry out to us, and we should stream out—to what? Struggle, slaughter, victory, the illusion of peace! Was that to be the eternal sequence in man's little world—struggle, peace, stagnation, boredom, struggle? Would some new and supersensuous revelation rescue us from the sense-scramble? I looked at Meona, and even her loveliness had a bleak, sharp edge. And if she loved me it was because I was a combative creature, not a tame sentimentalist spewing out vapid verses.

"Listen!"

The trumpets! I heard their sudden, brazen scream, distant yet significantly near in their challenge. So, that great, blond swaggerer Maximus had kept his word. Meona was pointing her spear at the gate and calling to the men to take down the bar. It was a huge oak beam, and two men were needed to slide it from its slots.

"Wait!"

My voice echoed sharply in that tunnel. I pushed my horse forward aand turned him across the noses of Meona's beasts.

"Wait! Red Beard will give us the signal."

For one moment her impatience blazed at me, and then she smiled, for I think she knew that my love was both wiser and more cunning than her hate.

Uproar! The German camp seemed to boil up like a cauldron and spill itself into a crackle of steam and noise. I could picture those savages grabbing their weapons and trying to hustle into some sort of order. It was like a kennel of hounds giving tongue. Our horses began to fidget, for there was elemental fear and fury in that animal uproar, and above it I could hear the trumpets screaming. Moreover, I fancied that I could sense the thunder of hoofs, and feel their hammer-beats vibrating through the earth. My horse had his ears cocked forward, and he began to paw the stones.

A shout came from the wall.

"Out, out!"

I pointed to the bar with my spear, and the men drew the bar from its slots and slid back the bolts. As the gates swung in I had to edge my horse back against the noses of Meona's whites, but that was a part of the plan. The arch framed the scene for us, all that sound and scud and frenzy. I saw a line of spears, helmets and horses' heads coming like a wave across the field, and moving to meet it a ragged cloud of men, confused, trailing out shreds of scattered colour, howling, cursing. I turned and rode out of the gate, keeping my horse in front of Meona's chariot. Then Geraint and his chosen men came round us in a boss of steel. I looked back for a moment at Meona's face. It had a fierce ecstasy. She was lashing her horses. Her mouth was open, but the cry that came from it was no more than a little, shrilling thread in the tumult and trampling of our charge.

Geraint had given orders to his three hundred to open out to the flanks so that the impetus of our charge should not be wasted, and we went forward in the form of a broad arrow or wedge. I could see a vast confusion ahead of us. Maximus's charge had got home and our enemies had had no time to form and close their ranks. The Germans had rushed blindly into battle, just like mad beasts whose first impulse was to charge. There had been hell's own uproar to begin with, but it struck me that this mass of humanity had become significantly silent. Killing can be silent, an affair of set teeth, and deep hard breathing. Maximus's men had ridden down and speared the first of their enemies, and now they seemed to be interlocked with the main mass. It was thrust against thrust, and the Germans were like a stubborn, sticky mass that held together and clogged the British spears. I realized that we had the crisis in our hands. Our enemies had neither heard nor seen the dreadful diversion we were providing. I think we must have been within thirty yards of their srug- gling, fuming rear, when I saw one or two hairy faces turned, faces stupid with fear and fury, open mouthed, shout- ing. "About! About!" But it was too late. Geraint and I had drawn together in front of Meona's horses, and with our picked men round us, we crashed in. I had expected some shock of impact, but we seemed to cleave like the ram of a ship into a soft, gelatinous substance. I remember spearing two men, and then my spear stuck in the belly of a third. I struggled to get my sword out, and a savage rushed at me with an axe. I saw a spear shoot out from somewhere and catch the German in the throat just as he was on me. Then, we were cutting, thrusting, bullocking our way forward. Once I glanced over my shoulder to see that Meona's chariot was safely in the thick of our iron phalanx. I saw her face. It was smiling. It seemed to dream.

Then, with a curious abruptness, the human mass caught between the weight and pressure of the double attack ap- peared to burst like a vast bladder. Its contents squirted right and left in splodges of confusion. We were going forward, and so were the Aurelii who were hacking their way towards us. The Germans seemed to be squeezed out, and to ooze away like butter between two boards.

We had smashed them, and like the two leaves of a door our bodies of cavalry swung opposite ways, sweeping the broken bodies of the German host before them. But that was only the beginning of the slaughter. Maximus's infantry had followed up the charge, and the men of Calleva, greatly bold now that the battle was going in our favour, came in behind us, and as we rode down the savages and broke them up into little knots of ferocity and despair, our footmen slew them. I'll give the beasts the credit of their courage. They stood and fought in little groups, in twos and threes, and when we saw a knot that still held out, we charged it, smashed it, and so let our footmen in. I remember Meona turning her chariot upon one of those cores of cohesion on the last fringe of the fight. I shouted to her, and called some of our men round me. There were bodies everywhere, blood, and a litter of weapons. I saw one wheel of her chariot bump over a corpse, and for a second I thought it was going to overturn, but she steadied herself and her horses, and drove straight for that little group of desperate men. I suppose there were about a dozen of us galloping hard after her. That was one of my last memories —fear, a kind of furious anger with her that she should risk so much when the day was so utterly ours.

I managed to push my horse level with her chariot, and our men were close behind us. I think my idea was to get hold of the reins and turn her horses aside, but when we were about twenty yards from that little group of Saxons, they broke and ran. They had had enough and could not face our charging horses. They scattered and legged it for the woods, and I thought the danger over.

"Let them go, Meona."

She did not look at me, but lashed her horses, and her face was the face of young Winged Victory.

"None must escape, none!"

A ride opened through the wood, and along it the rising sun was shining. I saw the Saxons plunge into this green way. We should lose them amid the trees, and again I called to Meona, and tried to stop her horses, but she was like a mad thing, and even threatened me with her spear. She drove straight for the opening in the wood. Our enemies had disappeared among the trees, and I knew that these wild beasts could be dangerous. They might turn on us, and have us at a disadvantage.

And so, it happened. I saw several of the Germans leap back into the ride, and one of them was the large and splendid person whom I had seen combing his hair. He had his shield up and his spear poised. There was a snarl on his face, and his blue eyes were fixed in a glare upon the white horses and the chariot. I pricked my horse with my sword, and managed to get him forward. One of the last things I remember was my swinging in front of Meona's horses, that poised spear, and those two blue, furious eyes.

Everything was growing dim, the sky, the trees. I was lying on my back with something in my throat. I was choking, smothering.

Meona was bending over me. Her face seemed to float above me, dim and pale. How very pale she was, with eyes—

I heard a voice.

"I will love you always. Can you hear me? I will—"

And that was all.

CHAPTER THIRTY-TWO

❧

𝓘 STILL am a very sick man, sick more, perhaps, in spirit than in body.

I am to be congratulated on being alive, I who am but half alive, a potential crock, and seemingly useless in this violent new world!

I cannot work yet, though my job is being kept for me, and both I and Lucy have a little capital. I am allowed to potter about in our garden, while aeroplanes fly overhead, the winged chivalry of our last crusade.

My car has been repaired, but Lucy will not let me drive it. My wife is very sad these days, for they are sad days for women. Sometimes I catch her looking at me with a questioning strangeness. What is she thinking, hoping? That I may never be fit to be involved in this chaotic war?

It is not a question of compulsion. I am burning to be in it, against the same enemy, the same savagery, the same faithlessness and arrogance.

A passionate restlessness consumes me. I, who so yearned with a feeling of desolation to be back in my own world, now yearn for that other world. I am always hearing, seeing, speaking to Meona. Will she grow dim to me? It is as though she had died, not I, and that I am clutching at a ghost, and pleading with it not to fade and leave me.

Our petrol is to be rationed! Can anything be an anti-climax in this world of ordered mendacity? I suppose that I should be considered a veritable Goebbels in romance. How could any man dream as I had dreamed, so consecutively, so vividly, so rationally, and at such length. In metapsychology my experience would be labelled as an extreme case of retro-cognition, a trick of time elaborated and exploited by a senti-mental liar! How could a whole page of history come to life and manifest itself in the person of one man? It might be said that I had dreamed a sex-dream and spun it into an extended day-dream; that my conscious self-control had been weakened, and that my subliminal self had seized the chance to take the stage and produce a play. How can one explain the unexplainable? How little do we know, save that our sensuous world is a world of appearances, and that we are fooled into accepting our sense-impressions as ultimate reali-ties. We have to plant poor Common Sense in the saddle and let him ride the donkey, but maybe the donkey, like Balaam's ass, may see more than his master.

Lucy has gone to town by train, complete with gas-mask. We have to save petrol. But an uncontrollable impulse takes possession of me. I remove the switch-key from its hook and sneak down to the garage, open the doors, and slip into the car. Three gallons of petrol in the tank. Good! I expect I shall receive a wounded scolding from Lucy when she looks at that dial and the speedometer, if she does so look. Poor

Lucy! Have I been so grossly disloyal to her in my dream? Hardly so. I was another man in that dream, and even though its bitter-sweet perfume remains with me, I know that Lucy is the one creature in this other world who matters to me.

Shall I ever tell her of my other world? Perhaps.

I press the self-starter, and back the car out into the lane. As I drive up the Heath Road I remember that morning when I came to the brow of this wild heath and stood like a scared and bewildered ghost trying to slip back into a warm and familiar world. I pass Vickers, a super-Vickers with its cars splurging everywhere, and that vast sandpit which is now being camouflaged. The Portsmouth Road. It seems quieter than usual, and the traffic consists mostly of lorries. I drive slowly, and I am getting along all right. An aeroplane passes overhead, and I think that if this new and chaotic era of violence and barbarism is to claim me actively, I shall choose to be an airman. Pellias fought those evil beasts on horseback; I would make of my horse an aeroplane.

Ripley. But I am balked at Clandon. For a year or more official progress has claimed its right to make a mess of the village highway. I have to go by way of Merrow. A strange feeling of suspense grips me as the car climbs the Downland road, and all that poignant country begins to shape itself. Newland's Corner. I park the car on the verge, get out, stroll across to the grass glacis of the Downs, and standing by a thorn tree, look across the valley.

Where is that temple?

I can pick out Farley Heath, with the woods at the back of it, and its slopes of bracken and heather. I feel something stab me. No temple, no Meona.

I drive on. I do not turn into Albury village. I shall go

there later. I take the Black Heath road past Albury Park, cross the railway line and down into the dip, and up and along the narrow, winding road. Somebody sells eggs here. I pass the green whose name I always forget, and take the heath road. Its heather slides up towards the sky, and I feel an acute pang of excitement stab me. If I lie in the heather and go to sleep, shall I wake up again in Meona's world?

I park the car on the stretch of grass by the wood. I have the place to myself. I notice that the familiar thorn tree has gone. Good lord, someone has been busy here! Archæologists? The bracken has been shaved away. There are sandy scars in the soil. Fragments of Roman tile lie scattered about. I find myself looking at a neat, new foundation plan laid out in the natural stone. Here stood the temple. I sit down close to it and stare at the horizon.

But that is not sufficient. I find a patch of heather and lie down in it, and close my eyes. Meona. Those last words of hers seem in my ears. Bitter Sweet! Had I picked the words out of Noel Coward's play? "I will love you always." What sort of trick had my subliminal self been playing?

What had happened to Meona? Where did she lie buried? I should not find my dead beloved's tombstone like the hero in *Berkeley Square*.

I keep my eyes closed and try to fall asleep, but sleep will not come to me. Why all this foolishness? Undoubtedly, my physician would tell me that I had cracked my skull, and just wallowed in unconsciousness for a matter of three weeks? I wonder? Where was I during those three weeks? My physical self may have rested like a corpse on a mortuary table, but my spirit self had broken out and escaped and found itself part of some strange old pattern. Why not? What is sleep?

Our essential self daily seems to die, and after hours of absence glides back into the body.

I give up trying to sleep, and lie and stare at the sky. I have a strange feeling that the sense veil is very thin, like gossamer or rice-paper spread over the sensuous world. The mystery of the mirror! We look into a mirror, and sometimes we seem to know that it is but a mirror, a sheet of silvered glass. When man dreams does he pass through the mirror? Is ecstasy a passing through the mirror into otherness? Have those many visionaries shed the senses, and floated into a world of other dimensions, poets and seers, those who make music? Words, words! But I have a feeling that I have been on the other side of the mirror.

A profound sense of peace steals over me. The September sun is shining, and I lie and look at the sky.

Peace, when the tragedy of Poland moves us all. What other savage tragedies are waiting to be reflected in the glass?

A sudden understanding of life comes to me. What a filthy mess man is making of things, and why? Because he cannot see beyond the mirror; he piles in front of it masses of raw flesh, and blood, and mechanical beastliness. Man is becoming standardized and mechanized. Where have these Totalitarians gone wrong? Why is Communism the enemy, a slime product, a cabbage cult, with an elemental brute like Stalin for its Christ?

I think I begin to understand. I do not belong to the Eugenic Society, but on the rare occasions when I have read their journal, it has seemed to me tainted with priggery. *Mens sana in corpore sano,* oh, certainly. Has not man through thousands of years struggled upwards with suffering and bloody sweat to refine and temper and liberate individual

man? Has it not all been a progress in personality, a trying
out of temperaments, a development of differences, even as
Nature loves her differences? I am a rather simple person,
but it seems to me that the whole life structure, the ultimate
significance of a community, rests upon individual values.
Why talk about the sanctity of the State, its right to regard
each individual as no more than an obedient brick built into
the structure? What nonsense! A community should be a
live entity, not a city of baked mud ruled by some Assyrian
bull-tyrant. If we enslave the individuals we build a slave
state, a debased beastliness, a horror of dead materialism.
Man should be the symbol; free, restless, questioning, articu-
late man, waving his little torch in the mysterious darkness,
yet somehow glimpsing the sheen of other mysteries about
the mountain top.

Yes, man is to be cherished, not the State, man the poet,
man the maker of music, man the craftsman, man the farmer.
What is the State if those who toil and explore and sing are
mere dumb and purblind beasts, crushed into a dreadful
docility, with all the free questioning of children bludgeoned
out of consciousness? Man is not steel and concrete and baked
mud. We have taken away from him the mysterious mirror
in which it should be his fate to gaze, and divine the glimmer
of angel's wings.

The September sun is warm on my face and body, and
with it a new inspiration seems to soak into my soul. I sit up
and remember that strange and frightening moment when I
had discovered those unfamiliar shoes upon my feet. But no
longer am I afraid. I turn and look at the place where the
temple stood. Yes, I had seen it, of that I am sure, just as sure
as I am of the other realities, the face of my other world

beloved. I have been behind the mirror, and no longer am I afraid.

I go and stand in the centre of that foundation pattern, and gaze upon the familiar hills, England in all its green tranquillity. Yet, I think of it as Meona's country. And war is with us as it was with her, blatant, bombastic war, a barbaric beastliness, a challenge to the free soul of man.

Yes, if the fates are kind to me I will fight in this war as I fought in that other war, for freedom, for the beauty and mystery and loveliness of things.

This is a crusade, and I would be part of its winged chivalry.

A NOTE ON THE TYPE
IN WHICH THIS BOOK IS SET

**DEVICE OF
ROBERT GRANJON**

This book is set in Granjon, a type named in compliment to ROBERT GRANJON, *but neither a copy of a classic face nor an entirely original creation. George W. Jones drew the basic design for this type from classic sources, but deviated from his model to profit by the intervening centuries of experience and progress. This type is based primarily upon the type used by Claude Garamond (1510–61) in his beautiful French books, and more closely resembles Garamond's own than do any of the various modern types that bear his name.*

Of Robert Granjon nothing is known before 1545, except that he had begun his career as type-cutter in 1523. The boldest and most original designer of his time, he was one of the first to practise the trade of type-founder apart from that of printer. Between 1549 and 1551 he printed a number of books in Paris, also continuing as type-cutter. By 1557 he was settled in Lyons and had married Antoinette Salamon, whose father, Bernard, was an artist associated with Jean de Tournes. Between 1557 and 1562 Granjon printed about twenty books in types designed by himself, following, after the fashion of the day, the cursive handwriting of the time. These types, usually known as "caractères de civilité," he himself called "lettres françaises," as especially appropriate to his own country. He was granted a monopoly of these types for ten years, but they were soon copied. Granjon appears to have lived in Antwerp for a time, but was at Lyons in 1575 and 1577, and for the next decade at Rome, working for the Vatican and Medici presses, his work consisting largely in cutting exotic types. Towards the end of his life he may have returned to live in Paris, where he died in 1590.

This book was composed, printed, and bound by H. Wolff, New York. The paper was manufactured by S. D. Warren Co., Boston.